A WINTER'S RECKONING

KADE DUTTON

CONTENTS

CHAPTER ONE

Dawn broke reluctantly over the West Texas plains, the pale, bruised light of the winter sky casting a somber glow over the endless horizon. The land stretched out in all directions, a stark canvas of frost-covered dirt, scattered mesquite trees, and rugged sagebrush. Here and there, nodding pump jacks—a reminder of Midland's oil-driven heart—broke the stillness, their rhythmic groaning blending with the soft whisper of the cold wind. Frost clung to the spindly branches of the mesquite, their jagged shadows painting the ground in skeletal patterns. This winter was unusually cold and wet for West Texas. Midland had already received the equivalent of three years' worth of snow, and more was forecast in the coming days.

Sheriff Roger Hartley drove his rust-red Chevy Silverado down the empty stretch of highway, the truck's old engine grumbling in protest with every bump and dip. He exhaled slowly, his breath fogging the windshield for a moment before disappearing.

The call had come in just before dawn, pulling him from a restless, dreamless sleep. A body had been discovered near Monahans Draw, where the land spread out in a vast, desolate sea of brush and dirt, broken only by the occasional rusted barbed wire fence. Jenny Pearson, the dispatcher, had sounded shaken, her normally steady voice strained. Roger had known then that whatever awaited him at the scene would be bad.

Roger, in his late fifties, looked every bit the seasoned sheriff of a small, hard town. His face was deeply lined, his blue eyes shadowed with the weight of things long past. A jagged scar split his left eyebrow, a relic from his days in the service, and his square jaw was rough with stubble that had turned almost entirely gray. Despite his age, he moved with purpose, his presence still commanding respect in a town that had seen more than its fair share of darkness.

But there were scars far deeper than the one visible on his face. During his military service, Roger had been awarded both the Purple Heart and the Silver Star. The Purple Heart had come from being wounded in battle—a bullet that tore through his side, leaving behind a lingering ache that winter weather made unbearable. The Silver Star, however, was harder to think about. It was awarded for saving the lives of five of his team members, pulling them from the chaos of an ambush despite his own injuries. Yet even with that honor, the three who hadn't made it was what stuck with him. The faces of those lost soldiers haunted his dreams, their names carved into his memory like the sharp edge of a blade. He carried their weight in the quiet moments when the adrenaline of his work as sheriff didn't mask the pain.

Those nightmares and the endless question of "Why them, not me?" often drove Roger to the bottle. He wasn't proud of it, but the burn of whiskey was sometimes the only thing that dulled the ache long enough to let him sleep. Between trying to make the world a better place during the day and battling his demons at night, his reliance on alcohol had cost him dearly. It had likely been the nail in the coffin of his marriage and was the reason any chance at meaningful relationships slipped through his fingers. He'd tried to stay close to his ex-wife, Kathy, and their daughter, Emily, but even that had become a strain he wasn't sure how to fix.

As he pulled into the gravel road leading to the site, he spotted Deputy Liz's cruiser parked at an angle, its blue and red lights flashing in rhythmic bursts that cut through the dim morning light. Roger parked behind her, killed the engine, and took a moment to collect himself. The cold was relentless, biting through his old denim jacket, and he tugged his hat down lower over his brow.

Liz stood by the edge of the scene, arms crossed over her chest, her breath visible in short, frosty puffs. In her late thirties, Liz was a striking woman, her features sharp and angular, and her blue eyes fierce and unyielding. Her blonde hair was pulled back into a tight bun beneath her sheriff's hat, and she wore the exhaustion of the job like a badge of honor. Growing up in Midland had taught her to be tough, but it was more than the town's hard edges that had shaped her.

Liz's childhood had been anything but easy. She grew up in a modest house on the outskirts of town, where the shouting between her parents was so constant it felt like the walls themselves were steeped in it. The fights started small—arguments over money, the pressure of dead-end jobs—but they escalated quickly, often culminating in smashed dishes or her father's fists leaving bruises that took weeks to fade. Liz learned early how to be invisible, tiptoeing through life to avoid the worst of her father's wrath.

When she was fourteen, her mother's quiet sadness turned into something unbearable. Liz would never forget the morning she woke up to the sound of breaking glass and found her mother standing in the kitchen, clutching an empty bottle of pills in one hand and a revolver in the other. Her mother's last words—apologies whispered through tears— were a scar Liz carried deeper than any bruise. The gunshot had been deafening, shattering not just the quiet of the morning but any semblance of safety Liz had clung to. She had called 911 in a daze, standing barefoot in a puddle of her mother's blood.

The trauma of that moment shaped Liz into the woman she is today. For years, the memory haunted her, and it still did, resurfacing in unexpected ways. The sharp crack of a gunshot or the sight of a person's lifeless body could pull her back to that morning, leaving her stomach twisted in knots. Instead of letting it destroy her, Liz used it as fuel. She swore she'd never let herself—or anyone else—be powerless again.

Determined to rise above the chaos of her upbringing, Liz worked tirelessly to put herself through college, earning a bachelor's degree in criminal justice. The nights were long, juggling shifts at a local diner with studying, but she refused to quit. She joined the Midland Police Department straight out of school, where her grit and sharp instincts quickly set her apart. Her transition to the Sheriff's Department felt like a natural progression, giving her the chance to work alongside people like Roger, who valued hard work and determination over pedigree.

Over the years, Roger became more than just her boss—he became a father figure, something she hadn't realized she needed until it was there. He saw the cracks in her armor, the weight she carried, and in his quiet, unassuming way, he looked out for her. Roger's tough, no-nonsense exterior reminded Liz of the parts of her father she had wished were stronger, but his steady presence and unwavering support gave her the kind of stability she'd never had growing up. She respected him deeply, not just as a sheriff but as a man who'd fought his own battles and come out on the other side, scarred but standing.

But even with Roger's guidance and the support of her colleagues, Liz still had trouble letting anyone truly in. Her current relationship with Jason was proof of that. What had started with passion and the hope of something lasting had begun to unravel, caught in the same trap as every other relationship she'd tried. Jason wanted to know her—to really know her—and Liz couldn't give him that. Every time he pushed, asking about her past, about the walls she built so carefully around herself, she pulled away. It wasn't that she didn't care for him—she did—but letting someone into the parts of herself, she fought so hard to keep buried felt impossible. And Jason wasn't the kind of man who wanted to live on the outside forever.

Still, she tried to focus on the job, to push everything else to the back of her mind. There was work to be done, and Liz had always been good at throwing herself into work when the rest of her life started to feel like it was slipping through her fingers. Today was no different, though there was something in the air, something about this scene that made it harder to shove everything else aside.

"Morning, Sheriff," Liz greeted him, her voice steady but tight. She didn't look away from the body that lay in the dirt as though forcing herself to confront the horror of it.

Roger gave her a brief nod and followed her gaze, his gut tightening at the sight.

He followed her gaze, his gut tightening at the sight. The victim was a young man, his body sprawled on the frost-bitten earth. His arms were raised above his head, fingers twisted in a final, desperate splay. The chest wounds were savage, a grotesque cross carved with a brutal hand. The ribs had been splintered, shards of bone sticking out like jagged knives. The victim's heart had been exposed, a dark cavity gaping open where it had been cruelly cut. His organs glistened wetly in the dim light. Blood had pooled beneath him, a thick, dark stain that had frozen in patches, forming glistening crystals that sparkled like a macabre version of morning dew.

The young man's face was a study in agony. His jaw had been shattered, bone protruding eerily through purpled skin, and his mouth had been stuffed full of sand and mesquite thorns. The sand had mixed with blood, forming a sludge that leaked from the corners of his cracked lips. Mesquite thorns protruded sharply, piercing his gums and cheeks, leaving dark, angry puncture marks. His tongue, swollen and dark, pushed against the thorns, creating an image of suffering that was almost too much to bear.

His eyes were wide open, clouded with a final, horrified stare. The eyeballs were slightly bulging, the capillaries ruptured and staining the whites a mottled red, as if the very act of seeing his own death had marked them. His cheeks were streaked with tears, leaving jagged tracks down his bruised and battered face.

His hands were another testament to his suffering. The fingers were twisted, the nails cracked and caked with dirt, as though he had tried desperately to claw at the ground, leaving deep gouges in the frost-bitten earth around him. The skin on his wrists was bruised, with deep ligature marks suggesting he had been bound tightly, the flesh torn and rubbed raw from the struggle.

Roger knelt beside the body, the denim of his jacket creaking. The brutality wasn't what unnerved him most; it was the methodical precision. Every wound, every detail seemed purposeful. Roger stood and looked around. The only thing close by was an old abandoned well. On the rusted old wellhead was a sign hanging from a single piece of rusted bailing wire. On the sign, one could barely make out a big red M. As he studied the scene, a memory tugged at the edge of his mind—something about an old photograph he'd seen years ago. It was frustratingly out of reach, but the feeling it left was unmistakable: a sense of unease, as if history were repeating itself in ways he couldn't yet understand.

The area around the body had an eerie stillness, broken only by the soft rustling of the wind through the brush. Roger scanned the surroundings, taking in every detail—the discarded beer bottles near the fence line, the remnants of an old campfire, and the tire tracks that led away from the scene. He made a mental note to have Liz photograph everything. Evidence was often buried in the mundane.

Liz swallowed hard, her breath catching. "Whoever did this," she said in a hushed voice, "they wanted him to suffer. And they wanted us to know."

Roger straightened, his knees aching from the cold, and turned to Liz. "What about ID?" he asked.

Liz shook her head, her hands clenched so tightly around her notepad that her knuckles had gone white. "Nothing," she said, "No wallet, no phone. He's a John Doe for now. Whoever did this stripped him clean."

Roger sighed, the cold settling deeper into his bones. Before he could respond, a familiar voice called out from nearby.

"Sheriff."

Roger turned to see Jim Bishop, a local rancher, standing a few yards away. Jim Bishop was the kind of man you couldn't picture anywhere but West Texas. In his late sixties, he'd lived through droughts, oil booms, and busts and had the weathered face to prove it. His hands, thick and calloused, spoke of decades of ranch work—mending fences, branding cattle, and coaxing a living out of unforgiving land. He had a stubbornness that fit his reputation, someone who wasn't afraid to argue with city folks who didn't understand ranch life. But this morning, Jim looked like a man who'd seen something he couldn't argue with, something he couldn't explain away.

Roger approached slowly, giving the man time to gather himself. The Sheriff had known Jim for most of his life—long enough to know that despite his gruff exterior, Jim was as steady as they came. If this crime had shaken him, it meant something.

"Jim," Roger said, his voice low and steady, "you found the body?"

Jim nodded, still clutching his weathered cowboy hat. The brim was frayed, the leather band darkened with years of sweat and sun. "Yeah," he said, his voice gravelly. "Was out feedin' the cattle. Thought maybe one of the calves had wandered off, so I came lookin'. Then I saw him."

His eyes flicked toward the body, and he quickly looked away, swallowing hard. "Ain't never seen anything like it, Roger. Not in all my years."

Roger tilted his head, studying the rancher. "You're sure you didn't see anyone else? No trucks, no footprints?"

Jim shook his head, his lips pressed into a thin line. "No one. Just him. Like he'd been…left there. Like someone wanted me to find him."

The Sheriff felt the weight of those words. "Why do you say that?"

Jim hesitated, glancing at the crime scene and then back at Roger. "You think the land remembers?" he asked quietly. "You think it holds onto things, even after we're gone?"

Roger frowned, unsure how to respond. It wasn't the kind of question Jim usually asked. "What do you mean?"

Jim hesitated, his gaze shifting toward the wellhead, the rusty frame swaying slightly in the cold wind. "This area's always had…a reputation," he said slowly, as if reluctant to voice old fears. "My granddaddy used to tell stories about the Permian Basin. Said there were parts of it you just didn't go to—places where bad things happened. Feuds, fights, disappearances. And sometimes, when someone went missin', folks'd say it was the land takin' what it was owed."

Roger's brow furrowed. "You mean like superstition? Curses?"

Jim gave a short, humorless laugh, shaking his head. "No, not curses. More like…unfinished business. He said the land remembers things we try to bury. Blood spilled here; don't stay hidden. Sometimes it comes back up, like oil seepin' to the surface, makin' us reckon with it all over again."

Roger's gaze shifted to the wellhead, its rusty, crooked frame swaying slightly in the wind. The faded red "M" on the sign dangled precariously, the wire creaking softly with each gust. "You're saying this isn't the first time something like this has happened out here?"

Jim hesitated, his brow furrowing as he chose his words carefully. "Not like this," he admitted. "Not this brutal. But bad things have happened in the Basin before. Folks just don't talk about it much. Maybe because they're afraid it'll stir somethin' up."

Roger studied the man, weighing his words. Jim wasn't prone to flights of fancy, and he certainly wasn't one to scare easily.

Roger nodded slowly, sensing there was more the man wasn't saying. "Jim," he said, his tone firm but understanding, "if there's anything else you know—anything that could help us—you need to tell me."

Jim met his gaze, and for a moment, the defiant old rancher was gone, replaced by a man carrying the weight of too many unanswered questions. "Sheriff," he said, his voice low, "I can't shake the feelin' that whoever did this…they ain't just tryin' to kill people. They're tryin' to say somethin'. To all of us."

Roger's stomach tightened at the words. He reached out, placing a hand on Jim's shoulder. "Go on home," he said gently. "If you remember anything else, you call me."

Jim nodded, slipping his hat back onto his head. He hesitated a moment longer, his eyes lingering on the wellhead and the body beyond it. Then, without another word, he turned and walked back to his truck, his boots crunching over the iced-over ground. The sound of his old engine starting echoed across the empty drawer before fading into the wind.

Roger watched him go, his gut churning with unease. Jim's words—about the land, about the killer's message—stuck with him. He didn't believe in curses or haunted places, but he did believe in patterns, in history repeating itself. And right now, it felt like Midland was caught in the middle of something dark that had been waiting in the shadows for far too long.

He turned back to Liz, who had been listening quietly from a few steps away. Her expression mirrored his own: wary, unsettled, and deeply concerned.

"You think Jim's right?" she asked softly. "About the land, remembering?"

Roger didn't answer right away. "I don't know," he admitted. "But I'm starting to think this isn't just about the bodies. It's about what they mean."

Liz nodded, her jaw tightening. "Then we better figure it out. Fast."

Roger nodded, the weight of her words settling heavily on him. He could feel it in his bones, a darkness that seemed to stretch beyond just one body, one scene. There was something larger at play, something that felt like it was only beginning to reveal itself.

Roger was about to speak when the rumble of another vehicle cut through the silence. The county coroner, Marla Decker, had arrived. She stepped out of her SUV, her breath forming small clouds in the frosty air. Marla was in her late forties, with dark hair pulled back in a messy ponytail and sharp eyes that missed nothing. She wore a thick coat over her scrubs, and her expression was tight with the weight of a long career spent dealing with death.

"Morning," Marla said, her voice brisk but grave. She approached the body, her leather bag clutched in one hand and knelt beside it. Her gloved hands moved with practiced precision, examining the shattered jaw, the deep chest wounds, and the sand and thorns crammed into the victim's mouth.

Roger and Liz watched her work, the silence thick with unspoken dread. Marla finally let out a slow breath, her brow furrowed. "This wasn't just a murder," she said, looking up at them. "It was a performance. Every detail was intentional, meant to send a message."

Roger felt his jaw tighten. "What can you tell us about the injuries?"

Marla pointed to the victim's hands. "No defensive wounds," she said. "He didn't fight back. Either he was unconscious or restrained. The chest wounds are deep and precise, made with something sharp—a knife, maybe a hunting blade. The shattered jaw was done with incredible force. Whoever did this took their time. And the sand and thorns…" She paused, her lips pressing into a thin line. "That's pure cruelty. Meant to silence him in the most brutal way."

Liz shivered, but she kept her voice steady. "You think there's more to come?" she asked, though she already knew the answer.

Marla looked back at the body, her eyes shadowed with worry. "I hope not," she said quietly. "But my gut says we're only at the beginning."

Roger's eyes drifted to the horizon, the pale light of the rising sun touching the frost-covered ground. He felt a pang of worry, not just for the victims but for Midland itself. It wasn't just the brutality of the crime that scared him; it was the way it seemed to pull at the fabric of the town, unearthing old fear and old stories that people had long tried to forget.

Roger turned back to the scene, his sharp eyes moving over every detail. The wellhead with its swaying red "M," the blood frosted in a dark halo around the body, and the disturbed earth told a fragmented story. Kneeling near the tire tracks that led away from the scene, Roger brushed a gloved hand over the marks, noting their depth and spacing.

"Liz," he called. "Get some shots of these tracks before the frost thaws. Looks like a truck—heavier tread."

Liz hurried over, her camera clicking rapidly as she documented the evidence. "You think it's local?" she asked, pausing to check the clarity of the images.

"Could be," Roger said, straightening. "But these tracks don't match anything Jim's driving. We'll compare them with what we've got back at the station." He glanced at the abandoned well again, his gut telling him it was more than just a backdrop. "And get shots of that wellhead. Every angle."

As Liz worked, Roger circled the body, careful not to disturb the ground. The twisted fingers, the chest wounds— it all screamed deliberate, purposeful violence. He crouched near the victim's head, studying the mesquite thorns protruding from the man's bloodied mouth. In all his years in the service and the sheriff's office, he'd never seen anything like this.

By the time they finished documenting the immediate area, the scene had taken on a more organized chaos. Crime scene tape fluttered in the wind, marking the boundaries of the investigation. Evidence bags lay neatly arranged near Liz's cruiser, each one containing a fragment of the killer's macabre performance. The victim's body, now partially covered by Marla's tarp, was ready for transport, though the grim details of his death would linger in everyone's mind long after the scene was cleared.

Roger stood back, taking in the full picture. The frosted landscape, the eerie quiet, the rusted wellhead—it all felt like the prelude to something much larger. The killer had taken great care, not just in the violence but in the staging. This wasn't just a murder; it was a statement.

As Marla's team began preparing the body for transport, Roger's radio crackled to life. Jenny Pearson's voice came through, high and strained. "Sheriff, we've got another one," she said, her words cutting through the cold like a knife. "A body at Beal Park. It's…it's bad, Roger."

Roger felt his heart drop, and the cold settling in his bones turned into a deep, hollow ache. Two bodies, two brutal scenes, and the morning was barely half over. This wasn't just a bad day. This was something far worse.

Liz's eyes widened, and she exchanged a look with Roger, one filled with fear and determination. "We need to get there," she said, her voice steady but tight.

Roger nodded, his mind already racing. The sun was creeping higher in the sky, casting pale light over the chilled landscape, but it did nothing to warm the chill that had taken hold of him. Midland was on the brink, and he knew this was only the beginning.

"Let's move," he said, and together, he and Liz headed for their vehicles, bracing themselves for the nightmare waiting for them at Beal Park.

CHAPTER TWO

Beal Park, a sprawling patch of green and playgrounds that once echoed with all the children's laughter and weekend family picnics, now lay shrouded in an eerie silence. The frost-covered grass crackled underfoot, and the wind whispered through the bare branches, carrying a sense of foreboding. The usual bustle of life had been replaced with crime scene tape fluttering in the cold breeze and the somber murmurs of police officers.

Liz stepped out of her cruiser, the adrenaline from the morning's first murder still coursing through her veins. Her gloved hands were balled into fists, and she took a moment to steady herself. Two brutal murders in a single morning in a town like Midland was unheard of, and the unease she felt was palpable, coiling in her gut like a snake ready to strike. She drew in a slow breath, trying to calm herself, the cold air stinging her lungs. The park that had once been filled with warmth and joy now seemed haunted, the shadows beneath the oak trees appearing as if they were hiding secrets.

Roger's battered Silverado pulled up behind her, the old truck rattling as it came to a stop. Roger climbed out, his face etched with exhaustion and disbelief. His blue eyes, already shadowed by the violence they had seen earlier, hardened as he took in the scene before him. The town he had dedicated his life to protecting was unraveling, and he could feel the weight of it pressing down on him. His boots crunched on the frosty ground as he approached Liz, his breath coming out in white puffs. He noticed how her eyes were fixed on the scene ahead, and he could see the tension in her posture.

"Two bodies," Roger muttered, his breath hanging in the frigid air. "Same morning. This is more than coincidence." His voice was heavy with the kind of dread that came from years of facing the worst humanity had to offer. He knew the difference between random acts of violence and something calculated. This felt orchestrated.

Liz didn't respond. Instead, she gestured toward the old oak tree at the heart of the park. The scene was far more brutal than anything she had imagined. The victim, an older man in his late fifties, had been tied to the tree, his limbs spread out and bound with thick, rough rope.

The ground beneath the tree was soaked in blood, the dark stain spreading out like a gruesome halo around the body. The frost on the ground had melted in places where the blood had pooled, creating patches of bare earth that contrasted starkly with the white of the surrounding grass. The man's eyes were open wide in an expression of terror, and his skin had taken on a bluish hue from the cold. His hands were swollen and bruised, the rope cutting so deeply into his wrists that the skin had split, revealing raw, torn flesh beneath. His fingernails were cracked and broken, some torn away entirely as if he had fought desperately against his restraints. Blood crusted around his fingernails, a testament to his futile struggle.

His face was a macabre portrait of suffering. The dirt and shards of glass that had been forced into his mouth had left his lips torn and shredded. Some of the glass had cut deep into the gums, causing thick rivulets of blood to freeze along his chin and neck. His teeth, visible through the torn skin, were chipped and cracked, with several missing entirely, likely broken during the brutal act. The glass protruded from his mouth like jagged, glistening teeth, catching the weak morning light in a twisted, shimmering display.

The deep slash across his throat was ghastly. The cut was not clean; the edges were jagged, indicating that the blade had been either dull or that the killer had intentionally made it brutal. The wound gaped open, exposing the muscles and tendons beneath, the severed trachea visible amidst the blood. The head, barely attached, lolled distortedly to one side, the neck muscles torn and frayed like shredded cloth. Blood had spattered the tree's bark in a dark, chaotic pattern, some of it still wet and glistening in the cold light.

His left arm had been twisted at an unnatural angle, the bone protruding through the skin in a sickening display. The exposed bone was stained with blood, and the flesh around it was a freakish mix of purple and black, the skin split and torn from the force. The flesh around his wrists was torn and mangled, evidence of a desperate attempt to free himself.

Roger took a slow breath, fighting the wave of nausea that threatened to rise. He had seen plenty of violence in his years—war zones, bar fights gone horribly wrong, domestic disputes that ended in tragedy—but this level of cruelty was different. It was calculated and deliberate, and somehow, it felt deeply personal. The methodical nature of the wounds, the ritualistic positioning, the sheer brutality of it—this was someone sending a message.

Liz stepped closer, her boots crunching over icy leaves. "It's the same as the scene at Monahans Draw," she said, her voice low and tense. "The method, the violence… they have to be linked." She stared at the man's face, her stomach churning at the sight of the dirt and glass packed into his mouth. Whoever had done this had wanted to degrade him, to strip him of his humanity.

Roger nodded, his mind racing. He scanned the area, taking in every detail—the old oak tree, its bare branches reaching skyward like skeletal fingers, the patches of trampled grass, the blood that had spattered the tree's bark. He could almost feel the echoes of violence in the air, the hatred that had fueled this act. "We need to ID this guy," he said, his voice gruff. "Did we find anything?"

Liz held up a clear evidence bag, inside an old, worn leather wallet. "Found this in his back pocket," she said. "Name's Thomas Anders. Local contractor. Been living in Midland for years, mostly kept to himself."

Roger took the evidence bag and studied the wallet through the plastic. The name was familiar, but he couldn't immediately place Anders. He knew that in a town like Midland, everyone's paths crossed eventually, but Anders's name didn't ring any alarm bells. Yet. He turned his attention back to the body, his eyes narrowing as he considered the violence that had been inflicted. There was something almost different about it, something that suggested a deeper meaning.

Before he could process further, the county coroner's SUV rumbled into the park. Marla Decker stepped out, her face set in a grim expression. Her eyes were sharp and tire and seemed to absorb the horror of the scene without flinching. Marla had seen her fair share of gruesome deaths, but this morning was testing even her resolve.

"Another one," she said as she approached Roger and Liz, setting her heavy leather bag beside the body. Her breath fogged in the cold air, and she pulled on a pair of latex gloves. "What's Midland coming to?"

Roger didn't respond, but his expression said enough. He watched as Marla knelt beside the body, her movements careful and deliberate. She examined the broken arm, the deep slash across the throat, and the dirt and glass packed into the victim's mouth. Her gloved fingers moved with practiced precision, her eyes narrowing as she assessed each injury.

"It's the same killer," Marla confirmed, her voice clinical but tinged with dread. "The arm was broken before he died. The throat wound was the fatal one, but it wasn't quick. The dirt and glass…" She trailed off, her eyes darkening. "That's pure degradation. Whoever did this wanted to silence him, humiliate him."

Liz's hands tightened around her notepad. She forced herself to take notes, even as her stomach churned at the details. "We're dealing with a monster," she said, her voice barely above a whisper. She glanced at Roger, her eyes searching his for some kind of reassurance, but all she saw was the same grim determination that she felt.

Roger nodded, his jaw clenching. Two brutal murders, two messages he couldn't yet decipher. Before he could dwell on it, his phone buzzed in his pocket. He pulled it out, frowning at the unfamiliar number. "Hartley," he answered, his voice gruff.

"Sheriff, this is Angela Ramirez over at Midland Memorial," a woman's voice said. "I think we might have a lead on that John Doe you found this morning. A young woman just came in, frantic, saying her boyfriend's missing. Matches your description."

Roger's pulse quickened. "We're on our way," he said, and he hung up, turning to Liz. "We might have a lead on the first victim. A woman at the hospital reported her boyfriend missing, and he matches our John Doe's description."

Liz's eyes widened. "If we can ID him, maybe we'll find a connection between the victims."

Roger nodded, though he felt the tension in his chest tighten. Two murders— both brutal, and still no clear connection. But they had to start somewhere. "Marla," he said, turning to the coroner, "let us know as soon as you have anything more from the autopsy."

Marla gave him a grim nod. "I'll do what I can. But you two be careful," she said, her voice heavy with warning. "Whoever did this isn't done. You can feel it."

Roger didn't need to be told twice. He and Liz made their way back to his vehicle, the wind rustling through the park's empty playground, and he couldn't shake the feeling that the whole town was holding its breath, waiting for something even darker to come.

Roger and Liz sped toward Midland Memorial Hospital on Andrews Highway, the tension between them palpable. The town felt different, like something had shifted beneath the surface, and every mile they drove seemed to bring them closer to whatever lay at the heart of it. The silence in the truck was heavy, both of them lost in their thoughts, replaying the morning's events in their minds. Roger could feel the weight of the situation pressing down on him, the responsibility of finding whoever was responsible before they struck again.

When they arrived, the emergency room was its usual mix of chaos and exhaustion. Nurses moved briskly between patients, and the smell of antiseptic hung heavy in the air. Angela Ramirez, a young nurse with tired eyes and a calming demeanor, approached them.

"Sheriff, Deputy," Angela greeted them, gesturing toward a waiting room down the hall. "She's in there. Name's Megan Castillo. She came in about an hour ago, crying, saying her boyfriend hadn't come home last night. She saw your description on the news and… well, she's not doing well."

Roger exchanged a look with Liz, and they both braced themselves. They had done this before—delivered terrible news to loved ones—but it never got easier.

Megan Castillo was a young woman, maybe in her early twenties, with dark hair pulled into a messy ponytail and eyes red from crying. She was sitting in one of the plastic chairs, her hands shaking as she held onto her phone like it was the only thing keeping her grounded. Her face was pale, her eyes hollow from sleepless hours spent worrying, and now the crushing weight of what she was about to hear.

Liz approached her gently. "Megan?" she said softly.

Megan looked up, her eyes filled with a desperate kind of hope that made Roger's heart ache. "Are you here about Caleb?" she asked, her voice cracking. "Please, tell me you found him."

Roger knelt in front of her, his hat in his hands. "Megan," he said, his voice heavy, "we found a young man this morning, but we need you to help us confirm if it's Caleb."

Megan's face crumpled, and she clutched her phone tighter, her whole body trembling. "No," she whispered, her voice breaking. "No, no, no…" Her shoulders shook as the weight of Roger's words hit her. Tears streamed down her cheeks, and she let out a choked sob that filled the quiet room. The desperate hope she had clung to for hours shattered, leaving only a hollow void in its place.

Liz sat beside her, placing a comforting hand on her arm. "We're so sorry," she said softly, her own eyes brimming with empathy. "We know this is hard, but we need your help, Megan. It's the only way we can make sure Caleb gets justice."

Megan sniffled, nodding as she tried to steady herself. She took a shaky breath and pulled up a photo on her phone. Her hands were trembling, and it took her a moment to get the screen to respond. "This... this is him," she said, showing them a picture of a smiling young man with sandy-blond hair and bright green eyes. He looked full of life, his face glowing with happiness in the photograph. It was almost impossible to reconcile the bright, lively person in the picture with the horrific image Roger had seen that morning.

Roger felt his stomach drop. It was the same face he had seen suspended in horror at Monahans Draw. Caleb. A name to go with the John Doe, a life reduced to a brutal crime scene. He closed his eyes for a brief moment, feeling the weight of it all pressing down on him. "Thank you, Megan," Roger said softly, though he knew the words offered little comfort. "We'll do everything we can to get justice for Caleb."

Megan sobbed, her grief raw and uncontainable, echoing in the small waiting room. Roger had to look away, his own emotions threatening to bubble to the surface. He had been a sheriff long enough to know that moments like this never got easier. They never should.

Roger and Liz grabbed two uncomfortable chairs and sat across from Megan Castillo, the sterile walls and fluorescent lights casting a harsh light on her tear-streaked face. Megan sat hunched forward, clutching a disposable cup of water between trembling hands, her knuckles white. Liz had insisted on giving her a moment to breathe, but time was a luxury they couldn't afford.

Roger leaned forward, his voice calm but firm. "Megan, I know this is hard. But anything you can tell us about Caleb's recent behavior or where he's been could help us catch whoever did this."

Megan sniffled, her lips quivering as she set the cup down on the table. "I don't know…" she began, her voice weak. "He… he didn't seem like himself these past few weeks."

Liz exchanged a quick glance with Roger. "What do you mean?" Liz asked gently. "Did something happen?"

Megan nodded, her eyes downcast. "He was stressed. More than usual. Caleb was always looking over his shoulder." She rubbed her hands together, her gaze distant. "I asked him what was going on, but he wouldn't tell me. He just kept saying he had to take care of something."

Roger's brow furrowed. "Take care of what? Did he say anything about who or what he was worried about?"

Megan shook her head, her voice trembling as she replied. "No. But he was spending a lot of time out at night. He'd leave after dinner and wouldn't come back until after midnight. When I asked where he was going, he said he needed to meet someone but wouldn't tell me who." She looked up at Roger, desperation in her eyes. "I begged him to let me in, but he just kept saying it was better if I didn't know."

Liz leaned forward slightly, her tone soft but probing. "Did he ever mention any specific places he went? Was there anyone new he started hanging out with?"

Megan hesitated, her brow creased in thought. "There was… one time," she said slowly. "Last week, he came home with dirt on his shoes and jacket, like he'd been walking somewhere in the middle of nowhere. When I asked him about it, he got defensive. He said it was nothing and that I shouldn't worry."

Roger's jaw tightened. "Megan, did he have any enemies? Anyone he didn't get along with?"

She shook her head quickly. "No. Caleb wasn't like that. He was kind and always tried to avoid conflict. But…" She hesitated, biting her lip.

"But what?" Liz pressed gently.

"There was this guy," Megan admitted, her voice barely above a whisper. "I don't know his name, but Caleb mentioned him a couple of times. He said the guy was 'bad news.' Caleb didn't want anything to do with him, but he said he didn't have a choice."

Roger and Liz exchanged a glance, the unspoken understanding passing between them. "Megan," Roger said carefully, "did Caleb ever say why he didn't have a choice? Did this man threaten him?"

Megan nodded, fresh tears spilling down her cheeks. "I think so. Caleb wouldn't say much, but I could tell he was scared. He kept saying he was trying to fix things and just needed a little more time."

"Thank you, Megan," Liz said, her voice steady. "This helps more than you know."

Liz's jaw tightened, and she stood, her resolve hardening as she looked at Roger. "We have to find whoever did this," she said, her voice low but fierce. "No one else needs to suffer like this."

Roger nodded, his blue eyes dark with determination. He had faced violence before, but this case was starting to feel different, like an old wound that was being torn open. He placed a steadying hand on Megan's shoulder. "We'll find them," he promised, though the words felt heavy with the weight of what they had yet to uncover. "We'll make sure they pay for what they did to Caleb."

Angela Ramirez, who had been watching quietly from the doorway, stepped in her gentle presence a small comfort as she knelt beside Megan. "Come with me," Angela said, her voice soothing. "Let's get you somewhere more private where you can rest."

Megan allowed Angela to lead her away, her sobs echoing down the hallway. The scene left Roger and Liz standing in the sterile hallway, surrounded by the chaos of the emergency room but feeling the silence between them like a living thing.

Roger ran a hand over his tired face, his jaw clenched. "Two murders, and now we have a name," he said, his voice taut. "Caleb Jennings."

Liz exhaled sharply, her breath fogging the air. "And Thomas Anders at Beal Park," she added, her mind already spinning with questions. "What's the link between them? We need to figure out why these two were targeted."

Roger thought about the crime scenes and the way the bodies had been brutalized and placed. There was a connection here, a thread he couldn't quite pull loose, but he could feel it tightening around them. "Let's get back to the station," he said. "We need to start piecing this together before whoever did this strikes again."

The Midland Sheriff's Office was buzzing with activity when they returned. Officers were huddled around maps, comparing notes and taking calls from concerned residents who had heard about the murders. The atmosphere was tense, a mixture of fear and determination, and Roger could feel the weight of every eye that turned toward him as he walked in.

Liz headed straight for the incident room, her boots echoing off the tiled floor. Roger followed, his mind racing. He didn't have the luxury of hesitation. Whoever was behind these murders was escalating, and they needed answers.

The incident room was cluttered with whiteboards, pinned maps, and stacks of files. Liz grabbed a marker and began scrawling details onto one of the boards: Caleb Jennings, 44, found at Monahans Draw. Thomas Anders, 58, was found at Beal Park. She stepped back, chewing her lower lip, a habit she had when she was deep in thought.

"Okay," Liz said, her voice steady despite the turmoil inside her. "What do we know about these men? Anything that ties them together?"

Roger rubbed his temples, his brain working overtime. "Caleb was young, likely with few enemies," he said. "A boyfriend, a life… nothing that screams high risk. Anders, on the other hand, was older. A contractor. We need to look at his history, see if there's anything that might have made him a target."

Deputy Eli Rivera, a young and eager officer with a wiry frame and a perpetually anxious demeanor, stepped into the room holding a file. "Sheriff, we've got some initial background on Anders," he said, pushing his glasses up his nose. "He did a lot of work around town. Mostly did residential construction, but he had some big clients, too. Worked on a few city contracts over the years."

Liz frowned. "City contracts? Anything controversial?"

Eli shook his head, his brows furrowed. "Not that I've found yet, but I'm still digging."

Roger tapped the marker against the board. "Keep looking," he instructed. "We need to know if Anders crossed the wrong person or if there's something about his work that made him a target."

Eli nodded and hurried out, leaving Roger and Liz alone once more. Liz stared at the names on the board, frustration etched across her features. "It doesn't make sense," she said. "Two completely different people, no obvious connection. But this kind of brutality… it's not random."

Roger didn't respond right away. He was staring at the board, his mind still circling back to that rusted sign, the memory it had stirred but refused to fully reveal. It was maddening, like trying to grasp smoke. He'd seen something like this before—he was sure of it—but where?

"Something's missing," Roger said finally, his voice heavy. "There's a piece of this puzzle we don't have yet."

Before Liz could reply, a knock at the door made them both turn. Jenny Pearson stood there, looking more anxious than Roger had ever seen her. Her usually calm face was pinched with worry, and she was clutching a piece of paper in her hand.

"Sheriff, you need to see this," Jenny said, stepping into the room and handing Roger the paper. "It's a fax that just came through from an unknown number. It's… strange."

Roger took the paper and scanned it, his frown deepening. It was a message, typed in an old-fashioned font, the kind you'd find on a dusty typewriter. The words were chilling in their simplicity:

"The land remembers. The debt must be paid."

Liz leaned over his shoulder, her eyes narrowing. "What the hell is that supposed to mean?" she asked, her voice low.

Roger's heart thudded in his chest. The land remembers. The words sent a chill down his spine, resonating with the unsettling feeling he'd had all day. He clenched his jaw, his grip tightening on the paper. Whoever had sent this knew something—something they were all missing.

"It means," Roger said, his voice grim, "that we're dealing with someone who thinks these murders are justified. And they're not finished yet."

The room seemed to grow colder, the weight of the message pressing down on them. Roger exchanged a look with Liz, and for a moment, he saw the same fear he felt reflected in her eyes. Midland was on the edge of something dark, and they had to figure out what it was before it consumed them all.

"Let's dig deeper," Roger said, his voice hardening with resolve. "Because if the land remembers, we need to find out why—and fast."

The investigation was far from over, but they had a new clue. And somewhere in the shadows of Midland, a killer was waiting.

CHAPTER THREE

The sky over Midland was a slate-gray canopy, heavy with clouds that pressed down on the town like an unspoken warning. Through the narrow windows of the Sheriff's Office, faint streaks of sunlight struggled to pierce the gloom, casting ghostly patterns on the walls. The air inside felt thick, weighed down by the tension simmering in every corner, while the hum of fluorescent lights buzzed faintly, almost drowned out by the relentless ticking of the wall clock.

Roger sat at the head of the long table in the incident room, his hands clasped around a mug of black coffee. His blue eyes, usually hard and steady, were tinged with exhaustion, the lines around them deeper than usual. The past twelve hours had been a nightmare, and the cryptic message they'd received earlier that morning—"The land remembers. The debt must be paid."—echoed in his mind, gnawing at the edges of his sanity. He kept replaying the scenes in his head: the gruesome bodies, the terrified faces of those left behind, and that haunting message.

"Damn it," Roger muttered, running a hand over his face, feeling the stubble rough against his palm. The stress of the job was something he had grown used to, but this case was dredging up something deeper. He knew Midland was a town with secrets, but he was starting to feel like they had been waiting for a moment just like this to come boiling to the surface—dark memories and untold stories buried in the dust of West Texas.

Across the room, Liz paced back and forth, her boots thudding rhythmically against the worn tile floor. Her arms were crossed over her chest, her brows knit in concentration. She chewed on the end of a pen, a habit she had picked up in high school and never managed to shake. Frustration rolled off her in waves, her thoughts a storm she couldn't seem to settle. Each step echoed her impatience, each thud of her boots a reminder that time was against them.

"It's not random," Liz said, more to herself than anyone else. "Whoever wrote that message—whoever killed Caleb Jennings and Thomas Anders—thinks they have a reason. We just can't see it yet." Her eyes darted to the whiteboard covered in photos, timelines, and hastily scribbled notes. The lines connecting victims, locations, and potential motives formed a chaotic web—so many strands, and yet none seemed to lead anywhere concrete.

Roger set down his mug, his fingers flexing as if he wanted to strangle the truth out of the air. "The problem is," he replied, his voice heavy, "the reason is buried somewhere we haven't looked. We need to know why these men were targeted. We need to know what ties them together." His voice cracked slightly, a testament to his deep weariness in his bones. Every new lead felt like another door slamming shut.

Liz stopped pacing and faced him, her eyes meeting his with a spark of determination. "We're looking for a thread," she said. "And we're running out of time." There was a fierce intensity in her gaze, a resolve that had carried her through more nights than she cared to remember. This case had become personal, not just because of its horror but because of what it represented—the darkness that could consume anyone, anywhere.

Roger's cell phone buzzed, and he glanced at the screen. It was a text from his ex-wife, Kathy: Call me when you have a moment. We need to talk about Emily. The message sat there like a weight on his chest, a painful reminder of the life he had failed to keep together. The stark words on the screen brought a rush of memories—Emily as a child, her laughter filling their house, her questions about his work that he had tried to answer without scaring her. The teenager she had grown into was angry at him for missing recitals, for the nights he came home smelling of whiskey, and for the fights he and Kathy tried to keep quiet but never quite managed.

Kathy had always been his anchor, but their marriage had unraveled slowly, like a frayed rope. The years of long hours, missed dinners, and the emotional distance created by Roger's dedication to the job had worn them both down. He'd tried to be there for Emily, but being a father to a bright, determined young woman like her was a challenge he hadn't always lived up to. Emily had inherited his stubbornness, and that had led to more than a few shouting matches, especially in recent years.

Their last conversation ended with Emily in tears and Roger feeling like the worst father in the world. She had begged him to take care of himself, to quit drinking, to prioritize his health. But the job was in his blood, and the whiskey helped dull the memories he didn't want to face.

Kathy, ever the mediator, had been trying to repair their relationship, but Roger couldn't shake the guilt.

"Everything okay?" Liz asked, her voice softer than usual, cutting through his thoughts.

Roger looked up, startled, and blinked, realizing he had been staring at his phone. "Yeah," he lied, slipping the device back into his pocket. "Just family stuff." His voice was gruff, the words scraping like shards of glass in his throat.

Liz nodded, her expression carefully neutral. She had known Roger long enough to sense that "family stuff" was a loaded topic for him. She also knew that pressing wouldn't help. Roger was a man who carried his burdens alone, whether or not they were breaking him. She noticed the cracks forming but also knew he was too proud—or stubborn—to admit it.

Liz's phone buzzed next, and she pulled it from her pocket, her heart sinking when she saw the name Jason. She had been dating Jason for a little over a year, and things had started off well. Jason was kind and dependable, and he made her laugh—something she desperately needed in a life filled with stress and darkness. Lately, he had been talking about the future and wanting more, and Liz found herself unable to promise him anything. The case was just the latest excuse to avoid facing the growing chasm between them.

Her mind drifted back to the night they met, almost like a scene from *The Comedy of Errors*. It had been a rare evening off, and she'd gone to Fast Freddy's with a few friends, eager for some laughter and distraction. She was at the pool table mid-game, leaning over to line up her shot when chaos struck. On his way back from the bar with a fresh beer in hand, Jason had been tripped by one of his friends, sending the entire glass spilling down her back.

Liz had straightened up, her temper flaring as she turned to confront him. "Are you kidding me?" she'd snapped, brushing beer off her shirt. But the anger fizzled as soon as she locked eyes with Jason—a sheepish, utterly apologetic look on his face that was somehow endearing.

"I'm so sorry," Jason had stammered, grabbing napkins from the nearest table. "I… I swear that wasn't on purpose. My idiot friend…" He'd glared over his shoulder at the culprit, who was doubled over in laughter.

Liz couldn't help it. Despite the sticky shirt and ruined moment, she'd laughed. "You're lucky I have a sense of humor," she'd said, taking the napkin from his hand. And that was how it had started—an accidental mess that had turned into an evening of drinks, conversation, and an undeniable spark. Jason had spent the rest of the night making it up to her, buying her drinks, and charming her with his wit. By the end of the night, he'd asked for her number, and Liz, against her usual better judgment, had given it to him.

Now, though, that spark felt dimmed by the weight of everything else. Jason wanted more, but Liz wasn't sure she had more to give. Her life felt like a precarious balancing act, and the thought of letting someone all the way in… scared her.

We need to talk, the text read, simple yet loaded with meaning.

Liz's throat tightened. She had been dodging this conversation for days, hiding behind her badge and her duty. Jason wanted to settle down and build a life together, but how could she commit to something like that when her life was built around uncertainty and danger? How could she bring someone she loved deeper into a world that had already taken so much from her?

"You good?" Roger asked, his voice breaking through her thoughts.

Liz slipped her phone back into her pocket and forced a smile. "Yeah," she said. "Just… distractions."

Roger didn't push her for more. They had both become experts at compartmentalizing their personal pain, shoving it into boxes they only opened when they were alone. But Liz couldn't help but wonder if she was making a mistake if she was letting the job take more from her than it already had.

Deputy Eli Rivera burst into the room, clutching a stack of printouts and looking like he hadn't slept in days. His wiry frame practically vibrated with nervous energy, and he adjusted his glasses, which were perpetually slipping down his nose. His face was drawn, exhaustion etched in his red-rimmed eyes.

"I've got something," Eli announced, setting the documents down on the table with a slap that echoed in the otherwise quiet room. "Background on Thomas Anders. He had some legal disputes over the years. Construction projects

36

have gone wrong, and there are a few angry clients. No violence, though—just accusations of cutting corners."

Liz flipped through the pages, her brow furrowing as she scanned each line. "So, he made some people angry," she said. "But angry enough to end up like that?" She gestured toward the crime scene photos pinned to the board, each one a haunting reminder of the brutality they were dealing with. The images of Anders, bound to the tree, his throat slashed, glass forced into his mouth—those were acts of rage, hatred, something far beyond a simple grudge.

Eli shook his head, looking uneasy. "No evidence of threats. It's not much, but it's something. I also found out that Anders was involved in a project near the old refinery site about five years ago. Thought it might be worth checking out."

Roger leaned forward, his interest piqued. "The refinery site," he echoed. That name tugged at the memory that had been plaguing him all day. Something about that location felt important, but he couldn't grasp why. It was like an itch in the back of his mind, something just out of reach, waiting for him to remember.

Liz's eyes lit up. "We'll need to look into that," she said. "Maybe Anders stirred something up there—something worth killing over."

Before they could dive deeper into the refinery lead, Jenny Pearson appeared in the doorway, her expression grim. "Sheriff, Deputy," she said. "We've got a problem."

Roger and Liz followed Jenny out of the incident room, down the dimly lit hallway, and into the evidence locker, where a small group of officers had gathered. The air smelled of metal and cold concrete, the kind of chill that seemed to seep into your bones, and everyone looked uneasy. Their faces were pale, and they exchanged nervous glances.

"What is it?" Roger asked, his voice sharp, cutting through the tension in the room.

Jenny led them to the evidence locker area in the back part of the sheriff's office. The evidence locker smelled of cold metal and damp concrete, the chill in the air sinking into Roger's skin. On the back wall, the message glared at them in jagged, dripping black paint: "No one is innocent. The land remembers." The words bled down the concrete in uneven streams as though alive, pulsating with malice. The letters were rough and chaotic, the strokes erratic as if painted in a frenzy. In the harsh glare of the locker's single overhead bulb, the black paint gleamed like fresh oil, sending a wave of unease through the gathered officers.

Liz's heart raced, and she took a step back, her breath catching in her throat. "How did this happen?" she demanded, her voice rising. "How did someone get in here?" Her mind raced with questions, the implications of what this meant sending a chill down her spine. The evidence locker was supposed to be secure, a fortress within the station.

Roger's hands curled into fists, his knuckles whitening. The message was similar to the one they had received earlier, but seeing it inside the station felt like a violation. It meant the killer—or someone connected to them—was closer than they'd thought. It meant they were being watched. It reminded them that they were playing a game where the rules were already set, and they were always a step behind.

"This isn't just a message," Roger said, his voice low, simmering with anger. "It's a warning. And it means we're getting close to something they don't want us to find." He looked around the room at the officers gathered there, their faces drawn and tense. The fear was palpable, but so was the determination. They all understood now that the stakes were higher than they'd imagined. Whoever was behind these murders wasn't just content with killing—they wanted to send a message, to strike fear into the hearts of those trying to find them.

Liz stepped forward, her eyes scanning the words scrawled across the wall. She could feel her heart pounding, her mouth dry. "They know we're onto something," she said. "This isn't just a threat. It's a challenge. They want us to know they're watching."

Roger nodded, his jaw tightening. "And we're going to take that challenge head-on. We don't back down." He turned to the officers. "I want a full sweep of the station. Check every camera and every entry point. Whoever did this knew exactly where to go and how to avoid detection. We need to figure out how they pulled it off."

The officers nodded, their resolve hardening. They dispersed to carry out Roger's orders, leaving him and Liz standing in the evidence locker, the words still glaring at them from the wall.

The atmosphere in the Midland Sheriff's Office had turned even more tense after the discovery in the evidence locker. Roger and Liz were back in the incident room, the dim light flickering slightly as they pored over the refinery notes. The pressure was mounting, and every new twist seemed to pile on more uncertainty. Roger could feel it in his bones—they were being toyed with, led down a path with no guarantee of what they'd find at the end.

The door to the incident room creaked open, and Deputy Eli Rivera entered, his face drawn, worry etched in every line. Roger looked up, already bracing himself for more bad news.

"Sheriff," Eli said, stepping closer to the table, his voice low. He adjusted his glasses nervously, a gesture that Roger knew well—Eli only did that when things were really bad. "I… I've got an update on the security footage from the evidence locker."

Roger's eyes narrowed, and he leaned back slightly, crossing his arms. "Go on," he said, his voice edged with impatience.

Eli took a breath, his gaze flicking to Liz, who had stopped what she was doing to listen. "It's all gone, Sheriff. The footage from every camera covering the office last night has been completely wiped. There's nothing left—no backups, no timestamps, nothing. It's like someone knew exactly how to erase it without leaving a trace."

A heavy silence settled over the room. Roger's jaw tightened, his fingers curling around the edge of the table. "All of it?" he asked, his voice barely above a growl.

Eli nodded, swallowing hard. "Yes, sir. I checked with IT—whoever did this knew what they were doing. It wasn't a simple hack; it was surgical. And…" He hesitated, his eyes flickering to Roger, then back down at the floor.

"And what?" Roger snapped, his patience wearing thin.

"We didn't find any prints," Eli said quietly. "Not on the evidence locker door, not on the wall where the message was painted—nothing. It's like they were never there."

Roger exhaled slowly, the air hissing between his teeth. He closed his eyes for a brief moment, trying to steady the anger bubbling up inside him. No footage. No prints. They were dealing with someone who knew exactly how to cover their tracks, someone who was meticulous, calculated, and fearless enough to break into a sheriff's station without leaving a single shred of evidence.

"They're mocking us," Liz said, her voice low, her eyes hard as she stared at the whiteboard covered in notes and photos. "They're showing us that they can get in and out whenever they want, and we can't even catch a glimpse of them."

Roger pushed himself up from the table, pacing across the room. His hands were clenched into fists at his sides, his mind racing. They had been outmaneuvered, and it stung more than he wanted to admit. The killer—or whoever was helping them—had resources and skills that went beyond what they were dealing with in Midland.

Liz took a deep breath, her hands clenched into fists at her sides. "We can't afford any more surprises like this, Roger. If they can get in here, they can get to any of us." The thought sent a chill down her spine. The killer—or killers—weren't just dangerous; they were audacious, willing to take risks that most wouldn't dare. And that made them even more unpredictable.

Roger glanced at her, his expression softening for a moment. "I know. But we can't let them get in our heads. That's what they want. Fear makes us sloppy." He reached out, resting a reassuring hand on her shoulder. "We'll find them, Liz. We just have to keep pushing."

Liz met his gaze, seeing the exhaustion etched into his features. She nodded, swallowing the fear that threatened to choke her. "You're right. We keep moving. We need to get to that refinery site. Whatever Anders and Caleb had in common—it's tied to that place."

Roger gave her a grim smile. "Then let's get moving. We're not giving them any more of a head start."

They left the evidence locker, the words on the wall still looming in their minds like a dark cloud. The station buzzed with activity, officers moving with renewed purpose, the tension in the air almost tangible. Roger and Liz moved with urgency, gathering what they needed for their visit to the refinery site.

As they stepped outside, the cold wind hit them, the sky still overcast, the heavy clouds hanging low as if mirroring the weight of what they carried. Roger pulled his coat tighter around himself, glancing at Liz. "You ready for this?"

Liz nodded, her eyes hard. "Let's go find out what secrets this town has been hiding."

They drove in silence, the tension between them thick but unspoken. The refinery site was on the outskirts of town, a desolate area that had long since been abandoned, and the skeletal remains of machinery and storage tanks looming in the distance. The place had an eerie stillness to it, a sense of forgotten history that made Liz's skin prickle as they approached.

Roger parked the Silverado near the rusted gates that marked the entrance to the site. The metal was covered in graffiti, years of neglect evident in the peeling paint and the tangled weeds that had grown up around the perimeter. He cut the engine, and they both sat for a moment, taking in the scene before them.

"Looks like it's been decades since anyone cared about this place," Liz said, her voice barely above a whisper. The wind whistled through the gaps in the old structures, the only sound breaking the silence.

Roger nodded, his eyes narrowing as he scanned the area. "Places like this... they hold memories. People come here to do things they don't want seen. We need to be careful." He reached for the flashlight on the dashboard and handed another one to Liz. "Let's take a look."

They stepped out of the truck, the gravel crunching beneath their boots as they made their way toward the entrance. The air was heavy with the scent of rust and decay, the wind carrying an almost metallic tang. Liz shivered, her eyes darting around, every shadow seeming to move, every creak of the old metal putting her on edge.

Roger pushed open the gate, the hinges groaning in protest. The path ahead was overgrown, the concrete cracked and split by years of neglect. They moved cautiously, their flashlights cutting through the gloom, casting long, wavering shadows that danced along the walls of the abandoned structures.

"If Anders was working here, there must be records," Liz said, her voice low. "Something that tells us what he was doing—who he was dealing with."

Roger nodded, his flashlight sweeping across a dilapidated building that looked like it might have once been an office. The windows were shattered, the door hanging off its hinges. "Let's start there," he said, nodding toward it. "If there are records, they'd be in there."

They approached the building, their steps slow and deliberate. Roger pushed the door open, the wood splintering as it swung inward. The inside was dark, the air musty, filled with the scent of mildew and rot. Papers were strewn across the floor, as were old blueprints and documents, most of them yellowed with age and covered in dust.

Liz knelt down, picking up a stack of papers, her eyes scanning the faded text. "These look like schematics," she said, squinting at the blueprints. "But they're old—pre-dating anything recent."

Roger moved further inside, his flashlight illuminating the corners of the room. He paused, his eyes catching something on the far wall—an old corkboard, papers pinned haphazardly, some of them torn, others barely clinging on. He stepped closer, his eyes narrowing as he focused on a faded photograph pinned to the center.

It was a group photo—men in hard hats standing in front of one of the refinery's massive tanks. Roger's breath caught in his throat as he recognized one of the faces. "Liz," he called, his voice tight. "Come look at this."

Liz stood, crossing the room to stand beside him. She leaned in, her eyes widening as she saw what Roger was looking at. There, in the center of the group, was Thomas Anders—standing beside another familiar face.

"That's Caleb," Liz whispered, her heart pounding. "They knew each other."

Roger nodded, his mind racing. "This isn't just a coincidence. They were here together—for some project. Something happened here, something that ties them together."

Liz's eyes scanned the rest of the board, her gaze falling on a faded map pinned beside the photo. Red circles marked several locations within the refinery site, each one numbered. She reached out, her fingers brushing against the paper. "These spots—they must mean something. Maybe they're areas they were working on or places where something happened."

Roger pulled the map down, folding it carefully. "We need to check these locations. Whatever they were doing here, it's connected to why they were killed."

Liz nodded, the weight of what they were uncovering settling heavily on her shoulders. "Let's go," she said, her voice steady despite the fear that gnawed at the edges of her resolve. "We need to find out what happened here—before it's too late."

They left the building, the wind howling through the empty refinery, the shadows lengthening as the day slipped further into darkness. Each step they took felt like they were walking deeper into the past—into the secrets that Midland had buried, secrets that someone was willing to kill to keep hidden.

Roger led the way, his flashlight cutting through the encroaching night, the map clutched tightly in his other hand. He could feel the tension between them, the unspoken understanding that they were getting closer to something dangerous. The refinery loomed around them, its rusted skeleton a reminder of the town's past, of promises made and broken, of the price that had to be paid.

The first location on the map was a storage building, the door padlocked and rusted. Roger pulled at the lock, but it held fast. He looked at Liz, who nodded, stepping back and delivering a swift kick to the door near the handle. The wood splintered, the door swinging inward with a crash that echoed through the empty yard.

Inside, the air was thick with dust, the beams of their flashlights catching motes that danced in the stagnant air. Shelves lined the walls, cluttered with old equipment, rusted tools, and stacks of paperwork that had long since been forgotten. Roger moved to one of the shelves, his eyes scanning the items, while Liz moved toward the back, her flashlight sweeping across the floor.

"Over here," Liz called, her voice echoing slightly in the enclosed space. Roger turned, his light finding her standing beside an old metal locker, the door slightly ajar. She pulled it open, her breath catching in her throat.

Inside the locker was a hard hat smeared with what looked like dried blood. Beneath it, a jacket was crumpled, the fabric stained and torn. Liz reached out, her fingers brushing against the jacket, her stomach turning at the sight of the dark, crusted stains. She turned to Roger, her eyes wide. "This is recent," she said. "Whoever was here—this happened not long ago."

Roger's jaw clenched, a cold fury building inside him. "They're taunting us," he said, his voice low. "Leaving us breadcrumbs—trying to lead us somewhere."

Liz nodded, the realization sinking in. "But why? What are they trying to show us?"

Roger didn't have an answer, but he knew one thing for certain—they couldn't stop now. The pieces of the puzzle were finally starting to fall into place, and despite the risks, they had to see it through. Not when they were finally starting to piece together the puzzle. He turned, his flashlight cutting through the darkness once more. "Let's keep moving. We need to see this through—whatever it takes."

They moved deeper into the refinery, the wind howling through the rusted skeleton of the old industrial complex—a mournful wail that seemed to echo the ghosts of its past. The flashlight beams cut through the gloom, revealing twisted pipes and rusted platforms that loomed like shadows against the dimming sky. The refinery was a labyrinth of decay, and every step felt like it was taking them closer to a truth that loomed ominously just out of reach—a truth neither of them was sure they wanted to face.

Roger led the way, his eyes scanning the map, checking the red circles that had been marked with precision. The refinery's abandoned machinery loomed over them— massive storage tanks, crumbling catwalks, and pipes that twisted like veins through the earth. Liz walked beside him, her eyes constantly moving, every creak of metal and shifting shadow putting her on edge.

They reached the next location—a set of large, rusted storage tanks that had long since fallen into disrepair. The metal was corroded, flaking away in places to reveal dark, empty interiors. A rusted but still intact ladder led to the top of one of the tanks. Roger glanced at Liz, and she nodded, already beginning to climb. Each rung groaned under her weight, the metal cold and slick beneath her gloves.

When she reached the top, she swept her flashlight across the flat surface. The wind whipped at her hair, the chill biting through her jacket. Her light caught something near the edge—a dark stain that spread across the rusted metal. Liz's stomach turned as she knelt to get a closer look, the faint metallic scent of old blood mingling with the acrid tang of rust. The stain was old, the edges dried and cracked, but it was unmistakably blood. She traced the trail with her eyes, following it to where it disappeared over the edge of the tank.

"Roger," she called down, her voice barely audible above the howling wind. "You need to see this."

Roger climbed up, his boots clanking on the ladder until he pulled himself onto the platform beside her. His eyes narrowed as he saw the stain, and he followed Liz's gaze to the edge. He moved closer, careful not to lose his footing, and looked over. Below, the ground was littered with rusted debris—twisted pieces of metal and shattered glass. But amidst the debris, he could see something else—a dark, crumpled shape.

Roger exchanged a glance with Liz before they both descended the ladder. They moved cautiously, picking their way through the debris until they reached the shape. Liz's heart pounded as her flashlight illuminated it—a bundle of fabric stained dark with old blood. She knelt beside it, her gloved hands trembling slightly as she pulled the fabric back.

Beneath the cloth was a small notebook, its cover battered and stained. Liz picked it up carefully, her eyes meeting Roger's. "This could be it," she said, her voice tight. "This might tell us what they were doing here."

Roger nodded, his eyes hard. The discovery confirmed what he had feared—there was more to this place than just its rusted ruins. "Let's get it back to the station. We need to see what's inside."

They made their way back to the truck, the refinery's looming structures casting long shadows across the ground. As they drove away, Liz flipped through the notebook, the pages filled with notes and sketches, many of them smeared and illegible. But there were words that stood out— references to "debt," "land," and something called "The Reckoning."

Roger glanced at her, his brow furrowed. "What the hell were they involved in?"

Liz shook her head, her eyes glued to the pages. "Whatever it was, it wasn't just a job. This was something else—something they believed in."

Roger's grip tightened on the steering wheel. "And now it's gotten them killed. We need to find out who else was involved—who's pulling the strings."

Back at the station, they spread the notebook out on the table in the incident room. The officers gathered around, their eyes scanning the pages. Eli Rivera leaned in, his glasses perched precariously on his nose. "Look at this," he said, pointing to a sketch of the refinery layout. Several areas were marked with symbols—circles, crosses, and arrows, each one labeled with numbers or short phrases.

Liz leaned closer, her brow furrowing. "These symbols—they look like they're marking something specific. Locations, maybe? Or something buried?"

Roger nodded, his eyes narrowing as he scanned the pages. "We need to go back. We need to check every one of these locations. Whatever they were doing out there—it's still there, and it's what got them killed."

Jenny Pearson appeared in the doorway, her shoulders tense and lips pressed into a thin line, her expression grim. "Sheriff, we've got a call. There's been another message."

Roger looked up sharply. "Another message? Where?"

Jenny swallowed, her face pale. "It was found at the community center. Painted on the wall—same handwriting as before. 'The debt grows. The land remembers.'"

Liz felt her heart drop. The community center is another place that connects Caleb and Anders. It was like the killer was taunting them, staying one step ahead. She exchanged a glance with Roger, her jaw set. "They're escalating," she said. "They want us to follow their trail. They're daring us."

Roger stood, his eyes hard. "Then we'll play their game. But on our terms. We're not going to let them control this." He looked at his team, the exhaustion evident in their faces, but also the determination. "We're going to find out what happened at that refinery, what happened at the community center, and we're going to bring whoever's doing this to justice."

As they moved out, Roger felt the weight of the case—a reminder of the lives already lost and the lives still at risk. The sky outside was dark, the storm clouds hanging low, and he knew the worst was yet to come. But they wouldn't back down. They couldn't. Not until they had answers. Not until they had justice for Caleb, for Anders, and for everyone else who had been caught in the crosshairs of whatever darkness had taken root in Midland.

The refinery, the community center, the cryptic messages—it was all connected. And as Roger and Liz prepared to face whatever lay ahead, they knew they were getting closer to the truth. But the closer they got, the more dangerous the game became. The land remembers what the message had said. And now, they were going to make sure that whoever was behind this would remember, too.

CHAPTER FOUR

The last of the daylight bled out over Midland, Texas, as the sun sank behind a line of skeletal trees, leaving the sky bruised and ominous. The cold had teeth now, gnawing through even the thickest coats and settling into bones. The Midland Community Center stood in the dying light like a mausoleum—a decaying relic from a time when the town had thrived. Now, shadows clung to the building's facade, curling around broken windows and graffiti-scrawled walls.

Roger parked his rust-red Chevy Silverado on the uneven asphalt of the parking lot, cutting the engine and letting the silence engulf them. Beside him, Liz shivered, clutching her flashlight as if it were a weapon.

"Never thought I'd come back here," Liz said, her voice barely more than a whisper. She swept her gaze over the ruins of what had once been the heart of the community: the basketball courts, now cracked and overgrown; the playground, where rusted swings creaked mournfully in the wind; and the once-pristine building itself, now crumbling and forgotten.

Roger glanced at her, reading the tension in her posture. "You and me both," he said. His blue eyes, usually so resolute, were haunted by memories. The community center had been a refuge, a place where Midland had come together. He remembered coaching his daughter Emily's basketball games here, remembered the way her laughter used to fill the air. That seemed like a lifetime ago.

They stepped out of the truck, their boots crunching on gravel. The air was heavy with the scent of decay and cold earth, and every gust of wind sent a shiver down Roger's spine. He couldn't shake the feeling that they were being watched. His instincts, honed over decades of police work, screamed at him to stay alert.

"Let's make this quick," he said, his voice gruff. Liz nodded, her face pale but determined.

They approached the building, their flashlights cutting narrow beams through the darkness. The side door had been forced open, the wood splintered, its rusted hinges hanging loose. Roger pushed the door wider with the barrel of his flashlight, and it creaked, the sound echoing down the empty hallways.

"After you," Liz said, attempting a smile that didn't reach her eyes.

Roger stepped inside, gun drawn, and Liz followed close behind. The interior was a graveyard of memories. Graffiti covered the walls in angry, erratic slashes, and water damage had left dark, spreading stains on the ceiling. Broken glass and old, yellowed papers littered the floor. The air was thick with dust and the scent of something sour—like rot mixed with mildew.

"Smells like death in here," Liz murmured, wrinkling her nose.

Roger nodded grimly but didn't respond. His mind was focused on the task at hand—finding any information that could tie the murders to the old refinery. His gut told him they were close to something, but what? He couldn't say. All he knew was that this place felt wrong, like a graveyard for secrets that had never truly been buried.

They moved cautiously down the main corridor, their flashlights playing over old posters announcing Family Fun Day and Youth Basketball Tournaments. The memories those posters stirred up made Roger's heart ache. Midland had been a different place then, full of life and laughter. Now, it was like the soul had been ripped out of it.

They reached the administrative offices. The door was ajar. Roger pushed it open, and they stepped into a room that had been thoroughly ransacked. Filing cabinets lay toppled over, drawers yanked out and emptied. The desk had been shoved against the wall, its surface scarred with deep gouges. Papers covered the floor in a chaotic mess.

But something about the room was off. Amid the disorder, there were signs of recent activity—too recent.

"Wait," Roger said, his flashlight sweeping the room. His beam stopped on a corner where a makeshift nest of old blankets and newspapers was piled. Empty water bottles and crumpled food wrappers surrounded it. A strong, acrid scent clung to the air—a mix of unwashed fabric, mildew, and stale sweat. "Someone's been staying here."

Liz grimaced, stepping closer to examine the area. "It's like they've been squatting here for a while," she said. Her flashlight caught something glinting near the pile. She crouched and picked it up carefully with gloved fingers—a long, thin knife, its blade clean but its handle worn. "Why leave this behind?"

"Maybe they left in a hurry," Roger said, his voice tight. "Or they didn't expect anyone to come looking."

Liz stood and shone her flashlight on the wall above the makeshift bedding. A chaotic scrawl of writing covered the peeling paint, words scratched in charcoal or soot. Phrases leapt out—*"They knew," "No one listens," "Justice for the lost"*—while others were fragmented, rambling, and incoherent.

"Looks like our guy has a flair for drama," Liz muttered, stepping back uneasily.

Roger moved past the corner toward the desk, where something else caught his eye—a neat stack of papers separate from the rest of the chaos. They were pinned down with a stone, as if deliberately left for someone to find. He lifted the stone and carefully spread the pages out. His stomach churned as he realized what he was looking at.

"It's city council memos," he said, his voice low. "Some dated as far back as 2001."

Liz joined him, her face tightening as she scanned the documents. "Look at this one," she said, pointing to a yellowed page stamped with the council's letterhead and marked "Confidential." "Complaints about contamination near the refinery. And here—notes on emergency evacuation protocols they never followed through on."

Roger flipped through the rest of the stack, his hands growing heavier with each page. "They buried it," he said bitterly. "Deferred it to Marathon Oil's legal team, told everyone to keep quiet. This is exactly what we've been looking for."

Liz picked up another sheet, her brow furrowing. It was a hand-drawn map of the refinery grounds and surrounding areas, with certain sections circled in red ink. "These markings," she said, trailing a finger over the map. "They're all areas where bodies were found."

Roger clenched his jaw. "Whoever's been staying here isn't just squatting. They're hunting."

As they sifted through more papers, the feeling of being watched grew stronger, almost suffocating. Roger's hands stilled on a stack of documents, and he lifted his head, listening. The building was full of creaks and groans, but this was different—a faint rustling sound, like feet shuffling across the debris-strewn floor.

"Did you hear that?" Liz whispered, her voice taut.

Roger nodded, his grip on his gun tightening. He rose slowly, gesturing for Liz to stay behind him. They moved out of the office and back into the hallway, their flashlights slicing through the dark. The rustling had stopped, replaced by an almost unbearable silence. Even the wind seemed to hold its breath.

"Who's there?" Roger called, his voice echoing.

No answer. But the feeling remained, prickling at the back of his neck. Liz's flashlight caught movement—a fleeting shadow vanishing around the corner at the far end of the hall. Roger's heart pounded, and he signaled for Liz to follow. They approached the corner cautiously, guns raised. Roger swung around, ready for anything.

But the hall was empty. The shadows seemed thicker here, pressing in on them, and the only sound was the steady drip of water from somewhere deep in the building.

"This place is messing with us," Liz said, her voice cracking slightly. "Feels like it's alive."

Roger didn't answer. He couldn't shake the sensation that whoever—or whatever—had been watching them was still there, hiding in the dark. But he forced himself to refocus. There was work to be done.

They finally reached the records room, a heavy metal door with a rusted, nearly illegible label. Roger tried the handle, but it was locked. He cursed under his breath. The feeling of being watched hadn't left, and he felt exposed, vulnerable, like prey.

Liz pulled an old, tarnished key from her pocket. "Let's see if this does the trick," she murmured.

Roger watched as she inserted the key into the lock. For a tense moment, nothing happened, and frustration surged through him. But then the lock clicked, and the door creaked open. They exchanged a look, and Roger pushed the door wide, his flashlight illuminating the room.

The records room was a mausoleum of Midland's past. Metal shelves lined the walls, sagging under the weight of dusty boxes and binders. The smell of paper and rust filled the air, and a thick layer of dust coated everything. Roger stepped inside, the floor creaking underfoot, and moved his flashlight across the shelves. Each label told a different story: *Employee Records, 1999*; *Financial Ledgers, 2000*; *Environmental Reports, 2001*.

Liz picked up a box labeled *Incident Reports*, her hands trembling slightly. "If there's anything here that ties to the refinery," she said, "it's in one of these."

They began sifting through the boxes, each document a fragment of the town's history. Roger's flashlight fell on a stack of ledgers bound with twine, and his gut told him to investigate. He untied the knot and flipped through the pages. They were financial records—payments made to families affected by refinery incidents. The amounts were significant, but the names of the recipients had been redacted.

"Look at this," he said, showing Liz the ledgers. "They paid people off to keep quiet. No wonder no one ever talked."

Liz's face darkened. "Blood money," she said. "And they got away with it for years."

As they searched, Liz's flashlight caught something wedged behind a stack of boxes. She pulled it free, revealing an old, leather-bound journal. The cover was cracked and worn, the initials *H.M.* embossed in faded gold lettering. Opening the journal revealed what the initials stood for.

"Harold Mercer," Liz whispered, her eyes wide. "This was his."

Roger took the journal, the leather cool against his fingers. He flipped it open, and the first few pages were filled with neat handwriting, detailing Mercer's work at the refinery. But the entries quickly turned darker, describing accidents, chemical spills, and a growing fear that the land itself had been poisoned. The final entry was chilling: *They won't listen. No one will. But the land remembers. And it will make them pay.*

A shiver ran down Roger's spine. The journal was a key to the case, but he didn't yet know how. All he knew was that Mercer had seen something—something that had driven him to the brink of madness.

Liz's flashlight flickered, and she cursed, tapping it until it steadied. But in that brief moment of darkness, Roger could have sworn he saw movement out of the corner of his eye—a figure, tall and shadowy, watching them from the doorway. He spun around, his gun raised.

But the hallway was empty.

"Roger?" Liz asked, her voice shaking.

He lowered his gun, his heart pounding. "Let's get out of here," he said. "We have what we need."

They hurried back to the entrance, the journal and the ledger clutched tightly in their hands. The feeling of being watched followed them, pressing in on all sides, and Roger knew that whatever they had discovered, it had put them in even greater danger.

Outside, the first flakes of snow had begun to fall, settling on the cracked asphalt and whispering against the metal frames of the old playground. Roger and Liz climbed into the truck, slamming the doors behind them. The warmth of the cab did little to chase away the chill that had settled in their bones.

Roger started the engine, his jaw clenched. "We have to find Harold Mercer," he said, his voice resolute. "And we need to be ready for whatever comes next."

Liz nodded, but her eyes kept flicking to the dark windows of the community center. "I just hope we're not too late," she whispered.

As they drove away, the building loomed in the rearview mirror, a monument to secrets and sins that refused to stay buried. The wind howled, carrying with it the echoes of a past that was not yet done with Midland—and a warning that the worst was yet to come.

CHAPTER FIVE

The snow was falling harder now, sweeping across Midland in thick, swirling gusts. Heavy flakes clung to windshields, streetlights, and rooftops, blanketing the town in an eerie silence. Everything felt unnaturally still, as if the town itself was holding its breath, waiting for the next blow to land.

Roger drove cautiously down North Big Spring Street, the truck's tires struggling for traction. He squinted through the windshield, the wipers pushing aside the snow in rhythmic yet futile sweeps.

Beside him, Liz sat with a stack of crime scene photos in her lap, her face illuminated by the soft glow of her flashlight. Her bloodshot eyes betrayed her exhaustion, but her mind was racing. Two brutal murders in less than a week, and now the killer had left a note: *The land remembers.* The connection to the old refinery was undeniable, yet the pieces refused to fit together.

They were nearly back at the sheriff's office when the radio crackled to life.

"Sheriff," came Deputy Jenny Pearson's voice, strained with urgency. "We've got a situation. Harold Mercer just walked in. Says he's turning himself in."

Roger's grip tightened on the steering wheel. "What?" he barked into the radio. "Turning himself in for what?"

Jenny's reply was edged with confusion and concern. "He didn't say. He's... he's terrified, Roger. Keeps saying someone is after him."

Roger and Liz exchanged a look, the same question hanging between them: *What could possibly make Harold Mercer, the reclusive former refinery worker, come out of hiding?*

"Ten-four," Roger responded. "We're two minutes out."

He pressed down on the gas, the truck skidding slightly on the icy road as they sped south on North Big Spring Street, past darkened storefronts and deserted sidewalks. The sheriff's office came into view, its lights glowing through the snowfall—a beacon in the night.

The building was a hive of activity. Snow had begun to pile up on the steps, and officers moved in and out, their breath fogging in the cold air. Inside, the tension was palpable. Townspeople crowded the lobby, seeking updates or safety, while deputies worked frantically to process information and answer the phones, which never seemed to stop ringing.

Roger and Liz pushed their way through the crowd and into the main area. Harold Mercer sat on a bench near the front desk, hunched over, his face buried in his hands. A frail, aging man, his gray hair was wild, and his canvas coat was soaked with melted snow. As they approached, he lifted his head. His eyes—wide with terror, bloodshot, and rimmed with exhaustion—met Roger's.

Roger's heart thudded. Mercer didn't look like a killer. He looked like a man being hunted.

"Harold," Roger said, his voice firm but measured. "Why are you here?"

Mercer's hands trembled as he pulled them away from his face. "I need protection," he rasped, his voice raw. "They're coming for me."

Liz crouched in front of him, studying his face. "Who's coming for you?" she asked. "And why would anyone be after you?"

Mercer's gaze darted around the room, as if expecting someone to burst in at any moment. His voice dropped to a whisper. "The land," he said, his throat tightening. "It remembers. It's demanding justice, and they think I know too much."

Roger exchanged a glance with Liz. The man was clearly terrified, but was it paranoia, or was there something more to it?

"All right," Roger said, motioning to a deputy. "Let's get him into the interrogation room. Somewhere safe where we can talk."

They led Mercer to a small, dimly lit room in the back, the air tinged with the scent of stale coffee and cigarette smoke. A large bulletin board covered in maps of Midland loomed over a dry-erase board filled with scrawled case notes.

Roger and Liz took their seats across from Mercer, their expressions serious.

Mercer's hands still shook as he clutched an old leather-bound folder to his chest. "You think I'm crazy," he murmured, his voice unsteady. "But I'm not. I tried to expose what happened near the refinery, but no one listened. And now, they're making sure the truth never comes out."

Liz leaned forward, her exhaustion momentarily forgotten. "What truth, Harold?" she pressed. "What happened that's worth killing over?"

Mercer's eyes filled with tears, his throat bobbing as he swallowed hard.

"The explosion," he whispered, his voice breaking. "It wasn't just an accident. It happened at one of the old wells near the refinery. The pressure built up, and they ignored all the safety protocols. When the blast hit… it was like hell on earth. Chemicals everywhere—leaking into the ground, into the water. It poisoned everything."

Roger's jaw tightened. He'd read about the explosion in old records, how it had been dismissed as an unfortunate industrial accident. Lives had been lost. Mercer had spent years trying to get someone—anyone—to hold those responsible accountable. But his claims had been ignored, buried beneath layers of corporate money and political influence.

"The well," Mercer continued, his voice growing desperate. "The explosion ruptured everything. Chemicals spilled everywhere. The ground, the water—it was poisoned. People got sick. My daughter got sick."

Roger's gut twisted. He knew about Mercer's daughter—how she had died of leukemia not long after the explosion.

"I documented everything," Mercer said, his voice shaking as he thrust the leather folder onto the table. Papers spilled out, their edges yellowed and brittle, carrying the faint scent of age and mildew. "The explosion, the chemical spills, the bribes to city officials, the reports they destroyed—it's all in there. But now… now they're coming for me because they think I know too much."

Liz picked up one of the documents, scanning it quickly. It was a report from 2003, detailing dangerously high levels of toxic waste in the groundwater near the well site. Stamped across the bottom were the words: **DO NOT RELEASE. HANDLE INTERNALLY.**

Roger felt his stomach tighten further. "Harold," he said, his voice low, steady. "Who is 'they'? Who's coming for you?"

Mercer's eyes flicked to the door, as if he expected his pursuers to burst in at any moment. "I don't know who they are," he admitted, his voice cracking. "But they're tied to what happened back then. Thomas Anders and Caleb Jennings were involved—either they orchestrated it, or their families did. And now someone thinks the only way to get justice is through murder."

Liz's grip on the paper tightened. "We've had two victims," she said, her voice sharp. "Both connected to the refinery and the explosion. Are you saying someone's avenging the land?"

Mercer swallowed hard, his face pale. "Yes," he whispered. "And if you don't stop them, more people will die."

Before Roger could press for more, the interrogation room door burst open. Deputy Eli Rivera rushed in, his face drawn with urgency.

"Sheriff," he panted, "we've got a situation."

Roger's pulse kicked up. "What now?"

Eli took a steadying breath. "Shots fired at Midland Park Mall. Multiple casualties reported."

Roger felt his blood turn cold. Midland Park Mall—one of the busiest places in town—sat at the corner of Loop 250 and North Midkiff Road. If someone had opened fire there, the damage would be catastrophic.

Liz shot to her feet, her exhaustion forgotten. "We need to move," she said, already reaching for her jacket.

Roger turned back to Mercer, who was trembling in his chair. "Stay here," he ordered. "We're not done with you. But for now, you're safe."

Mercer's wide, fear-filled eyes followed them as they rushed out. The sheriff's office was a storm of movement—officers grabbing rifles, dispatchers coordinating responses, townspeople pressing for answers. Roger and Liz shoved through the chaos and into the freezing night. The snow was falling harder now, thick flakes swirling in the wind.

Roger's truck roared to life, tires slipping on the ice as he pulled onto the road. The siren screamed through the storm, red-and-blue lights slicing through the darkness. The streets were eerily empty, the snow swallowing all other sounds.

Liz was already on the radio, her voice unwavering despite the urgency. "All available units, secure the perimeter of Midland Park Mall," she ordered. "We have an active shooter on site."

As they neared the mall, Roger's pulse pounded in his ears. The parking lot was a chaotic blur of flashing lights, people running in terror, and the deafening wail of sirens. Car alarms blared, doors slammed, and panicked voices filled the icy air.

Roger slammed the truck into park, and he and Liz jumped out, weapons drawn. The wind howled around them, whipping snow into their faces, but it couldn't drown out the fear gripping the town.

Somewhere inside, a killer was loose.

And Roger knew—whatever happened next would change everything.

The mystery of the land, the buried secrets, and the violence of the present had collided. Now, it was a race against time to stop a killer who believed they were delivering the justice the land demanded.

CHAPTER SIX

Snow pummeled Midland, Texas, in thick, relentless waves, transforming the town into a ghostly, snow-covered wasteland. The storm swallowed sound, but the chaos outside Midland Park Mall was loud enough to pierce through the white silence. Flashing red and blue lights bounced off the thick blanket of snow, and the air was thick with shouts, the panicked cries of families, and the shrill wail of emergency sirens. The frigid wind howled through the broken doors, carrying with it the sharp tang of blood and gunpowder.

Roger and Liz moved through the mass of terrified shoppers, pushing toward the shattered glass doors of the mall. Inside, the once-busy hub of holiday shopping had been transformed into a nightmare. Blood smeared the white tile floors, and toppled holiday decorations lay scattered, twisted, and broken. A plastic Santa Claus lay on its side, its face cracked, its hollow eyes staring into nothing, with fake snow dusted over a pool of dark, arterial red. The overhead speakers still played faint, distorted Christmas music, an eerie contrast to the horror before them.

"Stay close," Roger ordered Liz, his gun drawn as they stepped into the mall. Liz nodded, her own weapon held steady, her eyes scanning for any sign of the shooter. Every shadow seemed to move, every echo stretched long in the cavernous emptiness. Their breaths came out in short, visible puffs, the cold intensifying the sense of isolation.

"Food court's this way," Liz said, gesturing with her gun. They made their way through the empty, trashed corridors, their boots slipping slightly on the blood and snow tracked in by the panicked crowds. The scent of something burnt hung in the air—gunpowder, or maybe scorched fabric from where a bullet had struck.

They entered the food court, where first responders were already tending to the wounded. Paramedics knelt over victims lying on the ground, their cries of pain cutting through the icy air. Blood smeared the polished floors, mingling with the remnants of spilled drinks and shattered trays. Most of the victims appeared to have non-lethal injuries—gunshot wounds to the arms or legs, a few with gashes from the mad scramble to escape. A mother clutched her young son, both of them sobbing, while an older man lay groaning, a tourniquet wrapped tightly around his thigh.

Despite the chaos and the number of casualties, there was only one person who hadn't survived. And it was impossible to ignore him.

The victim, a man in his mid-forties, had been grotesquely staged in the center of the food court. He was propped up against an overturned table, his limbs twisted into unnatural positions. His mouth was frozen in a silent scream. Blood soaked his flannel shirt, spreading in a dark stain across his chest, but it wasn't just the gunshot wounds that caught Roger and Liz's attention—it was the way his body had been arranged.

The man's arms were stretched out wide, each wrist nailed to the table's wooden legs with what looked like long, rusted nails, pinning him in place like a human crucifix. The nails had been hammered through flesh and bone, leaving jagged tears where skin had split and muscle had been shredded. His fingers had been broken and splayed apart, the bones visible through torn, bloodied skin, with shards of bone protruding at odd angles. His eyes had been forced open, held wide by small, crude hooks pierced through his eyelids, ensuring his gaze was forever fixed upward. The hooks had ripped through the delicate tissue, leaving angry, red gashes that oozed blood, trailing in streaks down his hollow cheeks. A slurry of dried blood streaked his face, and his mouth was stuffed with a mixture of dirt, snow, and pine needles. His head was tilted at an impossible angle, as if his neck had been snapped and then carefully positioned to look skyward. The skin around his neck was bruised and discolored, evidence of the sheer force used to break it.

Blood pooled beneath him, congealing in thick, viscous patches around his legs. His torso was marred with several deep lacerations, as though the killer had taken the time to carve into his flesh, each cut deliberate and cruel. The flannel shirt he wore was shredded, the fabric soaked and stiff with dark, arterial blood. The metallic scent of blood mingled with the acrid smell of fear and gunpowder , a nauseating cocktail that made Liz gag as she tried to steady herself. She turned her head slightly, noticing a discarded shopping bag lying nearby, its contents—children's toys—spilled out onto the floor, a stark reminder of what this place had been before the massacre.

Liz covered her mouth, the bile rising in her throat. "Oh my God," she whispered, her voice muffled by her shaking hands. "Who would… who could do this?"

Roger swallowed hard, forcing down his own revulsion. The brutality of it was staggering, and the symbolism screamed a message he didn't yet fully understand. With a gloved hand, he reached forward and pulled a crumpled piece of paper from the victim's shattered, bloodied fist. The note was written in the same precise, typewritten font as before: "The land remembers. This debt is paid."

Roger's jaw tightened. The killer wasn't just murdering; they were staging these bodies with an almost religious fervor, sending a message about sins and debts and a land that demanded retribution. He looked at the dirt and snow forced into the man's mouth, a sick reminder of the poisoned land Mercer had written about.

"This isn't random," Roger said, his voice hard. "This is a statement."

Liz nodded, her face pale but determined. "And he's getting more theatrical, more violent," she said. "He wants us to pay attention. He wants to make sure we know."

The sound of crunching boots on the snow-covered floor announced the arrival of Marla, the county coroner. Her green eyes took in the horrific scene with a practiced, unflinching gaze, and she wore a thick black coat over her scrubs, a heavy medical bag slung over her shoulder.

Marla stepped carefully over the blood-slick tiles and knelt beside the body, her gloved hands moving with precision. "You two seem to find the worst crime scenes," she remarked, though there was no humor in her voice.

Roger and Liz stepped back to give her space. "Marla," Roger said, "this one's different. He's escalating, and we need any clues you can find."

Marla's lips pressed into a thin line. "I'll do what I can," she said. She examined the dirt and snow packed into the man's mouth, the crude hooks in his eyelids, the rusted nails driven into his wrists. Her face was impassive, but her eyes betrayed a flicker of unease.

She leaned in closer, her fingers tracing the line of the man's broken neck. Her hand stopped over a spot just beneath the jawline, and she frowned. "Wait a minute," she murmured. "There's something embedded in his skin here."

Roger and Liz leaned in, the tension thickening. With a pair of small surgical tweezers, Marla carefully extracted a thin, metallic object from the torn flesh. She held it up to the light, her eyes narrowing.

"It's a fragment of a coin," she said, her voice tinged with intrigue. The small, tarnished piece of metal was bent and crusted with dried blood.

Liz peered closer, her curiosity piqued. "A coin?" she echoed. "Why would he embed a coin in the victim's neck?"

Marla wiped the coin fragment clean, revealing a faint, worn engraving. "It's an old silver dollar," she said. "But it's been cut in half. And look at this—there's an inscription on the edge."

Roger took the coin fragment from her, squinting at the barely legible words etched into the metal: "In debt to the land." His pulse quickened. The message was clear—the killer was obsessed with the idea of debts owed to the land, debts paid in blood.

Liz shivered, despite the heat of the emergency lights and the adrenaline pumping through her veins. "This isn't just about revenge," she said. "It's a belief system. A twisted ideology."

Roger's face darkened. "We're dealing with someone who thinks they're delivering judgment," he said. "And they're not going to stop until every debt is paid."

Marla placed the coin fragment into an evidence bag, her expression grave. "I'll keep looking for more clues," she said. "But this killer is meticulous. He's sending a message, and it's up to us to decode it."

Before Roger could say anything more, his phone buzzed. He pulled it out, recognizing Deputy Eli Rivera's number. "Eli," he answered, his voice tense. "What did you find?"

Eli sounded breathless, as if he had been running. "Sheriff, I've got something," he said. "I was digging through the old refinery reports and cross-referenced the families who refused settlement money. One name stood out: Greg Dawson. He was a vocal activist, but he went silent after his wife died of cancer. He had a son, Michael Dawson, who would be in his thirties now."

Roger exchanged a sharp glance with Liz. "Michael Dawson," he repeated. "Where is he now?"

"That's the thing," Eli said, his voice tight with urgency. "Michael dropped off the map years ago, but I found a property in his name—an old farmhouse north of town, off East County Road 60. It's isolated, near some abandoned oil wells. It'd be the perfect place to hide."

Liz folded her arms, her expression unreadable. "If he's our guy, then this isn't just about revenge. It's a crusade."

Roger's jaw tightened. "And he's not done," he said. "Not by a long shot."

Before they could leave the scene, an officer called out to them. "Sheriff, you need to see this."

Roger and Liz followed the officer outside to a patio area, where a frozen fountain stood against the mall's outer wall. The fountain had frozen over in the unusual West Texas cold. Under the glare of emergency lights, a message was smeared across the ice in blood. The jagged letters, dripping with a mixture of fresh crimson and the bitter cold of the ice, were a taunting reminder that the killer was always one step ahead. The words sent a chill through Roger: "Only blood can cleanse the land."

Liz exhaled a shaky breath, her eyes darting around the mall as if expecting the killer to leap out from the shadows. "He's taunting us," she whispered. "He knows we're close, and he's daring us to stop him."

Roger felt the rage simmer beneath his skin. The killer's calculated cruelty, the elaborate staging of the body, the taunting messages—it all pointed to someone who had meticulously planned every move. Someone who was determined to make Midland pay for sins long buried.

He turned to the officer who had called them over. "Get this cordoned off," Roger ordered, his voice tight with barely contained frustration. "And have forensics document everything. We're going to need every piece of evidence we can get."

The officer nodded and hurried away, his breath fogging in the frigid air. Roger and Liz exchanged a look, the weight of the case pressing down on them both.

"This is more than just revenge." As the first flakes of snow drifted down, Liz rubbed her arms. "It's a crusade, like we said. But why the coins? Why embed them in the victims' bodies?"

Roger ran a hand over his face, exhaustion creeping in. "It's symbolism," he said. "A debt paid in blood. The killer is making sure the message is clear—every victim represents a debt owed to the land."

Liz frowned, her brow furrowed in thought. "But why these specific people?" she wondered. "What's the connection between them?"

They didn't have time to dwell on the questions. The lead Eli had given them about Michael Dawson needed to be followed up immediately. The old farmhouse north of town, near the abandoned oil wells, was isolated, and the snowstorm would only make the drive more treacherous.

Roger and Liz left the mall, the cold air biting at their faces as they climbed into Roger's truck. The engine roared to life, and the tires crunched over snow and ice as they pulled away from the chaos of Midland Park Mall.

As they drove, the tension in the truck was palpable. The snow fell heavier now, thick flakes swirling in the headlights, obscuring the road and making it difficult to see more than a few feet ahead. Roger gripped the steering wheel tightly, his knuckles white.

Liz's phone buzzed, and she glanced down at the screen. "It's Eli again," she said, answering the call. "Eli, what is it?"

Eli's voice was strained, filled with anxiety. "I've been digging into Michael Dawson's background," he said. "Turns out he had a history of mental health issues after his mother's death. He was hospitalized twice for severe depression and what the records describe as 'paranoid delusions.'"

Roger's jaw clenched. "Paranoid delusions?" he repeated.

"Yeah," Eli confirmed. "He believed the land was cursed, that the contamination from the refinery had awakened something ancient and vengeful. According to his medical records, he was obsessed with the idea that the land demanded a blood sacrifice to be cleansed."

Liz stared out at the snow-covered fields, unease settling in her stomach. "So he's not just angry—he genuinely believes he's carrying out some kind of ceremonial rite," she said.

Roger's mind raced. If Dawson truly believed that the land required blood to be cleansed, then he wouldn't stop until he felt the debt was paid. And if his delusions had taken root in something deeper, something darker, then everyone in Midland was in danger.

"Eli," Roger said, his voice hard, "stay at the station and keep digging. We need to know everything about Dawson's connections, his history, and anyone who might be helping him."

"Will do," Eli replied. "Be careful out there, Sheriff."

Roger ended the call, his grip tightening on the steering wheel. "This is worse than we thought," he said. "We're dealing with someone who's convinced he's doing the right thing, no matter how many people he has to kill."

Liz nodded, her face set with grim determination. "Then we'd better stop him before he turns this town into his personal altar."

The old farmhouse loomed in the distance, a dark shape barely visible through the swirling snow. It sat at the end of a long, winding dirt road, flanked by skeletal trees that groaned and creaked in the wind. The property was surrounded by fields that had long since gone fallow, the ground cracked and lifeless even under the thick layer of snow. A bitter chill clung to the landscape, the wind slicing through their coats like a blade. Off to the right, a cluster of rusting oil pumps stood like silent sentinels, their skeletal frames casting eerie shadows in the headlights.

Roger parked the truck at the edge of the driveway, cutting the engine. The sudden silence was deafening, broken only by the howling wind and the creak of the farmhouse's old weather vane. He and Liz stepped out, their boots sinking into the snow, and drew their guns.

"This place looks abandoned," Liz whispered, her breath misting in the air. The cold gnawed at her fingertips even through her gloves. "But I don't trust appearances anymore."

Roger nodded, his senses on high alert. The air felt heavy, charged, as if the land itself was holding its breath. They approached the farmhouse cautiously, their flashlights cutting through the darkness. The front door was slightly ajar, swinging on its hinges with a mournful creak.

Roger exchanged a look with Liz, and she nodded. They moved forward, guns raised, and pushed the door open.

The interior was dark and freezing, the air thick with the smell of decay and mildew. A damp, rotting scent clung to the walls. The walls were lined with peeling wallpaper, and the floorboards creaked under their weight. Dust motes danced in the beams of their flashlights, and the shadows seemed to shift and breathe around them.

"Dawson!" Roger called, his voice echoing through the empty rooms. "This is the sheriff's department! Come out with your hands up!"

The silence that followed was oppressive, almost mocking. Liz moved carefully through the front room, her flashlight sweeping over old, broken furniture and newspapers scattered across the floor. Her light caught something strange—a dark stain near the base of the stairs, faded but unmistakable. She frowned and swept her beam across the floor again. That's when she saw it. A series of symbols carved into the wooden floorboards. They were crude, jagged, and arranged in a circular pattern.

"Roger," she said, her voice tight. "You need to see this."

Roger joined her, his eyes narrowing at the carvings. The symbols were familiar, similar to those they had seen in old refinery documents linked to warnings about the contamination sites. The symbols seemed to radiate a sense of unease, as if they carried a power that defied logic.

"This is a ritual site," Liz whispered. "He's been performing ceremonies here."

Roger's stomach twisted, but before he could respond, a noise from the back of the house made them both spin around, guns raised. It was the sound of footsteps, heavy and deliberate, echoing through the empty halls.

Liz inhaled sharply, her grip tightening on her weapon.

"Stay sharp," Roger said, his voice low. They moved deeper into the house, every nerve on edge, as the shadows seemed to close in around them.

The hunt for Michael Dawson had begun, and with each step, the land seemed to whisper its secrets, urging them forward into a darkness from which they might never return.

CHAPTER SEVEN

The old farmhouse stood eerily around Roger and Liz, its long shadows shifting with the wind, almost alive. The swirling snow had finally begun to subside, leaving a heavy, bone-chilling stillness in the air, as if the storm had merely set the stage for something worse. The skeletal trees surrounding the property groaned under the weight of ice, their creaking branches whispering in the cold night. In the distance, abandoned oil pumps loomed, their jagged silhouettes a grim reminder of Midland's past—a town built on oil and the sacrifices it demanded.

Roger and Liz stepped cautiously through the farmhouse, the floorboards groaning under their boots. Dust hung thick in the air, swirling in their flashlight beams and catching in their throats. The walls, covered in peeling wallpaper, revealed rotted wood and gaping holes where time had eaten away at them. The entire house smelled of decay, mildew, and something more elusive: a sharp, metallic scent that raised the hairs on their necks. Old blood. It lingered like an accusation in the shadows.

Liz's flashlight caught on old photographs crookedly hanging on the wall. She stepped closer, the light revealing faded images beneath layers of grime. A family—a hollow-eyed man, a gentle-faced woman with a fragile smile, and a young boy whose solemn gaze made him seem older than his years. Michael Dawson. He couldn't have been more than ten in these photos—a child frozen in time, a haunting reminder of what this place once was. The weight of the past pressed heavily around her, and she wondered if that boy had ever imagined he'd be part of a nightmare like this.

Roger led them through the front room into a narrow hallway.

"Dawson!" he called, his voice echoing off the cracked walls before fading into the void. "Michael Dawson, come out with your hands up!"

Silence. Thick. Suffocating.

Liz followed closely, her gun raised, finger lightly on the trigger. The symbols carved into the front room floorboards had set her nerves on edge, and now, every shadow felt like a potential threat. Chaotic spirals and jagged lines marred the wood—deep, hurried cuts made by someone desperate to finish before something found them.

They reached the back of the house, where a narrow staircase led to the basement. The wooden steps leaned at odd angles, and an unsettling chill seeped from below, pulling them in. Roger hesitated, his flashlight revealing cobwebs draped over the cracked banister like funeral veils. The air grew colder with each breath, thick with a creeping dread neither of them could shake.

"Think he's down there?" Liz whispered, barely moving her lips.

Roger nodded. "Only one way to find out."

They exchanged a look, then Roger started down, his boots heavy on the warped steps, each creak a reluctant warning. Liz followed, her pulse thudding in her ears. The staircase groaned beneath them, their flashlights cutting through the cavernous dark.

The basement swallowed them whole. Rows of rusted shelves stood like forgotten sentinels, their surfaces coated in dust. Old, decaying tools lay abandoned, their edges dulled by time. Glass jars lined the shelves, their contents dried into unrecognizable remnants.

The room felt alive—not with a person, but with something left behind. A memory, an echo of desperation and fear. Symbols, like those upstairs, were carved into the concrete walls, their frenzied strokes vibrating in the dim light.

A rhythmic dripping sound echoed in the darkness. Roger's flashlight followed the noise to a cracked, rusted sink in the far corner. Water—or something darker—dripped slowly from a damaged faucet, each drop splattering into a shallow pool on the concrete floor. The sound was hypnotic, a steady metronome marking time in this forsaken place.

Then, in the center of the room, their flashlights landed on him.

Roger exhaled sharply, reached for his phone, and quickly dialed.

"Marla, it's Roger. We need you out here off East County Road 60," he said, his voice tight with urgency. "We've got another body—Michael Dawson. The farmhouse basement."

Michael Dawson lay crumpled on the cold concrete; his limbs twisted in a grotesque imitation of movement. One arm was bent at an unnatural angle, his face frozen in an expression of utter terror. Blood had pooled beneath him, seeping into the cracks like the house itself was drinking it in. But something about the scene felt... wrong.

His mouth was stuffed with charred, brittle paper, the blackened fragments jutting from his lips, crumbling at the edges as if burned in some kind of ritual. His unseeing eyes glistened with dried tears, his hands bound tightly with coarse rope, the fibers biting into his wrists, leaving deep, raw welts. The rope was drenched in something dark and sticky, a sickening mixture of blood and an unidentifiable black residue that shimmered in the flashlight beams.

Roger's light swept over the body, revealing more horrors. Deep lacerations crisscrossed Michael's torso, the jagged edges suggesting a blade meant to cause pain rather than a quick death. Around his neck, a thin wire had been looped, cutting deep into his flesh, leaving behind a trail of bruises. His torn, bloodstained clothes were streaked with a dark, oily substance—an unsettling echo of the refinery's contamination.

Roger swallowed hard, his stomach twisting. "Damn it," he muttered. "He was supposed to be our lead. Now he's just another victim."

Liz knelt beside the body, her hands steady despite the unease gnawing at her. She reached for one of the paper fragments, the brittle edges crackling as she carefully pried it free. She held it up to her flashlight, her pulse quickening.

"What is this?" she murmured.

The paper was scorched, its edges curling inward, but the center remained intact. Faded ink revealed a few surviving words:

"A settlement paid to silence the truth."

Liz's breath hitched. She looked up at Roger, her voice tight. "Settlement agreements." She swallowed hard. "The ones his family tried to fight. The killer stuffed them in his mouth, just like the dirt and snow in the other victims' mouths."

Roger's mind raced, fitting the pieces together. Whoever had done this knew Midland's dirtiest secrets—the kind people spent decades trying to bury. The symbols, the staging, the message burned into the paper—this wasn't just a murderer. This was someone with a vendetta.

Footsteps crunched against the cold, damp basement floor. Marla Decker, the county coroner, arrived, her expression unreadable but her eyes sharp. The bitter cold didn't seem to faze her as she knelt beside the body, her breath fogging in the dim light.

"Another one," she said quietly, her voice steady but laced with a grim certainty. "Whoever did this took their time. This wasn't just about killing—it was about sending a message."

Roger and Liz stepped back, giving Marla room to work. She pulled on a pair of latex gloves, her movements swift and practiced. Her fingers traced the deep wounds, the taut rope, the wire at his throat.

"The ligature marks suggest strangulation," she said, studying the dark bruising around his neck. "But not before he suffered. These cuts—they weren't meant to kill him right away. The killer wanted him to feel it."

Liz shivered, her stomach knotting. "It's like they wanted to make him suffer." Her voice dropped. "Like… an offering."

Marla's fingers froze mid-examination. Her brows knitted together as she tilted Michael's chin, revealing something just beneath his jawline.

"Wait," she murmured. "There's something else here."

She lifted the flashlight closer, revealing a small, circular mark—burned into the flesh. The symbol was intricate, its sharp lines unmistakable, almost ceremonial. It bore a chilling resemblance to the symbols carved into the basement walls.

Roger's stomach turned to lead. "What the hell is that?"

Marla leaned in, studying the mark. "A brand," she said, her voice lower now. "Fresh, too. The skin is still seared." She exhaled sharply. "This was deliberate. The killer didn't just leave a message—they marked him."

Liz swept her light across the basement, the symbols etching themselves into her mind like scars.

"These carvings," she said, her voice tight, "they're not random. They're connected. It's a language. And now he's branding his victims with it."

Marla's hands moved to Dawson's chest, where something glinted beneath the blood-soaked fabric.

"What's this?" she murmured, carefully extracting a small, rusted key attached to a frayed leather cord. The metal was darkened, stained with blood, and the leather worn thin, as if it had been carried for years before finding its way here.

Roger took the key, turning it over in his gloved hand. It was old and heavy, its ornate design suggesting it once belonged to something important.

"What does this open?" he wondered aloud.

Liz's mind raced. "It has to be a clue," she said. "Something the killer wants us to find. But why leave it here, on the victim? Is it leading us somewhere?"

Marla sealed the key in an evidence bag, her expression grim. "Whatever it opens," she said, "it's not random. The killer left it for a reason. Either it's meant to lead us somewhere… or it's part of the game he's playing."

Roger stood, the rusted key cold and heavy in his palm. He turned it over again and again, the intricate design catching in the dim light. A deep unease settled in his gut—whatever this key led to, it wouldn't be anything good.

Liz's flashlight swept across the room, landing on a shattered glass jar, its contents spilled across the floor. Among the shards and dark, viscous sludge was a small, yellowed envelope, its edges stained with something that smelled faintly of motor oil and rot.

She crouched, carefully prying the envelope free with gloved fingers. "What's this?" she murmured, easing it open.

Inside was a faded photograph, creased and brittle with age. It showed a group of men standing proudly in front of an oil rig, their faces weathered but beaming with pride. Behind them, the Marathon Oil Company logo—a bold, red "M"—stood prominent and unmistakable.

But Liz's breath hitched when her eyes locked onto one familiar face in the center.

Harold Mercer.

The man they'd been watching, the man who had buried more secrets than he'd ever told. Only in this photo, he wasn't the broken man they knew. He was younger, sharper, his expression filled with the kind of determination and control he had long since lost.

Roger leaned over her shoulder, his jaw tightening. "Mercer," he muttered. "He just keeps coming up, doesn't he?"

Liz exhaled slowly, the pieces of the puzzle shifting into place. "What if he knew something about the refinery that no one else did?" she said. "Something he's been hiding for decades?"

Before Roger could answer, his phone buzzed. He pulled it from his pocket, frowning at the name flashing on the screen. Deputy Eli Rivera.

He answered, and Eli's voice came fast, strained with urgency. "Sheriff, we've got a problem. It's Harold Mercer."

Roger's stomach dropped. "What about him?"

Eli's breath was shaky. "He's missing."

Roger stiffened. "What do you mean, missing?"

"He was in the living room area at the station," Eli said. "We checked on him five minutes ago—he was there. Now he's gone. And, Sheriff... there's blood. A lot of it."

Liz froze, her knuckles whitening around her flashlight. "They got to him," she whispered. "The killer took him."

Roger's grip tightened on the phone. The killer wasn't just taunting them anymore—he was erasing their leads, one by one.

"Lock down the station," Roger ordered. "I want every available deputy searching the area. Follow the blood trail. And Eli… be careful."

"Yes, sir." Eli's voice was tight, and then the line went dead.

Roger lowered the phone, his jaw clenched. The situation was unraveling faster than they could keep up. Dawson, dead. Mercer, gone. The killer was always one step ahead, pulling them deeper into his twisted game.

Liz rubbed a hand over her face, trying to steady her breath. "If they can get to someone inside the station… what's stopping them from coming after the rest of us?"

Roger didn't answer right away. His mind worked through the connections, the missing pieces. The photo. The key. The symbols. The refinery.

"Mercer was our last link," he said finally, "but we still have the key. Whatever it opens, it's part of this."

Liz nodded, her expression hardening. "Then let's find out what it leads to before the killer takes their next target."

Roger didn't hesitate. They had no more time to waste.

As they stepped out of the farmhouse into the freezing night, the wind howled through the skeletal trees, and the snow crunched beneath their boots. The land felt alive—watching, waiting.

Somewhere in the darkness, the killer was waiting, too.

Always ahead. Always ready to strike.

The land remembered. And it wasn't just seeking justice—it was demanding retribution.

CHAPTER EIGHT

The truck's tires skidded over the snow-slicked road as Roger and Liz sped back toward the sheriff's station. The heater in the cab was on full blast, but the chill that gripped them was more than just the bitter winter cold. Something thick and suffocating lingered between them, an unease neither could shake. The rusted key in Roger's pocket pressed against his thigh, a silent reminder of the secrets they were unraveling—and the danger that lurked in every shadow.

Snow flurries spun across the windshield, and the skeletal branches of the trees lining the road swayed in the wind, their jagged arms reaching for something unseen. The land looked serene under its blanket of white, but Roger knew better. Beneath the snow lay history—the kind that refused to stay buried. He glanced at Liz, her gaze fixed on the road ahead, her fingers clenching the steering wheel just a little too tightly.

Liz shifted uneasily in her seat, her eyes flicking between the road and the dark vastness beyond. "Do you think Mercer's still alive?" she asked, her voice low, almost as if she was afraid of the answer.

Roger gripped the steering wheel tighter. The truth was, he had no idea. Harold Mercer was a key figure in the town's dark history, and it was becoming painfully clear that anyone with ties to the old Marathon Oil scandal was in danger. But this wasn't just about covering tracks. The brutality of the acts, the symbols, the careful staging—it all pointed to someone forcing them to see something, understand something.

"I don't know," Roger admitted, his voice gravelly with frustration. "But if he is, we need to find him fast."

The landscape rushed by, a blur of white and dark silhouettes. That feeling again. Roger couldn't shake it—the sensation of being watched, of something unseen just beyond the reach of his headlights. His gut twisted. The land felt restless. Waiting.

When they pulled into the sheriff's station, the place was alive with movement. Deputies rushed around, their faces set in grim determination. The usual stillness of the station had been replaced with a frantic energy that made Roger's stomach churn. Deputy Eli Rivera stood at the center of it all, barking orders, his glasses fogged, breath visible in the cold. Flashlights cut through the dark, illuminating deputies combing the surrounding area, searching for any sign of Harold Mercer.

Roger stepped out of the truck, the snow crunching under his boots, and strode toward Eli. "Eli!" he called, his voice cutting through the chaos. "What's the situation?"

Eli turned, his face pale beneath the station's harsh lighting. "Sheriff, we followed the blood trail," he said, pointing behind the station. "It leads out there, but then it just… stops. There are no footprints, no vehicle tracks, nothing. It's like whoever took Mercer vanished into thin air."

Roger's jaw clenched. That was impossible. "And the security footage?" he asked.

Eli's expression darkened. "Gone," he said. "Wiped clean. Whoever did this knew exactly what they were doing. They got in, took Mercer, and left without leaving a trace."

Liz let out a sharp breath, crossing her arms. "How is that even possible?" she demanded. "We had officers on duty, the building is secure, and we've never had anything like this happen before. It doesn't make sense."

Eli ran a hand through his hair, clearly shaken. "Trust me, I know." He exhaled sharply, shaking his head. "It's like they were a ghost. We're still sweeping the area for anything—hair, fibers, anything at all—but so far, we've got nothing."

Roger felt the rusted key in his pocket, its weight a reminder of how little they truly understood. He looked at Eli, then Liz, a determination hardening his gaze. "Keep at it," he ordered. "Tighten security. I don't want anyone else disappearing on our watch."

Eli nodded and turned back to the search, shouting more orders to the deputies.

Roger and Liz stepped inside, the warm air of the station doing little to thaw the chill that had settled deep in their bones. Inside, the tension was just as thick. Desks were cluttered with files, maps of Midland spread out across every surface, marked with circles and crisscrossing lines that charted the horror unraveling in their town. Phones rang non-stop, deputies spoke in hushed tones, and beneath it all, a quiet, creeping sense of dread had taken root.

In the conference room, Marla Decker was waiting for them. The county coroner was usually unshakable, a woman who had spent years dealing with death and the ugliness it left behind. But now, dark circles shadowed her eyes, and she gripped a clipboard like it was the only thing keeping her upright. She looked exhausted—more than that, unsettled.

"Roger, Liz," she greeted, her voice tight. "I came straight in from the Dawson place. I've been going over Michael Dawson's preliminary. My assistant is downstairs working on him now, and there are some… disturbing details."

Roger exchanged a look with Liz before focusing on Marla. He wasn't sure he wanted to hear this. "Go on," he said.

Marla set the clipboard down and flipped through her notes. "The lacerations on Dawson's wrists," she began, "weren't made with a typical knife. The edges are jagged, almost as if the blade was serrated but crude—like a piece of broken metal." She paused, taking a steadying breath. "And the oily residue we found? It's not just motor oil. It's a mixture of petroleum contaminants, the kind you'd find seeping out of old refinery sites. Specifically, the land around the Marathon refinery."

Liz leaned forward, her brow furrowed. Pieces of the puzzle were starting to come together—but the picture they formed was nothing short of terrifying. "So the killer is using elements from the contaminated land," she murmured, more to herself than anyone else. A slow exhale left her lips. "They're literally turning the poison of the land into a weapon."

Marla nodded, her lips pursed. "And that symbol branded onto Dawson's neck," she continued, lowering her voice. "It matches the insignia used by The Land's Vengeance—a radical environmental group from the 1980s. They believed the contamination of the land was a sin that could only be cleansed through blood."

Roger stilled. The Land's Vengeance. The name hit him like a slow-burning memory. He remembered hearing about them when he was younger—stories of environmental protests that had spiraled into violence, of people who believed that the earth itself demanded retribution.

"I thought they disbanded," he said, his voice unreadable. "After a few of their leaders were arrested."

Marla's gaze was heavy. "That's what we were led to believe." She crossed her arms, staring down at her notes. "But it seems their ideology didn't die. Someone has picked it up again, and they're using it to justify these murders."

Roger reached into his pocket and pulled out the rusted key, placing it on the table. The metal was ice cold, heavier than it should have been, like it carried the weight of something more than steel. The ornate design suggested it had been made decades ago—maybe longer.

"This was around Dawson's neck," he said. "It's the only clue we have, but we still don't know what it unlocks."

Liz picked it up, running her fingers over the rusted grooves. It was old, worn by time and neglect, but solid. Something about it unsettled her, like she was holding a relic from a past best left forgotten. "We need to find out," she murmured. "It looks like it belonged to something important." Her mind raced through possibilities— a vault, a cellar, maybe even an old industrial lock, the kind built to keep people out. "If the killer left it for us to find, it has to lead somewhere."

Marla nodded. "If it's tied to The Land's Vengeance or the refinery," she said, "we need to check historical records. Maybe there's a hidden location, something that was sealed up and forgotten after the contamination scandal."

Roger rubbed his temple, the weight of exhaustion pressing down on him. His body begged for sleep, but there was no time for that. He looked at Marla, then Liz. "Then that's what we'll do," he said, his voice filled with grim resolve. "But we need to move fast. The longer Mercer is missing, the worse this is going to get."

Armed with flashlights and a renewed sense of urgency, Roger and Liz made their way out back to follow the blood trail. The night was deathly quiet, the snow absorbing sound, muting their movements as they ventured deeper into the dark. Orange flags, placed by the deputies, marked a winding path that led into the dense forest, where the trees stood like silent sentinels, their bare limbs stretching toward the sky.

The air was thick with the scent of damp earth, sulfur, and something else—something faintly metallic. Blood. Liz shivered, her breath fogging in the cold air. "This doesn't feel right," she whispered. "It's too quiet."

Roger's hand rested on the grip of his gun, his eyes scanning the surroundings for any sign of movement. Something about this place set his nerves on edge. The shadows seemed to close in around them, and the wind made the branches creak and groan like old bones settling in their grave.

"Stay alert," he said, his voice low. "If the killer is watching, we can't let them catch us off guard."

The blood trail led them to a small clearing, where the snow had been disturbed. Dark smears spread across the ground, pooling in irregular patterns—signs of a struggle, of someone fighting for their life. Branches were broken and scattered, and the scene told a story Roger could picture too well: Mercer, trapped, dragged, overpowered. And now? Now, nothing.

Roger knelt, his flashlight illuminating the bloodstains. It hadn't yet turned brown. He could almost hear it— Mercer's panicked breaths, the sound of his boots kicking up the snow, a struggle cut short. Then silence.

"How does a man vanish without a trace?" he muttered. He wasn't expecting an answer, but the thought gnawed at him. No footprints. No vehicle marks. Nothing.

Liz's flashlight beam flickered across something half-buried in the snow. A glint of metal, dull and corroded. She knelt and brushed the snow away, revealing a small, rusted metal plate bolted to a rock. The plate was weathered and pockmarked with rust, but the words beneath the grime were still legible:

MARATHON REFINERY SITE B-12.

Liz's eyes widened. She recognized that name. "Site B-12," she whispered. "That was one of the old refinery locations. It was decommissioned and buried after the contamination scandal. No one's been out there for years."

Roger's pulse quickened. The key. The refinery. It wasn't coincidence.

"Maybe that's what the key opens," he said, his voice tight. "A door, a vault, or something hidden at Site B-12. Something they never wanted found."

Liz nodded, but there was a flicker of something in her expression— hesitation. Not doubt, not fear, but the cold realization that they weren't in control of this anymore. The killer was pulling the strings.

"We're heading straight into the heart of this," she said. "And if we're not careful, we might not come back out."

Roger stood, the rusted key clenched in his hand. The area around them was silent. Too silent. The kind of quiet that didn't just come from an empty forest but from something unseen. He could feel it pressing down on them.

The land remembered.

And whatever was waiting for them at Site B-12—

It wasn't finished yet.

CHAPTER NINE

The snow fell in thick, heavy flakes, muffling the world in an eerie silence as Roger and Liz prepared to set out for the abandoned Marathon Refinery Site B-12. The rusted key sat between them on the truck's dashboard, a cold, foreboding talisman that seemed heavier than metal alone, as if it carried the weight of what lay ahead.

As they drove deeper into Midland's forgotten outskirts, the landscape grew more desolate. Snow clung to rusted chain-link fences, and long-dead machinery lay half-buried in drifts, like the skeletal remains of something long forgotten. The weight of history hung in the air, pressing down on them, a silent reminder that they were heading straight into one of Midland's darkest chapters.

Liz adjusted her scarf, her face pale in the dim glow of the dashboard lights. "Site B-12," she murmured, her breath fogging the air. "I remember hearing about the explosion when I was a kid. People used to whisper that the area was cursed. That the land was poisoned, the people sickened. My dad used to warn me not to play near there." Her voice was even, but something in the way she spoke told Roger that the warnings had never fully left her.

Roger glanced at her, the lines on his weathered face deepening. "I remember, too," he said. "When the contamination scandal broke, everyone in Midland was scared. They buried the site, sealed it off, and hoped we'd all forget. But some things don't stay buried." His voice was heavy, a reflection of the unspoken truth—they were driving straight into a place haunted by the failures of those who came before them.

They had just passed the old stadium on E Loop 250, the snow thickening around them, when Liz's phone buzzed. She pulled it from her pocket, frowning.

"It's dispatch," she said, answering the call. Her face paled as she listened.

"What? You're sure?" She looked at Roger, her grip tightening on the phone. "They've found Harold Mercer's cell phone. It's pinging from his house on Green Tree Boulevard."

Roger's hands tightened on the wheel. Green Tree Boulevard. That wasn't where they expected Mercer to be.

Green Tree cut through one of the wealthiest neighborhoods in Midland, where manicured lawns and sprawling estates lined the wide streets. Harold Mercer's house was an imposing mansion, a reminder of the fortune he had once built before everything crumbled.

"If Mercer's back there—or if the killer is—we need to check it out," Roger said, voice tight.

He swung the truck around, turning back onto W Loop 250. The snowstorm made the usually busy road eerily empty, the city's lights blurred and ghostly in the distance. They drove in tense silence past Midland Park Mall, its parking lot buried under a layer of snow, then onto Midland Drive, where the affluent Green Tree neighborhood loomed, shrouded in icy darkness.

***

Mercer's House

Green Tree Boulevard was lined with towering oak trees, their branches heavy with snow. The houses were grand, set back behind wrought-iron gates, each one a silent monument to old money and power.

Mercer's mansion sat at the end of a long, winding driveway, its brick facade illuminated by security lights that cast long shadows across the snow. The windows were dark. The house seemed to crouch in the cold, a predator waiting in the dark.

Roger pulled the truck near the gate, letting the engine idle as he scanned the house.

Something felt wrong.

"Stay close," he told Liz. "If the killer's here, we need to be ready."

They stepped out into the freezing air, their breath fogging in the darkness. Snow crunched beneath their boots, the silence so profound that every sound seemed magnified.

Then they saw it.

The front door was slightly ajar, a sliver of darkness yawning beyond the threshold.

Roger drew his gun instantly, every instinct honed by years of knowing when a scene was off. He glanced at Liz, who nodded, gripping her own weapon tightly.

The house swallowed them whole as they entered.

The grand foyer stretched before them, its sweeping staircase and gleaming marble floors untouched by time— but something was off. Expensive artwork lined the walls, a crystal chandelier hung above, catching the dim light, but the air felt stale, unnatural, like the house had been holding its breath for too long.

"Mercer?" Roger called, his voice low but firm, echoing into the vast space.

Nothing.

Liz's flashlight swept across the living room. The shelves were lined with dusty books, a fireplace with logs that hadn't seen flames in years. A grandfather clock ticked softly in the corner, each chime a grim reminder of time slipping away.

Her beam landed on the dining room table.

She froze.

Papers were scattered haphazardly across the polished wood, some overturned, others crumpled as if someone had been rifling through them in a hurry.

Roger stepped forward, picking up a document. Old financial records, legal papers.

"Someone was looking for something," Liz said. "And they weren't exactly careful about it."

Roger's jaw tightened. "Let's check his study. If Mercer was hiding anything, that's where we'll find it."

They made their way deeper into the house, past closed doors that led to darkened rooms. Each door they passed felt like it was concealing some malevolent presence, something waiting for the right moment to strike.

When they reached Mercer's study, the door was shut tight Roger hesitated for a moment, then twisted the knob and pushed it open.

Something in his gut told him to be ready.

Liz stepped inside first, her boots crushing crumpled paper as she moved.

Chaos.

Books and papers were strewn across the floor, the massive oak desk buried under folders left half-open, documents spilling onto the carpet. The heavy curtains over the large bay window shifted slightly, caught in a cold draft.

Liz approached the desk, her flashlight illuminating the chaos. Papers lay scattered across the surface, some crumpled, others torn as if someone had gone through them in a hurry. A chair had been knocked over, its wooden legs scraping against the dusty floor.

"Looks like someone's been here," she said, her voice tense. "Maybe Mercer. Or maybe the killer."

Roger moved to a tall filing cabinet that had been left half-open, its drawers full of folders labeled with names and dates. He pulled one out, flipping through the pages, his eyes narrowing as he scanned the contents. "These are all refinery records," he said. "Employee files, contracts, legal documents. Mercer wasn't just paranoid—he was gathering evidence."

Liz turned her attention to a leather-bound notebook lying on the floor, its cover creased and worn. She picked it up, flipping through the pages filled with Mercer's frantic handwriting, words scrawled in jagged, uneven strokes. She exhaled sharply.

"He was convinced someone was watching him," she murmured, while reading Mercer's notes. "He thought he was being followed. He was documenting everything, but none of it is finished. It's like he ran out of time."

Roger's flashlight beam swept over a bookshelf, and something caught his eye—a metal box, tucked behind a row of old hardcovers. He pulled it out and set it on the desk. Liz moved beside him, glancing at the rusted lock securing it shut.

Roger reached into his pocket, his fingers curling around the small, rusted key they had found around Dawson's neck. For a moment, he hesitated, glancing at Liz. Neither of them wanted to get their hopes up—it was too much of a long shot. He slid the key into the lock, twisting it.

The soft click echoed in the stillness of the room.

They exchanged a brief look of shock before Roger lifted the lid. Inside, old photographs, newspaper clippings, and a crumpled map of Midland lay piled together. Some of the documents were yellowed with age, others had been folded so many times the creases had worn thin.

Liz dug through the photos, her fingers tightening around the edges as she sifted through them. Then she saw it.

One photograph—buried beneath a stack of refinery documents, tucked away as if someone had wanted it hidden.

She held it up to the light. It was black and white, grainy, and creased, but horrifyingly clear.

The Marathon Oil refinery explosion.

A massive fireball consumed the background, thick, inky smoke curling into the sky. In the foreground, chaos. Oil pooled in slick rivers across the snow, reflecting the fire in its shimmering surface. Steel beams lay twisted and mangled, broken machinery thrown about like discarded scraps.

And the bodies.

Liz's stomach turned. The victims of the explosion were frozen in twisted, unnatural positions. A man slumped over a pipeline, his back arched grotesquely. A woman sprawled in the snow, her face contorted in a silent scream, her hands reaching toward something unseen. The devastation stretched across the entire image, a haunting snapshot of the past, one Midland had tried to forget.

Liz's hands trembled as she turned the photograph toward Roger. "This is it," she said, her voice barely above a whisper. "The explosion that poisoned everything. The contamination, the sickness… it all started here."

Roger's face had gone pale, his eyes locked on the photo. His mind flashed back to the first murder—the way the victim had been posed. The old Marathon Oil sign. Something about it had been nagging at him, and now he understood why. A wave of nausea twisted in his gut.

"That's why it felt familiar," he murmured, his voice thick with dread. "The first body we found… it was staged exactly like one of these victims."

Liz's breath caught in her throat as realization set in. Her eyes darted to another victim in the photograph, and the memory of the second murder scene flashed through her mind. "And the second murder," she whispered, her voice unsteady. "That one was posed like another body in this picture."

Roger's jaw tightened as he grabbed the photograph and counted the bodies. Eight in total. His stomach churned.

"The killer isn't finished," he said, the realization settling over him like a weight. "There are five more victims to go."

Liz swallowed hard, the implications sinking in. "This isn't just a killing spree," she said, her voice hushed. "The killer is recreating the explosion. One victim at a time."

Roger's mind reeled. Each murder was deliberate, methodical—a grotesque tribute to the past. The killer wasn't just avenging something; they were crafting a perverse kind of justice, tying the past and present together with blood and oil.

Before they could process what they had uncovered, a sudden noise shattered the silence.

A loud crash.

Glass breaking.

The sound came from somewhere deeper in the house.

Roger and Liz froze, their bodies tensing as their instincts took over. Liz's grip on her gun tightened as she turned toward the sound.

"Someone's here," she whispered.

Roger's heartbeat thundered in his ears. He stepped cautiously toward the noise, his flashlight cutting through the darkness. The sound hadn't come from upstairs. It was coming from the back of the mansion.

They moved swiftly, carefully, their eyes scanning the shadows for movement. The sound had led them to a set of glass doors that opened onto the back patio. The glass had been shattered inward, shards scattered across the polished wood floors.

Liz pointed her gun at the broken door, her jaw tight. "They broke in."

Roger stepped out onto the patio, the cold air biting at his skin. His boots crunched against the snow as he noticed fresh footprints. Leading away from the house.

Liz joined him, scanning the tree line. The tracks cut through the snow, disappearing into the land behind the property.

Whoever had been inside had already fled.

"Damn it," Roger muttered, frustration mounting.

Liz exhaled sharply. "We need to follow those tracks," she said. "This might be our only chance to catch them—or find Mercer."

Roger nodded, his pulse pounding. The game was accelerating, the stakes rising. The message was clear.

The past wasn't done with them.

And the land would not rest until its debts were paid in full.

Back in the truck, they followed the footprints through Green Tree, turning onto Holiday Hill Road. Snow fell harder now, their visibility narrowing, but the urgency burning in their veins kept them moving.

The killer was leading them somewhere.

Deeper into the darkness.

Roger gripped the wheel, his jaw clenched. He knew one thing for certain—whatever lay ahead would either reveal the truth or bury them with it.

CHAPTER TEN

The snow fell in thick sheets, a rare but brutal occurrence in Midland, Texas. The land around them was sparse, stretching into the dark with only mesquite trees and rusted oil equipment breaking the emptiness.

Roger drove down E Loop 250, gripping the wheel, his jaw tight. The truck's headlights cut through the swirling white, revealing the thorny mesquite branches reaching from the night.

The footprints they had been following were gone, swallowed by the storm. Roger muttered a curse under his breath, his fingers flexing on the wheel. Beside him, Liz held her gun and flashlight ready, scanning the snow-covered expanse. She exhaled slowly, her breath fogging up her scarf. Every part of her was tense.

"Do you think we're still on the right path?" Liz asked, voice tight.

Roger glanced at the faint tire tracks barely visible through the storm. "We have to be," he said, more to himself than to her. "The tracks lead toward the old refinery site. Whoever we're after wants us there."

Liz pulled her coat tighter, a shiver running through her—not just from the cold. "Feels like a setup," she murmured. "But we don't have a choice, do we?"

Roger's knuckles whitened on the wheel. "No. We don't."

They turned onto a bumpy, snow-covered service road leading to Site B-12. The refinery loomed in the distance, a rusting skeleton of pipes and metal, once the lifeblood of Midland's oil boom. Now, it stood forgotten.

Roger parked at the edge of the site and killed the engine. Silence followed. Not the kind of silence that's peaceful. The kind that waits.

Snow gathered in drifts against rusted machinery, shadows flickering against the walls of the abandoned buildings. It felt like stepping into another world—one where things lingered, watching.

They stepped out, their boots sinking into the snow-covered sand. The wind bit at their faces. Roger adjusted his coat, shaking off the unease. He wasn't the type to believe in ghosts, but something about this place felt off.

"Stay close," Roger said, voice low. He looked at Liz— her fingers were wrapped tight around her gun, her breath quick. She met his gaze and nodded. She wasn't scared. Not exactly. But she knew enough to be wary.

The main refinery building stood ahead, a rust-streaked husk of steel and concrete. Graffiti covered the walls, and the roof caved in places. The heavy metal entrance door hung slightly open, creaking in the wind.

Roger and Liz exchanged a look before stepping inside.

The refinery's interior was a maze of corroded catwalks, cracked concrete, and rusting machinery. The air was thick with the smell of oil and decay. Their flashlights cut through the dimness, revealing footprints in the dust. Recent ones.

Roger's pulse quickened. Whoever had brought them here wasn't far.

They moved carefully, their boots crunching against debris as they followed the footprints deeper inside. Liz kept her breathing steady, but her heart pounded.

They passed through rooms filled with rusted oil drums and overturned filing cabinets. Papers littered the floor, some yellowed with age, others freshly disturbed.

"Someone's been here recently," Liz murmured. "But where did they go?"

Roger didn't answer. His gut told him this wasn't just about following a trail. They were being led.

The footprints stopped outside a heavy metal door marked 'Control Room.' Roger pressed his back to the wall beside it, motioning for Liz to do the same. He reached for the handle, inhaling sharply before pushing it open.

The control room was cavernous. Rows of shattered glass, rusted panels, and dust-covered screens stretched before them. The room had once been the nerve center of the refinery, but now it was a hollow shell, echoing with the ghostly hum of the wind.

In the center of the room, a crude, makeshift altar had been set up. Candles, some burned down to waxy nubs, stood in a circle around a wooden table. On the table lay an assortment of objects: tarnished coins, pieces of machinery, and a photograph.

Roger approached the altar, his flashlight casting long, shifting shadows as he leaned in. His gut tightened. Something about this felt... personal. The photograph in the center caught his attention—it was another image of the Marathon Oil explosion, but this one had been defaced. Red

"X" marks slashed over most of the victims' faces—except for five who remained untouched.

Liz's breath hitched. She stared at the photograph, her voice barely above a whisper. "The unmarked faces..." She swallowed hard. "Those are the next victims. We have to find them before it's too late." Her fingers curled into fists.

Roger picked up the photograph, his hands tightening around the edges. The unmarked faces stared back at him, frozen in time, almost pleading. His throat went dry.

Before either of them could say another word, footsteps echoed through the building. Heavy. Unsteady.

Roger and Liz spun toward the sound, guns raised, flashlights slicing through the darkness. Their breathing went still.

Out of the shadows, a figure stumbled forward—disoriented, swaying like a man half-conscious.

Liz exhaled sharply. "Eli?"

Eli Rivera, one of their own deputies, emerged into the dim light. His face was pale, bruised, smeared with blood. His uniform was torn, and his wide, frantic eyes darted around the room.

Roger lowered his gun slightly but didn't holster it. Something was wrong.

"What the hell happened to you?" Roger asked, his voice laced with both shock and suspicion.

Eli staggered a few steps closer, his trembling hands reaching out—before his knees buckled beneath him. He collapsed, chest heaving, eyes wild with panic.

"You… shouldn't have come," he choked out. His voice was raw, like he had been screaming for hours. His gaze flicked toward the darkness. "They're watching. They're everywhere."

Liz knelt beside him, her heart hammering. "Eli, who's watching? What happened?" Her fingers pressed against his shoulder, grounding him.

Eli's breath came in short, ragged bursts. "They… they knew I was close," he gasped, his voice breaking. His hands clenched into the fabric of his torn uniform as if trying to hold onto something—anything.

"I followed a lead about Mercer. Came here to find him, but... but they ambushed me." He coughed, the sound scraping his throat. His gaze flickered toward the altar, and something in him snapped. His entire body recoiled.

"The land…" His voice dropped to a whisper, barely audible. His pupils shrank, fixated on the symbols carved into the wood. "It's cursed. It's taking its revenge."

Roger's jaw clenched. Dammit. He had heard enough about curses to last a lifetime. But Eli's fear wasn't some drunken superstition—it was real.

"Eli, focus," Roger said firmly. "Who ambushed you? Was it the killer?"

Eli's eyes rolled back, and his body went limp.

Then—

CRACK.

The air exploded with gunfire.

Bullets tore through the rusted metal walls, sending sparks flying. The cavernous room amplified the noise, turning it into a deafening roar.

Roger barely had time to react before instinct took over. He lunged forward, throwing himself over Liz as they hit the ground. The impact knocked the breath from his lungs, but a sharper, searing pain cut through it—white-hot, burning. His upper arm.

"Shit!" He clenched his teeth, pressing a hand to the wound. Warm blood seeped through his coat.

"Get down!" he barked, forcing himself to stay sharp.

Liz was already moving. She twisted, gun aimed, firing toward the shadows. Muzzle flashes lit up the room, catching glimpses of movement—a dark figure ducking behind a rusted oil drum.

"They're trying to pin us down!" Liz yelled, her voice strained but steady.

Roger gritted his teeth and pushed himself up, his vision blurring for a second from the pain. He aimed, squeezing off a few shots. The shooter, masked and dressed in heavy clothing, moved like a ghost—quick, deliberate.

Then, just as fast as they had appeared—

They were gone.

The room fell silent again, save for the ringing in Roger's ears and the pounding of his heart. His breath came in short, uneven bursts, the adrenaline refusing to let go. He swayed slightly, the mix of pain and exhaustion making his vision blur.

Liz rushed to his side, her face pale but set with determination. She grabbed his uninjured arm, grounding him.

"Are you okay?" she asked, her voice tight with concern.

Roger nodded, jaw clenched. "It's just a scratch," he muttered, but the way he winced said otherwise. "We need to keep moving."

Liz didn't buy it, but she didn't argue. They didn't have time.

Minutes later, an ambulance pulled up at the edge of the refinery, sirens wailing, lights flashing. The paramedics worked quickly, cleaning Roger's wound and wrapping his arm in a makeshift bandage.

"You're lucky," one of them said. "Could have been a lot worse."

Roger barely acknowledged them. His mind was stuck on Eli's words. The land… it's cursed. And the killer—they had been right there, watching, waiting.

"I'm fine," he insisted. The pain barely registered anymore. "We need to find Harold Mercer. There's no time to waste."

Liz's expression hardened. She felt it too—the weight of urgency pressing down on them.

"Let's go," she said. "If Eli's right, Mercer is running out of time."

They pushed deeper into the refinery, guided only by the dim emergency lights and Eli's disjointed warnings. The air grew colder, heavier. A sense of unease settled over them like a thick fog.

Their boots crunched over broken glass and snow-covered concrete as they neared one of the oldest storage buildings.

Roger and Liz exchanged a look.

Neither of them spoke. They just knew.

Roger took a steadying breath and pushed the door open.

The metallic groan of the hinges made Liz's stomach twist. The air inside was different—thick, suffocating. And then they saw it.

Harold Mercer's body hung from a rusted metal beam, strung up by chains that bit into his wrists and ankles. His weight made them creak under the strain, the sound barely audible over the oppressive silence.

His mouth was stuffed full of thick, black sludge—old oil, forced down his throat, spilling from his lips, staining his face and neck. The viscous liquid clung to him, mixing with his own blood, turning everything a sickening shade of tar-like black.

His torso had been flayed open. The flesh peeled back, exposing glistening ribs. His insides weren't just spilled; they had been arranged—meticulously placed around him, as if part of some twisted ritual. The crude oil mingled with his blood, pooling beneath him in thick, inky puddles.

Liz clamped a hand over her mouth, her stomach lurching violently.

Symbols had been carved into Mercer's skin—deep, deliberate, mirroring the ancient markings they had seen before. The edges of the wounds were darkened with oil, making them look almost burned into him. Whoever did this hadn't just wanted him dead. They wanted him to suffer.

His eyes were wide, frozen in terror. His mouth stretched in a silent scream.

The stench of blood and decay coated the air. It wasn't just death—it was desecration.

Roger felt his knees threaten to buckle. He had seen murder. He had seen cruelty. But this? This was something else.

"Jesus Christ," he whispered, voice hoarse. "This… this isn't just a murder. It's a goddamn massacre."

Liz stumbled back, hand still pressed to her mouth. Her breath came in sharp, shallow bursts.

"Oh my God," she choked out. Her mind reeled, trying to comprehend the level of brutality before her. "How… how could someone do this?"

An hour later, Marla Decker, the county coroner, arrived. Even she, a veteran of countless gruesome autopsies, looked shaken. Her usual detached professionalism faltered the moment she stepped inside.

She moved closer to the body, her breath catching.

"The oil," she murmured, reaching out with gloved fingers. "This wasn't just torture—it was symbolic. They used the very thing that poisoned the land and ruined lives to silence him."

She bent down, carefully tracing the symbols carved into Mercer's flesh.

"These symbols... they're not random," she murmured. "Whoever did this knew exactly what they were doing."

She pointed at a particularly deep gash across Mercer's chest. "This one here… it's almost like they were trying to mark him as some kind of offering."

Her eyes flicked up to the chains suspending him.

"These chains—they're industrial, the kind you'd find in an oil rig or heavy machinery." She exhaled sharply. "It's like they used the tools of his own industry against him."

She hesitated, her gaze sweeping over the arrangement of organs, and the meticulous placement of symbols.

Her voice dropped to a near whisper. "The positioning of the body, the way his organs were arranged... of course they want their presence known…."

She turned to Roger, her expression grim.

"This is more of a warning than revenge. They are making sure that what happened years ago, no one ever dares to repeat it," she said and swallowed hard. Her fingers curled slightly as if trying to steady herself.

"This is the worst thing I've ever seen," she admitted, her voice wavering.

"Whoever did this… they're more than killers. They're monsters."

Roger turned away, his mind racing. The symbols. The ritualistic display. The message.

This wasn't over.

The killer had left them something more than just a body. They had left a promise.

A promise that demanded payment in blood.

The question wasn't just who was behind this.

It was how many more would die before it ended.

CHAPTER ELEVEN

The icy Midland air stabbed at Roger's exposed skin as he stepped away from the brutal murder scene at the refinery. The coroner, Marla Decker, worked silently, her movements precise, but Roger could see it—the tension in her jaw, the way her gloved hands gripped the instruments a little too tightly. No amount of experience prepared anyone for a sight like this.

Liz stood near one of the rusted support beams, arms crossed tight against her chest. Her face was pale, eyes distant, locked onto something only she could see. The cold dug into her, but it wasn't just the wind—it was the image of Mercer's shredded, lifeless body burned into her mind. She wiped at her eyes, not sure if the dampness was from the wind or tears. Her fingers, stiff with cold, curled and uncurled at her sides. The thick fabric of her gloves barely made a difference.

Roger approached, his bandaged arm throbbing in protest. He ignored it. There wasn't time for pain. "Liz." He spoke gently, placing a hand on her shoulder. Even through her coat, he could feel her trembling. "We need to regroup. The killer is still out there, and we're running out of time."

Liz turned slowly, her jaw clenched so tight he thought she might break it. Her eyes, usually sharp, were bloodshot, clouded with anger and exhaustion.

"This isn't just about catching a murderer anymore." Her voice was quieter than he expected, but the weight behind it was heavy. "It's like… they're trying to make us feel the land's pain. To suffer like the victims of the refinery explosion."

Roger exhaled, his breath a cloud of white. He looked past her at the refinery—looming, skeletal in the swirling snow. Red and blue lights threw jagged shadows across the rusted beams.

"And they're succeeding." His voice was low, measured. If fear took hold, they were finished. "But we can't let them win. Eli mentioned something about a curse, about the land taking its revenge. We need to figure out what he meant—fast."

They found Eli sitting in the back of an ambulance, a wool blanket wrapped around him like a cocoon. His face was pale, hands trembling despite the medication he'd been given. His uniform, soaked with snow and blood, made him look more like a man barely holding onto reality than a deputy.

Roger and Liz approached cautiously. Roger crouched in front of Eli, searching his face. The terror there wasn't fading. His eyes darted around, scanning the darkness beyond the lights.

"Eli." Roger's voice was steady but urgent. "We need you to tell us everything. Why were you here? What did you mean when you said the land is cursed?"

Eli's gaze flicked to Roger, but his expression was hollow as if his mind was still trapped in what had happened.

"I... I was following a lead." His voice was barely a whisper, raw with exhaustion. "It came through the tip line. A man called in and said he had information about Harold

Mercer, the explosion, and the refinery contamination. He said it was all connected. That the land was angry. That we were all in danger. He told me to go to Site B-12 if I wanted to understand the truth."

Liz crouched beside Roger, her breath curling in the freezing air. "Did he give you a name?"

Eli's lips barely moved. "No," he murmured. His hands clenched in his lap. "He said the truth was there, buried under the sins of Midland."

Roger frowned. "And when you got here?"

Eli's shoulders hunched, and his breath hitched. He looked down at the snow-covered ground. "They were waiting for me," he whispered. "Not just one person— shadows moving through the snow, slipping between the beams like ghosts. They ambushed me and chased me through the refinery. I tried to fight back, but they… they knew this place too well. It was like they were using the building itself to trap me."

Liz shot Roger a look, her face tight. "The land taking its revenge," she murmured. "Do you think the killer is using this story—this supposed curse—to justify the murders?"

Eli let out a shaky breath. "The man… he said the explosion and the contamination poisoned the land. That the spirits of the dead wouldn't rest until the people responsible paid in blood." He swallowed hard, eyes locking onto Roger's. "I thought he was crazy, but now… I'm not so sure."

A chill ran through Roger, and for once, he wasn't sure it was just the cold. The idea of a curse was absurd. But the murders… the brutality…

Something about this was different.

"Whoever this killer is, they're using these stories to send a message." His voice was grim. "We need to find the truth. Supernatural or not."

Before Liz could respond, the sound of hurried footsteps crunching through the snow cut through the air.

Tim Fletcher, a young deputy, ran toward them, breath puffing in frantic bursts. "Sheriff!" His voice cracked with urgency. "We've got something. It's important."

Roger straightened, heart hammering. "What is it?"

Tim handed over a sealed evidence bag containing a small, rusted key and a crumpled piece of paper. His expression was tight, the kind that said he already had a bad feeling about it. "A local resident named Maria Sandoval called in. She said she found these in her backyard this morning, half-buried in the snow. Her house is near the old water treatment plant off West Cuthbert Avenue. She's seen strange people lurking around there at night and thought it might be connected."

Liz's eyes widened as she examined the paper through the plastic. It was stained with something dark, and scrawled across it in jagged handwriting were the words: *The debt must be paid in blood.*

It was that message and the key…… *Again.*

Her stomach tightened. "That's…ominous."

Roger inspected the rusted key, a cold weight settling in his gut. "This key… it looks old," he murmured, turning it in his gloved hand. "And it's covered in oil residue. Could it be from the water treatment plant?"

Tim nodded. "That's what we think. The lab tested it and confirmed the oil matches the type used at Marathon Oil decades ago. Whatever this unlocks… someone wanted it hidden."

Liz exhaled sharply, her mind racing. "So Maria's backyard is right near the plant," she said, piecing it together. "That place has been abandoned for years, but if people are still hanging around…" Her gaze flicked to Roger. "What if it's a hideout? Or worse?"

Roger's jaw clenched. His gut told him they were already behind. "Then we don't waste any more time." He turned to Liz. "Call it in. I want backup on-site. We're heading there now."

***

The water treatment plant loomed ahead, a relic of Midland's past. Its silhouette cut jagged lines against the night sky, the storm making the rusted structures groan like something alive.

Roger and Liz arrived with two patrol units, their headlights slicing through the swirling snow. The deputies spread out, flashlights sweeping over the skeletal remains of the facility.

Inside, the damp air clung to them like a second skin. The scent of rust and stagnant water filled their lungs, and every step echoed, making it feel like the whole place was listening.

"Stay sharp," Roger whispered, his voice barely audible over the wind slipping through broken vents. His grip tightened around his gun. Places like this had a way of swallowing people whole.

They moved cautiously, beams of light cutting through the gloom. The deeper they went, the thicker the air became—heavy, metallic. Liz swallowed against the bile rising in her throat.

They entered what had once been the main filtration chamber. The space yawned before them, filled with rusted tanks and collapsed machinery. Then, the beam of Roger's flashlight caught something that made his pulse stutter.

A body.

Suspended from the ceiling, chains biting deep into pale, exposed flesh. Limbs twisted at unnatural angles.

Liz sucked in a breath, willing herself to keep her focus. She moved closer, her flashlight skimming over the scene, and stopped when she saw a laminated ID card swinging from a chain around the man's neck. Her gloved fingers trembled slightly as she reached for it.

Her voice came out thin, disbelieving. "Franklin Weaver."

She turned to Roger. "It's him. The main safety officer for Marathon Oil. You knew him."

Roger's eyes narrowed, his stomach knotting as he focused on the victim's face. Recognition crawled over him like a slow, sickening wave. Franklin Weaver. He had spoken to the man not long ago—routine safety protocols, just another call in a long line of responsibilities. Now, Weaver was here, strung up like a grotesque warning.

Roger exhaled sharply. This wasn't just murder. This was a spectacle.

Weaver's chest had been torn open, ribs spread like grotesque petals. His organs—**placed, not discarded—**formed a perfect circle around him, each one impaled on long, rusted nails hammered deep into the concrete. Not chaos. Deliberate.

Blood had pooled beneath him, dark and slick, spreading in jagged streaks. Like ink seeping through old paper.

Roger's grip on his flashlight tightened. He forced himself closer, his breath steady, but his gut twisted in protest. The symbols carved into Weaver's flesh were deep, too precise to be rushed. The same ancient runes they had seen before. But these—these were different. More intricate. More refined. The killer had taken their time.

Liz gagged, turning away just long enough to steady herself. She wiped at her mouth, her hand trembling. "This is… worse than Mercer," she whispered, voice barely audible over the distant sound of dripping water.

She met Roger's gaze—fear, fury, and something sharper beneath it. Realization.

"They're escalating, Roger. The killer is getting bolder."

Roger nodded, his pulse steady despite the rage simmering underneath. His eyes swept the scene, catching something glinting in the pool of blood beneath Weaver's body. Gold. Small. A coin.

Carefully, he knelt down, reaching for it. The tarnished surface was stained with blood, the image of an oil derrick barely visible beneath the grime. The words stood out, though. Crisp. Deliberate.

"Marathon Oil Company."

"Another coin," Roger muttered, holding it up for Liz to see. A bitter taste settled on his tongue. "Same as the one at the refinery. This has to be their calling card."

Liz's gaze drifted back to the nails, to the way Weaver's organs had been arranged with disturbing precision.

Roger's thoughts raced, too. The symbols. The coins. The victims.

The connection clicked into place.

The explosion.

The contamination.

The people it had poisoned.

"I don't know what to think of these murders anymore, honestly. No matter how gruesome they are….it's just,…." he paused to take a deep breath and continued, "….the killer wants us to understand the pain of those victims. I don't know what to make of it," he said. His jaw clenched.

"They're recreating the suffering the explosion caused. Using these victims to represent the people who were responsible."

Liz swallowed hard, her throat tight. "They think they're restoring balance. And even though I do get the sentiment, this is too disturbing. They can't make whatever happened back then right by doing this…."

Her gaze flicked to the rusted pipes, to the darkened corners where shadows stretched and lingered. "They want the ones who profited from the refinery's destruction to pay in blood."

Roger didn't respond. He didn't have to. The truth settled between them like an anvil.

A sudden noise shattered the silence.

A metallic clang. Hurried footsteps.

Both of them snapped to attention, guns raised.

Roger and Liz exchanged a quick glance, an unspoken agreement. No hesitation.

"Stay close," Roger murmured, his voice low but firm.

They moved quickly through the maze of rusted machinery and corroded pipes. The air felt thicker now, heavy with something beyond just damp decay. Their flashlights carved through the darkness, beams bouncing off the rust and pooling in shadows.

Footsteps were faster now. Leading them.

They reached a narrow corridor. The sound grew sharper, more frantic.

Roger's heart pounded as he rounded the corner, his flashlight catching the briefest glimpse of movement. A figure.

A shadow slipping through the far doorway.

"Stop! Sheriff's Department!" Roger barked, voice slicing through the cavernous space.

He took off, boots pounding against the slick floor. Liz was right behind him, breath sharp, controlled.

The figure darted through the door. Roger slammed into it a second later, stepping into a wide, open space.

Wind howled through broken windows. Snow swirled in the air.

But the room was empty.

Roger's flashlight swept across the space—remnants of old equipment, scattered crates, the bones of a place long abandoned.

Nothing. No sign of the person they had chased.

"Damn it," he muttered, frustration curling at the edges of his voice.

Liz stood beside him, scanning the darkness, her body tense but her mind still working.

"They're toying with us," she said, voice low, angry. "They know this place better than we do. They're leading us in circles."

Roger exhaled, steadying himself. "We need to pull back. Regroup." He turned toward the exit, the weight of the night pressing into his shoulders. "This isn't over—not by a long shot."

Liz nodded, her jaw set, eyes burning with determination.

"We'll stop them, Roger," she said, voice firm, unwavering. "No matter what it takes."

CHAPTER TWELVE

Roger and Liz sat in the cruiser, the heater blasting to ward off the winter chill that had gripped Midland. The snow fell steadily outside, blanketing the streets in white as they watched people move in and out of a diner, oblivious to the darkness they were chasing. The headlights of passing cars reflected off the snow, while the muffled sounds of the city made an eerie contrast to the storm.

Roger adjusted his hat and broke the silence. He said in a low voice, "You know, the killer's not just picking random targets. Everything points back to Marathon Oil. The symbols, the locations, the victims. There's a pattern, Liz. It's all connected."

Liz nodded, her eyes staring out at the falling snow, her mind racing. The memories of each crime scene replayed in her head: the blood, the symbols carved into the victims, the coins left behind like some twisted calling card. "We're missing something, though," she said. "It's more than just revenge. Whoever's doing this, they want to send a message. But why go to these lengths?"

Roger rubbed his jaw. "They see themselves as some kind of avenger. All the victims were tied to that explosion, to the cover-up. Maybe they think they're bringing justice— their version of it—to the people who covered up what happened."

Liz frowned. "An avenger, maybe. But it's more than just cold vengeance. It's like they're trying to make everyone remember what happened. Like they think the world forgot.

And these murders—they're meant to force people to see it." She shook her head, the weariness visible in her eyes. "The victims, the symbols, the staged scenes... it's all meant to tell a story. But what's the endgame?"

Roger turned to look at her, his eyes serious, the weight of his years in law enforcement etched into his features. "The message is clear, Liz: 'The truth lies in the ashes of greed.' That's what they carved on Franklin Weaver's wall. Whoever this is, they think they're delivering some twisted kind of justice. But we can't let them keep escalating. We have to stop them before more people get hurt."

Liz's fingers drummed against the steering wheel, her eyes narrowed as she stared at the diner, watching the patrons inside. "The oil residue and sulfur compound we found—it matched one of the old Marathon Oil sites, near Cotton Flat and Industrial. Maybe they're hiding there, using it as some kind of base." She sighed. "It makes sense. It's isolated, forgotten... just like what happened."

Roger said, "The lab said it's a match. If they're still out there, that's where we need to be. We can't keep chasing their tail. We must head them off before they decide on their next target."

Liz gave a short nod, contemplating what would lie ahead for them. "We keep finding traces, but we keep missing them. It's like they're always two steps ahead of us, Roger. It's frustrating as hell." She felt tensed, the constant weight of failure bearing down on her. "Every time we think we're close, they slip away."

Roger's jaw tightened, the lines on his face deepening. "They're too careful. They've been planning this for years, maybe even decades. We're talking about someone who believes they're the hero in this twisted story. Every clue, every murder, it's all part of some larger plan we haven't quite put together yet." He looked at Liz, his voice softening slightly. "But we will. We have to."

"And if we don't figure it out soon, they'll just keep going. We need to end this." Her voice was barely above a whisper. "We can't let more people die because of this."

Roger nodded. "We will. We'll go out there, to that site, and we'll find whatever it is they want us to see. Or whoever. But we're not going to let them dictate the game anymore. This ends with us bringing them in." He looked out at the snow-covered streets. His mind raced with possibilities and plans.

The resolve between them was palpable, the weight of the responsibility shared equally. Liz shifted the cruiser into gear, and said after a deep thought, "Let's finish this, Roger." Roger gave a curt nod.

Suddenly, their radios crackled to life. "Sheriff Hartley, this is Deputy Fletcher," came the voice, strained but clear. "We've got something from the lab. The key you found in Maria Sandoval's yard was analyzed. It has traces of a specific oil residue and sulfur compound that matches an old Marathon Oil storage site. The site is on the outskirts of town, near the intersection of Cotton Flat Road and West Industrial Avenue."

Roger's pulse quickened, his instincts screaming at him. "That site's been abandoned for years," he said, his voice tight. "But if the killer's been using it, we need to move fast."

"The evidence keeps pointing us to these old Marathon Oil properties," she said with a steady voice. "Whoever this is, they're making sure their message is heard loud and clear. They want us to follow the trail."

Roger nodded. "We need to get out there," he said. "But first, let's finish clearing this place. If the killer's been hiding here, there might be something we missed. Let's get to that Marathon Oil site. If the killer is still trying to send a message, that's where we'll find our next clue… or our next victim."

They didn't waste another moment. They sped through the snow-covered streets of Midland. The city lights blurred past, the world outside the windows a wash of white and gray, and Roger couldn't shake the feeling that time was running out. The killer was escalating, and the closer they got to uncovering the truth, the more dangerous things became. The land, scarred and silent, waited for them, holding secrets that had festered for decades. The snow continued to fall, the wind howled across the open expanse, and Roger knew that whatever they found there, it would bring them one step closer to ending the nightmare that had gripped Midland.

"We're close," he said, his eyes meeting Liz's.

Liz pulled the cruiser to a stop. The headlights illuminated the darkened site before them. They exchanged a final look, the silent understanding passing between them.

Together, they stepped out of the vehicle. "One way or another," Roger muttered, his voice barely audible over the wind. "We're ending this."

They moved cautiously through the abandoned Marathon Oil storage site, the snow crunching under their boots, their flashlights cutting through the darkness. The site was eerily quiet, the wind whistling through gaps in the old structures, the air thick with the scent of rust and decay. They swept their lights over rusted tanks, piles of old, weathered equipment, and the skeletal remains of buildings that had long since fallen into disrepair.

Roger's breath fogged in the cold air as he scanned the area. Liz stayed close, their footsteps echoing off the crumbling concrete.

They searched every building, every possible hiding place. The old storage site was a labyrinth of rusted metal and forgotten machinery. Every corner turned up nothing but remnants of the past. They found empty oil drums, broken tools, and faded hazard signs. The deeper they went, the more it became clear that the site had not been touched by anything but time and the elements.

Liz sighed. "Nothing. No sign of anyone. If they were here, they're long gone now." She kicked at a piece of debris, the sound echoing in the emptiness.

Roger paused. He could feel the disappointment settling in his chest. "They're always one step ahead," he said, his voice grim. "They knew we'd come here. This was just another dead end."

Liz turned to face him. "We'll keep going, Roger. We're getting closer, piece by piece. They can't hide forever." She looked around one last time. "We need to regroup, go over everything again. There's something we're missing, and we're going to find it."

"You're right. We'll figure it out." He took a deep breath, the cold air stinging his lungs. "Let's get back. We need to come at this from a different angle."

They made their way back to the cruiser, the sense of urgency still gnawing at them but tempered now by the bitter realization that the killer was still out there, watching, waiting. Roger opened the door and slid into the passenger seat, the heater humming to life as Liz started the engine.

As they pulled away from the abandoned site, Roger looked out at the snow-covered landscape, his mind already worked through their next move. They were close—he could feel it.

Liz glanced over at him, her eyes meeting his for a brief moment. "We'll get them, Roger. We're not giving up. Not now, not ever."

CHAPTER THIRTEEN

Snow continued to fall over Midland, a relentless cascade that coated the city in a thick, white blanket. The cold night air was sharp but it was nothing compared to the chill that had settled in the hearts of the sheriff's department. Roger and Liz had been running on pure adrenaline for days, each lead dragging them deeper into a twisted game of cat and mouse. Exhaustion settled over them like a heavy, sodden cloak.

Roger glanced at Liz, who was slumped in the passenger seat of his pickup, her head leaned back against the headrest. Her face was pale and the strain of the case was etched into the lines around her normally bright eyes. Her dark hair fell messily around her face. She had been his rock through all of this, always ready with a sharp mind, but even she had her limits.

"Liz," Roger said softly as they bounced along the rutted road, his voice rough with fatigue. "You need to get some rest. We both do."

Liz opened her eyes and gave him a tired smile, though it didn't reach her eyes. "I'll rest when we catch this bastard," she replied.

Roger shook his head. "We won't be any good to anyone if we can't think straight," he insisted. "Let's start fresh tomorrow morning. We need to be sharp."

Liz sighed. She knew he was right. "Fine," she agreed reluctantly. "But only a few hours. I want to be back on this as soon as possible."

Roger nodded, though he couldn't help but feel the weight of their situation pressing down on him. The killer had been playing with them, taunting them, and now it felt as if they were running out of time. As he drove Liz home, the city lights glowed through the snowfall, casting a muted, almost serene picture of Midland that belied the horror lurking in its shadows.

When they pulled up in front of Liz's small house on Ohio Avenue, the street was silent, the snow muffling the distant hum of the city. The old craftsman-style house stood alone, its porch light flickering in the wind. Liz climbed out of the truck, her entire body aching from the long hours they'd spent chasing shadows and staring at crime scene photos. She glanced back at Roger, giving him a small, grateful smile.

"Try to get some sleep, Sheriff," she said. "I don't want you falling apart on me."

Roger chuckled softly, though the sound was hollow, strained. "You too, Trujillo," he replied. "I'll see you in the morning."

Liz nodded, her eyes lingering on Roger for a moment longer before she turned and made her way up the icy steps to her front door. The warmth of her home enveloped her as she stepped inside, and for a moment, she closed her eyes, savoring the reprieve from the bitter cold outside. The heater hummed softly, and Max, her orange tabby, appeared from the hallway, rubbing against her leg. She scooped him up, pressing her face against his fur, the simple warmth of the cat offering her some comfort.

She had just locked the door behind her when her phone buzzed. Liz pulled it out, her heart skipping a beat when she saw the name: Jason. Her boyfriend. Her anchor in the storm. Jason was a local EMT, and though their relationship had always been complicated by their demanding careers, he was one of the few people who truly understood her.

Hey, his text read. Just finished my shift. Want me to come over and check on you?

Liz felt a wave of emotion crash over her—relief, exhaustion, and a desperate need for comfort. Yes, she replied, her hands shaking. Please.

It wasn't long before there was a soft knock at the door. Liz opened it to find Jason standing there, his blue eyes filled with concern. His short brown hair was damp from the snow, and he wore his EMT jacket, which he quickly shrugged off as he stepped inside. The warmth of the house was a stark contrast to the cold outside, and Jason pulled Liz into a tight hug.

"God, Liz," he whispered, his voice rough with worry. "I've been so scared for you."

Liz clung to him, burying her face in his chest. The strength of his embrace and the familiar scent of him—a mix of antiseptic and cedarwood—washed over her, and for the first time in days, she felt a flicker of safety.

"I'm okay," she said, though her voice cracked. "It's just… this case is killing me, Jason. It's so much worse than anything I've ever worked on."

Jason pulled back slightly, cupping her face in his hands. "I'm here," he said, his eyes searching hers. "Whatever you need."

Liz's lips trembled. What she needed was an escape, even if just for a moment. She leaned up and kissed him, and he responded immediately, his lips warm and familiar, a lifeline in the chaos. The kiss deepened, and Liz felt the tension begin to melt away, replaced by a burning need for closeness, for anything that made her feel human again.

Jason guided her gently toward the living room. They moved together, shedding layers of clothing as they went, and by the time they reached the couch, the urgency of their need had taken over. Liz pulled him down with her, her fingers threading through his hair as they kissed with a passion fueled by fear and relief. The world outside, the snow, the horror—it all faded away, leaving just the two of them.

Their lovemaking was intense. Liz let herself get lost in the moment, in Jason's touch, in the way he whispered her name like a promise. She needed this—needed him—to remind her that there was still light in the world, even amid so much darkness.

When it was over, they lay together on the couch, wrapped in each other's arms. Liz rested her head on Jason's chest, listening to the steady rhythm of his heartbeat. For a little while, the case, the murders, and the killer felt distant, as if they couldn't touch her here in this small, sacred moment of peace.

But the respite was brief. As Jason stroked her hair, Liz's mind wandered back to the horrors she had witnessed. The images of the victims, the symbols carved into their flesh, the cold, calculated way the killer operated—all of it lurked at the edges of her thoughts, waiting to pull her back under.

Jason seemed to sense her unease. "Hey," he murmured, pressing a kiss to her forehead. "You're safe right now. Let yourself be here, with me."

Liz closed her eyes, willing herself to believe him, even as a nagging sense of dread refused to leave her.

Across town, Roger parked his truck in the driveway of his modest ranch-style house on North Baird Street. The house felt emptier than ever without Kathy. His ex-wife had left years ago, and while he tried not to dwell on it, nights like these made it hard to avoid the memories. The laughter, the warmth, the family dinners that used to fill the home— all of it felt like a different life, one that had slipped through his fingers while he wasn't paying attention.

He stepped inside, greeted by the familiar creak of the wooden floorboards and the faint scent of leather and old coffee. The living room was neat but sparse, decorated with only a few framed photographs: his daughter, Emily, from her high school graduation, and a family portrait from years ago when she was just a little girl. Emily lived in Dallas now, working as a journalist, and he missed her fiercely. Their calls had grown infrequent, and he often wondered if she'd ever truly forgiven him for choosing the job over family too many times.

Roger poured himself a glass of whiskey. The burn in his throat felt good, like a reminder that he was still alive, still fighting. He leaned against the counter, and stared out the window. The silence of the house pressed in on him.

"Get it together, Hartley," he muttered to himself. He was too old to dwell on what couldn't be changed. The only thing he could do now was catch the monster terrorizing his town.

Setting the empty glass down, Roger made his way to the living room. He collapsed into his leather armchair. His gun and badge were within arm's reach, as always. With a heavy sigh, he closed his eyes, the exhaustion finally dragging him under.

At her home, Liz woke with a start. The room was dim, the early morning light just beginning to filter through the blinds. Jason was still asleep beside her, his arm draped protectively over her waist. Max, her orange tabby, sat rigid on the coffee table, his fur bristled, eyes wide and fixated on something.

Her instincts sharpened immediately, a wave of unease replacing the fleeting warmth of sleep. Liz reached for her gun on the end table, her breath held as she scanned the room. Everything seemed in place—except for the stack of photographs sitting neatly on the coffee table, right beside her badge.

Her heart pounded as she leaned forward, her fingers trembling as they hovered over the top photo. She picked it up, the glossy surface cold against her skin. The image showed her crouched at the scene of Franklin Weaver's murder, captured from a shadowed vantage point. She froze, her stomach twisting in knots as she flipped to the next picture. It was of her and Roger at a different crime scene, taken during what they had thought was a private moment of discussion. Picture after picture showed them, unguarded and vulnerable, as if the killer had been toying with them all along.

Then she reached the last photo—a polaroid of her and Jason making love on the couch just hours earlier. The air seemed to vanish from her lungs. Her hands shook violently as she stared at the image. The intimacy, the invasion of their sacred moment, sent a wave of nausea rolling through her.

She flipped the polaroid over, revealing a jagged, handwritten note: *I've been watching you. Leave me alone, or I'll show you how close I can get.*

Liz's knees buckled, and the photo fluttered to the floor. Jason stirred awake. His brow furrowed as he took in her pale face and shaking hands. "Liz?" he said, his voice thick with concern. "What's going on?"

She couldn't speak, couldn't find the words, so she simply handed him the polaroid. Jason's face went rigid as he stared at it. His fingers tightening around the edges. "What the hell is this?" he demanded, anger and fear sharpening his voice.

"The killer," Liz whispered, her voice cracking. "He was here. He watched us, Jason." She gestured to the photos still on the table, her breath shallow. "We're not safe. Not even here."

Jason pulled her into a fierce embrace, his jaw clenched, his heart hammering in his chest. "We'll figure this out," he said, though his voice trembled. "I'm not going to let anything happen to you."

But Liz couldn't shake the sense that they were already too late.

Jason sat stiffly on the couch, his fists clenched as he stared at the photos spread across the table. His mind raced, a cacophony of anger, fear, and helplessness battling for dominance.

"That son of a bitch," he muttered. "He was here. In your house." He looked up at Liz, his expression fierce. "He was watching us, Liz. *Watching you.*"

Liz nodded, her face pale, her hands still trembling. "I know," she whispered, her voice barely audible. "I can't stop thinking about it. How close he was. How—how vulnerable we were." She shivered, her arms wrapping tightly around herself.

Jason leaned forward, his elbows on his knees, his eyes dark with determination. "I should've stayed with you last night. Hell, I should've been here every night since this started."

"This isn't your fault," Liz said, her voice firmer now, though her hands still shook. She reached out to him, her fingers brushing his arm. "You couldn't have known. Neither of us could."

Jason covered her hand with his, his grip solid and grounding. "Then we'll know now. We'll be ready. He's not going to get near you again. I promise."

Liz wanted to believe him, wanted to cling to the strength in his voice, but the chill in her chest refused to thaw.

On the other end, Roger was jolted awake by the sharp ring of his phone. His hand darted out, grabbing it from the side table. "Hartley," he answered, his voice thick with sleep.

"Sheriff," came the urgent voice of Deputy Fletcher. "We've got a situation. A package was delivered to the front steps of the sheriff's office. It's addressed to you."

Roger sat upright, his exhaustion evaporating in an instant. "What's in it?" he asked, already swinging his legs off the chair.

"We haven't opened it yet, but it doesn't look good," Fletcher said, his tone shaken. "You need to see it for yourself."

Roger scrubbed a hand over his face, trying to clear the lingering haze of sleep. As he stood, something on the kitchen table caught his eye. He froze, his heart skipping a beat.

There, in the center of the table, was a stack of photographs. His badge lay neatly on top.

His hands trembled as he approached the table, dread coiling in his gut. The photographs showed him in unsettling detail: leaning against his truck at a crime scene, standing by his kitchen window, even asleep in his leather armchair. Each image was more intimate, more invasive, than the last.

But it was the final photo that sent a chill down his spine. His badge, carefully removed from his pants, had been placed in the killer's hand for a close-up shot.

Beneath the photographs was a handwritten note: *I slipped your badge off while you slept. I'm always closer than you think. Leave me alone, or there will be consequences.*

Roger's stomach churned, and his grip tightened on his phone. "Hartley," Fletcher repeated, his voice echoing distantly. "Are you on your way?"

Roger's voice was raw when he answered. "The killer was in my house, Fletcher. I'm coming now."

As Roger ended the call, he looked back at the photos, his breath heavy in the silence of the house. His hand hovered over the badge.

He grabbed it, his fingers curling around the cool metal. "This isn't just a game anymore," he muttered to himself, his voice barely above a whisper.

His jaw clenched as he stormed out of the house, the snow crunching under his boots. Somewhere out there, the killer was watching, laughing. Roger swore he'd put an end to it—even if it cost him everything.

CHAPTER FOURTEEN

Snow continued to blanket Midland. The rising sun cast an orange glow across the horizon, but the beauty of the morning did nothing to chase away the darkness that had settled over the town. The snowflakes fell in swirling patterns, covering the rooftops and the barren streets.

Roger stepped out of his house. His heart still pounding from the discovery of the photographs and his stolen badge. The violation was a terrifying reminder that the killer wasn't just a shadowy figure lurking in the distance but someone who could breach the most private of spaces without a sound. The cold air stung his face, and he could feel the weight of his badge now, heavier than ever. He locked the door behind him, his eyes scanning the street, the familiar surroundings suddenly feeling alien and threatening. The neighborhood that had always been a place of solace now felt like a hunting ground.

He climbed into his truck, his mind racing as he gripped the steering wheel so tightly his knuckles turned white. The sound of the phone call with Liz played on repeat in his mind. He had to get to the sheriff's office, but the knowledge that the killer had been inside his home, mere feet away from where he slept, gnawed at him. He could almost feel the shadow of the killer's presence, lingering in the corners of his mind, reminding him that no place was safe.

Roger knew the stakes had never been higher, and he had to act fast. The lives of his team, his family, and the people of Midland depended on it.

When Roger arrived at the sheriff's office, the snow was still falling. Deputies huddled together in the lobby, their faces pale and tense. The package that had been delivered sat ominously on a table in the center of the room, a thick, black box that seemed to pulse with a quiet menace.

Deputy Fletcher, a young but competent officer with sandy blond hair and anxious eyes, approached Roger. "Sheriff," Fletcher said, his voice taut, "the package arrived just before dawn. We've kept it secure, but we haven't opened it yet." Fletcher's eyes darted nervously to the box, his fear palpable.

Roger nodded. The room seemed to hold its breath as he carefully lifted the lid. The sight inside made his stomach turn. A collective gasp echoed through the room as the contents were revealed.

A pristine, white envelope lay atop a mound of shredded, bloody fabric. Roger recognized the shirt immediately; it was the same shirt Franklin Weaver had been wearing the day his body was discovered. The symbolism was clear: the killer was sending a message, one that tied directly to the gruesome murders. A chill ran down Roger's spine as he realized the killer was not only playing a game—he was escalating, becoming bolder with each move.

Roger picked up the envelope, his hands steady despite the storm of emotions inside him. He slid a knife through the flap and pulled out a single sheet of paper. The note was typed, it read: *You think you can catch me? Think again. I'm everywhere, and I'm always watching.*

The room was deathly silent as Roger read the note aloud. Liz arrived just as he finished, her face pale, her hair still disheveled from the hurried drive over. She had left Jason behind, too shaken by the events of the morning to think about anything but the case.

Liz exchanged a glance with Roger, the worry and exhaustion clear in her eyes. "This bastard is taunting us," she said, her voice low but steady. "He wants us to feel helpless, to feel like we're always a step behind."

Roger set the note down, anger flaring in his chest. "He's playing a game," he said, his voice a growl.

The sheriff's office conference room felt colder than usual, even with the heater running. Roger and Liz sat at the head of the table, their team assembled around them. Deputies murmured in hushed tones, the tension thick and suffocating. The usually bustling office was now filled with the weight of fear, and Roger could feel it bearing down on all of them.

"We need to start connecting the dots," Roger began. "We know this killer is targeting people tied to the Marathon Oil explosion and its cover-up. But now, he's escalating. He's making this personal. He's showing us that he can get to us whenever he wants."

Liz leaned forward, rubbing her temples. "The photographs he left at my house," she said, her voice cracking slightly, "they weren't just pictures of me at the crime scenes. There was… a Polaroid of me and Jason. In a private moment." Her eyes flickered with a mix of shame and fury, and she clenched her jaw, trying to maintain her composure.

The room fell silent, the weight of her words pressing down on everyone present. The killer's invasion of their lives was no longer abstract; it was painfully real. The deputies exchanged uneasy glances, the reality of the situation settling heavily on their shoulders.

Roger's jaw tightened. "He's watching all of us," he said. "We need to operate under the assumption that we're being monitored at every turn. This bastard wants us to be scared, to make mistakes. We can't give him that."

Deputy Fletcher cleared his throat, his face pale. "Sheriff, what about your house? Did he leave anything else?"

Roger hesitated, his gaze darkening. He could feel the eyes of his team on him, waiting for his answer. "He left my badge," he admitted. "Took it off me while I was sleeping. If that doesn't show how bold he's gotten, I don't know what does."

The deputies looked at one another, fear written across their faces. The sense of security they had clung to was shattered. Not only was the killer targeting strangers, but he was now coming for them, for their families, their homes.

Liz took a deep breath, her hands shaking despite her best efforts to appear composed. "We need to regroup," she said. "Go over every piece of evidence again, re-interview witnesses, look for anything we missed. He's not invincible. There's something we're overlooking, and we need to find it."

Roger nodded, feeling the weight of leadership pressing heavily on his shoulders. His team was looking to him for guidance, and he couldn't afford to show weakness. "Fletcher," he said, turning to the young deputy, "I want extra patrols around the houses of everyone involved in this case, especially the families of our team. If the killer is targeting us, we need to make sure our loved ones are safe."

Fletcher swallowed hard but nodded. "Yes, Sheriff."

After the meeting, Roger found Liz standing by the window. Her arms were wrapped around herself, and she looked smaller and more vulnerable than he had ever seen her. The usually unshakeable deputy had always been the epitome of strength, but this case was unraveling her bit by bit. Her reflection in the glass seemed almost ghostly, her eyes hollow from lack of sleep.

"Liz," he said softly, not wanting to startle her.

She turned, and he could see the glint of unshed tears in her eyes. "I can't shake the feeling that he's always watching," she admitted, her voice barely above a whisper. "Even now, standing here, I feel exposed." She shivered slightly, as if the chill of the killer's presence had seeped into her bones.

Roger's heart ached at the sight of her so shaken. He wanted to comfort her, but he knew there were no easy words that could make this better. "We're going to catch him," Roger said, his voice firm, though the doubt lingered in the back of his mind. "He wants us to feel powerless, but we're not going to let him win."

Liz wiped at her eyes. "It's hard to keep fighting when it feels like he's always a step ahead," she said. "But I won't give up. I can't."

Roger placed a comforting hand on her shoulder. "You're one of the strongest people I know," he said, his voice filled with genuine admiration. "You've faced things that would break most people. We're going to stop him. Together."

Liz opened her mouth to reply, but her phone buzzed in her pocket. She pulled it out and saw a text from Jason: Hey, just wanted to check in. Are you okay? I can't stop thinking about this morning.

Liz felt a lump form in her throat. Jason had seen her at her most vulnerable, and now he was worried about her, too. She typed out a quick reply: I'm hanging in there. Thank you for being there for me. I'll call you later.

She slipped her phone back into her pocket, her eyes meeting Roger's. "Jason's worried," she admitted. "I hate that this is affecting him, too. He didn't sign up for any of this."

Roger nodded, understanding all too well the toll the job could take on loved ones. "This job takes pieces of us," he said quietly. "And it takes pieces of the people who care about us. But we will keep going because it's the only way to make sure they stay safe." Liz sighed and smiled half-heartedly, to assure him so he doesn't worry about her.

Later that day, as Roger sat in his office, trying to piece together the latest clues, his phone rang. He glanced at the screen and saw Emily's name. His heart leapt, a mixture of relief and guilt flooding through him. He hadn't spoken to his daughter in weeks, and the distance between them was something that ate at him constantly.

"Emily," he answered, trying to keep his voice steady.

"Dad," she said, her voice soft but strained. "I saw the news. The murders… they're talking about them all over the state. Are you okay?"

Roger's chest tightened. Hearing the worry in his daughter's voice made him feel both comforted and ashamed. "I'm okay," he lied. "We're working hard to catch this guy. You don't need to worry."

Emily sighed. "That's not true, and you know it. I know how dangerous this is. I just… I wish you'd be careful."

"I am careful," Roger insisted, though he knew it wasn't enough. His job had always put him in harm's way, and it had cost him too much. "I promise I'll come out of this in one piece."

There was a long pause on the other end. "I miss you," Emily finally said.

Roger's throat tightened. "I miss you too, Em," he said. "When this is all over, I'll come to Dallas and visit. We'll spend some real time together."

Emily's voice wavered. "You'd better keep that promise," she said. "Because I'm holding you to it."

Roger closed his eyes, the weight of his failures as a father pressing down on him. "I will," he whispered. "I love you, kid."

"I love you too," she replied before hanging up.

Roger put the phone down, his heart heavy. The call had been a lifeline, but it also served as a painful reminder of what he stood to lose if he didn't catch the killer soon.

As the day wore on, the tension in the sheriff's office only grew. Roger and Liz pored over the case files, looking for any connection they had missed. Every piece of evidence was scrutinized, every lead reconsidered. The walls of Roger's office were covered in photos, maps, and notes, each one a piece of the puzzle that seemed impossible to solve. The photographs, the bloody shirt, and the ominous notes were all reminders that time was running out. The fear in the room was palpable, the kind of fear that made people question every decision, every move.

Roger knew they were in a race against a monster who thrived on fear, and the stakes couldn't have been higher. Deep down, he couldn't shake the feeling that they were being watched, that the killer was closer than any of them realized, waiting for the perfect moment to strike again. And when that moment came, Roger knew he had to be ready, because the cost of failure was too great to bear.

CHAPTER FIFTEEN

The heavy snowfall had slowed to a light dusting, but the sky remained a steely gray, as if Midland itself were holding its breath. The sheriff's office was a hive of activity. Phones rang off the hook, deputies scrambled to follow up on leads, and the tension in the air felt almost suffocating. The stale smell of coffee mixed with the anxiety that permeated the building. Roger stared at the evidence board in his office. Strings of red yarn crisscrossed from one photograph to another. Despite hours of analysis and speculation, the connections between the victims still felt tenuous, like trying to hold onto smoke. The photos of victims, locations, and potential suspects stared back at him. Liz entered the office. She held a steaming cup of black coffee, which she set down on Roger's desk. "You look like hell, Sheriff," she said, though there was no humor in her voice. She glanced at the evidence board. Roger glanced at her. His eyes were rimmed with red, and the lines on his face seemed deeper than usual. "I feel worse," he admitted, rubbing a hand over his weathered face. The stubble on his chin scratched against his palm "Any luck with the new witness interviews?"

Liz shook her head. "Nothing substantial. Everyone we've talked to either claims to know nothing or is too scared to speak up." She sighed, crossing her arms and leaning against the edge of his desk. "I don't blame them. The killer has everyone terrified. People don't want to stick their necks out when they know they could be next."

Roger let out a slow breath. He knew the feeling all too well. The killer's presence felt like a constant shadow. "We're missing something," he said, his voice low, almost as if he were speaking to himself. "Something right in front of us. We're just not seeing it."

Liz's phone buzzed, and she glanced at the screen. It was another message from Jason: Still thinking about you. Be safe. The words were simple, but they carried a weight that made her chest tighten.

Liz felt a pang of guilt for the worry she was causing him. She quickly texted back: I will. Promise. She slipped the phone back into her pocket, her thoughts briefly drifting to Jason—to the look on his face that morning when she had left, the concern etched in his eyes. He hadn't signed up for this kind of danger, and she hated that he was being pulled into it.

Roger noticed the look on her face. "Jason?" he asked, his voice gentle, softer than she had heard it in a while.

Liz nodded, slipping her phone back into her pocket. "He's worried. I can't blame him." She forced a smile, but it didn't quite reach her eyes.

Roger gave her a sympathetic look. He turned his attention back to the evidence board. The photos of the victims stared back at him, their eyes almost telling a story of a final moment of terror. "Let's go over what we know about the Marathon Oil explosion again," he said, his voice taking on a new urgency. "We need to understand exactly what happened back then. Who was responsible, and who covered it up?"

Liz grabbed a file from the overflowing stack on Roger's desk. She opened it, flipping through the documents, her brow furrowed. "The official story," she said, her voice laced with skepticism, "was that a gas leak caused a catastrophic explosion. But there have always been rumors that it was more than that—something to do with cost-cutting measures and unsafe working conditions." She pulled out a page with a list of names. "There were several complaints filed by workers before the explosion. Safety violations, ignored maintenance requests. It was all swept under the rug."

Roger frowned, scanning the list. "And who was in charge at the time?"

Liz pulled out an old photograph of the Marathon Oil Company board of directors. The black-and-white image showed a group of stern-faced men in suits, standing in front of a company banner. Their expressions were cold, detached. "Several of these men have passed away," Liz continued, "but a few are still alive, living quiet lives in and around Midland." She tapped on one of the faces. "James Barrett. He's one of the survivors. He's kept a low profile, but he's still here."

Roger studied the photograph, his eyes narrowing as he considered the implications. "If the killer is targeting people connected to the explosion," he said, "then we need to talk to these board members. Find out if they know something— or if they're next on the killer's list."

Before they could continue, a knock sounded at the door. Officer Ramirez stepped in, her usually calm demeanor replaced by unease. Her eyes darted between Roger and Liz, her voice tinged with urgency. "Sheriff, we have a problem," she said. "We just received a call from the Midland Community Center. There's been another body found."

Roger felt his stomach drop. "Damn it," he muttered, grabbing his hat and coat. His heart pounded as the fear set in. "Liz, let's go."

The ride to the community center was tense, the silence between them thick with dread. The windshield wipers swept away the light dusting of snow, the world outside a blur of white and gray. As they pulled up, the sight of police tape and flashing lights greeted them, cutting through the still morning air. A small crowd had gathered despite the cold.

Roger and Liz made their way past the onlookers and approached the crime scene. The victim lay sprawled near the entrance to the community center, the body arranged in a statuesque pose. The snow around the corpse was stained crimson. The blood seeped into the white powder and spread like a macabre halo. The body had been deliberately positioned, with the limbs splayed out unnaturally, the head twisted at an odd angle, and the face petrified in a final expression of sheer terror. The killer had carved deep symbols into the flesh, each cut cruelly, spelling out a message that only made sense to the monster who had done this.

The symbols had precise lines and angles that formed an intricate pattern across the victim's chest and abdomen. The cuts were deliberate, as though the killer had taken his time to ensure every stroke was perfect. The victim's hands had been posed, palms up, with fingers bent in what seemed like an unnatural, almost pleading gesture. There were traces of dirt under the fingernails, and the fingertips were bruised, suggesting the victim had fought back, even if only briefly, before being overpowered.

Liz swallowed hard. She forced herself to focus, to look at the scene with a detached eye. "Same pattern," she said, her voice steady despite the horror. "It's him."

Roger knelt beside the body, taking in every detail. The victim's face was pale, the eyes wide open, glassy, reflecting the gray sky above. The cold had stiffened the limbs, and the smell of blood hung heavy in the air. Roger reached into his coat pocket and pulled out the old photograph of the Marathon Oil Company board members.

"It's him," Roger said, his voice hollow. "One of the board members. James Barrett."

Liz's eyes widened. She looked at the photograph, then back at the body, her mind racing. "The killer is working his way through the people responsible for what happened at Marathon Oil," she said. "He's not just targeting random victims. He's following a plan."

Roger felt a chill crawl up his spine. The methodical nature of the murders, the precision with which the killer was working—it all pointed to someone who had been planning this for a long time. This wasn't just about revenge. It was about making a statement, about exposing the truth in the most brutal way possible.

Roger looked closer at the symbols carved into Barrett's flesh. They were different from the ones they had seen in previous killings. These were more intricate, with additional lines and overlapping shapes. The precision of the symbols, combined with the almost ceremonial way the body had been displayed, suggested a killer who was intelligent and utterly ruthless.

"Get the coroner here," Roger ordered. "And start canvassing the area. Someone must have seen or heard something. We're not going to let this bastard slip away again."

As they worked the scene, Roger's phone buzzed. He pulled it out and saw an incoming call from an unknown number. His instincts prickled with unease, but he answered, his voice sharp. "Sheriff Hartley."

There was a pause, and then a low, distorted voice crackled through the line. "You think you're so close, don't you?" the voice taunted. "You think you can catch me, but you're still playing my game."

Roger's grip on the phone tightened. "Who are you?" he demanded, his voice rough with anger. "Why are you doing this?"

A cold, mocking laugh echoed through the speaker. "You already know why," the voice said. "You just haven't put the pieces together yet. But don't worry—I'll help you understand when the time comes."

Roger's free hand curled into a fist. "You're not as untouchable as you think," he shot back. "We're coming for you."

The voice paused, and then it spoke, lower and more menacing than before. "I've watched you, Sheriff. Watched you sleep, watched you drown your sorrows in whiskey. I could've ended you anytime I wanted. But where's the fun in that? You're nothing but a puppet in my little show."

Roger's blood ran cold, the reality of the threat sinking in. The killer had been closer than he'd imagined.

"Leave my people alone," Roger said, his voice shaking with barely controlled rage. "If you want someone, come after me."

The voice laughed again, colder this time. "Oh, Sheriff," it whispered. "You should know by now—it's not that simple. I'll see you soon."

The line went dead, and Roger stood there, the phone pressed against his ear, his heart pounding. He felt Liz's eyes on him, her expression tight with worry.

"What is it?" she asked, her voice barely above a whisper.

Roger lowered the phone, his face pale but his jaw set in determination. "The killer," he said, his voice grim. "He just called me. He's been watching us. Watching me. He thinks he's in control."

Liz's hands curled into fists at her sides. "Then we need to take that control away," she said, her voice hard. "We need to stop him before he hurts anyone else."

Roger nodded, but the weight of the killer's words hung heavy in the air. The threat was a declaration of war, and the clock was ticking.

Back at the sheriff's office, Roger and Liz gathered their team for another emergency briefing. The latest murder had shaken them all, but Roger refused to let fear rule the investigation.

"We need to focus," he said, his voice strong despite the exhaustion that gnawed at him. "We're dealing with someone who has a deep, personal connection to the Marathon Oil explosion. We need to track down everyone who was involved, and we need to do it fast."

Liz spoke up, her voice steady but urgent. "I'll start with the surviving board members," she said. "Maybe one of them knows something—or remembers someone who held a grudge."

Deputy Fletcher nodded. "I'll work with Ramirez to cross-reference any unsolved cases from around that time," he said. "See if there's a pattern we missed."

Roger felt a flicker of hope. They were running out of leads, but they weren't out of the fight. Liz gave him a determined look. "Let's make sure we finish this."

As night fell over Midland, a sense of unease settled over the town. The killer was out there, somewhere in the shadows, waiting for his next move. Roger and Liz worked late into the night, driven by the knowledge that time was slipping through their fingers.

But even as they combed through the evidence, a sense of dread loomed over them. The killer had made it clear: he was always watching, always one step ahead.

And somewhere, in the dark corners of Midland, he was preparing to strike again.

CHAPTER SIXTEEN

The early morning light had barely begun to seep into the sky. The world appeared silent, the snow muffled every sound, but inside the sheriff's office, there was no sense of calm. The tension was palpable. The fluorescent lights flickered, and every officer felt on edge, feeling the weight of the investigation.

Roger stood at the head of the conference room table, his shoulders hunched and his eyes shadowed with stress and lack of sleep. He knew his team was running on fumes. They'd been chasing the killer for days, and with each new body, the stakes only grew higher. The latest victim, James Barrett, had made it clear: the killer was targeting the people involved in the Marathon Oil explosion, and they were closing in on the final players in this deadly game.

Roger cleared his throat, drawing the team's attention. "We've got new priorities," he announced, his voice rough but steady. The weight of leadership pressed on him, but he knew he had to keep his team focused. "Our focus is on the remaining members of the Marathon Oil board who are still alive. We need to protect them, question them, and find out if any of them have received threats or noticed anything suspicious."

Deputy Fletcher spoke up, his face drawn and serious, lines of worry etched across his forehead. "What if the killer's already gotten to them?" he asked. "We're always one step behind."

Roger shook his head. "We can't think like that," he said, his voice firm. "If we start assuming we're already too late, then we will be too late. We need to move fast and stay vigilant. We owe it to the victims to not give up."

Liz leaned forward, pulling a list of names from her file. "I've identified three surviving board members," she said, spreading the pages on the table. "Henry Lawson, Robert Withers, and Gerald Simmons. They're all retired, living quiet lives here in Midland. We need to reach them before the killer does." Her voice was steady, but Roger could see the tremor in her hands as she laid the papers down.

Roger nodded. "Fletcher, you and Ramirez take Gerald Simmons. He lives near the Old Course at Ranchland Hills Golf Club on Fairgrounds Road. Liz, you and I will take Henry Lawson. He lives over in the Warwick neighborhood off of N. Garfield Street. I'll have another team head to Robert Withers, who's out by Green Tree Country Club off of W. County Road 60 and Holiday Hill Road. Let's keep these men under constant watch until we know more."

Fletcher rose from his chair, his face set in determination. "Understood, Sheriff," he said, motioning for Ramirez to follow him. The two deputies left the room, their expressions grim.

Once they were gone, Roger turned to Liz. "Are you ready for this?" he asked. He knew how much pressure she was under.

Liz gave him a tight smile. "Ready as I'll ever be," she replied.

Roger and Liz drove down Wadley Ave, passing familiar Midland landmarks—the strip malls, the gas stations, the quiet suburban houses. The road was nearly empty, with most people still inside, huddling away from the bitter cold. As they turned onto N. Garfield Street, the houses grew larger and more spaced out, each one tucked behind carefully manicured lawns. The snow-covered branches of mesquite trees cast long shadows across the driveways, and the occasional car passed by.

Roger kept his eyes on the road, but his mind was racing. The killer's taunts echoed in his head: I've watched you, Sheriff. He couldn't stop replaying the sinister call, the way the voice had lingered on his weaknesses and fears.

"Do you think we're making any progress?" Liz asked suddenly, breaking the silence.

Roger gripped the steering wheel tighter as he turned onto Mockingbird Lane. "We're getting closer," he said, though he wasn't sure if he believed it. "We know more now than we did a week ago. We know who the targets are." He tried to sound confident, but the doubt lingered beneath his words.

Liz sighed, her breath fogging up the window. "But is it enough?" she asked, her voice tinged with worry. "This guy always seems to be ahead of us. Every time we think we've got a lead, he's already moved on."

Roger's jaw clenched. "We don't have a choice but to try," he said. "We owe it to the victims—and to ourselves."

Henry Lawson's house was a modest brick home on the outskirts of the Warwick neighborhood, surrounded by barren mesquite trees and a chain-link fence. The lawn was overgrown, the driveway cracked, and the windows were dark, giving the house an abandoned feel. Roger parked the car at the curb, and approached the front door.

Roger knocked firmly, his other hand resting on his holstered gun. The door creaked open a few moments later, revealing an older man with thinning gray hair and a lined face. Henry Lawson's eyes widened when he saw their badges, and he pulled his robe tighter around himself.

"Sheriff," Henry greeted, his voice wary. "Is something wrong?"

Roger glanced around, scanning the quiet street for anything suspicious. The sense of unease was growing with every second, the silence of the neighborhood almost too complete. "Mr. Lawson, may we come in?" he asked. "We need to talk to you about something important."

Henry stepped aside, his expression troubled. "Of course," he said, ushering them into the living room. The room smelled of old books and wood polish, and a fire crackled in the fireplace, casting flickering shadows on the walls. The walls were lined with shelves filled with dusty books, and a few faded family photographs sat on the mantel, their colors washed out by time.

Liz took a seat on the worn couch, while Roger remained standing, his eyes never straying far from the windows. He could feel the weight of the situation pressing down on him, the urgency of the moment. "Mr. Lawson," Liz began, her voice gentle but firm, "do you know about the recent murders that have taken place in Midland?"

Henry's face paled, his hands gripping the arms of his chair. "I've heard," he said, sinking into an armchair. "It's horrible, what's happening. But what does it have to do with me?"

Roger exchanged a glance with Liz. "The victims," he explained, "are people connected to the Marathon Oil explosion from years ago. We believe the killer is targeting individuals who were involved in the company or the aftermath of the incident."

Henry's hands trembled slightly, his eyes widening in shock. "You think I'm a target?" he asked, his voice barely above a whisper.

Liz nodded. "We don't want to take any chances," she said. "Have you noticed anything unusual? Any threats, strange calls, or someone following you?"

Henry rubbed his forehead, looking older and more fragile than ever. The lines on his face seemed to deepen as he spoke. "I haven't noticed anything," he admitted. "But that explosion… it was a nightmare. So many lives lost, and so many secrets buried."

Roger's ears perked up, his eyes narrowing. "What kind of secrets?" he pressed.

Henry's eyes darted to the window, as if he were afraid of being overheard. He leaned in closer, his voice dropping to a whisper. "The kind that ruined lives," he said. "Marathon Oil was cutting corners left and right. The equipment was old, faulty, and the safety measures practically nonexistent. We warned them—God, we warned them—but the higher-ups didn't care. They only cared about the bottom line. Profits over people."

Liz's eyes narrowed, her focus sharpening. "And the explosion?" she asked. "What really caused it?"

Henry swallowed, his throat working visibly. "A leak," he said, his voice cracking. "A gas leak we knew about. We begged them to shut down the operation and fix it, but instead, they ordered us to keep quiet. They said the company couldn't afford another setback. So we kept running it, pretending everything was fine, until it all went to hell."

Roger's expression darkened, anger simmering beneath his calm exterior. "And after the explosion?"

Henry nodded, his gaze distant, as if he were reliving the nightmare. "They covered it up. Paid off families, silenced the survivors, and made us sign non-disclosure agreements. They threatened us—said if we ever spoke out, we'd lose everything. Some of us wanted to go public, but... we were scared. Martin Caldwell, the regional director, was ruthless. He would do anything to protect the company's reputation."

Before Roger could press for more details, the sound of glass shattering exploded through the room. Roger's instincts kicked in, and he shoved Liz to the floor as a bullet tore through the window.

Chaos erupted. Roger drew his gun, heart pounding, and scrambled to pull Henry behind the couch for cover. Liz had her weapon out, her eyes scanned the broken window for any sign of the shooter.

"Stay down!" Roger barked. "Liz, can you see anything?"

Liz crawled toward the window, peeking over the edge. The front yard was empty, but fresh footprints in the snow told a different story. "Someone was out there," she hissed. "They're gone now."

Henry was shaking, clutching his chest as he tried to catch his breath. "I-I don't understand," he stammered. "Why now? Why would they try to kill me?"

Roger's mind raced. The killer had to know they were closing in, that Henry might have the answers they needed. "They're trying to silence you," Roger said, his voice grim. "But we won't let that happen."

Liz rose cautiously, gun still drawn, and moved toward the door. "We need backup," she said. "And we need to get Henry somewhere safe."

Roger nodded, pulling out his phone to call for reinforcements. The killer was more ruthless than they'd imagined, and the ambush had only solidified how desperate they were to keep the past buried.

Once backup arrived and the scene was secured, Roger and Liz stood outside, watching as officers combed the area for evidence. The sun had risen higher, but the morning light felt harsh.

Roger's phone buzzed, and he felt a surge of dread when he saw another unknown number. He answered, putting it on speaker so Liz could hear. "Hartley," he said, his voice rough.

This time, the distorted voice was not taunting—it was seething with rage. "You just couldn't leave it alone, could you?" the killer spat, the anger crackling through the line like static. "You think you're a hero, Sheriff? You think you can stop me from getting justice?"

Roger clenched his jaw, his voice calm but cold. "You call this justice? You're murdering people."

The killer let out a harsh, ugly laugh. "You have no idea what justice is," he snarled. "These people buried the truth, let innocent men and women burn while they lined their pockets. They deserve to suffer."

Liz's eyes met Roger's. Roger took a deep breath. "We're not going to let you keep doing this," he said. "We'll find you."

The killer's voice dropped, turning darker, more menacing. "If you keep interfering, Sheriff," he warned, "I'll come after the people you care about. Your precious daughter, Emily. Or maybe your deputy's sweet little boyfriend, Jason. How would you like that? To see your loved ones bleed, just because you couldn't leave well enough alone?"

Liz's hands trembled. Roger's vision went red with fury. "You stay away from them," he growled. "If you touch them—"

"Oh, Sheriff," the killer interrupted, his voice dripping with mockery. "You're not in control here. I am. And by the way…" There was a pause, and Roger and Liz both felt their skin prickle with fear. "I'm watching you right now."

Roger's eyes darted to the surrounding area, searching for any sign of movement. Liz did the same, her heart pounding in her chest. But the street was empty, eerily quiet in the aftermath of the ambush.

The call ended, and the silence that followed was suffocating. Roger and Liz stood there, the realization sinking in: the killer was close. Closer than they'd ever imagined.

CHAPTER SEVENTEEN

The chill of the Midland morning seemed to seep into everything: the air, the ground, even the people. Roger had never felt the weight of a case like this before. The killer's threats were definitely not futile—the last call proved that.

He stood in his office. The call from the killer still echoed in his mind: *I'll come after the people you care about.* His daughter Emily was far away in Dallas, but his ex-wife Kathy and Liz's boyfriend, Jason, were too close for comfort. The killer's reach seemed limitless, and now the threat felt more suffocating than ever.

The room felt smaller with each passing second, the walls closing in as Roger's thoughts spiraled. His desk was littered with photographs and notes—remnants of a case that refused to give up its secrets. He could see Kathy's face in one of the photographs, a family picture taken years ago, back when things were simpler, before the job had cost him so much. The sight of her smile twisted something deep in his chest, a mix of regret and raw determination.

Liz entered the office. She'd had little sleep, but she pushed through the exhaustion with the same fierce will she always showed. Her hand hovered over her holstered weapon as if it were a lifeline. Her eyes met Roger's, and for a moment, neither of them spoke, the weight of the situation hanging between them.

"What's our next move?" she asked.

Roger took a deep breath. "We need to get to Robert Withers and Gerald Simmons," he said. "They could be next, and we have to be there before the killer strikes. And there's another name we need to track down: Martin Caldwell."

Liz's eyes widened slightly. "Caldwell?" she repeated. "The regional director who ordered the cover-up?"

Roger nodded grimly. "Henry Lawson confirmed he was the one who called the shots and kept everything buried. If anyone has answers—or if anyone could be a prime target—it's him."

Roger and Liz sped down Midland Drive, the sheriff's SUV cutting through the morning traffic. They approached the more affluent neighborhoods of Midland, the houses there reminded them of the wealth that had been built on the oil industry. Green Tree Country Club sat at the heart of one of these neighborhoods, sprawling and pristine even under a layer of snow.

Liz checked her phone as they neared the turn into the Country Club. "Fletcher and Ramirez are still with Gerald Simmons," she reported. "No signs of trouble yet, but they're staying on high alert."

Roger grunted in response, his mind already turning over a thousand possibilities. If the killer was watching them, it wouldn't be long before he made another move. Every second counted.

The houses along Midland Drive were impressive, their large front yards blanketed with snow. The crisp air carried a sharp edge, and the cold seemed to seep into their bones. They pulled into the long driveway leading up to Robert Withers' estate, a grand, two-story house with a snow-dusted lawn and a view of the golf course. Roger parked the SUV, and he and Liz exchanged a look before stepping out, their hands never straying far from their weapons.

"Stay sharp," Roger warned. "We don't know what we're walking into."

Liz nodded, her eyes scanning the property. The front door loomed ahead, solid and dark, and a single light was on in the front window. The house was quiet, but there was an unnatural stillness to the air as if something unseen was lurking just out of sight.

Roger knocked firmly, and the door opened after a few tense moments. Robert Withers stood there, his face drawn and wary. He was a man in his late seventies, with thinning white hair and a body that had once been powerful but was now frail. He wore a heavy sweater, and deep lines of worry were etched into his face. Behind him, his wife, Margaret, appeared. She was a petite woman with neatly styled gray hair and tired eyes that spoke of sleepless nights.

"Sheriff Hartley," Withers said, his voice rough. "I wasn't expecting company this morning."

Roger stepped forward, his gaze steady. "We need to talk, Mr. Withers. May we come in?"

Withers hesitated at first, then stepped back, allowing them into a spacious, well-decorated foyer. The house smelled of wood polish and old leather, and a fireplace crackled in the distance. Margaret led them into the living room, where the warmth of the fire was a stark contrast to the cold fear that had settled in Roger's gut.

Liz kept her hand close to her weapon as she followed Roger inside. "Mr. Withers," she began, "we're here because we believe you're in danger."

Withers exchanged a look with Margaret, who sat down beside him, her hands clasped tightly in her lap. "Danger?" he repeated, his voice skeptical. "What kind of danger?"

Roger's eyes hardened. "The murders," he said. "The victims are people connected to the Marathon Oil explosion and its cover-up. You were on the board at the time, and that makes you a target."

Withers' face paled, and he swallowed visibly. "I thought I was done with that chapter of my life," he muttered. Margaret reached out and gripped his hand, her eyes brimming with concern.

"What happened back then?" she asked, her voice trembling. "It's haunted him for years."

Withers let out a shaky breath, his shoulders slumping under the weight of his memories. "What happened back then… it was more than just an accident. We knew the rig was unsafe, but the higher-ups didn't care. They ordered us to keep things running, no matter the risk. We tried to speak up, but they shut us down."

Liz leaned forward, her expression intent. "Who gave those orders?" she pressed.

Withers' eyes filled with guilt and fear. "Martin Caldwell," he whispered. "He was ruthless. He threatened to ruin us and destroy our families if we didn't comply. When the explosion happened, he was the one who orchestrated the cover-up. We paid off grieving families, destroyed records, and silenced anyone who tried to speak out."

Margaret's hand tightened on his. "He's had nightmares for years," she said softly, her voice cracking. "The guilt has eaten him alive."

Withers' voice broke as he continued. "We buried the truth, Sheriff. We buried it deep, but it never went away. The memories, the faces of the people we failed… they haunt me. And now, it seems someone is making us pay for our sins."

Roger's fists clenched. He could feel the weight of Withers' confession, the decades of buried secrets and lives ruined for corporate greed. "Where is Caldwell now?" he asked.

Withers swallowed hard. "Last I heard, he was living out near the outskirts of town," he said. "A gated property on FM 1788, near the oil fields. He's a paranoid man—never trusted anyone. But if he's on the killer's list, he won't be safe."

Before Roger could respond, Liz's phone buzzed with a call from Deputy Fletcher. She answered, her face going tense as she listened. "Got it," she said, hanging up. "Fletcher said they spotted a suspicious vehicle circling Gerald Simmons' neighborhood. They're trying to track it now."

Roger's gut twisted with anxiety. The killer was circling, looking for any opening to strike. They had to be faster, smarter, more vigilant.

Just then, Roger's phone buzzed. He saw another unknown number flashing on the screen and felt his pulse spike. He exchanged a grim look with Liz, then put the call on speaker. "Hartley," he said, his voice rough.

The distorted voice that came through was colder and more venomous than before. "You're playing a dangerous game, Sheriff," the killer said, seething with anger. "I warned you to stay out of this."

Roger's jaw tightened. "You can't scare us off," he shot back. "We're not backing down."

The killer let out a snarl, the sound twisting into something almost inhuman. "You think you're brave? You think you can save them all? You're wrong. I can strike whenever I want, wherever I want. You're just a puppet on my strings."

Liz stayed silent, her hand steady on her gun. Roger's voice was ice. "If you're so powerful, why don't you face us?" he challenged. "Stop hiding."

The killer laughed, a sound that dripped with malice. "Oh, I will," he promised. "But first, I'll punish you. You'll know what it feels like to lose. To see your loved ones suffer because of your stubbornness."

Roger's chest tightened. "Leave them out of this," he growled. "If you touch them—"

"I'll do more than just touch them," the killer interrupted, his voice dropping to a menacing whisper. "Your ex-wife, Kathy… you think she's safe in her little world, don't you? And Deputy Trujillo's boyfriend, Jason… so fragile, so easy to break. How long will it take before you realize you can't protect them?"

Liz's knuckles turned white, but she refused to let fear take over. Roger's vision went red with fury. Before he could respond, both their phones buzzed simultaneously.

Roger and Liz exchanged a look, dread pooling in their stomachs as they opened their messages. The photographs that greeted them sent icy shivers down their spines.

Roger's phone displayed a picture of Kathy standing on her front porch, bundled in a heavy coat and scarf, her breath visible in the cold morning air. The timestamp indicated it had been taken mere minutes ago. Another picture followed: Kathy was bent down, retrieving the morning paper, completely oblivious to the danger lurking in the shadows.

On Liz's phone was a photograph of Jason, standing outside his office, his hands stuffed into his pockets, looking distracted. The message beneath it read: So easy to reach, Deputy. How much will you sacrifice before you learn?

Roger's grip on his phone tightened, his knuckles turning white. The muscles in his jaw worked as he fought to contain the rage that threatened to consume him. "If you hurt them—" he began, his voice shaking.

The killer interrupted, his voice dark with satisfaction. "Consider this your last warning," he sneered. "Stay out of my way, or next time someone you love will bleed. You're on borrowed time, Sheriff. The game is only just beginning."

The line went dead. The weight of the threat hung heavy in the air, and the living room seemed to close in around them. Roger's heart pounded with fury and fear. He glanced at Liz, who looked equally shaken, her face pale and her hand trembling slightly as she lowered her phone.

Margaret Withers, who had been listening to the conversation in horror, clutched at her husband's arm. "What is happening?" she whispered, her voice breaking. "Why is this happening to us?"

Robert Withers looked stricken, guilt and terror etched into every line of his aging face. "It's my fault," he murmured, barely audible. "This is all because of what we did… because of the secrets we kept."

Roger turned to Withers, his voice hard. "We're going to do everything we can to protect you," he promised. "But right now, we need to move fast. The killer isn't bluffing, and we have to act before he makes good on his threats."

Liz swallowed hard, her resolve hardening despite the fear that clawed at her insides. "We need to get a protection detail on Kathy and Jason," she said. "We can't take any chances."

Roger nodded, already formulating a plan. His mind was racing, torn between his duty to protect the people of Midland and the desperate need to keep his loved ones safe.

Roger stepped outside, the icy wind biting at his skin as he called the station. He barked orders into the phone, instructing deputies to be dispatched immediately to both Kathy's and Jason's locations. Every second felt like an eternity, and the fear gnawed at him, relentless and unyielding.

Liz followed him out, her breath visible in the cold air. "I'll call Jason and tell him to stay put until help arrives," she said, her voice steady despite the strain in her eyes. She pulled out her phone, dialing Jason's number with shaking fingers.

Roger listened as Liz spoke to Jason, her voice taking on a softer, protective tone. "Jason, it's me. Listen carefully. You need to stay inside your office and lock the doors. Deputies are on their way to you, and I need you to promise me you won't go anywhere until they get there."

Jason's voice was faint but worried. "Liz, what's going on? Are you in danger?"

Liz's eyes filled with tears she refused to shed. "I'm okay, just worried about you. Promise me, okay? Stay safe. I love you." Liz hung up, she took a shaky breath, her resolve hardening once more.

Roger placed a hand on her shoulder. "It's okay," he said. "They'll be fine now."

Back inside the Withers' house, Margaret had made tea, her hands trembling as she poured the steaming liquid into delicate porcelain cups. It was futile to restore some sense of normalcy, but the fear in the room felt deeply etched. Robert Withers sat with his head in his hands, the weight of his past sins pressing down on him.

"I never thought it would come to this," he whispered, his voice cracking. "I thought… I thought time would bury what we did. That we could live out the rest of our days in peace. But I was wrong."

Roger sat across from him, his voice hard but compassionate. "You may have made mistakes," he said, "but right now, we need you to stay strong. The more you can tell us, the better chance we have of stopping this."

Withers looked up, his eyes filled with anguish. "Caldwell was the architect of it all," he said. "He knew how to cover his tracks, how to keep us all under his thumb. But there were others—men who turned a blind eye, who let it happen because it was convenient. We were all complicit, and now… now we're paying the price."

Roger exchanged a look with Liz.

She took a steadying breath. "We'll find Caldwell," she said, her voice resolute. "And we'll find the killer. But we need to be ready for whatever comes next."

Roger nodded, his jaw set. The clock was ticking, and the killer was always one step ahead. But they weren't about to back down. They had too much to lose, and the fight was far from over.

As they prepared to leave, the tension in the air was almost suffocating. Midland was a town on edge, the shadow of the killer looming over every street, every home.

CHAPTER EIGHTEEN

The drive down FM 1788 felt longer than usual. The vast West Texas landscape stretched endlessly around them. The open sky above was a dull, heavy gray, pressing down on the horizon, and neither of them could shake the sense of foreboding that had settled in their chests.

Roger glanced over at Liz, noting the way her jaw clenched, as if she were trying to bite back her frustration. The killer had made everything personal, and their failure to protect the people on the killer's list felt like a weight they could barely carry. The relentless snowfall outside the window only added to the feeling of isolation, like the world had been cut off from any hope of help.

When they finally reached the gates of Martin Caldwell's estate, the grandeur of his wealth was on full display. The wrought-iron gates were massive, adorned with intricate designs of interlocking oil rigs and the family crest, depicting the Caldwell dynasty's grip on the oil industry. Behind the gates, a long, snow-covered driveway wound through the groomed grounds to the mansion, a sprawling architectural marvel of stone, glass, and steel. The building loomed over the landscape like a fortress.

Roger pulled the SUV to a stop at the intercom. He pressed the button and waited, the wind howled around them and sent chills down their spines. A crisp, disinterested voice crackled over the speaker. "Yes?"

"This is Sheriff Roger Hartley and Deputy Liz Trujillo," Roger announced. "We need to speak with Martin Caldwell. It's urgent."

There was a long pause, and Roger exchanged a look with Liz, who raised an eyebrow, her hand hovering near her weapon. After a few seconds, the gates groaned open as if begrudgingly granting them access. Roger drove up the driveway.

A uniformed security guard awaited them at the top of the driveway, standing stiffly with his hands clasped in front of him. He was a tall, broad-shouldered man with a stoic expression, and he gestured for them to follow as he led the way into the mansion. The front doors were heavy oak, carved with scenes of oil derricks and the Caldwell family crest, and they swung open to reveal a foyer that reeked of old money and privilege.

The marble floors gleamed under the light of crystal chandeliers, and a sweeping staircase curved up to the second floor, its railing wrought in gold filigree. Priceless artwork adorned the walls—landscapes and portraits, each one a testament to the power and influence Caldwell wielded. A grand piano sat in one corner of the room, its polished surface reflected the firelight from the massive stone hearth. The entire place felt like a shrine to wealth and power, a witness to the fact that Martin Caldwell was a man who didn't just live in Midland but ruled over it.

Martin Caldwell was waiting for them in a sitting room just off the main hall. He lounged in a high-backed leather chair, dressed in a tailored charcoal suit despite the early hour. His silver hair was perfectly styled, and he held a crystal tumbler of whiskey in his hand. A fire crackled in the hearth behind him, casting shadows across his face, but there was nothing warm about his expression.

He barely looked up as Roger and Liz entered. He took a leisurely sip of his drink before setting the glass down on a mahogany side table. "You have five minutes," he drawled, his voice conveying superiority. "Make them count."

Roger's jaw tightened, and he fought to keep his irritation in check. He'd dealt with powerful men before, but Caldwell's arrogance felt suffocating. "Mr. Caldwell," Roger began, "we're here because your life is in danger. Several people connected to the Marathon Oil explosion have already been murdered. We have reason to believe you could be next."

Caldwell's mouth twisted into a smirk. "A target?" he repeated as if the idea were ridiculous.

Liz stepped forward, her patience wearing thin. Her eyes flashed with anger, and her voice was sharp. "This isn't a joke," she said firmly. "The killer is targeting former board members—people who were involved in the cover-up. This person has bypassed sophisticated security before. You need to take this seriously."

Caldwell's smile widened, but there was no humor in it. "Ah, yes, the cover-up," he said, leaning back in his chair and steepling his fingers. "I remember it well. We did what needed to be done. Sacrifices were made, but that's the cost of doing business. If you're expecting me to show remorse, I'm afraid you're wasting your time."

Roger took a step forward, his voice hardening. His eyes locked onto Caldwell's, refusing to back down. "People died," he said, his eyes narrowing. "Lives were destroyed. And now someone is out there making sure you and the others pay for what you did. This isn't about guilt—it's about survival. Yours."

Caldwell raised an eyebrow, clearly unimpressed. He leaned back in his chair, his gaze almost bored. "Survival?" he echoed, his voice dripping with mockery. "Let me tell you something, Sheriff. The world is built on hard decisions. People like me thrive because we're willing to do what others won't. The weak fall, and the strong rise. What happened with Marathon Oil was a necessary sacrifice. Those people were collateral damage, and that's just how the world works."

Liz's face flushed with anger, and she clenched her fists at her sides, her body practically vibrating with fury. "You're talking about human lives," she snapped. "Families, children, people who trusted your company to keep them safe. And now someone is coming after you for what you did, and you're too arrogant to see the danger."

Caldwell's expression darkened, and he leaned forward, his voice dropping to a menacing whisper. "Deputy, I built this empire on decisions you can't even fathom. I don't regret a single one of them. I've outlasted every enemy, every challenge. If someone thinks they can scare me, they're welcome to try."

Roger's phone buzzed in his pocket, and he pulled it out, feeling a wave of relief when he read the text: Kathy is safe. Deputies are stationed outside her home.

It was a small comfort, but it did little to ease the tension in the room. He slipped his phone back into his pocket and met Caldwell's icy gaze.

"We're not here to scare you," Roger said, his voice steady but filled with barely controlled frustration. "We're here to warn you. If you know anything—anything at all—that could help us catch this killer, now is the time to speak up."

Caldwell's eyes narrowed, and he stood abruptly, the movement sharp and controlled. He seemed to tower over them with a dark, oppressive energy. "I have nothing to say to you," he said coldly. "You've wasted enough of my time. I won't be intimidated in my own home."

Liz stepped closer, her own anger simmering just beneath the surface. "You might think your money makes you untouchable," she said, her voice like ice. "But this killer doesn't care about your wealth or your power. They've already taken down people who thought they were safe. You need to take this seriously."

Caldwell's lip curled into a sneer. He took a step toward Liz, his voice low and dangerous. "Get out of my house," he ordered, his voice echoing through the cavernous room. "If this so-called killer wants to come after me, they can try. But I'm not afraid, and I certainly don't need protection from you."

Roger exchanged a look with Liz. He'd dealt with difficult people before, but Caldwell's utter disregard for human life, his complete lack of remorse, was almost too much to bear. The air between them was electric, a dangerous tension crackling just beneath the surface.

Without another word, Roger and Liz turned and walked out of the mansion. As they stepped outside, the cold wind hit them like a slap, and Roger let out a long, shaky breath. The mansion loomed behind them, its windows dark and unwelcoming, as if it had absorbed the darkness of the man who resided within.

They reached the SUV, and Roger yanked the door open, sliding in with a force that made the door creak in protest. Liz got in beside him.

"He's not going to take us seriously, is he?" she asked, her voice filled with frustration and a hint of disbelief. "Even with everything that's happened, he still thinks he's untouchable."

Roger shook his head, his jaw clenched. "Men like Caldwell think they're above consequences," he said, his voice low. "They think their money and power make them invincible. But he's wrong. The killer's not playing by his rules, and Caldwell is too arrogant to see it."

Liz nodded, her expression grim. "We can't force him to cooperate," she said, her fingers drumming against the dashboard. "But we need to keep an eye on him. He's a target, whether he wants to admit it or not."

Roger started the engine, the SUV rumbling to life as he pulled out of the driveway. The wrought-iron gates slowly creaked open once more, and he drove through, the mansion disappearing from view behind them.

CHAPTER NINETEEN

The drive away from Martin Caldwell's estate was tense. Roger's mind was a whirlpool of thoughts, each one more frustrating than the last. Caldwell's arrogant, dismissive attitude had struck a nerve, and the man's lack of remorse for the lives destroyed in the Marathon Oil explosion only made things worse. The way he'd sat there, casually sipping whiskey, talking about human lives as if they were nothing but collateral damage—Roger could still feel the rage simmering in his chest.

Liz sat beside him, silent but seething. Her hand rested on her thigh, her fingers tapping an anxious rhythm as she replayed the conversation in her head. The sheer audacity of Caldwell's indifference was infuriating, and it only made their job more difficult.

"You think he's going to change his mind?" Liz finally asked, breaking the silence.

"No," he admitted. "Men like Caldwell don't change. They think they're invincible until they're not. And by then, it's too late." He glanced over at her, his expression grim. "He's not going to take any precautions. He'll keep living his life like nothing's wrong, and we're going to be left cleaning up the mess."

Liz chewed her bottom lip, her anger simmering just beneath the surface. "I hate that he's so confident," she said. "Like he's untouchable. But I have a feeling he'll learn the hard way." She shook her head, the frustration evident in her eyes. "It's just a matter of whether we can stop it before it's too late."

Roger nodded. "Let's just hope we catch the killer before that happens," he said. But even as he spoke, he couldn't shake the feeling that they were running out of time. Every moment they spent chasing leads felt like another moment the killer was planning their next move, always staying one step ahead.

The SUV's radio crackled to life. "Sheriff Hartley, this is Dispatch. Over."

Roger picked up the radio. "This is Hartley. Go ahead."

"We've got an update on Gerald Simmons," Dispatch reported. "His security detail spotted an intruder on the property but lost them in the property behind the house. Simmons is unharmed, but he's shaken up."

Roger's pulse quickened, and he exchanged a glance with Liz. Her eyes widened, the worry clear on her face. "Understood," he replied. "We're on our way."

Liz straightened in her seat. "If the killer's getting bolder, we need to be ready for anything," she said. "They're escalating."

Roger nodded, his mind already working through the possibilities. "And that means Simmons might not be the only one in immediate danger," he said. "We need to be proactive." He made a sharp turn and headed toward Gerald Simmons' estate.

Gerald Simmons lived in another upscale part of town, his property sprawling but more understated compared to Caldwell's ostentatious mansion. The estate was nestled among a series of gently sloping hills, with a long driveway that curved through groves of leafless trees. The house itself was a stately, two-story colonial with dark shutters and a wraparound porch, the kind of home that whispered of old wealth and generational privilege.

As Roger and Liz pulled up, they saw two squad cars parked near the front entrance, their lights flashing a warning to anyone who might try to approach. Deputies Fletcher and Ramirez were stationed by the front steps, both of them looking tense and alert. Their breath formed small clouds in the cold air, and the weight of the situation was written all over their faces.

Fletcher stepped forward as Roger and Liz got out of the SUV. He was a burly man with a thick mustache, and he looked tired but focused. "Sheriff, Deputy," he greeted them, his voice gruff. "We've had our hands full. Simmons' housekeeper spotted someone lurking near the tree line, but they disappeared before we could get a good look."

Liz frowned, her eyes scanning the property. "Did you find any footprints?" she asked.

Ramirez, a wiry young deputy with sharp eyes, nodded. "We did, but they were erratic," he said. "Like the person was trying to throw us off. They led us around in circles and then just… stopped. It's like the intruder vanished into thin air."

Roger felt a chill run down his spine, but he forced himself to stay focused. "Where's Simmons now?" he asked.

Fletcher jerked his head toward the house. "Inside. He's pretty shaken up. Keeps saying he doesn't know why anyone would target him."

Roger and Liz exchanged a look. Simmons' involvement in the Marathon Oil explosion cover-up was undeniable, but the man had always kept a lower profile than someone like Caldwell. He was the type to play the part of a humble benefactor, donating to charities and sitting on boards, but Roger knew that didn't absolve him of his sins.

"Let's talk to him," Roger said, and he and Liz made their way up the porch steps and into the house.

Inside, the warmth of the house was a stark contrast to the cold dread that had settled in Roger's gut. The interior was tastefully decorated, with expensive Persian rugs, antique furniture, and art that probably cost more than a deputy's annual salary. Crystal light fixtures cast a soft, golden glow over the room, but it did little to dispel the shadows clinging to the corners.

Gerald Simmons was sitting in the living room, slumped in a high-backed armchair. A heavy wool blanket was draped over his shoulders, and his trembling hands clutched a glass of whiskey that sloshed dangerously close to the rim with every nervous movement. His eyes, framed by wire-rimmed glasses, were wide and bloodshot, and his pale skin had a sheen of cold sweat.

Roger took a seat across from him. Liz stood nearby, her stance protective and her eyes scanned the room for any signs of danger.

"Mr. Simmons," Roger said, keeping his voice calm, "we need to talk. We understand that you're frightened, but you have to be honest with us. The people being targeted are all connected to the Marathon Oil explosion and the subsequent cover-up. We believe you could be next."

Simmons looked up, his gaze darting between Roger and Liz. His mouth opened, but no sound came out at first. He swallowed hard, his throat working, and finally managed to speak. "I... I don't understand why this is happening," he stammered. "Why now? After all these years?"

Liz's expression hardened, and she stepped closer, her voice firm. "Because people don't forget," she said. "Especially not when they've lost everything. You might think time has erased the past, but for some, the pain never goes away."

Simmons' hands tightened around his glass, and a tear slipped down his cheek. "Do you think I haven't suffered?" he whispered. "Do you think the guilt hasn't been eating away at me every day since it happened?" His voice broke, and he looked down, his shoulders shaking. "I've tried to make up for it," he continued, his voice thick with emotion. "Donations, charity work, scholarships in the names of the victims. But nothing... nothing erases the memories."

Roger watched him closely, searching for any hint of deceit. But Simmons looked like a broken man, haunted by the ghosts of his past. "Guilt doesn't change what happened," Roger said gently. "But right now, we need you to focus. We need any information you have, no matter how small."

Simmons' gaze lifted, his eyes filled with desperation. "There was a man," he said, his voice barely above a whisper. "Walter Granger. He was one of the foremen on the rig. He was… vocal about the safety issues. He tried to warn us, but no one listened. When the explosion happened, he lost everything. His wife and his two daughters… they were trapped in the fire."

Liz's throat tightened, and she exchanged a grim look with Roger. "Granger?" she repeated. "What happened to him?"

Simmons' face crumpled. "He couldn't live with the grief," he said. "He… he took his own life a few years later. But I always wondered if someone in his family would come for us one day. His brother was furious, swore revenge. And his sister—she was never the same after the accident. I heard she moved away, but I don't know where."

Roger leaned forward, the pieces of the puzzle beginning to fall into place. "You think one of them might be responsible for the murders?" he pressed.

Simmons shook his head, his eyes brimming with tears. "I don't know," he choked out. "I've spent years looking over my shoulder, waiting for the past to catch up with me. But I don't have any way to contact them. I've tried to forget, but the guilt never goes away."

Liz's voice softened, but her resolve didn't waver. "We're going to need everything you have on Granger and his family," she said. "Documents, correspondence, anything that might help us track them down."

Simmons nodded shakily, his fingers clenching around the blanket. "I'll give you what I can," he said. "But please… promise me you'll stop this person. I can't live like this anymore. I can't."

Roger stood, his expression grim. "We're doing everything we can," he said. "But you need to stay vigilant. Trust your security detail, and don't take any risks. If anything feels off, call us immediately."

Simmons nodded, but the fear in his eyes was unmistakable. He looked like a man on the edge of a breakdown, and Roger couldn't help but wonder if they would be too late to save him.

As Roger and Liz stepped outside, the winter wind hit them hard, biting through their coats. The last light of day was fading, and the shadows stretched long and thin across the snow-covered ground.

Liz pulled her coat tighter around herself, her breath visible in the cold air. "Granger's family," she said thoughtfully. "It's a lead, but it's a long shot. We don't have much to go on."

Roger nodded, his jaw tight. "No," he agreed. "But it's a start. And right now, we need every piece of the puzzle we can get."

CHAPTER TWENTY

Night had fallen over Midland, Texas, shrouding the town in an eerie silence. The city seemed to hold its breath, waiting, anticipating, as if it too, sensed the imminent danger lurking in the shadows.

Roger and Liz drove away from Gerald Simmons' estate, their SUV cutting through the darkness. They had received word that the supposed intruder in the back area of the property was just a false alarm: neighborhood kids fooling around with flashlights, unaware of the tension gripping the entire town.

"There was no one else out there," Deputy Fletcher had reported, sounding equal parts annoyed and relieved. "Just some kids trying to spook each other. We've sent them home, but we're staying on high alert."

The update had done little to ease the tight coil of anxiety in Roger's chest. The fact that it was a false alarm didn't mean they were safe; it just meant the killer hadn't struck yet.

Liz sat beside Roger, her laptop balanced on her knees as she combed through records. The glow from the screen highlighted her fatigue, the lines of stress etched deeply into her features. Just as she was about to start a new search, her phone buzzed. She glanced at the screen and saw Jason's name. Her heart clenched.

She answered, her voice trying to be calm and steady. "Hey, Jason."

There was a pause, and then Jason's voice came through, raw and frayed with fear. "Liz," he breathed, and she could hear the strain in his words. "I... I couldn't sleep. I keep thinking about those pictures. The ones the killer took."

Liz felt a wave of nausea, the memory of those Polaroids flashing vividly in her mind: photos of her and Jason in the most intimate, vulnerable moments, taken from the shadows while they were completely unaware. The invasion had been more than physical; it had shattered their sense of safety.

"I'm so sorry," Liz whispered, her voice cracking. She closed her eyes, the guilt pressing down on her. "I never thought... I didn't know anyone was watching."

Jason's voice trembled. "I can't get it out of my head," he admitted. "The idea that someone was there, so close to us, and we never knew. I keep checking the windows and the doors. Every noise makes me jump. I've never felt so... helpless."

Tears prickled at the corners of Liz's eyes, and she wiped them away quickly. "You're not helpless," she said, her voice thick with emotion. "We're doing everything we can to catch this bastard. I won't let them hurt you, Jason. I promise."

Jason was silent for a moment, and then he spoke, "What about you?" he asked. "I'm worried about you too, Liz. You're in the middle of this, and I can't do anything to protect you. It's killing me."

Liz's heart ached, but she forced herself to stay strong. "I know," she said softly. "But I'm being careful. Roger and I are taking every precaution. You just have to trust me."

"I trust you," he said. "But promise me you'll keep looking over your shoulder. Don't let your guard down, even for a second."

"I promise," Liz said, her voice firm. "And I'll call you when I can, just to check in."

There was another pause, and then Jason's voice softened, though the fear still lingered. "I love you," he said, the words carrying an almost desperate need.

Liz felt her throat tighten. "I love you too," she replied. "Stay safe."

When the call ended, Liz sat in silence for a moment, her hands trembling. The fear Jason felt mirrored her own, and the weight of it was suffocating. But she couldn't let it break her. She had to keep going, for him and for everyone else who was counting on her.

Roger glanced at her, his eyes filled with understanding. "He's still shaken up?" he asked gently.

Liz nodded, slipping her phone back into her pocket. "Yeah," she said, her voice wavering. "The photos… they really got to him. To both of us."

Roger didn't say anything for a moment, but the compassion in his eyes was clear. The constant fear, the threats hanging over them—it was enough to break anyone. But Liz was strong. Stronger than anyone he knew. "It's hard," he finally said. "But we keep going. We have to."

Roger pulled into the parking lot of the sheriff's department. He parked the SUV but didn't move to get out. Instead, he pulled out his phone, hesitating for a moment before dialing Kathy's number. The line rang twice before she picked up.

"Roger?" Kathy's voice came through, a mixture of exhaustion and concern.

"Kathy," Roger said, his voice softer than usual. He exhaled, trying to find the right words. "I wanted to check in. Are you okay? Are the deputies still there?"

Kathy sighed, and he could almost see her running a hand through her hair. "Yes, they're here," she said. "But Roger, what's going on? You don't put a protection detail on me unless it's serious."

Roger rubbed his forehead, the guilt gnawing at him. "It is serious," he admitted. "We're dealing with a serial killer. Someone targeting people connected to the Marathon Oil explosion. I... I couldn't take any chances with you or Emily."

There was a pause, and then Kathy's voice softened. "Emily," she whispered, the worry evident. "She's safe, right?"

Roger's throat tightened, but he forced himself to stay composed. "I got word from Dallas," he said. "They've got a detail watching her. She's safe, Kathy. But I'm so sorry for dragging you into this. You don't deserve this."

Kathy was silent for a moment, and when she spoke again, her voice was tinged with an emotion he couldn't quite place. "Roger, you've always done everything you could to protect us," she said. "Even when we weren't on good terms. I know this job has cost you a lot, and I'm sorry for that. But just… please, take care of yourself. Emily needs her dad."

Roger's chest ached, a flood of memories of the life they'd once shared washing over him. The laughter, the warmth of family dinners, the way Emily used to look at him like he was her hero. It all felt so far away now, like a different lifetime. "I promise," he said, his voice thick with emotion. "I'll do everything I can to keep you both safe. Just stay inside, stay vigilant. If anything feels off, call me right away."

"I will. Be safe, Roger."

The line went dead, and Roger sat there for a moment, the phone still pressed to his ear. He took a deep breath, trying to shake off the heaviness.

Liz watched him, her expression soft with understanding. "You okay?" she asked quietly.

Roger nodded, though the tension never left his face. "Yeah," he said, his voice steady but strained. "Let's get inside. We have a lot to do."

The sheriff's department was quieter than usual, the late hour and the snowfall keeping most of the staff at home or out on patrol. Only a few deputies remained there.

Roger and Liz returned to the conference room they had claimed as their base of operations. Maps of Midland, stacks of case files, and hastily scrawled notes covered the table. The whiteboard was a mess of names, connections, and question marks, the case's complexity laid bare.

Liz set her laptop down and reopened her search, her fingers flying over the keys. "We need to dig deeper," she said, her voice resolute. "Miriam and Thomas Granger have to be somewhere. If we can find a trace, anything at all, it might give us the upper hand."

Before they could make any real progress, the door to the conference room burst open. Deputy Ramirez rushed in, his face pale, and his eyes wide with urgency. "Sheriff, Deputy," he said, his voice cracking. "We just got a 911 call from Martin Caldwell's residence."

Roger and Liz sprang to their feet, adrenaline coursing through their veins. "What happened?" Roger demanded.

Ramirez swallowed, his hands trembling. "The dispatcher said the call came in about two minutes ago. A man's voice, panicked, said something about an intruder. Then there was a scream, and the line went dead."

The words hit like a physical blow, and Roger's mind raced. He grabbed his radio, barking orders. "Get every available deputy out there, now," he said. "Approach with caution. This could be a trap."

Liz's hand moved to her gun, her eyes blazing with determination. "We need to go. It is at least a 20-minute drive to his residence from here, and who knows what damage the killer can do with that much extra time!" she said, her voice steady but full of urgency.

Roger nodded, his pulse pounding as he and Liz rushed into the freezing night. The storm was coming, and they were racing straight into it.

CHAPTER TWENTY ONE

The SUV tore through the icy streets of Midland, the wailing sirens and flashing lights slicing through the oppressive darkness. Roger's heart hammered in his chest, adrenaline surging through his veins. He couldn't stop thinking about the last time he had felt this kind of dread—the middle of a firefight overseas, the sudden silence before an explosion tore through his unit.

The city, which had seemed so festive only days ago with holiday lights twinkling on rooftops, now felt haunted, each decorated house a silent, ghostly reminder of a world that felt increasingly distant and dangerous. Roger could almost hear Kathy's voice, soft and worried, urging him to be careful. He pushed the thought away, forcing himself to focus.

Roger's voice crackled over the radio, slicing through the tension. "Dispatch, this is Sheriff Hartley," he barked. "What's the status at Caldwell's residence?"

The radio hissed with static before the dispatcher's anxious voice came through. "Sheriff, first responders are on site, but they're holding the perimeter. No signs of movement inside. All security personnel are unresponsive."

Roger's jaw clenched so hard that he thought his teeth might shatter. He glanced at Liz, who had gone even paler, but her eyes remained fierce. They both knew what "unresponsive" likely meant. It was the kind of word that blurred the line between hope and horror, and he hated it for that.

"Tell them we're one minute out," Roger said, his voice taut with dread. "No one enters until we arrive."

"Copy that, Sheriff."

The mansion came into view, its iron gates gaping wide like the jaws of some great beast. The lights from the squad cars reflected off the snow, turning the entire scene into a hellish tableau painted in flashing reds and blues. Roger slammed on the brakes, bringing the SUV to a skidding halt behind the line of police vehicles. He glanced at Liz, giving her a sharp nod. It was the only reassurance he could offer before they stepped into the unknown.

The cold air hit them like a slap as they stepped out, guns drawn. The snow in front of the mansion was painted in streaks of crimson, and the bodies of Martin Caldwell's security team lay scattered across the once-pristine driveway. The scene was a nightmare of calculated violence. Blood splattered the snow, staining the white ground with vivid red. One guard had fallen against the iron gate, his head tilted at an unnatural angle, eyes wide open and staring into the storm as if in disbelief. Another lay face-down near the central fountain, his weapon still clutched in his cold, dead hands.

A third guard lay closer to the mansion's front steps, bullet holes riddling his chest and neck. His blood had pooled and then begun to freeze, forming dark, glistening patches in the snow. His face was twisted in agony, his mouth slightly open as if he had died mid-scream. The snow beneath him was marred by a dark trail, as though he had tried to crawl towards the mansion before succumbing to his injuries. The scene was eerily silent, save for the distant wail of more sirens approaching.

Liz swallowed hard, the bile rising in her throat. "Jesus Christ," she whispered, her voice cracking. "This is… carnage."

Roger forced himself to keep moving. His gun felt heavy in his grip, but he kept it steady. His eyes searched for any sign of movement. He knew the killer could still be here, watching, waiting for the next victim to cross their path. "Stay focused," he muttered, more to himself than to Liz. "The killer could still be here."

The front doors of the mansion had been violently kicked in, the splintered wood scattered across the marble entryway. The house loomed before them, dark and foreboding, the once-opulent estate transformed into a silent house of horrors.

Roger and Liz stepped inside, and the metallic scent of blood hit them like a physical blow. The air was thick with the smell, mingled with the acrid tang of fear and the musty scent of expensive wood and upholstery. The grand foyer, with its marble floors and sweeping staircase, was in utter disarray. An antique vase lay shattered, its fragments dusted with bloody fingerprints. The elegant railing of the staircase was splattered with sticky patches of blood.

The trail led them deeper into the house, past overturned furniture and broken glass, until they reached Caldwell's study. The heavy oak doors were ajar, one of them hanging crookedly on broken hinges. Roger pushed the doors open, and what they found inside made both of them freeze in horror.

Martin Caldwell was bound to a high-backed leather chair in the middle of the room, but he was no longer the arrogant and powerful oil magnate they had encountered only days before. His body was slumped forward, wrists tied behind him, his blood-soaked clothes hanging in tatters. His chest was a mess of deep, jagged gashes, and the word PAYBACK had been carved into his flesh, the letters rough and uneven, as if the killer had relished every cut. The skin around the cuts was ragged, as though the blade had been twisted deliberately to maximize pain.

Wadded-up $100 bills had been shoved into Caldwell's mouth, his lips stretched around the crumpled currency, and his throat bulged, suggesting that more bills had been forced down his throat. Blood seeped from his mouth, soaking into the crumpled money, turning the once-valuable paper into a sickening symbol of greed and corruption. His teeth had been broken, likely during the forced feeding, the jagged remains visible between his bloodied lips.

But the most disturbing detail was Caldwell's eyes—or rather, the gaping, bloody holes where his eyes had once been. The killer had used shards of broken glass from one of Caldwell's prized Marathon Oil retirement awards to carve them out. The award itself lay shattered on the floor, the glass glittering with dark red stains. Blood had run down his face in thick rivulets, streaking his cheeks and pooling in his lap. The skin around his empty sockets was torn and ragged, the edges suggesting that the killer had taken their time, savoring the act.

Liz's knees went weak, and she had to brace herself against the doorframe. "Oh my God," she whispered, her voice barely audible. "They used his own award… to blind him."

Roger's hands shook with barely contained rage. His stomach churned, but he forced himself to stay focused. The scene was an act of utter sadism. He moved closer, his boots squelching in the blood that had pooled and begun to congeal on the once-polished floor. The floor beneath Caldwell's chair was a mess of blood and urine, the evidence of the prolonged and brutal torture he had endured.

The acrid scent of smelling salts hung in the air, and Roger's eyes fell to the shattered capsules littering the base of Caldwell's chair. The realization made his blood run cold. "The killer kept him conscious," he said, his voice thick with revulsion. "They woke him up over and over, just to keep torturing him."

Liz's hands trembled, but she took a step closer, scanning the room for anything that might give them a clue. Her gaze fell on the mahogany desk, where a piece of paper lay, stark white against the dark, blood-streaked wood. She picked it up carefully, using a pen to lift it, and read the message scrawled in bold, taunting letters:

"Killing him was a bonus—just for fun. The real game is far from over."

Liz's breath caught in her throat, and she handed the note to Roger. He read it, his eyes narrowing with fury. The killer wasn't just exacting revenge—they were enjoying every second of this game.

"This... isn't part of the pattern," Roger said, his voice low and urgent. "Caldwell's death doesn't match the staged bodies from the explosion photo."

Liz looked at him, confused. "What do you mean?"

Roger gestured to the scene before them. "The previous victims were staged to match the accident photo from Marathon Oil. They were deliberate recreations of the people who died in the explosion. But Caldwell? His death isn't posed like anyone from that photo. This isn't about revenge for him."

Liz's eyes widened as the realization sank in. "You're right," she whispered. "The killer didn't need to make Caldwell suffer for revenge. This... this was personal. They did it because they wanted to."

Roger's jaw clenched, and a cold, sick feeling settled in his gut. "This was a bonus for the killer. A thrill. Caldwell was tortured for the sheer pleasure of it."

The deputies and forensic team began arriving in a wave. Crime scene photographers snapped pictures, the harsh flash lighting up the horror in brief, glaring bursts. Every step had to be carefully taken, and every piece of evidence was meticulously documented.

Forensic specialist Marla Decker, the same coroner they had worked with before, entered the room. She wore a thick winter jacket over her scrubs, but her gloved hands were already busy, her practiced eyes assessing the scene.

"Marla," Roger greeted her, his voice strained. "This is… beyond anything we've seen. I swear it seems like it couldn't get worse."

Marla took a deep breath, the smell of blood filling her nostrils despite the mask she wore. "It's a slaughterhouse," she said, her voice steady but low. She knelt beside Caldwell's mutilated body, examining the deep gashes and the carved word on his chest. "Whoever did this knew exactly how to inflict maximum pain. These cuts... they're not just meant to kill. They're meant to make him suffer, slowly. The angles, the depth... they took their time, and they knew what they were doing."

Liz gestured to the scattered smelling salts. "The killer kept waking him up," she said. "They wanted him conscious through all of it."

Marla's eyes narrowed as she took in the shattered glass from the retirement award, now stained with Caldwell's blood. "And they used this to blind him," she murmured, her voice filled with both horror and professional detachment. "The level of premeditation here… it's calculated and deeply personal. They wanted him to feel every moment of it. These are the actions of someone who enjoys the suffering of others. This is beyond revenge. It's sadism."

She pointed to the broken capsules of smelling salts, her eyes meeting Roger's. "The fact that they used smelling salts... that tells us something important. They wanted him lucid. They wanted to look in his eyes as they did this, to see the fear and the pain. That kind of psychological element— this killer wanted to derive pleasure from every second."

Liz exchanged a glance with Roger, both of them shaken but refusing to let it show. She stepped back from the gruesome scene, needing a moment to collect herself.

Back in the foyer, deputies were busy securing the perimeter and marking evidence trails that led out into the snow-covered grounds. Roger and Liz stepped outside, the chill was almost a relief compared to the suffocating atmosphere inside.

Roger took a deep breath. "The escalation," he began, his voice thoughtful but urgent, "it doesn't make sense for this to be only about revenge. If it were, Caldwell's death would have matched the pattern."

Liz shivered, but whether it was from the cold or the fear, she couldn't tell. "You think there's something more going on?" she asked, her voice laced with both curiosity and dread.

Roger nodded slowly. "I think the explosion at Marathon Oil was the catalyst, but something else is driving this killer now. Something personal."

Liz frowned, her mind racing as she tried to piece together the puzzle. "Then we're missing something," she said, her frustration bubbling to the surface. "There has to be another connection. We just have to find it."

Roger's phone buzzed with an update from another deputy, but he ignored it for a moment, looking at Liz with grim determination. "We'll find it," he said. "Before this killer gets to anyone else."

CHAPTER TWENTY TWO

Roger and Liz had just finished debriefing the deputies outside Martin Caldwell's mansion. The brutal, haunting scene they had witnessed still clung to them, like the metallic scent of blood that seemed to linger in their nostrils.

Liz pulled her coat tighter around her shivering frame, but the cold wasn't what had her trembling. The call from Jason still echoed in her mind, a reminder that everyone she loved was now a potential target. She couldn't shake the feeling that every second counted, that they were running out of time.

"There's something we're missing, and we can't afford to overlook anything," Liz said.

Roger's breath came out in visible puffs of steam. He nodded, his jaw set with determination. "Agreed. Let's get back to the department. We need to reexamine every detail."

Inside the operations center, a large conference room converted into their command post, the atmosphere was thick with tension.

Liz dropped her bag onto a chair and rubbed her hands together for warmth. Her laptop, already open, buzzed to life, and she dove back into her research, scrolling through old property records, corporate filings, and archived news articles. "We need to look at this from every angle," she said, not looking up from the screen. "There's something we've overlooked, something we're missing."

Roger stood in front of the whiteboard, his arms crossed, eyes narrowing as he studied the names and connections they had pieced together. At the center was the explosion at Marathon Oil, a tragedy that had claimed countless lives and left many more scarred. Photos of the victims had been pinned there, each one a reminder of the devastation that had set this chain of events in motion. The red lines connected those victims to recent murder scenes, each one staged to mimic the explosion's aftermath.

But Martin Caldwell's photo was off to the side, a rogue piece that didn't quite fit. His death was brutal, horrific, and filled with a sadistic pleasure that the other murders didn't have. It was a puzzle that Roger couldn't solve, and the weight of it pressed down on him.

"This killer has a deep-seated grudge," Roger said, his voice thoughtful yet taut with frustration. "But the way they escalated with Caldwell... it doesn't fit the pattern of the others. What if there's another motive? Another layer we haven't uncovered yet?"

Liz's gaze flicked up from her laptop, her brow furrowed. "You mean, what if this isn't just about revenge for the explosion? What if the killer is motivated by something even deeper, something more personal?"

Roger nodded slowly. "Exactly. We need to dig into everyone connected to Marathon Oil, not just the victims. Survivors, executives, anyone who had something to gain or lose from the explosion. There has to be a link we're missing."

Liz's eyes fell on a thick stack of records sitting at the edge of the table, freshly delivered from the city's archives. The documents were old, some of them yellowed and fragile, but they promised answers—or at least more clues. "These are the records Ramirez found," she said, pulling the folder closer. "Let's see what Marathon Oil was so desperate to hide."

They sat side by side, hunched over the folder, each document revealing another piece of a corrupt and broken system. The thick, musty smell of old paper filled the air, and the yellowed edges of the documents crumbled slightly under their fingers. Each page was a testament to the lengths Marathon Oil had gone to protect itself in the wake of the explosion.

Liz flipped through a series of internal memos, her eyes narrowing as she read. "Look at this," she muttered, her voice a mix of anger and disbelief. She pushed the memo toward Roger. "They knew the safety protocols were inadequate. They ignored multiple warnings from their own engineers."

Roger took the paper and scanned it, his jaw tightening. The memo detailed a series of risk assessments performed by an internal safety officer six months before the explosion. The officer had raised alarms about the deteriorating conditions at the drilling site, highlighting the risk of a catastrophic failure if immediate action wasn't taken. But in the margins, someone had scribbled dismissive notes: Too expensive. Not a priority. Handle internally.

"Unbelievable," Roger said, his voice low and dangerous. "They were more worried about their bottom line than the lives of their workers."

Liz's hands shook with barely contained fury as she pulled out another report, this one from a private investigator hired by a group of grieving families after the explosion. "This investigator found evidence of Marathon Oil paying off city officials to sweep the investigation under the rug," she said. "And they weren't subtle about it, either. Look—there's even a list of payments."

Roger leaned in. Each payment was significant, enough to ensure silence from people who should have been seeking justice. The names on the list included building inspectors, city council members, and even a high-ranking member of the fire department who had ruled the explosion an accident.

"This whole thing stinks," Roger muttered, his frustration mounting. "It's corruption on a scale we couldn't even imagine."

Liz set the report down, her fingers now carefully peeling open a redacted government file. The words were blacked out in thick, ominous stripes, but she could still piece together some of what was being hidden. "They even had friends in high places," she said. "Government agencies willing to look the other way. How deep does this go?"

She flipped to the next page, her breath catching as she uncovered a faded photograph clipped to the document. The image was grainy, black and white, and showed a group of Marathon Oil executives standing in front of a drilling rig. The men were smiling, their hands in their pockets, their suits crisp and spotless despite the muddy ground beneath their feet. One of them was Martin Caldwell, his smile wide and self-assured, as if he owned the world.

Liz's voice dropped to a whisper. "They acted like nothing could touch them."

Roger picked up the photograph, his fingers curling into fists. "And they got away with it. For decades."

The next document Liz pulled out was a thick, typed report on something called the Blackpine Facility. Her eyes widened as she read the details. "This wasn't just any drilling site," she said, her voice tight with dread. "It was an experimental project, something they were testing on the outskirts of Midland. High-pressure drilling techniques that had never been used before. There were reports of workers getting sick, strange environmental phenomena, and unexplained accidents."

Roger's brow furrowed, and he leaned closer, reading over her shoulder. The Blackpine Facility had been a state-of-the-art operation, designed to maximize oil extraction in a particularly rich but dangerous patch of land. But as Liz read on, the details became more sinister. There were mentions of toxic exposure, chemical leaks, and unexplained disappearances. Workers had suffered from debilitating respiratory illnesses, skin lesions that wouldn't heal, and neurological symptoms that left them unable to function.

"There's more," Liz continued, her voice trembling slightly as she read on. "They brought in specialists to try and contain the situation, but the damage was already done. The chemicals they used contaminated the groundwater. People living nearby reported mysterious illnesses, and livestock started dying off. Some families just... disappeared, with no explanation."

Roger felt the weight of the horror pressing down on him. "And they covered it all up," he said, his voice thick with rage. "They buried it because admitting the truth would have ruined them."

Liz's hands trembled slightly as she flipped the page, revealing a list of names: workers who had been assigned to the Blackpine Facility. Next to each name was a note about their fate: deceased, missing, permanently disabled. The list went on, and with each name, the horror of what had happened there grew.

"They tried to bury this," she whispered, her voice cracking. "They relocated the workers who survived, paid them off, and shut the facility down without any explanation. And anyone who tried to speak out… just vanished."

Roger's face hardened, and his hand slammed down on the table, causing the papers to rustle. "This is it," he said, his voice thick with emotion. "This is what triggered the killer. The Blackpine Facility wasn't just a danger to the workers. It was a death sentence. And Marathon Oil tried to pretend it never existed."

Liz's eyes filled with determination. "If the killer or someone they loved was connected to Blackpine, it explains everything. The explosion, the murders, the rage. It's all tied to this place."

She continued digging through the documents, her mind racing. Every piece of evidence painted a clearer picture of a company that had built its empire on the backs of the powerless and the dead. Marathon Oil hadn't just caused a tragic accident—they had orchestrated a cover-up so thorough that the truth had almost disappeared.

But now, things started to add up, and the truth was emerging.

Liz reached for another document, this one was a letter written by a desperate widow. Her husband had been one of the workers at Blackpine, and in the letter, she begged Marathon Oil for compensation after he had fallen ill and died. The letter was heart-wrenching, the words filled with grief and anger. The company had ignored her, and she had been left to raise three children alone.

Roger's hand tightened around his pen. "This isn't just about revenge," he said, his voice trembling with suppressed rage. "It's about justice. The killer is doing what no one else had the courage to do—making these people pay for what they did."

Liz looked up at him, her eyes glistening with unshed tears. "But it's still murder," she said. "And it won't bring those people back."

Roger met her gaze, the weight of their responsibility pressing heavily on him. "No," he agreed. "But we have to understand it if we're going to stop it. And we have to do it before the killer strikes again."

Just as they were starting to piece things together, the door to the conference room burst open. A young deputy stood there, his face pale and eyes wide with worry. "Sheriff," he said, his voice strained, "we just got a call from one of Kathy's neighbors. They brought in a security video from their home camera. It shows someone standing outside her house.”

Roger’s heart stopped, the world seeming to slow for a split second. “Did they try to break in?” he demanded, his voice rough.

The deputy shook his head. “No, sir. They just… stood there. Watching. For almost ten minutes. Then they disappeared into the yard behind the property.”

Roger’s hands clenched into fists, rage and fear coursing through him. “Get that video to our tech team,” he ordered. “I want it analyzed for every detail. And double the patrols around Kathy’s house. We can’t take any chances.”

The deputy shifted uncomfortably. “There’s more,” he said. “We also got footage from Jason’s house. The killer was there too, watching from the shadows. But Jason’s home security system triggered an alert, and the cameras scared them off before they could do anything.”

Liz’s face had gone pale. Her stomach knotted at the thought of Jason being so close to danger. The killer had been there, lurking, watching, just waiting for the perfect moment.

Roger’s eyes burned with a mixture of guilt and anger. “We never moved Kathy or Jason,” he admitted, his voice thick with regret. “I thought they’d be safer at home, with deputies watching the place. But now…” He swallowed hard, the weight of his decision pressing down on him.

Liz placed a reassuring hand on his arm, her grip strong. “We’ll catch this bastard,” she said. “But we need to move fast. This isn’t just about the past anymore. It’s about now.”

The tension in the room thickened, the sense of urgency almost suffocating. The mention of Blackpine Facility had cracked open a terrible secret, but now the killer was sending a message that no one was truly safe. The thought of Jason and Kathy being hunted made the stakes feel even higher.

CHAPTER TWENTY THREE

Snowflakes continued to swirl in the frigid Midland air. The snowstorm had been relentless, a rare occurrence in West Texas that felt almost ominous, as if nature itself had conspired to deepen the mystery Roger and Liz were trying so desperately to solve. The landscape, once familiar, had been transformed into something eerie and otherworldly.

Inside the sheriff's department's operations center, Roger and Liz huddled around their case files, the room bathed in the harsh glow of fluorescent lights. Liz was hunched over her laptop, her fingers flying across the keyboard as she searched for any digital trace of the Blackpine Facility. Her face was lit by the blue glow of the screen, eyes squinting with concentration. "I've found references to the Blackpine Facility in some old environmental reports," she said, her voice tense with excitement. The details on her screen were fragmented and cryptic, but each clue built on the last, painted a chilling picture of what had happened there.

"It looks like Blackpine was more than just an oil drilling site," Liz continued, her voice growing quieter, almost as if she were speaking in reverence to the horror she was uncovering. "It was an experimental facility hidden behind the guise of a standard operation. Marathon Oil's internal documents reference something called 'Project Deep Surge.'"

Roger's interest piqued, and he leaned closer, his tired eyes sharpening. "Project Deep Surge?" he echoed, his voice gruff with a mix of curiosity and anger. "What the hell were they doing out there?"

Liz clicked on a link, and a series of old, scanned documents filled the screen. She squinted, reading aloud. "High-pressure fracking experiments, using a combination of chemical and heat-based extraction methods. They were trying to access deeper oil reserves that conventional drilling couldn't reach." She paused, her expression hardening. "But the chemicals they used were untested, volatile. There are reports here about methane pockets and hydrogen sulfide releases. Extremely dangerous gases."

Roger's hands tightened into fists, his knuckles turning white. "They were playing with fire," he said, his voice low and dangerous. "And they didn't care who got burned."

Liz scrolled down, her fingers trembling. "It gets worse," she said, swallowing hard. "The environmental reports from that time flagged massive contamination of the groundwater. People living nearby reported strange odors, unexplained health problems—rashes, respiratory failure, neurological damage. Even animals were affected: livestock dropping dead overnight, fish kills in the nearby creeks."

Roger's brow furrowed deeply. "And Marathon Oil covered it all up?" he asked, though the answer was already clear.

"Looks like it," Liz confirmed, her voice tinged with disgust. "The reports disappeared, and the people who tried to raise concerns were silenced. Some of them just vanished. Others signed non-disclosure agreements and were paid off, but their families still suffered. And here's the kicker—there are records of whistleblowers being threatened or even mysteriously dying."

The room seemed to grow colder, despite the warmth of the heaters. Roger could feel the rage simmering just below the surface. "They sacrificed this town," he said through gritted teeth. "All for profit."

Liz's eyes filled with anger and sorrow. "And the worst part is, some of the people affected didn't even know what was happening. There's a mention of a family that lived closest to the facility—the Jennings family. Caleb Jennings's father, David, was one of the lead engineers, and he went missing right after Blackpine was shut down. His disappearance was labeled a suicide, but now…" Her voice trailed off, a deep sadness settling into her expression.

Roger's jaw clenched tighter, the name Jennings bringing back the image of Caleb's broken body out near Monahans Draw. "That family never stood a chance," he said, his voice rough with grief. "David Jennings was probably killed for knowing too much, and his son was the first victim in this twisted revenge scheme."

Liz nodded, her gaze hardening with determination. "This killer isn't just avenging the victims of the explosion. They're avenging everyone who was affected by the Blackpine contamination. The sins of the past have come back with a vengeance."

Roger rubbed his temples, trying to process the magnitude of what they were dealing with. "And Project Deep Surge," he murmured. "If this was their secret weapon for deeper oil extraction, then Blackpine was part of a much larger plan."

Liz's fingers flew across the keyboard, pulling up more documents. "Look at this," she said, her voice taut with urgency. "Marathon Oil had plans to replicate the Blackpine experiments at other sites. They knew the risks, and they were willing to gamble with people's lives. They covered up test results, forged safety reports, and bribed government officials to keep everything under wraps."

"This is a goddamn atrocity," he growled. "They didn't care about ruining lives. The people of Midland have been paying the price ever since."

Liz leaned back, her face pale and exhausted. "And now someone is making sure they pay for it in blood," she whispered. "The killer is methodical. He's targeting both the families who suffered and the executives who caused that suffering."

They sat in silence for a moment, the weight of their discovery pressing heavily on them. Roger finally broke the silence, his voice steady but grim. "We need to get this information to the team," he said. "Every deputy needs to know what we're up against. If this killer has a hit list, we need to be prepared."

Liz nodded, but her eyes were distant, haunted by what they had uncovered. "This town has been living with ghosts," she said softly. "And now, those ghosts have come back to claim justice."

The room felt smaller, as if the walls were closing in on them. Each piece of evidence, each shattered life, was a reminder of the darkness that had festered in Midland for decades. And now, that darkness was coming to light, one brutal murder at a time. The exhaustion caught up to them, and everything they'd learned pressed heavily on their shoulders.

Liz finally broke the silence, her voice softer than before. "Have you checked in on Kathy?" she asked Roger, genuine concern etched across her features. "With the killer targeting our loved ones, she's got to be terrified."

Roger's shoulders sagged, the stoic mask he always wore slipping slightly. "I called her last night," he admitted, the guilt heavy in his voice. "She tried to sound brave, but I could hear the fear. Emily's back in Dallas, under heavy protection. But Kathy... she's never had to deal with anything like this before."

Liz's expression grew somber. "It's hard," she said, her own voice cracking slightly. "Knowing we're the reason the people we care about are targets."

Roger met her gaze, a flicker of vulnerability in his usually hardened eyes. "How's Jason?" he asked quietly.

Liz sighed, her fingers gripping the edge of the table. "He's trying to be strong, but I can tell it's eating him up inside. The pictures the killer took of us... it shattered whatever illusion of safety we had. We haven't had a moment to just be together, to breathe, without the threat hanging over us."

Roger reached out and squeezed her hand, a rare and tender gesture. "We're going to end this," he said, his voice resolute, though his eyes betrayed the worry gnawing at him. "We have to."

The clock struck midnight, and tiredness finally began to overtake them. Roger knew they needed rest, even if their minds were still racing and their bodies coiled tight with anxiety. "Let's call it a night," he said, his voice rough with fatigue.

They gathered their things and headed to their homes.

Roger drove slowly through the icy streets, the familiar landscape of Midland transformed into something alien by the snow. His truck's tires crunched over the fresh powder, and he felt the weight of every mile as he made his way to Kathy's house. Each turn of the wheel felt like he was pushing through something far heavier than the snow.

When he pulled into Kathy's driveway, he sat there for a moment, gripping the steering wheel and staring at the warm glow of the porch light. The light felt like a beacon, drawing him out of the darkness he carried with him. Finally, he took a deep breath and stepped out, his boots crunching on the snow-covered path.

Kathy opened the door at his knock, her eyes widening with a mix of relief and worry. She was wearing a soft, oversized sweater, and her hair fell loosely around her shoulders. The sight of her, so familiar and warm, nearly broke him.

"Roger," she said, her voice trembling. "Come in. You look exhausted."

Inside, the house smelled like cinnamon and pine, the remnants of the holiday season lingering in the air. Roger hesitated before sinking onto the couch, his shoulders hunched. His hands shook slightly as he rubbed his face, trying to hold back the flood of emotions threatening to break free.

"I'm sorry, Kathy," he whispered, his voice cracking. "I'm so sorry for everything. For putting you in danger, for dragging you into this nightmare… for everything I did to hurt you. I never wanted this for you."

Kathy knelt in front of him, her hands gently cupping his face. Her eyes were filled with unshed tears, but there was a strength in them, too. "We've both made mistakes," she said softly. "But you're here now. And I'm here. That's what matters."

Their eyes locked, and the tension dissolved into something fragile and intimate. Roger leaned forward, and their lips met in a kiss that was both desperate and healing. Years of pain and longing melted away, leaving only the raw, honest need for comfort and connection. They held each other tightly, as if afraid to let go, and what followed was a release of all the emotions they had kept bottled up for far too long. Their intimacy was tender and full of unspoken promises, a sanctuary in the middle of the storm.

Liz drove home through the empty streets, her heart pounding with a mixture of fear and longing. The sight of the snow blanketing her neighborhood felt surreal, as if the world had become an entirely different place overnight. When she pulled into her driveway, the glow from her house was a small comfort against the oppressive darkness.

Jason was waiting for her, pacing the living room, his worry evident in the tight lines of his face. The moment she stepped inside, he pulled her into a fierce embrace, his arms wrapping around her with a desperation that mirrored her own. "I've been so scared something happened to you," he whispered, his voice thick with emotion.

Liz pulled back slightly, looking up at him. His eyes were full of love and fear, and she felt the tension in her chest loosen just a little. "Can you stay with me tonight?" she asked, her voice small and vulnerable. "I don't want to be alone. Not with everything that's happening."

Jason cupped her face in his hands, his touch gentle but firm. "Of course," he said. "I'm not going anywhere."

They climbed the stairs together, the house eerily silent except for the occasional creak of the old wood under their feet. In the bedroom, Liz changed into a soft, worn t-shirt and climbed into bed, pulling the covers up to her chin. Jason slid in beside her, wrapping his arm around her waist. His warmth seeped into her, and she pressed her face into his chest, inhaling the familiar, comforting scent of him.

The bed felt like a safe haven, a small island of warmth in a sea of fear and uncertainty. Liz closed her eyes, trying to focus on Jason's steady heartbeat instead of the whirlwind of thoughts racing through her mind. "I don't know what I'd do without you," she whispered.

Jason kissed the top of her head, his lips lingering there. "You won't have to find out," he said. "We'll get through this. Together."

They lay there, holding each other as the snow continued to fall outside, the rare and unsettling storm painting a picture of a world that was beautiful and dangerous in equal measure. But in that moment, they had each other, and that was enough to keep the darkness at bay, if only for a little while.

CHAPTER TWENTY FOUR

Roger stood at the head of a long conference table, his weathered hands pressed firmly against the polished wood. His face was hard, the lines deepened by exhaustion and anger. Around the table sat the remaining members of the old Marathon Oil board: Robert Withers, Henry Lawson, and Gerald Simmons. Each man wore a tailored suit, but the fabric looked out of place against the backdrop of the grim reality they faced.

Liz sat beside Roger, her laptop open. Her eyes were sharp, taking in every nuance of the men across from her. The three board members shifted uncomfortably under her unwavering gaze. The only sounds in the room were the groan of the old building's heating system and the muffled hum of traffic outside.

Roger let his gaze linger on each of the men, his blue eyes cold and unforgiving. These were men who had once wielded significant power, men who had made decisions that sacrificed lives for profit. The silence stretched on, heavy and suffocating, until Roger finally broke it.

"Thank you all for coming," he said, his voice a low, dangerous rumble. The civility in his words was a thin veneer, barely masking his contempt. None of the board members had come willingly, and they all knew it. The pressure to attend this meeting had been immense, and the threat of being dragged in forcibly loomed large.

Robert Withers, the eldest of the three, with thinning gray hair and wire-rimmed glasses that slipped down his nose, cleared his throat. He adjusted his tie, trying to compose himself. "Sheriff Hartley, I'd like to remind you that we're here voluntarily. And we expect to be treated with respect."

Roger leaned forward, his palms pressing harder into the table. "You'll get the respect you deserve, Mr. Withers, once we get some answers," he shot back, his voice sharp and unyielding. "We need to know everything about Blackpine and Project Deep Surge. No more half-truths. No more lies."

The board members exchanged uneasy glances. Gerald Simmons, a broad-shouldered man with a thick mustache and a habit of tapping his fingers when nervous, shifted uncomfortably. Henry Lawson, a man in his sixties with lines etched deeply into his face from years of worry and guilt, ran a hand over his mouth, his expression grim. The silence was thick, and it took quite an effort for one of them to speak.

Finally, Henry Lawson sighed. "We knew this would come back to haunt us," he murmured, almost to himself. He looked like a man haunted by more than just bad memories.

Henry shifted in his chair, his gaze darting to the security camera in the corner. The knowledge that everything he was about to say would be recorded seemed to press on him, making him visibly uncomfortable. "Project Deep Surge," he began, his voice cracking, "was supposed to be a revolutionary way to access oil reserves that were considered unreachable. The oil beneath Blackpine was trapped in shale layers too deep and too tough for traditional methods, so we had to innovate."

Roger crossed his arms, his muscles tense. "Innovate," he repeated, his voice dripping with disdain. "That's your word for endangering lives and poisoning this town?"

Henry winced but didn't look away. "Yes," he said softly. "We used high-pressure fracking, long before fracking was thought of, combined with chemical injection. We developed heat-based extraction techniques to break down the shale, but we didn't fully understand the chain reactions we were setting off."

Gerald Simmons leaned forward, his face flushed with both guilt and defensiveness. "We were promised this technology would change the industry," he said, his voice rising slightly. "We had scientists assuring us that the risks were manageable, that the benefits far outweighed any potential consequences."

Liz's eyes flashed, and she leaned in, her voice cutting like a blade. "Explain," she demanded. "What kind of consequences are we talking about?"

Henry rubbed his temples, as if trying to ease an invisible pain. "The kind that spiraled out of control," he said. "Methane gas pockets ignited without warning. There were hydrogen sulfide releases—highly toxic gas that we couldn't contain. The chemicals we pumped into the ground seeped into the aquifer, contaminating the water supply. People started getting sick: dizziness, seizures, skin lesions. And the worst cases were neurological, affecting children. We… we ruined lives."

Liz clenched her fists, her knuckles white. "Children," she spat. "You knew you were poisoning children, and you did nothing to stop it. You let families suffer while you counted your profits.”

The silence was suffocating, and Henry’s next words made it even worse. “It all came to a head the day of the explosion,” he said, his voice cracking. His eyes were wide, haunted by the memory. “It was a warm afternoon. Pressure readings spiked beyond anything we’d ever seen. Methane gas had built up in pockets, and we couldn’t vent it fast enough. There were alarms, people screaming. We tried to shut everything down, but the system failed. And then… it all blew.”

Gerald’s face turned ashen, his eyes unfocused as he remembered. “The ground cracked open, and flames shot up into the sky,” he said, his voice raw with anguish. “Workers ran, engulfed in flames. Some were burned alive, some suffocated in the poisonous gas. I can still hear their screams. The heat was so intense, it felt like hell itself had erupted.”

Robert Withers took off his glasses, his hands trembling. “The sound,” he whispered. “It echoed for miles. The explosion was deafening. We were 25 miles away from Midland, and the blast shook houses in town. It blew out every damn window in the area. People tried to escape; those who couldn’t were incinerated where they stood. We lost good men that day, men who had no idea they were part of something so monstrous.”

“And instead of taking responsibility,” Roger said, his voice dangerously low, “you covered it all up. You buried the evidence, paid off survivors, and made sure no one knew how bad it was.”

Henry's voice broke. "We didn't have a choice," he pleaded. "The people pulling the strings wouldn't let us come clean. We were told to stay quiet, or we'd end up like David Jennings."

Liz's gaze darkened. "How much were you paid to keep quiet?" she asked, her voice cold as steel.

Robert Withers's face went pale, and he hesitated before answering. "They gave me $50 million," he confessed, his voice thick with regret. "Deposited into offshore accounts. It was blood money, and I knew it. I've never been able to spend a dime of it without feeling the weight of those lives."

Henry Lawson swallowed hard. "I received $65 million," he admitted, his hands clenching and unclenching. "They called it a 'special compensation package' for my silence. I tried to tell myself it was to secure my family's future, but no amount of wealth can erase what we did."

Gerald Simmons's face flushed with guilt. "I took $40 million," he said, his voice breaking. "At the time, I thought I was protecting my loved ones, but the money is tainted. I can't touch it without remembering the people who suffered."

Liz's stomach turned, her anger boiling over. "Over a hundred million dollars between the three of you," she said, her voice trembling with rage. "While families in this town lost everything. While children died. And you still want to paint yourselves as victims?"

Roger exhaled slowly. The anger in his veins felt like molten fire, barely contained. "You all knew," he said, his voice dangerously calm. "You knew what was happening, and you chose to do nothing. You let this town bleed, let families be destroyed, because you were too greedy or too cowardly to do the right thing."

Henry's hands shook, his voice cracking. "We didn't have a choice," he insisted. "It was about survival. People who tried to expose the truth disappeared or died under suspicious circumstances. We had families to protect. We were terrified."

Roger's fist came down on the table with a resounding crack, and the board members flinched as one. "Don't talk to me about survival," he growled. "The people of this town didn't have a choice. The families who lost loved ones didn't have a choice. You took millions and let this community suffer. That blood is on your hands, and you'll answer for it."

The room fell into a stunned silence, the board members visibly shaken. Gerald Simmons looked like he might vomit, his face glistening with sweat. Robert Withers buried his face in his hands, and Henry Lawson slumped back in his chair, defeated.

Liz leaned forward, her voice ice-cold. "We need every piece of documentation you have," she said. "Every email, every memo, every record. If we're going to stop this killer, we need to know exactly who might be next on their list. We need to know every name, every deal, every detail."

Robert Withers lifted his head, his eyes hollow. "We'll give you everything," he whispered. "Every record, every file. But you have to understand… we were victims too."

Roger's eyes blazed with fury. "Victims?" he repeated, his voice low and menacing. "Don't you dare call yourselves victims. The real victims are the people whose lives you destroyed. If I find out you're hiding anything, I'll make sure you face the full weight of the law. Do you understand me?"

The board members nodded and the meeting ended with a sense of finality that left no room for redemption. The dark truths had been dragged into the light, and now Roger and Liz had to find a way to stop the killer before the sins of the past claimed even more lives.

As the board members filed out of the room, their heads down and shoulders slumped, Roger and Liz sat in the suffocating silence that followed. The weight of everything they had just heard pressed down on them, suffocating and relentless.

CHAPTER TWENTY FIVE

Roger and Liz walked side by side, making their way back to the sheriff's department. Steam curled from the tops of their coffee cups, the warmth seeping into their chilled fingers.

They had just come from a small coffee shop, one of the few places still open despite the storm. The interior of the coffee shop had been cozy, filled with the smell of roasted beans and the faint sounds of a classic rock station playing softly in the background. The barista had smiled at them, her own exhaustion evident as she served their drinks. Roger had thanked her, his voice heavy, and Liz had offered her a small smile in return. But the warmth, the smell, and the sense of normal life had vanished the moment they stepped back into the storm, replaced by the weight of what they had to do.

Liz sipped her coffee. "I still can't believe how quiet it is," she said, her voice low. "It's like the whole town is holding its breath, waiting for something to happen."

Roger's expression was grim as he adjusted his hat, his breath visible in the freezing air. "Something is going to happen," he said. "This killer isn't done, and they're not going to stop until we catch them or they finish whatever twisted plan they have."

"I just wish we knew what that plan was," she said.

They reached the front of the sheriff's department, and the sight of Deputy Ramirez standing just inside the entrance, looking tense, immediately put them on high alert.

Ramirez stepped outside as they approached, his face pinched with urgency.

"Sheriff, you need to see this," Ramirez said, ushering them inside.

Roger and Liz followed Ramirez to his desk, where a series of security camera feeds were displayed on a monitor. Ramirez rewound the footage to a timestamp from earlier that evening, then hit play. The grainy video showed a figure approaching the sheriff's department through the falling snow. The person wore a long, dark coat and a wide-brimmed hat that cast deep shadows over their face. They moved deliberately, carrying a small package that they placed on the back steps before vanishing into the night.

Liz's grip tightened around her coffee cup. "That package wasn't there when we left for the coffee shop," she said. "Did anyone touch it?"

Ramirez shook his head. "No, ma'am. We secured the area and kept everyone back. It's still outside, untouched."

Roger exchanged a look with Liz, both bracing themselves for what they knew would be another grim message from the killer. "Let's go," Roger said, setting down his coffee and pulling on his gloves.

The package sat on the back steps, looking deceptively harmless under its layer of fresh snow. Roger knelt down and carefully picked it up, his movements deliberate.

The note taped to the top was written in the same precise, elegant handwriting as before. Roger read it aloud, his voice steady. "Leave them alone. This is your final warning."

Liz's stomach churned, her pulse quickening. "He knows we're getting close," she whispered. "He's trying to scare us off."

Roger unwrapped the package, his hands steady despite the dread pooling in his gut. Inside was a stack of photographs, and he flipped through them with a growing sense of unease. The first photos were of Roger and Liz, taken from various locations around town. They showed the two of them leaving the sheriff's department, standing at crime scenes, and even through the windows of their homes. Each image was invasive, a violation that made Liz's skin crawl.

But there were more photos. One showed Liz sitting on her bed, her head in her hands, with Jason in the background, his face etched with concern. Another captured Roger standing in his living room, his shoulders hunched, looking older and more weary than he ever let himself feel.

Then came the most disturbing photo yet: a picture of the board members—Robert Withers, Henry Lawson, and Gerald Simmons—leaving the sheriff's office after their meeting. The camera had caught them in the harsh glow of the streetlights, their expressions tense and haunted.

Liz's hands began to shake. "He was here," she said, her voice cracking. "Watching them. Watching us. He's always there."

Roger's jaw tightened, and he felt a flash of anger so intense it almost burned through his fear. "We're not taking any more chances," he said. "I'm putting extra protection on you and Jason. We'll have deputies stationed at both of your homes."

Liz swallowed hard, trying to suppress the rising panic. "And what about you?" she asked. "You're a target too, Roger. This isn't just about us."

Roger's blue eyes met hers, filled with a fierce determination. "I can handle myself," he said. "But I'm not losing anyone else. Not you, not Jason, and not Kathy."

The conference room inside the sheriff's department had never felt so claustrophobic. The usually sterile, fluorescent-lit space was heavy with tension, the air thick enough to choke on. The deputies, who had once joked and swapped stories over coffee and stale donuts, now sat stiff and silent, their faces shadowed with lack of sleep and fear.

Roger stood at the front of the room, the lines on his weathered face etched even deeper in the harsh light. His blue eyes, usually warm with a steady calm, now burned with a fierceness that no one dared question. He looked over his team—men and women he had worked with for years, people he trusted with his life—and knew that they all felt the same growing sense of helplessness. But he couldn't afford to let that show.

"We're dealing with a killer who's calculated he began, his voice low but carrying a commanding presence that demanded attention. "This isn't some impulsive madman. This person has been watching us, studying us. They know our routines, our vulnerabilities, and they're using that information to stay ahead of us."

The room was so quiet that Roger could hear the hum of the old heating system, the occasional creak of the building settling. Deputy Ramirez, who normally had a laid-back demeanor, sat rigid in his chair, his knuckles white as he gripped his notepad. Even the youngest deputies, who hadn't been on the force long enough to grow jaded, looked worn out, shadows darkening their eyes.

"We have to assume that the killer knows more about us than we'd like to think," Roger continued, his gaze sweeping the room. "They've proven that they can get close—too close. They've invaded our homes, taken photos of us when we thought we were safe. This is psychological warfare, and they're using fear as a weapon."

Liz, standing near the back, crossed her arms tightly over her chest. She hated feeling vulnerable, but she hated seeing her team afraid even more. She cleared her throat. "That means we don't take any chances," she said. "From now on, we travel in pairs. No one goes anywhere alone—not even to the bathroom. We check in regularly, and we keep our loved ones safe. If you notice anything out of the ordinary, no matter how small, you report it immediately."

Deputy Harris, a burly man with a no-nonsense attitude, leaned forward. His brow was furrowed, a deep line etched between his eyes. "Sheriff," he said, his voice gravelly. "If this bastard is targeting people tied to Blackpine, then the board members are sitting ducks. Shouldn't we be doubling up on their protection?"

Roger's jaw clenched, the muscles in his neck tightening. Protecting the board members—men who had taken millions to cover up a disaster that had poisoned the town—felt like swallowing broken glass. But he knew Harris was right. The killer's vendetta was clear, and they had to be strategic.

"We don't have the manpower to spread ourselves too thin," Roger admitted, his voice heavy with the weight of their responsibility. "But we'll check in with Withers, Lawson, and Simmons. If they don't have adequate security, we'll assign deputies to them. We must stop this killer before more lives are lost."

A murmur ran through the room, and Liz could see the discomfort in her colleagues' faces. They all knew how much suffering the board members had caused, and the idea of protecting them didn't sit well. But they were law enforcement, and that meant protecting lives—even those of people who didn't deserve it.

Roger took a deep breath, trying to steady the rage simmering inside him. "Our priority," he said, "is each other and our families. We're all targets now, and that means we protect our own. But we also need to keep an eye on anyone connected to this case. The killer is escalating, and if we don't stay ahead of them, we're going to lose more people."

Liz stepped forward, her expression resolute. "I've been going through the environmental reports we pulled," she said. "There are names of people who knew about the contamination and tried to speak out. Whistleblowers, families who were affected. We need to track them down. Maybe someone knows something we haven't figured out yet."

"Do it," Roger said. "We need every piece of information we can get. If there's a pattern we're not seeing, we have to find it. This killer has made it personal, and they're not going to stop until we give them what they want—or until we stop them."

Deputy Ramirez spoke, his voice cracking slightly. "Sheriff, what about our families?" he asked. "My wife's been asking if we should leave town, just until this is over."

Roger's heart ached at the question. He knew how many families were living in fear, how many people were thinking of packing up and fleeing. "I can't tell you what to do," he said, his voice gentle but firm. "But I can tell you that we're stronger together. If your family needs to leave to feel safe, I understand. But if they stay, we'll protect them. We'll protect each other."

Liz's voice cut through the room, strong and unwavering. "We're a team," she said. "We look out for each other, and that means looking out for our families too. If anyone needs help, you call. No one is alone in this."

The room fell into a heavy silence, but there was a newfound sense of resolve. They were scared, but they were united. Roger watched his team, feeling both pride and a bone-deep exhaustion that made him wish, just for a moment, that he could set down the burden he carried.

But he couldn't. Not yet. Not while the killer was still out there, watching, waiting, and planning their next move.

CHAPTER TWENTY SIX

Robert Withers sat in his sprawling, two-story home, the walls lined with art pieces that looked out of place in a town built on oil and grit. His study, a testament to his wealth, was filled with dark mahogany furniture, plush Persian rugs, and floor-to-ceiling bookshelves crammed with leather-bound volumes he never read. He sat at his massive desk, sipping on a glass of brandy, the expensive liquor barely taking the edge off his frayed nerves. The meeting with the sheriff and his deputy had shaken him more than he wanted to admit. The truth of what he'd done—and the lives he'd helped ruin—clawed at the edges of his conscience, refusing to be silenced. He had told himself over and over that the money he'd taken had been for his family, for their security, but the lie had worn thin over the years. Now, he was just a man with too much money and too little peace.

The wind howled outside, a long, mournful wail that seemed to seep into the cracks of the house. Robert flinched at the sound, his hand tightening around the glass until his knuckles went white. The cold, creeping dread that had been his constant companion over the past few days grew stronger, coiling in his gut. He cursed himself for being so jumpy, but fear had a way of burrowing deep, especially when the past refused to stay buried.

He set the brandy down, the glass clinking against the polished wood, and leaned back in his chair, his gaze drifting to the shadows that gathered in the corners of the room. It was then that he heard it—a creak, subtle and low, like the sound of a floorboard protesting under someone's weight. His heart stuttered, and he sat up, every muscle in his body tensing.

"Hello?" he called out, his voice cracking. The house remained silent.

He stood slowly, wiping his damp palms on his tailored trousers. "I'm armed," he bluffed, though his gun was locked away upstairs in his bedroom. He cursed himself for not keeping it closer, for underestimating the danger that had crept so insidiously into his life. "Whoever you are, get out of my house!"

Another creak, this one closer, and the hairs on the back of his neck stood on end. His eyes darted around the room, searching for a weapon—anything he could use to defend himself. His gaze landed on the heavy brass letter opener on his desk, and he grabbed it, the cold metal feeling woefully inadequate in his shaking hand.

"Get out!" he shouted, his voice trembling. He was met with silence, thick and suffocating, and for a moment, he thought he had imagined the sound. But then he heard it—a low, raspy breath, like the sound of someone exhaling deeply, slowly, savoring his fear.

A figure emerged from the shadows, moving with a predatory grace that made Robert's blood run cold. The killer wore a black mask, the eyes behind it dark and merciless. Robert barely had time to scream before the attacker lunged, a gloved hand clamping over his mouth. The force of the assault sent them crashing into the bookshelves, volumes of leather-bound books toppling to the floor, their spines cracking against the hardwood.

Robert fought desperately, his limbs flailing, but the killer overpowered him with terrifying strength. He felt sheer terror as the killer pulled a long, serrated hunting knife from their belt. The blade caught the light from the fire, gleaming with a deadly promise. Robert's muffled scream was cut short as the knife plunged into him, over and over, the sound of tearing flesh and the wet, sickening splatter of blood filling the room.

By the time the police were called, alerted by a frantic neighbor who had heard the sound of breaking glass and muffled screams, it was too late. Roger and Liz arrived on the scene, the flashing lights of patrol cars casting harsh shadows over the pristine snow. The front door of Robert Withers's house was ajar, the wood splintered and hanging from its hinges, as if the house itself had been violated.

Roger stepped inside first, his gun drawn, Liz right behind him. The house was eerily quiet, the kind of quiet that felt unnatural, as if the violence that had taken place had sucked all the life out of the air. They moved carefully through the foyer, past expensive vases that had been smashed on the marble floor, and into the study.

The study was a scene of absolute horror, a nightmare brought to life. Blood splattered the walls in thick, violent arcs, as if a tornado of gore had torn through the room. The metallic tang of blood mixed with the acrid scent of fear and death, making the air feel suffocating.

Robert Withers's body had been arranged to mimic the positions of the victims from the old explosion photo. His torso was twisted at an unnatural angle, one arm bent unnaturally behind his back, while the other was outstretched, the fingers clawing at nothing. His face was a mask of terror, forever in a silent, agonized scream.

He had been tied to his desk chair with barbed wire, the sharp metal biting deep into his flesh, leaving raw, bloody gashes. His throat had been slashed so deeply that his head lolled back, barely attached by sinew and torn muscle. Blood pooled on the polished mahogany desk, dripping slowly onto the plush, cream-colored carpet below, turning it a dark, sodden red. The contrast of the rich furnishings and the brutal violence made the scene feel even more obscene.

Carved into his chest, with deep, jagged letters that split the flesh and exposed the raw muscle underneath, was the word: **LIAR**. The cuts were so deep that the letters gaped, the edges ragged and glistening.

The killer had gone further, making sure the scene mirrored the explosion photo in every grim detail. Shards of glass had been driven into Robert's face, his eyes gouged out and replaced with broken pieces of his own shattered brandy glass, leaving trails of blood that glistened in the dim light. His mouth had been forced open, stuffed full of wadded-up hundred-dollar bills, blood soaking through the currency. Next to his mutilated body, a copy of his bank statement lay on the desk, the bolded transaction numbers a reminder of the millions he had accepted to stay silent.

Roger swallowed hard, the bile rising in his throat. He forced himself to look away from the carnage. He had seen violent crime scenes before, but this was something different. This was personal, a message written in blood and agony.

Liz knelt beside the body, her face pale but resolute. She noticed something clutched in Robert's lifeless hand, his knuckles bloodied and broken from the struggle. Carefully, she pried his fingers open and pulled out a torn scrap of paper. It was stained with blood, but she could still make out a few words.

She handed it to Roger, her voice shaking. "Looks like he tried to leave us a clue," she said. "But whatever he knew… he took it to his grave."

Roger studied the paper, his mind racing. The words were smudged, but he could make out fragments: **"Deep Surge"** and **"Henry."**

Before they could analyze it further, a soft, muffled sob caught their attention. Roger and Liz turned, their hearts pounding, and followed the sound to a corner of the study. There, tied to a heavy armchair with duct tape around her wrists and ankles, was Robert's wife, Margaret Withers. Her eyes were wide with terror, her face pale and streaked with tears. Duct tape had been placed over her mouth, but her muffled cries were unmistakable.

Liz rushed over, pulling out a pocketknife to cut the bindings. "We've got you," she whispered, her hands gentle but efficient as she freed Margaret. "You're safe now."

Margaret ripped the tape from her mouth, her sobs breaking free. "He made me watch," she choked out, her whole body trembling. "He made me listen to every second of it. I couldn't do anything. I couldn't save him."

Roger knelt beside her, his voice gentle but urgent. "Did you see his face? Did he say anything that might help us?"

Margaret shook her head, her eyes haunted. "He wore a mask. But his voice... it was calm. He said Robert had to pay for his sins. That the past always catches up to people like him."

The coroner, Marla Decker, arrived shortly after. She wore a heavy parka over her scrubs, and the smell of antiseptic clung to her, a sharp contrast to the stench of blood and death that permeated the air. Her face was pale but composed, the practiced calm of someone who had seen too many scenes like this but still found herself unsettled by the brutality.

Marla knelt beside Robert Withers's body, snapping on a pair of latex gloves with practiced efficiency. She leaned in to examine the deep gashes, her flashlight illuminating the jagged letters carved into his chest. "Whoever did this took their time. They wanted to make sure every cut sent a message," she said in a low, clinical voice.

Liz, who had been trying to keep Margaret from collapsing in shock, took a shaky breath. "What kind of person does this?" she muttered, more to herself than anyone else.

Marla moved the flashlight to Robert's face, the shards of glass glinting like dark jewels embedded in his eye sockets. "The glass… it's from the brandy decanter," she said, her brow furrowing. "It wasn't just shoved in randomly. It was placed with care, almost as if the killer wanted to make a point about Robert being blind to the consequences of his actions."

Roger stood nearby, his arms crossed tightly over his chest, his jaw clenched. He was doing everything he could to keep from letting the horror of the scene get to him. "And the money in his mouth?" he asked. Marla carefully pulled one of the blood-soaked bills from Robert's mouth, inspecting it with a grim expression. "This is a statement about greed," she said. "The killer wants to make sure we understand that Robert's wealth came at the expense of others. They wanted him to choke on the very thing that drove him to make those choices."

Roger turned to one of the officers who had arrived with the crime scene team. "Get the rest of the forensic team in here," he ordered. "I want every inch of this room combed for evidence. Even the smallest detail could be important."

The officer nodded and hurried off, leaving Roger to return to Marla. "Can you tell anything about the knife?" he asked, his voice tight.

Marla examined the gashes on Robert's chest, her flashlight casting long shadows across the torn flesh. "It was a serrated hunting knife," she said. "Deep, jagged cuts. The killer knew how to use it to inflict maximum pain." She looked up at Roger, her eyes filled with a mixture of weariness and determination. "This murder was a warning."

Roger took a step closer, his gaze hardening. "Marla, you've seen a lot of violent crime scenes," he said, his voice dropping. "But this one... this feels different. It's not just rage. It's calculated."

Marla nodded. "I was thinking the same thing. Look at the precision of the cuts, the way the barbed wire was wrapped around him. Whoever did this, they knew what they were doing."

Liz, her eyes still on Margaret as she tried to comfort her, glanced up. "So, what are we looking at here, Marla? Someone with medical training? Military?"

Marla considered it for a moment, her eyes narrowing as she looked over the body again. "It's possible," she said slowly. "The cuts are deep but not sloppy. There's an understanding of anatomy here—they knew exactly where to cut to cause the most damage but also to prolong the suffering. It could be someone with a background in medicine or someone who's spent time studying it. Or even someone who's hunted before. The use of a hunting knife isn't accidental either; it's meant for inflicting damage in a way that's visceral, primal."

Roger's frown deepened, his mind piecing together what little they knew. "So, we're looking for someone who not only has a vendetta but also the skill to carry out something like this. Someone who wants us to know they're in control." He paused, glancing at the carved letters on Robert's chest. "The word 'LIAR'... it's like they're trying to expose him, to show the world what kind of man he really was."

Marla stood, peeling off her gloves and tossing them into a biohazard bag. "I'll get the full autopsy done as soon as possible," she said. "Maybe there's something I'll find that can give us a lead. But right now, we're dealing with someone who has a deep-seated need to make a point. They won't make this easy."

Roger nodded. "They might think they're smarter than us," he said, "but everyone makes mistakes. We just have to find theirs."

Marla gave a small, grim smile. "Let's hope they slip up soon," she said. "Because whoever did this… they're not finished yet."

Roger glanced at Liz, who was helping Margaret to her feet, her hand on the woman's shoulder. They exchanged a look, both of them knowing that the road ahead was only going to get darker. The killer had left them a puzzle, a brutal, bloody puzzle, and they were running out of time to put the pieces together.

Roger took a step back, running a hand over his face. His phone buzzed, pulling him from his thoughts, and he answered it with a tense, "Hartley here."

Deputy Ramirez's voice came through the line, tight with urgency. "Sheriff, I've got security details stationed outside Henry Lawson's and Gerald Simmons's homes," Ramirez reported. "Lawson is refusing protection, but we've got a deputy staying on-site, regardless."

"Good," Roger replied. "Keep me updated. And make sure those deputies know to be on high alert. This killer isn't playing around."

"Understood, Sheriff," Ramirez said before hanging up.

Roger shoved his phone back into his pocket, his gaze hardening. "We need to move fast," he said to Liz. "This killer is escalating, and I don't want to walk into another scene like this."

Liz nodded, though her expression was haunted. She glanced at Margaret, who was still shaking, her face pale and tear streaked. "We'll get her to safety," Liz said softly. "But what's our next move?"

Roger looked at the blood-soaked room, at the broken man who had once been powerful and untouchable, and felt a surge of anger and determination. "We'll talk to Henry Lawson," he said. "Whether he wants protection or not, he's going to tell us everything he knows about Deep Surge. Because if he doesn't, he might be the next body we find."

Roger and Liz stood on the porch, the breath fogging in front of them as they tried to process everything they had just seen.

Liz's eyes were distant. "They're not done," she whispered. "We're being led somewhere, and I'm scared of what we're going to find when we get there."

Roger's phone buzzed again, and he glanced at the screen. Another update from a deputy. He listened as he was informed that Gerald Simmons was reluctantly cooperating but still seemed nervous and agitated.

"Stay with him," Roger ordered. "Make sure he doesn't slip away."

He ended the call and turned to Liz, his blue eyes burning with determination. "We need to talk to Lawson. Now."

They exchanged a look, the unspoken fear and resolve shared between them. The killer was out there, watching, waiting, and they had to stay one step ahead—or risk becoming part of the gruesome game.

Roger took one last look at the house, at the blood-stained snow glistening under the streetlights. The past had come back with a vengeance, and the clock was ticking. They needed answers—and they needed them fast.

Together, they climbed into the cruiser, the engine roaring to life as they braced themselves for whatever nightmare awaited them next.

CHAPTER TWENTY SEVEN

Roger gripped the steering wheel tightly, his jaw clenched, his eyes focused intently on the road ahead.

Liz glanced over at Roger, noting the deep furrows on his brow, the way his knuckles had turned white from his grip on the wheel.

"We should have pushed harder earlier," she murmured, breaking the tense silence. "Maybe if we had, Robert would still be alive."

Roger's lips thinned into a grim line. "We can't think like that," he replied, though the guilt gnawed at him just as fiercely. "We did what we could with what we knew. But now… now we make sure we don't lose anyone else."

They turned onto North Garfield Street, heading into the Warwick neighborhood. The houses here were modest yet solid, each one reflecting the no-nonsense practicality of Midland's long-time residents. There were yards filled with barren mesquite trees and patches of scrubby grass, now blanketed in snow. The chain-link fences that surrounded some of the properties sagged in places, looking worn and rusted under the harsh winter sky.

Roger took a sharp right onto a quieter street, his eyes scanning for Henry Lawson's home. When they arrived, they found the small, unassuming brick house at the very edge of the neighborhood, surrounded by a chain-link fence and framed by the twisted branches of leafless mesquite trees. A single porch light illuminated the front of the house, casting long, skeletal shadows across the snow.

Roger parked the cruiser, and he and Liz stepped out. They approached the front door cautiously, the quiet pressing down on them.

The front door opened before they could knock, and Henry Lawson appeared in the doorway. The man was tall and wiry, with thinning gray hair and deep lines etched into his face. His eyes were shadowed with exhaustion and fear, and he wore a worn-out sweater over jeans, looking far less composed than the image he had tried to project when they had last met.

"What is the meaning of this?" Lawson demanded, his voice cracking with both irritation and barely concealed anxiety. "I've told your deputies already—I'm perfectly safe here."

Roger climbed the porch steps, his boots echoing loudly on the wooden boards. "You're not safe," he growled, his voice hard as steel. "Robert Withers is dead, murdered in his own home. The killer is coming for you next, and if you don't take this seriously, your stubbornness won't save you."

Lawson's face blanched, and he took an unsteady step back. "Robert... dead?" he whispered, the disbelief mingling with fear. "But... but why? We did what we had to. It was all for the company, for our families..."

Liz stepped forward, her eyes blazing with frustration. "Whatever your reasons were, someone wants you to pay," she said. "And they're not just killing—you've seen the news. The way they're staging these murders, it's like they want to make a statement."

Lawson's composure cracked, and he ran a hand over his face. "I have security," he insisted weakly. "Guards, cameras… this place is locked down."

Roger's jaw tightened. "So did Robert," he said coldly. "And look where it got him. We're coming inside, and you're going to tell us everything you know about Project Deep Surge. If you want to stay alive, you'll stop pretending this will all blow over."

Lawson hesitated, then finally allowed them inside. The interior was simple and utilitarian, with mismatched furniture and faded rugs covering the hardwood floors. A single old recliner sat in front of a TV, and the walls were lined with family photos from decades past. The warmth of the small space was inviting, but the tension in the air was palpable.

They moved into the living room, where a space heater hummed quietly, doing its best to fight off the chill. Lawson sank into the recliner, his hands shaking as he reached for a glass of water on the coffee table. He took a long drink, his Adam's apple bobbing, then set the glass down with a trembling hand.

Roger crossed his arms, his gaze unrelenting. "We already know the basics about Deep Surge," he said. "But we need the real story. What aren't you telling us?"

Lawson let out a shuddering breath, his shoulders slumping. "Deep Surge," he began, his voice hollow. "It was more than just a high-risk drilling project. We were venturing into one of the most dangerous formations beneath the Permian Basin. It was an area that geologists had warned us about for years, a volatile pressure trap that had remained untouched for good reason."

He rubbed his temples, his hands shaking. "The potential reserves were massive," he continued. "Billions of dollars in oil. We were under enormous pressure from Marathon Oil's board and shareholders to stay competitive. Other companies were making breakthroughs, and we couldn't afford to fall behind. So we authorized Deep Surge, despite every red flag."

Liz leaned forward, her voice tight with anger. "What kind of red flags?"

Lawson's eyes flickered with guilt. "The pressure in that formation was unlike anything anyone had ever encountered," he said. "The risk of a blowout was astronomical. Our engineers begged us to reconsider, to delay until we could develop safer methods. But we ignored them. We were blinded by the promise of wealth, by the fear of losing our place at the top. We pushed forward, and… the inevitable happened."

He swallowed hard. "When the explosion occurred, it was like a bomb had gone off beneath the earth. The shockwave was so powerful it caused tremors that could be felt miles away. The drilling rig was obliterated in seconds, and every worker on site was either killed instantly or horribly injured. The flames burned for days, and the environmental damage was catastrophic."

Roger's expression darkened. "And the cover-up?" he prompted.

Lawson rubbed his face with trembling hands. "We had to act fast," he said. "The board pulled every string they could. We paid off families, manipulated the media, and had environmental impact reports falsified. We even bribed government inspectors to certify that the area was safe. But it wasn't. The ground around the site is still contaminated, leaking toxic chemicals into the water supply. We just buried the evidence, hoping no one would notice."

His voice grew more frantic. "But it wasn't just about money. We ruined communities. People who lived near the site got sick, children were born with defects, and families were torn apart. We knew, and we did nothing. We silenced anyone who tried to speak out, made them disappear if they caused too much trouble."

Liz's eyes flashed with disgust. "So the killer isn't just avenging the workers," she said. "They're avenging everyone whose life was destroyed by your greed."

Lawson's face crumpled, and he buried his head in his hands. "I know," he whispered. "I know we deserve it. But I don't know who's doing this. We hurt so many people. It could be anyone. I had trouble even spending the money that I received from the payoff. That's why I don't live in a huge mansion like everyone else in this area."

Liz's expression softened slightly, though her eyes were still hard. "You're going to have to give us names," she said. "People you think might have had a reason to come after you. Anyone who was vocal about what happened, anyone you or the board silenced."

Lawson looked up, his eyes hollow and filled with a mix of fear and resignation. "There was a man," he said after a long pause. "Daniel Moore. He was one of the lead engineers. He tried to blow the whistle before the explosion. We… we made him disappear. And then there was Mary Caldwell. She lost her husband and her two sons in the blast. She kept protesting and always spoke out. We ruined her life. Last I heard, she was living in some rundown motel, completely broken. I… I wouldn't be surprised if she wanted us dead."

Roger exchanged a glance with Liz, their expressions grim. "We'll need their information," Roger said. "Addresses, phone numbers, anything you've got. And anyone else you can think of."

Lawson nodded, his hands trembling as he reached for a notebook on the coffee table. He flipped through the pages. His fingers shook as he scrawled down names and addresses.

Suddenly, a loud crash echoed from the front of the house, and everyone froze. The security guard's voice came through Lawson's old intercom system, panicked and breathless. "Sir! There's someone—"

The line went dead, and the house plunged into a tense, suffocating silence.

Roger drew his gun, his heart racing, and Liz did the same, adrenaline surging through her veins. The two of them moved in practiced synchrony, their footsteps silent on the worn hardwood floors. The house creaked and groaned around them, each sound amplified by the tension. The thin, frosted windows let in only the pale glow of the streetlights, casting long shadows that danced eerily across the walls.

As they approached the front of the house, the shattered remains of a side window came into view. Snowflakes swirled through the broken pane, glittering in the dim light. A cold wind howled through the opening, causing the curtains to billow like ghostly shrouds. The security guard who had been stationed outside lay crumpled on the floor, his flashlight still rolling in lazy circles. Blood pooled beneath him, spreading out over the wood and seeping into the cracks.

Liz knelt down, her gun still trained on the darkened hallway and checked the guard's pulse. She looked up at Roger, her face pale. "He's alive," she whispered, relief mingling with the horror of the moment. "But barely. The blow to the head must have been hard. I am calling for an ambulance now."

Roger nodded grimly, motioning for her to stay alert. Whoever had done this was still nearby, and the chill in the air felt more menacing than ever. His ears strained for any sound—footsteps, a rustle, the subtle shift of shadows.

And then he heard it. The unmistakable creak of a floorboard from somewhere deeper in the house.

Roger signaled to Liz, and they advanced cautiously, moving toward the source of the noise. They rounded the corner and entered the dimly lit kitchen. The space was cramped and cluttered, with dishes piled up in the sink and a half-empty pot of coffee sitting on the counter. The back door was ajar, swaying gently with the wind. Snowflakes had already begun to drift in, dusting the floor with a thin layer of white.

Roger's eyes narrowed. The killer was clever—using the distraction at the front to sneak in through the back. He crept toward the door, gun raised and gently pushed it open. The backyard was a winter wasteland, the snow covering every blade of dead grass and the barren mesquite trees casting jagged shadows in the moonlight. The chain-link fence at the property's edge rattled in the wind, but there was no sign of movement.

Liz stepped up beside him, her breath coming out in short, visible puffs. "They're toying with us," she muttered, her frustration evident. "Keeping us off balance."

Roger scanned the yard, his eyes searching for any sign of a disturbance in the snow. His gut told him that the killer was still nearby, watching, waiting for the perfect moment to strike. The silence felt like a coiled spring, ready to snap at any second.

Suddenly, a rustling sound came from the side of the house. Both of them spun, guns trained in that direction. Roger motioned for Liz to circle around to the right while he went left. Roger's pulse thundered in his ears as he rounded the corner, gun at the ready.

He stopped short, his breath catching in his throat. A lone figure stood at the far end of the yard, shrouded in darkness. The figure wore a black mask, the eyes obscured and emotionless, and their silhouette was tall and lean, almost spectral against the snow.

"Freeze!" Roger shouted, his voice cracking through the silence like a gunshot. The masked figure didn't move, didn't flinch. For a moment, time seemed to stand still, the world holding its breath.

And then the figure did move—suddenly and with purpose. They took a single step forward, and Roger's finger tightened on the trigger. But before he could react, the figure dropped something onto the snow. It was a small object, barely noticeable, but the sound it made when it hit the ground was unmistakable: the sharp, metallic clink of a grenade.

"Get down!" Roger bellowed, diving to the side and grabbing Liz as he pulled her with him. They hit the snow just as the grenade detonated with a deafening roar. The explosion sent a shockwave through the yard, a blinding flash of light, and a wave of heat that tore through the iced landscape. Shards of ice and debris flew in all directions, pelting them like shrapnel.

Roger's ears rang as he struggled to his feet. The snow around him was churned up, blackened by the explosion, and the chain-link fence had been blown apart. Liz groaned beside him, clutching her arm where a piece of debris had cut through her jacket. Blood stained the snow, vivid and jarring against the white.

The masked figure was gone, vanished into the chaos. The yard was a wasteland of smoke and broken fencing, and the killer had left behind nothing but destruction and another unanswered question.

Roger helped Liz to her feet, his heart hammering. "Are you okay?" he asked, his voice rough.

Liz winced, but she nodded. "I'll live," she said, though her face was pale, and she was clearly in pain. "But we need to get back inside. If Lawson is still alive, he's in more danger than ever."

They stumbled back toward the house, adrenaline fueling their movements. The front door was still open, and Roger's mind raced as he considered the killer's tactics. They had been outplayed—distracted and nearly killed. But he refused to let the killer win, to let this nightmare continue without a fight.

Bursting into the living room, they found Henry Lawson exactly where they had left him, trembling in his recliner, his eyes wide with terror. He had heard everything, and the shock had aged him another decade in just a few short minutes.

Roger holstered his gun and grabbed Lawson by the arm, yanking him to his feet. "We're not safe here," he said, his voice hard and urgent. "We need to move you somewhere secure—now."

Lawson nodded mutely, too terrified to argue. Liz clutched her injured arm but remained alert, her eyes scanning the room for any other threats.

"We're being hunted," she whispered, more to herself than anyone else. "And this killer knows exactly how to push us to our limits."

Roger didn't respond. He couldn't afford to waste another second. The game had changed, and the stakes had never been higher.

CHAPTER TWENTY EIGHT

The snow had finally stopped in Midland. The wind, however, continued to whip through the streets, cutting through every layer of clothing and making the cold feel even more brutal. It howled around corners, turning every breath into a ghostly mist. The eerie quiet of the city was occasionally broken by the distant sound of emergency sirens, echoing through the otherwise empty streets.

Roger and Liz moved with urgency, adrenaline masking the tiredness and pain that gripped their bodies. They loaded Henry Lawson into the back of the cruiser and slammed the doors shut as emergency medical personnel worked nearby to stabilize the injured security guard. The flashing red and blue lights cast shadows that seemed to flicker and dance. The stillness of the night contrasted sharply with the chaotic scene, with earlier events pressing down on them.

Roger turned to Liz, concern etched deeply in his features. Liz clutched her injured arm, the fabric of her jacket stiff with dried and fresh blood. Pain lined her face, but her grip on her gun was firm nonetheless.

"I'm fine," she insisted, seeing Roger's worried gaze. Her voice was tight but strong. "We have to move now."

Roger nodded, his voice low and resolute. "We'll get you medical attention as soon as we're safe," he said. "But stay sharp."

Liz gave a curt nod, swallowing her discomfort. "I'm ready."

Roger climbed into the driver's seat and Liz slid into the passenger side, her gun resting in her lap, her senses on high alert. Henry Lawson sat hunched over in the backseat, his hands trembling and his face pale and haunted.

Roger started the engine, and the cruiser roared to life, its tires slipping momentarily before gaining traction on the ice-packed road. The wind battered the vehicle, making it shudder as he pulled away from the curb. His eyes flicked constantly between the road and the mirrors, every nerve on edge.

"Where… where are you taking me?" Lawson stammered.

"The sheriff's office," Roger replied, his eyes never leaving the road. "It's the safest place right now."

Lawson let out a hollow, humorless laugh. "Safe?" he echoed, his voice tinged with hysteria. "You think anywhere is safe from someone like that?"

Roger clenched his jaw. "We'll make it safe," he said firmly, though doubt gnawed at the edges of his mind. The killer had always been one step ahead, a phantom haunting their every move.

The cruiser sped through Midland's dark, silent streets, passing shuttered storefronts and darkened homes. The city felt unnatural, as though it were holding its breath, waiting for the next act of violence. Roger's gut twisted, every nerve on high alert. Something was coming; he could feel it.

Then he saw it—a dark SUV with tinted windows speeding toward them, headlights blazing.

"We've got company," Roger said, his voice tight with tension.

Liz turned, wincing at the pain in her arm, and her heart sank at the sight of the SUV. Its engine roared as it closed the distance, headlights glaring. "They're not going to let us go," she said, her voice steady but grim.

Roger pressed harder on the accelerator, the cruiser struggling for speed on the icy road. The SUV stayed right on their tail, relentless. The wind screamed around them, and the slick streets made every maneuver dangerous.

"They're going to ram us," Liz warned, her grip tightening on her gun.

Roger took a sharp right, the cruiser skidding as it rounded the corner. The SUV followed, its tires screeching on the ice. Roger's pulse pounded, and he knew they couldn't keep running.

"They're not giving up," he muttered. "We have to make a stand."

He slammed on the brakes, and the cruiser skidded to a stop. The SUV overshot them, losing control and crashing into a streetlight. The sound of metal crumpling filled the air, and steam hissed from the damaged vehicle.

Roger and Liz jumped out of the cruiser, guns drawn. The cold wind cut into them, and their breaths fogged in the icy air. Roger's shoulder throbbed with pain, but he forced himself to focus as the driver's side door of the SUV creaked open.

A single figure stepped out, dressed in black, a balaclava obscuring their face. The assailant moved with eerie calm, raising a handgun. Roger barely had time to react before the gun fired.

The bullet struck his shoulder, a burst of searing pain that sent him to his knees. His gun slipped from his grasp, and he crumpled onto the snow. The world tilted, his vision blurring, and the cold seeped into his bones. Blood soaked through his shirt, hot against the freezing air.

"Roger!" Liz screamed, her voice breaking with fear and fury.

Roger's world dimmed, but he could still see Liz, her gun raised. The assailant turned their weapon on her, and Liz dove behind a parked car, bullets shattering windows and spraying glass over the snow. Her chest heaved, and the pain in her side flared where a bullet had grazed her, but she kept moving.

She steadied her breathing, focusing through the pain. "Come on," she whispered, waiting for her chance.

The assailant stepped forward, gun trained on her. Liz took a deep breath and, in one swift motion, popped up and fired. Her shots hit the attacker's vest, making them stumble but not fall.

"Damn it," she muttered, realizing they were armored.

The assailant fired again, and Liz felt the impact as a bullet struck her vest, knocking the wind out of her. Another bullet grazed her side, and she gasped, clutching the wound. But she refused to go down. Summoning the last of her strength, she lunged from cover, firing two more shots.

One bullet struck the assailant's neck, and the second found a gap above the vest. The attacker crumpled to the ground, their gun slipping from their hand.

Liz kept her gun trained on the motionless figure, her breath coming in ragged gasps. When she was sure the threat was over, she dropped to her knees beside Roger, her hands trembling.

"Roger," she whispered, her voice cracking. "Come on. You're okay. You're going to be okay."

Roger's eyes fluttered open, and a weak, pained smile crossed his lips. "Not… leaving," he whispered.

The sound of sirens filled the air, and backup arrived, officers flooding the scene and EMTs rushing to help. Liz slumped onto the snow, pain crashing over her.

The coroner, Marla Decker, arrived not long after, bundled against the cold but moving with practiced efficiency. She approached Liz, her face pale but composed. "Jesus, Liz," Marla said, taking in the scene. "Are you okay?"

Liz gave a weary nod. "I'm okay," she replied, her voice hoarse. "But… check on Roger."

The EMTs were already working on him, and Marla glanced over before kneeling beside the assailant's body. With a steady hand, she pulled off the balaclava, revealing the face beneath. Her eyes widened in surprise.

"It's Eli Chambers," she said, her voice filled with disbelief. "He's one of the local troublemakers. Ran with some bad crowds but… murder? I wouldn't have pegged him for this."

Liz leaned back. "Well, we got him," she said, her voice heavy with finality. "It's over."

Henry Lawson stumbled out of the cruiser, his body shaking. He looked from the dead assailant to Liz and Roger, his voice trembling. "It's… it's over," he whispered, more to convince himself than anyone else. "Thank God, it's over."

Liz looked around at the scene—the flashing lights, the officers standing down, the dead assailant. The danger felt like it had passed, the nightmare finally ending. And for the first time in days, she allowed herself to believe it.

CHAPTER TWENTY NINE

The hospital room was quiet, save for the rhythmic beeping of Roger's heart monitor. Pale morning light filtered through the thin curtains, casting soft, golden stripes across the room. The sterile scent of antiseptic clung to the air, a harsh reminder of everything they'd endured. Roger lay in bed, his shoulder heavily bandaged. The painkillers dulled the ache but couldn't fully silence the storm of thoughts racing through his mind.

Liz sat in a chair beside him, her arm in a sling, and a thick bandage wrapped around her side where a bullet had grazed her. Dark bruises marred her skin, deep and angry, a physical manifestation of the hell they'd been through. Her face was pale, but her eyes burned with worry and confusion. Her fingers absentmindedly traced the edges of her sling, a nervous gesture that betrayed the turmoil beneath her calm exterior.

"I don't get it," Liz said, breaking the heavy silence. Her voice was hoarse, and she winced as she adjusted herself in the uncomfortable chair. The ache in her muscles flared, but she ignored it. "Eli Chambers… it doesn't add up."

Roger turned his head slightly, managing a faint, tired smile. Even with the painkillers, he felt every pull and throb of his injury. "We got him, didn't we?" he replied, though his voice was rough and weary. "Isn't that what matters?"

Liz frowned, the crease between her eyebrows deepening. "Maybe. But Eli?" She shook her head, the frustration evident in her tense posture. "The guy was a

"

troublemaker, sure. Petty theft, vandalism… but murder? And not just murder, but this whole elaborate revenge scheme? It doesn't make sense."

Roger sighed, the movement making his injured shoulder scream in protest. He gritted his teeth, trying to push the pain aside. "Maybe he was more dangerous than we knew," he suggested, though he sounded unconvinced. "People can snap."

Liz wasn't buying it. "Snapping?" she echoed, her voice sharpening. "Snapping doesn't explain the level of planning this took. The precision, the way the bodies were staged… This wasn't random. Whoever did this had a purpose, a vendetta. And Eli… he doesn't fit."

Roger's smile faded, and he closed his eyes for a moment, the overtiredness pressing down on him like a heavy weight. "I know," he admitted softly. "I know it doesn't fit. But we're both lucky to be here, so maybe we should just take the win."

Liz leaned forward, her good hand gripping the edge of her chair. The intensity in her gaze never wavered. "Taking the win is one thing," she said, her voice low but fierce. "But ignoring what doesn't make sense? That's not how we do this. We owe it to the victims—and to ourselves—to get it right."

Roger opened his eyes and looked at her. Despite the bruises and bandages, the fire in Liz's eyes was unextinguished. It was that relentless will that made her one of the best damn deputies he'd ever worked with. And more than that, she was a friend he trusted with his life. He could see the weight of the investigation etched into her face, the lines of fatigue framing her eyes, and he knew she wouldn't rest until they found the truth.

"I don't know what to think anymore," he said, his voice tinged with defeat. "We've been chasing shadows, and now we're here, barely holding it together, and we still don't have all the answers."

Before Liz could respond, there was a soft knock at the door. It opened, and Kathy, Roger's ex-wife, stepped inside. Her eyes were wide with concern, and her hair was pulled back in a loose ponytail. She wore a heavy coat, and the cold of the winter morning still clung to her, visible in the pink of her cheeks. She hesitated at the threshold, her eyes taking in the scene, the bruises, the bandages, the toll the past few days had taken on the people she still deeply cared about.

"Roger," Kathy breathed, her voice breaking. She rushed to his side, her hands trembling as she reached for him. "Oh my God, are you okay?"

Roger's face softened, and he reached out to take her hand. "Hey, Kathy," he said, his voice gentler. "I'm alive. It looks worse than it is."

Kathy's eyes filled with tears, and she pressed a hand to her mouth. "You scared me half to death," she whispered, her voice cracking. "When I heard what happened... I thought..." She couldn't finish the sentence, her fear too raw. She took a shaky breath, her other hand brushing a strand of hair away from her face.

Roger squeezed her hand, guilt gnawing at him. "I'm sorry," he said quietly. "I never wanted to drag you into this."

Kathy shook her head, tears slipping down her cheeks. "You didn't drag me into anything," she said. "I still care about you, Roger. Even if we're not together anymore." Liz watched the exchange, her expression softened. Despite the enervation and pain, she felt a pang of respect for the quiet strength Kathy had. Even after everything she and Roger had been through, Kathy's love for him was undeniable. Liz couldn't help but admire how Kathy, despite everything, still showed up when Roger needed her most.

The door opened again, and Jason, Liz's boyfriend, entered. His gaze found Liz immediately, and he crossed the room in quick strides.

"Liz," Jason said, his voice tight with worry. He knelt in front of her, his hands gently cupping her face. "Are you okay?" His eyes scanned her, taking in every bruise, every bandage, the tiredness etched into her features.

Liz managed a small smile, her heart aching at the concern in his eyes. "I'm okay," she said, though the exhaustion and pain were evident in her voice. "Just... a little worse for wear."

Jason's jaw clenched, and he pulled her into a careful embrace, mindful of her injuries. "I've been worried sick," he murmured. "When I heard you were in the hospital..." His voice broke slightly, and he took a deep breath, holding her close.

"I'm here," Liz whispered, resting her head against his shoulder. The comfort of his presence was something she desperately needed, a small reprieve from the chaos. She closed her eyes, letting herself relax, if only for a moment, in the safety of his arms.

Kathy glanced over at Liz and Jason, a sad but knowing smile tugging at her lips. "Looks like we're both here for the people we care about," she said softly.

Liz pulled back slightly, meeting Kathy's eyes. "I guess we are," she replied, her voice gentler than usual. Despite the pain and fatigue, there was a moment of shared understanding between them. It was a rare moment of connection, forged through the shared fear of losing someone they loved.

The quiet moment shattered when the door opened once more. Marla Decker, the county coroner, walked in, looking exhausted but resolute. Dark circles under her eyes betrayed sleepless nights, but her gaze was sharp. Walking just behind her was Eli Rivera, the young man who had survived a brutal attack days earlier. His arm was still in a sling, and he looked sleep-deprived.

Jason and Kathy exchanged glances, but neither reacted protectively. They were here to support, and the weight of the room's tension was already suffocating enough.

Marla cleared her throat and set a thick folder on the rolling tray table. "Sorry to interrupt," she said, her voice steady. "But I thought you'd want to know what we've found."

Eli Rivera stepped forward, his eyes filled with lingering trauma but also a glimmer of courage. "I needed to be here," he said, his voice soft but steady. "I have to know."

Liz straightened in her chair, biting back the pain. "What did you find?" she asked, her voice tight.

Marla opened the folder, revealing crime scene photos, evidence reports, and documents detailing Eli Chambers' background. "We've dug into Eli Chambers' history," she began. "And here's what we have: Chambers was a well-known troublemaker. Vandalism, petty theft, breaking and entering… a list of minor offenses a mile long. But—and this is important—nothing in his past ever hinted at violence. No assault charges, no outbursts, nothing to suggest he was capable of the kind of calculated brutality we saw in these murders."

Roger's eyes narrowed. "Then why does everything point to him?" he asked, his frustration clear.

Marla sighed, rubbing her temples. "That's the thing. Every piece of physical evidence points to him. His fingerprints were on the murder weapon, we found DNA linking him to the scenes, and his SUV was identified as the vehicle involved. The evidence is overwhelming, almost too perfect."

Liz leaned forward, her jaw tight. "Too perfect," she repeated. "Like someone wanted it that way."

Eli Rivera spoke up, his voice trembling. "I knew Eli Chambers," he said. "We grew up in the same neighborhood. Sure, he was reckless, but he wasn't… a killer. When I was attacked, it felt like someone had been planning it for a long time. Watching me.”

Jason placed a supportive hand on Liz’s shoulder, his concern deepening. “If everything points to Chambers, but he doesn’t fit the profile…” he trailed off, the implication hanging heavy in the air.

Marla’s expression darkened. “We’ve got another problem,” she said. “The District Attorney and the Mayor are putting immense pressure on us to close this case. They’re willing to accept Eli Chambers as the sole culprit. They want a neat, tidy resolution.”

Kathy’s eyes widened in disbelief. “Even if it’s the wrong one?” she asked, her voice thick with emotion.

Jason’s face hardened. “Politics,” he muttered. “They’d rather have a convenient scapegoat than dig deeper for the truth.”

Liz clenched her fists, the frustration boiling over. “So we have a dead suspect, overwhelming evidence, and political pressure to make it stick. But our instincts tell us it’s wrong.” Her voice broke. “This isn’t justice.”

Roger rubbed his temples, feeling the exhaustion settling deeper into his bones. “If we push back, we risk going up against the DA and the Mayor. But if we let this go…”

Marla nodded, her worry evident. “Whoever the real mastermind is, they’re out there. And they’re dangerous.”

Liz’s gaze met Eli Rivera’s, a spark of determination igniting. “We owe it to the victims—and to Eli Chambers, if he really was just a pawn—to find the truth,” she declared.

Kathy squeezed Roger's hand, her eyes shimmering with tears. "Please, Roger," she whispered. "Be careful. We can't lose you."

Roger looked at her. "I'll be careful," he promised.

Liz leaned forward, her voice filled with quiet resolve. "We need to talk to the DA and the Mayor," she said. "Try to buy some time. Convince them to hold off on officially closing the case."

Roger nodded, though the thought of confronting them made his head pound even more. "We'll have to make them see reason," he said. "Or at least enough doubt to get an extension."

Kathy's worry deepened, but she nodded, understanding the necessity. "Just... be careful," she repeated, her voice soft but firm.

Outside, the world looked deceptively peaceful, the snow glistening under the morning sun. But inside the hospital, shadows of doubt and fear loomed, the sense of unfinished business suffocating them all. And now, with the added political pressure, the stakes had never been higher.

CHAPTER THIRTY

Two weeks had passed since the chaos and terror that had gripped Midland seemed to come to an end. The city was trying to move forward, to rebuild a sense of normalcy. People went back to their routines, but the lingering tension could be felt in the tight smiles of shopkeepers and the wary glances exchanged by neighbors.

Roger stood in front of the large, red-brick façade of Midland's City Hall. The crisp, cold air stung his face, and he shivered slightly, though he couldn't tell if it was from the wind or the feeling in his gut that something was off. His dress uniform was freshly pressed, every button and badge polished to a mirror shine. The sling that cradled his injured arm was a stark reminder of the brutality he had survived. Yet, he stood tall, resolute, though every movement still sent twinges of pain radiating through his body. His eyes scanned the crowd, the unease he felt deep within making him hyper-aware of every movement and sound.

Beside him stood Liz, similarly dressed in her formal uniform. Her left arm was also in a sling, her side still aching from the bullet that had grazed her. The bruises on her body had turned from deep purples to ugly greens and yellows, and she had learned to mask her pain with a practiced smile. Her hair was pulled back in a sleek bun, and her eyes, though shadowed with lack of energy, were steady and alert.

Rows of folding chairs had been arranged in front of the stage, where citizens of Midland sat bundled in heavy coats and scarves. Children clutched their parents' hands, wide-eyed and curious. Elderly men and women, some of whom had lived in Midland their whole lives, watched with tear-filled eyes, grateful to see their community finally reclaim some semblance of peace. The tension that had gripped the town for weeks was still present, but it was softened by the sight of families together, by the sense of hope that maybe the worst was behind them.

The ceremony was a grand affair. Red, white, and blue bunting draped the edges of the stage, and the American flag fluttered in the icy breeze. A brass band stood off to the side, their instruments gleaming under the pale winter sun, ready to play a triumphant tune. Volunteers had set up tables of hot chocolate and coffee, steam rising in thin wisps from paper cups. The atmosphere was one of cautious celebration, an attempt to lift the heavy cloud that had hung over Midland for too long. Conversations were hushed, but laughter occasionally broke through.

The Mayor of Midland, a tall, broad-shouldered man with a commanding presence and a neatly trimmed silver mustache, stepped up to the podium. Beside him stood the District Attorney, a stocky man with thinning hair and a serious expression. Both men had been instrumental in shaping the narrative surrounding the case, eager to reassure the public that the nightmare was over. They had worked tirelessly to maintain control, to restore a sense of security, and now they stood before the crowd as the faces of hope and leadership.

The Mayor adjusted the microphone and offered the crowd a warm smile. "Ladies and gentlemen," he began, his deep voice carrying across the plaza, "we are gathered here today to honor two of Midland's finest, Sheriff Roger Hartley and Deputy Liz Trujillo. Their courage, resilience, and unwavering dedication brought an end to one of the darkest chapters in our city's history."

The crowd erupted into applause. It was loud and heartfelt, a wave of gratitude that washed over Roger and Liz. Roger stood still, the weight of the moment pressing down on him. He searched the sea of faces, taking in the smiles and the expressions of relief. And yet, somewhere deep in his chest, a familiar unease simmered. He could feel Kathy's eyes on him, her presence a warm, steadying force. He glanced briefly in her direction, catching her small, encouraging smile, and it helped him hold his ground.

Liz stood rigid beside him, the applause a dull roar in her ears. She leaned slightly toward Roger, her voice a whisper. "This feels… wrong," she murmured, her lips barely moving. The smile she wore was practiced and forced. Her eyes darted across the crowd, searching for any sign of a threat, something out of place, but all she saw were grateful faces.

Roger's jaw tightened, but he kept his expression neutral. "I know," he whispered back. "But we've done what we could. Maybe… maybe it really is over."

Liz's eyes flickered with doubt, but she nodded, forcing herself to consider the possibility. The past two weeks had been eerily quiet. No new leads, no new bodies, no cryptic threats. Perhaps Eli Chambers really had been the killer, and maybe they had been too close to the case to see it clearly.

Maybe the terror really was over. But the quiet felt unnatural, like the calm before a storm, and Liz couldn't shake the feeling that something was still lurking in the shadows.

The Mayor continued, his voice strong and confident, each word a reassurance to the anxious crowd. "Sheriff Hartley and Deputy Trujillo risked their lives to bring a dangerous murderer to justice, and today, we honor them not only for their bravery but for their selfless commitment to our community. Midland owes them a debt of gratitude."

The applause swelled again, louder this time, echoing off the brick buildings that lined the streets. Roger scanned the crowd again, feeling as though he was looking for something he couldn't name. The faces blurred together, but there was no sign of anything out of place. Only grateful citizens, their expressions a mix of relief and pride.

The Mayor turned toward Roger and Liz, presenting them with framed awards, the gold lettering catching the sunlight. Roger stepped forward, accepting his award with a nod, the unease in his chest never quite settling. Liz did the same, her smile unwavering even as her mind raced. She could feel the weight of the frame in her good hand, the metal cold against her skin, a tangible reminder of everything they had endured.

As the Mayor handed over the awards, he leaned in and lowered his voice, just enough for Roger and Liz to hear. "You both did this city proud," he said, his tone sincere but carrying an undercurrent of finality. "Let's hope we can finally put all of this behind us."

Roger met the Mayor's gaze, his expression unreadable. "Thank you, sir," he replied, the words leaving a bitter taste in his mouth. He wanted to believe it was over, but a part of him knew better.

The Mayor straightened, turning back to the crowd. "Please join me in giving another round of applause to our heroes," he called out, and the crowd responded with fervor, the sound rolling over the plaza like a wave.

As the ceremony wrapped up, people began to approach Roger and Liz, offering handshakes, hugs, and words of gratitude. Jason made his way through the crowd, his face breaking into a proud grin as he reached Liz.

"You did it," Jason said, his voice warm and full of admiration. He looked at her as if she were the most remarkable person in the world. "You both did. You deserve this."

Liz looked up at him, her eyes softening. She felt the tight knot of tension in her chest loosen, if only a little. "Thanks, Jason," she said, her voice cracking slightly. "I don't know what I'd do without you."

He pulled her into a careful embrace, his touch gentle but reassuring. "I'm just glad you're okay," he murmured, his lips brushing against her temple. "I was so scared…"

Liz closed her eyes, allowing herself to lean into his warmth. "Me too," she whispered. "But we made it through." She held onto him for a moment longer, drawing strength from his presence, the noise of the crowd fading into the background.

Meanwhile, Kathy approached Roger, her eyes glistening with pride and something else—something deeper. "You were amazing up there," she said, her voice thick with emotion. "I'm so proud of you."

Roger's throat tightened, and he swallowed hard, feeling the guilt and love collide in his chest. "I couldn't have done it without you," he said quietly. "Even now… I don't think I could do any of this without knowing you're here."

Kathy's smile wavered, but she squeezed his hand, grounding him. "I'm not going anywhere," she promised. Her words felt like a lifeline, and he clung to them, the warmth of her touch cutting through the cold that had settled in his bones.

Just then, the two remaining board members of the Marathon Oil Company stepped forward, each of them wearing somber expressions. Henry Lawson and Gerald Simmons stood out in the crowd with their tailored coats and expensive leather gloves.

Henry Lawson, a man with salt-and-pepper hair and normally a stern demeanor, surprised Roger and Liz by stepping forward with genuine emotion in his eyes. "I owe you both my life," he said, his tone raw. "You saved me. When I think about what could have happened…" He trailed off, visibly shaken. "I can't thank you enough."

Liz's hardened expression softened as she looked at Lawson. She hadn't expected such vulnerability from him, and it caught her off guard. "We're glad you're safe," she replied.

Gerald Simmons, the youngest and most polished of the two, stepped forward, a faint but practiced smile on his lips. "Thank you for your service," he said smoothly. "Your bravery has inspired us all." His eyes, however, didn't quite match his words, and there was something calculating in the way he regarded them.

Roger and Liz exchanged a look, and Roger's grip on his award tightened. "Thank you," Roger said, his voice even. "But we were just doing our job."

Henry Lawson took a deep breath, his hands trembling slightly before he clasped them together. "You did more than that," he insisted, his voice cracking. "You gave me a second chance to be here with my family. That means everything to me."

Simmons placed a hand on Lawson's shoulder, nodding in agreement. "It's hard to believe it's really over," he murmured, almost as if speaking to himself. "After all these years…"

Simmons's smile faltered for a moment, and he cleared his throat. "Let's hope it stays that way," he said, his voice a bit too cheerful. "For all our sakes."

Roger felt the prickle of unease return, and he forced himself to remain calm. "We'll do whatever it takes to keep this town safe," he said. The words were a promise, though he couldn't shake the feeling that the board members knew more than they were letting on.

As the two men walked away, Roger and Liz exchanged another knowing look. The ceremony might have been a celebration, but the shadows of the past were still very much alive. Liz's eyes followed Simmons and Lawson, her instincts telling her that this wasn't over, that something still lingered just beyond their grasp.

A cold wind swept through the plaza, rustling the American flag. He pulled his coat tighter, the fear of unfinished business pressing down on him. Maybe the city could rest easy, but he and Liz knew better. There were still too many unanswered questions, too many loose threads. And until those threads were tied, neither of them could truly move on.

The brass band began to play a hopeful melody that filled the plaza, but to Roger and Liz, it sounded almost hollow. They shared a look of silent understanding—whatever lay ahead, they would face it together. The applause, the accolades, the speeches—it all felt like a curtain being drawn over a play that had yet to reach its final act. And in their hearts, they knew the story wasn't over yet.

CHAPTER THIRTY ONE

The celebration had wound down, the applause fading into the cold evening air, and the streets of Midland had begun to empty. The warmth of the sun had long since vanished, leaving a chill that made people walk a little faster and hug their coats tighter. But for Roger, Kathy, Liz, and Jason, the night was far from over.

Roger drove them in his old truck, the engine rumbling as they made their way through the familiar streets of Midland. The four of them had decided to continue the evening together, heading to a local diner they all knew well. It was a place that hadn't changed in decades, with red vinyl booths, a jukebox that still played classic country songs, and the smell of fried food that clung to the air like a comforting memory.

They settled into one of the corner booths. Roger slid in beside Kathy, his hand brushing hers as they both removed their coats. Across from them, Liz leaned into Jason, resting her head on his shoulder while he wrapped his arm protectively around her. The jukebox hummed in the background, playing an old Willie Nelson tune, and the low murmur of conversation from other patrons filled the space.

The waitress, an older woman named Shannon who had worked at the diner for as long as any of them could remember, came over with a friendly smile. "Well, if it isn't our hometown heroes," she said, her voice warm with admiration. "I don't know how y'all do it, but we're sure grateful you do. What can I get you folks tonight?"

Roger smiled, a tired but genuine expression. "We'll take a round of coffees to start," he said. "And four orders of your famous chicken-fried steaks, if you've still got some back there."

Shannon laughed. "You bet we do," she said, jotting down the order. "Coming right up." She gave them another warm smile before heading back to the kitchen, her voice calling out the order to the cook.

As she left, the four of them sat in comfortable silence for a moment, the sounds of the diner washing over them. The clatter of dishes, the sizzle of the grill, and the soft strains of country music made it feel almost surreal, sitting there as if nothing had changed, as if their lives hadn't been shattered and pieced back together in the past few weeks.

Liz was the first to speak. "Today was... a lot," she admitted, her eyes flicking to Roger. "Standing up there, pretending like everything's fine. Like we're not still carrying all of this with us."

Roger rubbed his free hand over his face. "Yeah," he said quietly. "I keep waiting for the other shoe to drop. For something to happen, or for something we missed to come back and bite us." His gaze drifted to the window, where he could see the reflection of their small group in the glass, framed by the night outside.

Kathy reached over and took Roger's hand, her touch gentle but grounding. "Maybe it's okay to breathe a little," she said softly. "Just for tonight. Maybe we need this."

Roger turned to look at her, taking in the sincerity in her eyes. "Maybe you're right," he replied. "But it's hard. Hard to let go of the fear that's been driving us." He squeezed her hand gently, feeling the warmth of her fingers against his.

Jason glanced at Liz, his thumb gently rubbing circles on her shoulder. "You both deserve a night to feel normal," he said. "To laugh, to relax, to remember what it feels like to be happy."

Liz's lips curved into a small smile. "You make it sound so easy," she teased lightly, though her voice trembled just a bit. She lifted her head to meet his eyes, the love and support she saw there made her chest tighten with emotion.

Jason leaned down and kissed her forehead. "It's not," he said. "But you've been through so much. We both have. It's okay to let yourself feel something good."

Liz closed her eyes for a moment, feeling the tension in her body begin to ease. "Thanks, Jason," she whispered. "For being here. For being you."

He pulled her closer, and they sat that way for a moment, drawing strength from each other. The simple contact, the warmth of his arm around her, was enough to remind her that they weren't alone—that they still had each other, no matter what.

Roger glanced between them and then back at Kathy. "I was thinking about what you said earlier," he murmured. "About trying to work things out. One day at a time."

"I meant it, Roger," she said. "I know we've been through a lot, and I know I've been hurt. But seeing you today, hearing you say you'd do whatever it takes to keep this town safe… It reminded me of the man I fell in love with. The man who would do anything to protect the people he cares about."

"I'm not perfect," he said, his voice rough with emotion. "I've made so many mistakes. But I never stopped loving you. Even when things got bad. Even when I didn't know how to fix it."

Kathy reached up and cupped his face. "One day at a time," she repeated. "We don't have to have all the answers tonight. But I want to try."

Roger covered her hand with his, feeling a spark of hope he hadn't felt in a long time. "I want to try, too," he said.

Shannon returned then, carrying a tray loaded with steaming plates of chicken-fried steak, mashed potatoes, and green beans. She set the plates down with a smile. "Enjoy, you four," she said. "And thank you again for everything you do."

"Thanks, Shannon," Liz said, her smile warm.

As they dug into their food, the conversation turned lighter. They shared stories from the past, laughing at memories that had been buried under the weight of everything that had happened. Roger told a story about one of his earliest cases, where he'd accidentally locked himself in the back of his own patrol car, and how he'd had to radio for help, much to the amusement of his fellow officers. Liz countered with a tale of the time she had to chase a goat down Main Street after it escaped from a petting zoo; the animal proved surprisingly fast and agile.

Kathy laughed until tears filled her eyes. Even Jason, who hadn't known the full extent of their stories, couldn't stop grinning. For a moment, it was as if the weight of the world had lifted, and they were just four people enjoying a meal together, the warmth of the diner wrapping around them like a comforting blanket.

When Roger and Kathy arrived back at his house, the night had settled into a deep, cold stillness. The house felt warm and welcoming. He couldn't help but feel a sense of peace as he locked the door behind them, the familiarity of his home grounding him in the moment.

Kathy slipped out of her shoes and wrapped her arms around herself. "It feels strange, being here again," she admitted. "Familiar but different."

Roger set his keys on the kitchen counter and looked at her. "I never thought I'd get the chance to have you back here," he said honestly. "But if we're going to try… I want to make this place feel like home for you again."

Kathy stepped closer, her eyes searching his. "You don't have to change anything," she said softly. "Just… be you. Be the Roger I know you are."

He reached out and pulled her into a gentle hug, his chin resting on the top of her head. "I'll do my best," he promised. "One day at a time." The warmth of her body against his was a comfort he hadn't realized he'd missed so deeply, and he held her close, not wanting to let go.

Jason and Liz made their way back to her small house, the wind howling against the windows as they stepped inside. Liz sighed as she sank onto the couch, her body aching from the day's events. Jason knelt in front of her, helping her take off her boots and rubbing her feet gently, his touch careful and soothing.

"You know," he said, "I never thought I'd be dating someone who could kick my ass while half-injured."

Liz laughed, the sound bubbling up from deep inside her, a release of all the tension she had been holding. "I don't think I could take you on right now," she admitted. "But give me a week."

Jason's smile softened, and he took her hands in his, his fingers brushing over her knuckles. "You're incredible," he said. "You're strong, brave, and you never give up. And I…" He hesitated, his cheeks flushing slightly as he looked down, gathering his courage.

Liz tilted her head, her heart thudding. "What is it?" she asked, her voice soft, her eyes searching his.

Jason took a deep breath and reached into his coat pocket, pulling out a small velvet box. Her eyes widened, and her breath caught in her throat as he opened the box to reveal a simple, elegant diamond ring. The light caught the stone, making it sparkle, and Liz felt her heart swell with emotion.

"Liz Trujillo," he began, his voice thick with emotion, "I have loved you from the moment I met you. You make me want to be a better man. You make every day brighter, even when the world feels dark. I don't want to wait any longer to tell you how much you mean to me. Will you marry me?"

Tears filled Liz's eyes, and she clapped a hand over her mouth, her whole body trembling. "Jason," she whispered, her voice breaking. "Yes. Yes, I'll marry you."

Jason slipped the ring onto her finger, his own hands shaking with excitement and relief. He pulled her into a careful embrace, mindful of her injuries, and kissed her deeply. Liz wrapped her arms around his neck. The kiss was full of love and promise, a moment that seemed to erase all the pain and fear they had endured.

They pulled back, both of them laughing through their tears, and Liz looked at the ring on her finger, her heart swelling with happiness. "I never thought I'd be this happy," she said, her voice trembling. "Not after everything."

Jason cupped her face in his hands, his eyes filled with love. "You deserve this," he said. "We deserve this."

They held each other for a long time, the world outside forgotten.

CHAPTER THIRTY TWO

The morning air was crisp, the kind of cold that bit at your skin. Roger stood on the front porch of his house, a steaming mug of black coffee in his hand. The warmth seeped into his fingers, but it did little to chase away the chill that had settled deep inside him.

He sipped his coffee slowly, savoring the quiet of the morning. Kathy was still asleep inside, and he had left her bundled up in blankets, her breathing soft and even. It had been a long time since he had felt her presence in his home, and he couldn't help but feel a sense of cautious hope. They had a lot of healing to do, but the thought of having her back, even just for moments like this, filled a void he hadn't realized was still so deep.

The street was mostly quiet, a few early risers out walking their dogs or scraping frost off their windshields. The normalcy of it all felt surreal. After weeks of terror and uncertainty, seeing his neighbors going about their routines was both comforting and disorienting. He watched Mrs. Palmer from two houses down struggle with her dog's leash as it tugged her toward a tree, her laughter carrying across the stillness of the morning. It was these small moments that reminded Roger what he was fighting for—the sense of community, the quiet routines, the safety of people just living their lives.

Roger's phone buzzed in his pocket, and he pulled it out, squinting at the screen. It was Liz. He couldn't help but smile, remembering the call he had received from her the night before.

It had been late, and Roger was sitting in his living room, nursing a glass of whiskey, when his phone had rung. He picked up immediately, concern flaring in his chest.

"Liz?" he had answered.

On the other end, there was a pause, and then Liz's voice came through, trembling but filled with something he hadn't heard in a long time: pure, unfiltered joy. "Roger, he proposed," she whispered, her voice cracking. "Jason proposed, and I said yes."

Roger had sat up straighter, the fatigue falling away. "What?" he'd said, a grin spreading across his face. "Liz, are you serious?"

She laughed, the sound clear and bright. "Yes, I'm serious. It just happened, and I couldn't wait to tell you."

Roger had felt an unexpected surge of emotion. After everything they had been through, hearing Liz happy, truly happy, was like a balm to his weary soul. "Liz, that's amazing," he said. "I'm so damn happy for you. You deserve this."

Her laughter softened, and he could almost picture her smiling through tears. "Thank you, Roger," she said. "For everything. I couldn't have made it through these past weeks without you."

"You're family, Liz," Roger had replied, his voice thick. "And Jason's a lucky man."

Now, standing on his porch, Roger replayed that conversation in his mind. It had given him hope, a reminder that even in the darkest of times, good things could still happen. He took another sip of his coffee. She deserved this joy after everything they had endured.

His phone buzzed again, pulling him out of his reverie. It was Liz, and this time her voice was tired but focused.

"Morning, Sheriff," she greeted, trying to inject some lightness into her voice.

"Morning, Deputy," Roger replied, smiling. "How's the newly engaged life treating you?"

Liz let out a small laugh. "It still feels surreal," she admitted. "I keep looking at the ring and wondering if it's all real. Jason hasn't stopped smiling."

Roger chuckled. "He's a good man," he said. "You both deserve this happiness."

"Thanks, Roger," Liz said, her voice softening. "But… that's not why I called."

The humor in Roger's eyes dimmed, replaced with a seriousness that came easily to him these days. "What's going on?" he asked, his voice low.

Liz hesitated, and Roger could almost picture her running a hand through her hair, her brow furrowed in thought. "I got a call from the station," she finally said. "There's been a break-in."

Roger's grip on his coffee mug tightened. "Where?"

"City records office," Liz replied. "They're still assessing the damage, but it looks like someone was after something specific. Nothing else was disturbed."

Roger's jaw tightened, his mind already racing. "I'll meet you there," he said.

The City Records Office was a squat, unassuming building tucked between a bank and a small insurance agency. It wasn't the kind of place that drew attention, and yet, as Roger and Liz approached the entrance, they could see the telltale signs of forced entry: splintered wood around the doorframe and shards of glass littering the sidewalk. A police cruiser was parked nearby, its lights flashing, and an officer stood guard, looking harried and cold.

Liz was already there, waiting for Roger. She had her hands stuffed in her pockets, but her eyes were sharp, scanning the scene with a practiced vigilance.

Roger pulled up beside her, nodding a greeting. "What do we know?" he asked, skipping the pleasantries.

Liz motioned toward the door. "Not much yet," she said. "The alarm was tripped around three this morning. The responding officer found the door kicked in, but whoever did it was long gone. They're going through the records now to see if anything's missing."

Roger frowned, stepping closer to the building. "It doesn't make sense," he muttered. "Why would someone break into the records office now? After everything that's happened?"

Liz's expression darkened. "I've been thinking the same thing," she admitted. "If the case was really over, if Eli Chambers was the killer, then why does it feel like we're still being pulled in?"

Roger didn't answer right away. He stepped inside and took a look around. The interior of the records office was a mess: filing cabinets had been pried open, papers were strewn across the floor, and a cold draft whispered through the shattered windows. It looked chaotic, but there was a sense of deliberateness to the mess, as if the intruder had known exactly what they were looking for.

"Whoever did this was in a hurry," Roger observed. "But they weren't just here to cause damage."

Liz followed him inside, her eyes narrowing as she took in the scene. "They had a purpose," she agreed. "But what?"

A clerk approached them, wringing his hands nervously. "Sheriff, Deputy," he said, his voice shaking. "I don't understand. Who would want to break in here?"

Roger studied the man, noting the way his hands trembled and the sweat beading on his forehead despite the cold. "That's what we're here to find out," he said calmly. "Have you noticed anything missing?"

The clerk swallowed hard, glancing at the wreckage around him. "I… I don't think so, but it's hard to tell. We're still doing an inventory. But there are some records from the 1990s and 2000s that were definitely pulled out and left in a pile. It's almost like whoever did this was focused on that era."

Roger and Liz exchanged a glance, the same thought occurring to both of them: the Marathon Oil explosion and the old cover-ups that had haunted their investigation.

"Do you have a list of those records?" Liz asked.

The clerk nodded, his hands still shaking. "We're working on it," he said. "But it'll take time."

Roger nodded, his mind working overtime. "Let us know as soon as you have anything," he said. "Anything at all."

The clerk nodded and scurried off.

"What are you thinking?" Liz asked, her voice low.

Roger's jaw clenched. "I'm thinking that someone out there doesn't want us to forget," he said. "And if they're willing to break into the records office, then this isn't over."

Before Liz could respond, a black SUV pulled up to the curb, and the Mayor stepped out. He was bundled in a long overcoat, his breath fogging in the cold, but his expression was more curious than upset. He walked toward them.

"Sheriff Hartley, Deputy Trujillo," the Mayor greeted. "I came as soon as I heard. What's going on here?"

Roger exchanged a quick glance with Liz before stepping forward. "We had a break-in at the City Records Office, Mayor," he explained. "The door was kicked in early this morning, and we're still assessing the damage."

The Mayor frowned, looking at the broken door and the officers inside cataloging the mess. "A break-in? That's unusual," he said. "But break-ins happen. Probably just some troublemakers looking for something to sell."

Liz shook her head, her eyes narrowing. "It's more complicated than that, sir," she interjected. "Whoever did this knew exactly what they were looking for. It wasn't random."

The Mayor's eyebrows lifted in mild surprise, but his demeanor remained calm. "What do you mean?"

Roger took a breath, choosing his words carefully. "The intruder seemed focused on records from the 1990s and 2000s," he said. "We've confirmed that some of the files related to that time period were disturbed, maybe even stolen."

The Mayor's brow furrowed, but his reaction was still measured. "Records from the 1990s and 2000s?" he repeated, sounding puzzled. "Why on earth would anyone be interested in those?"

Roger exchanged another look with Liz, both of them knowing this was the moment to tread carefully. "We think it might be connected to our case," Roger said, his voice steady. "The one involving Eli Chambers and the murders. There were a lot of secrets from that era, especially concerning the Marathon Oil explosion and potential cover-ups. Whoever broke in might be trying to protect those secrets."

The Mayor's face darkened, the calm slipping away to be replaced by a sharp glare. "Hold on," he said, his voice now tinged with irritation. "Are you suggesting this break-in is connected to that case? I thought we agreed that the case was closed. Eli Chambers was the killer. You made a public statement."

Roger straightened, his shoulders squaring. "We did make that statement," he acknowledged. "But that was before this break-in. Before someone decided to dig up old records. It doesn't feel like a coincidence."

The Mayor's jaw tightened, and a flash of anger sparked in his eyes. "With all due respect, Sheriff," he said, his voice growing cold, "the city needs closure. We've been through hell, and the people of Midland deserve to feel safe. We can't afford to stir up more panic."

Liz stepped forward, unable to hide her frustration. "We understand that, sir," she said, her voice firm but respectful. "But our job is to follow the evidence. If this break-in is connected to the murders, we can't just ignore it."

The Mayor took a step closer, his face flushed with anger now. "I don't care what you think," he snapped. "The city needs closure. We declared the case closed, and that's what the public believes. If you go around suggesting there's more to this, you'll only make things worse. The last thing we need is another wave of fear."

Roger's patience wore thin, and his voice dropped, dangerously calm. "You're asking us to ignore evidence," he said. "To turn a blind eye when someone might be trying to cover up the truth. We can't do that. Not if there's still a threat out there."

The Mayor's eyes flashed. "You think you're the only one who wants this town safe?" he retorted. "I'm trying to protect Midland from more chaos, from people losing their minds over some conspiracy theories. You have no concrete proof that this break-in is connected to anything."

Roger clenched his fists, the tension radiating from him. "We don't have concrete proof yet," he admitted. "But we can't afford to wait until we do. If there's even a chance that someone's still out there, planning God knows what, we have to act."

The Mayor's face was a mask of fury now. "You're playing with fire, Sheriff," he said through gritted teeth. "You think you can run this town without consequences? If you keep pushing this, don't expect any support from my office. You'll be on your own."

Liz bristled, her jaw set. "Our duty is to the people," she said, her voice steady despite the anger simmering beneath the surface. "Not to politics."

The Mayor took a deep breath. "Fine," he spat. "Do what you want. But mark my words: if this blows up in your face, it's on you."

With that, he turned on his heel, storming back to his SUV and slamming the door. The vehicle roared to life, and the Mayor drove off, leaving a cloud of exhaust in his wake.

Roger let out a breath he hadn't realized he was holding, the anger still coursing through him. "That went well," he muttered sarcastically.

Liz crossed her arms, her face flushed with frustration. "I hate politics," she said. "But he's wrong, and we know it. We can't stop now."

"No, we can't," he agreed. "And we won't."

Roger glanced at the records office one last time, his eyes narrowing with determination. "We need to dig deeper," he said, his voice barely audible over the wind. "If there are still secrets out there that someone's willing to protect this desperately, then we need to find out what they are."

Liz nodded, and they turned together, walking toward the unknowns that awaited them. As they moved, Roger couldn't shake the feeling that whatever lay ahead was going to test them even further. But as long as Liz was by his side, he knew they'd face it head-on—no matter the cost.

CHAPTER THIRTY THREE

The tension from the confrontation with the Mayor clung to Roger and Liz as they drove back to the sheriff's office. The drive was silent, save for the occasional sigh of frustration or the hum of the engine.

Roger's mind was racing, each thought darker and more urgent than the last. He had faced pressure from politicians before, but there was something about the Mayor's reaction that left a sour taste in his mouth. The insistence on keeping the case closed felt less like a desire for peace and more like a cover-up.

"Do you think he knows something?" Liz finally broke the silence, her voice steady but tense.

Roger didn't take his eyes off the road. "I don't know," he said, his voice low. "But he's hiding something, or at the very least, he's terrified of what we might find. That much is clear."

"It's hard to believe this all started with Eli Chambers," she murmured. "If he wasn't the mastermind, if he was just a piece of the puzzle... then who's pulling the strings?"

"That's what we need to figure out before anyone else gets hurt," he said grimly.

They pulled into the parking lot of the sheriff's office, the building looming ahead, sturdy and familiar but now feeling more vulnerable than ever. The office was busy, a low hum of activity buzzing through the air. Roger and Liz made their way to their desks, shedding their coats and preparing for what would undoubtedly be a long day.

Deputy Garcia, a young officer, approached them. He looked slightly nervous, shifting from foot to foot. "Sheriff, Deputy," he said, nodding. "We've got the preliminary list from the records office."

Roger motioned for Garcia to hand it over. The deputy gave him a thin folder, the pages inside filled with hastily scribbled notes. Roger flipped through the documents, his eyes scanning the contents. Liz leaned over his shoulder, her expression growing more serious with each line they read.

"It's all related to the Marathon Oil explosion," Liz said. "Safety reports, internal memos, lists of board members… even some early investigation notes from the police at the time."

"Whoever did this was looking for something to protect or something to exploit," Roger said. "These aren't just random records. They're pieces of a story someone doesn't want us to put together."

Liz frowned, her mind racing. "We need to talk to Henry Lawson again," she said. "He was deeply involved in everything back then. If anyone knows what those records contain, it's him."

"Call him," he instructed. "See if he's willing to come in and talk. If not, we'll pay him a visit."

Liz nodded, heading off to make the call. Roger sat down at his desk, staring at the pile of papers and evidence they had amassed over the past few weeks.

His phone buzzed, and he glanced at the screen. It was Kathy. A small smile pulled at his lips, and he picked up. "Hey," he said, his voice softening.

"Hey," Kathy replied, her voice warm but concerned. "How are you holding up?"

Roger leaned back in his chair, closing his eyes for a moment. "It's been a rough morning," he admitted. "The Mayor's breathing down our necks, and we're still chasing shadows."

Kathy was silent for a moment. "I know you'll figure it out," she said. "But you need to take care of yourself too. Promise me you'll get some rest tonight."

Roger chuckled, the sound dry. "I'll try," he promised. "But you know how it is."

"I do," Kathy said, her voice softening even more. "Just… be careful. And remember, I'm here if you need me."

Roger's heart clenched, the warmth of her words filling some of the cracks that had formed over the years. "Thanks, Kathy," he said quietly. "I don't know what I'd do without you."

They ended the call, and Roger sat there for a moment, letting the silence wash over him. But he didn't have time to dwell. Liz returned, her expression serious.

"Lawson won't come in," she said. "But he agreed to let us visit him. He didn't sound happy about it."

Roger nodded. "Then let's not waste any time."

They drove to Henry Lawson's house. The sky had lightened slightly, but the heavy gray clouds still loomed, promising more trouble. They turned onto N. Garfield and wound their way through the quiet streets until they reached the outskirts of the neighborhood.

Lawson's house was a modest brick home surrounded by barren mesquite trees, a chain-link fence marking the property line. It looked just as it had the last time they were here—unassuming but carrying a shadow of unease. It was the same place where Eli Chambers had chased them down, a reminder of how close danger had come.

Roger parked the cruiser, and he and Liz exchanged a knowing look. Memories of that harrowing night still lingered, but they pushed the past aside and approached the front door. Roger knocked, the sound echoing through the cold, still air.

The door opened, and Henry Lawson stood there, looking more worn than ever. He wore a thick cardigan over his clothes, and he regarded them with a mixture of irritation and fear.

"What now?" Lawson asked, his voice rough. "I thought this nightmare was behind us."

Roger's expression was serious. "We need to talk," he said. "May we come in?"

Lawson hesitated, his eyes flicking between them before he stepped aside, letting them in. The house was as sparsely decorated as they remembered, with old photographs lining the walls and an air of melancholy hanging heavy in the space. There was a faint scent of dust and something more bitter, perhaps old coffee left too long in a pot.

Lawson led them to the living room, where he motioned for them to sit. He remained standing, his posture stiff, as though the weight of his secrets were pressing down on him.

His eyes darted around the room, never quite settling on either of them.

"I've told you everything I know," Lawson said defensively, his voice cracking slightly. "What more do you want from me?"

Liz's eyes didn't miss the way his hands trembled. "Someone broke into the City Records Office last night," she said, her voice calm but firm. "They were looking for files related to the Marathon Oil explosion. Whoever did this is still trying to cover up the past, and we need answers before more people die."

Lawson's face went pale, and he sank slowly into a worn armchair, his hands gripping the armrests as if to steady himself. "That explosion..." he whispered, his voice shaking. "I've spent decades trying to forget it. The cover-up... it was supposed to be buried."

Roger leaned forward, his gaze unyielding. "What exactly were you covering up, Henry?" he demanded. "People have already died because of this, and the killer isn't done yet. We need the whole truth."

Lawson's hands trembled visibly, and he closed his eyes. "We were desperate," he began, his voice thin and brittle. "The explosion was an accident, but it was catastrophic. Marathon Oil was on the brink of collapse. If the truth came out, it would have ruined thousands of lives—jobs, families. We falsified safety reports, paid off inspectors... It was all a desperate attempt to salvage what we could."

Roger's jaw tightened. "You lied to save a company and a few fortunes," he said, his voice tinged with disgust. "And now people are paying the price."

Lawson's eyes snapped open, and for the first time, there was a flash of defiance. "You think I don't know that?" he snapped, his voice rising. "You think I haven't been haunted every day since? We thought we were doing the right thing. We thought… we thought we were saving lives in the long run."

Liz leaned forward, her voice steady but relentless. "Who else was involved?" she pressed. "Who else knew the extent of the cover-up and might be trying to keep it buried?"

Lawson's defiance crumbled, and he looked away, his face ashen. "Robert Withers and Gerald Simmons," he admitted. "They were just as involved as I was. Simmons handled the payoffs, and Withers managed the PR nightmare. But there were others—people who made millions off the lies, who would do anything to keep it quiet."

Roger and Liz exchanged a glance, the urgency in their eyes clear. "Why didn't you come forward when the murders started?" Roger demanded. "You had to know it would come back to haunt you."

Lawson's voice broke. "I was scared," he whispered, his eyes glistening with unshed tears. "Scared of losing everything. Scared of facing what we did. But now… now I realize that holding onto the past has cost more than I ever imagined."

Roger stood, his expression hard but resolute. "We need you to stay available," he said. "If we're going to stop this, we need to know everything. No more secrets."

Lawson nodded, his shoulders slumping in defeat. "I'll do what I can," he said, his voice hollow. "But I don't know if it'll be enough."

"It has to be," she said. "Because if we don't stop this, more people will die."

As they left Lawson's house, the sky remained heavy with gray clouds, and the wind howled through the mesquite trees. Roger climbed into the driver's seat, and Liz sat beside him, her eyes full of determination.

"Do you think he told us everything?" Liz asked.

Roger gripped the steering wheel, his knuckles whitening. "I think he told us enough to know that we're not done," he said. "And that we're running out of time."

They pulled out of the driveway, the weight of the day pressing down on them. The past was haunting Midland, and the shadows were closing in. But Roger and Liz weren't about to let the truth slip away, not when so much was at stake.

"We should go over those records again," she said. "There might be something we missed—some name or connection we didn't realize was important."

Roger exhaled, the weight of it all pressing down on his chest. "We're running out of time," he said, echoing his earlier sentiment. "But we're not backing down. Not now."

They continued driving in silence, the gravity of their situation sinking in. The clouds above seemed to grow even heavier, the promise of a storm looming over them. They reached the sheriff's office again, and Roger parked the cruiser, but neither of them moved to get out right away. They shared a moment of silence, both knowing that the stakes had just been raised higher. Liz took a deep breath, breaking the stillness.

"We have to be ready for anything now," she said, her voice filled with determination. "No more assuming this is just going to fade away."

Roger nodded. "We'll need to keep our circle tight. Only people we know we can trust. This is personal."

Liz leaned back in her seat, her eyes focused on Roger. "Garcia and a few others—Johnson, Marla—they're with us," she said. "But anyone else... I'm not sure who we can trust."

"Then we work with who we know. I'll talk to Garcia, get him on Lawson's house. We'll have to move fast—if they're watching us, they might already know our next steps."

"I'll start cross-referencing those records we got from the break-in. There has to be a thread we're not seeing yet—a name, a transaction, something that connects all of this together."

Roger looked at her, and for a moment, the exhaustion seemed to fade from his eyes. There was something else there now—a resolve, a determination to see this through. He reached over, giving her shoulder a firm, reassuring squeeze. "We're going to find them," he said, his voice low but fierce. "No matter what it takes."

Liz returned the gesture with a small, tired smile. "Together," she said. "We're in this together."

They both stepped out of the cruiser, the cold air biting at their faces. Roger led the way inside, and they split off—Liz heading towards the records room and Roger to find Garcia. The office was still bustling, the noise and movement a backdrop to the silent battle that was now raging under the surface.

Roger found Deputy Garcia in the briefing room, going over notes with a few other deputies. He motioned for Garcia to join him, and the young deputy's eyes widened slightly at the serious expression on Roger's face.

"Sheriff, what's going on?" Garcia asked as he followed Roger into a quieter corner of the room.

"Garcia, I need you to listen carefully," Roger said. "This isn't official yet, but Lawson's in danger. Someone's watching us, and they're making moves to keep this all buried. I need you to keep an eye on Lawson—discreetly. Don't let anyone know what you're doing, and don't trust anyone you're not sure of."

Garcia's expression grew serious, and he nodded. "You've got it, Sheriff. I won't let anything happen to him."

Roger clapped him on the shoulder. "Good. And be careful. If they know about Lawson, they might come after anyone who's working this case. That means you, me, Liz, all of us."

"I'll watch my back, Sheriff. And I'll make sure Lawson's safe."

Roger gave him a tight nod, then watched as Garcia headed out of the office, determination in his steps. Roger knew they were taking a risk—trusting anyone was dangerous now—but he also knew they couldn't do this alone. They needed all the help they could get, and Garcia was one of the few he could trust.

He turned, making his way to the records room to join Liz. She was already there, surrounded by papers and old files, her eyes scanning line after line, her brow furrowed in concentration. She barely looked up when Roger entered, too focused on the task at hand.

"I think I've found something," she said, her voice tinged with excitement. She pointed to a document—an old memo from Marathon Oil, dated just a few months before the explosion. "This memo mentions an external consultant—someone who was brought in to assess the risks of the drilling project. But there's no name, just initials: 'J.R.'"

"J.R.?" he repeated. "That could be anyone."

Liz nodded, her eyes sharp. "Exactly. But it's someone they didn't want to name directly. And look here—" she flipped to another page, an old financial ledger, with a list of payouts and consulting fees. "There's a large payment made to 'J.R.' just days before the explosion. It's listed as a consulting fee, but the amount is unusually high—almost like a payoff."

Roger's eyes narrowed as he studied the document. "If this J.R. knew something—something dangerous—they might have been paid off to keep quiet," he said. "Or worse, they might have been part of the cover-up."

"We need to find out who J.R. is," she said. "They could be the key to everything."

"Let's start with the board members and the key players from that time. Cross-reference anyone with those initials. If we can find J.R., we might finally get the answers we need."

Liz grabbed a fresh notepad, jotting down the initials and the details they had. "I'll start digging through the personnel records and see what I can find," she said. "This could be the break we've been waiting for."

Roger gave her a grim smile. "Let's hope so. Because if we're right, J.R. might be the one who's been pulling the strings all along."

CHAPTER THIRTY FOUR

The shrill buzz of Roger's work phone shattered the predawn silence, jolting him awake. He fumbled for the device on his nightstand, blinking against the darkness. Kathy stirred beside him, her voice groggy with sleep.

"Roger?" she murmured, her hand brushing his arm.

"It's work," he muttered, sitting up and answering the call. "Hartley."

"Sheriff, it's dispatch," came the voice on the other end, tense and clipped. "We've got a report of a body at Centennial Plaza. Witnesses say it's… bad. You and Deputy Trujillo need to get there immediately."

Roger swung his legs over the side of the bed, already reaching for his jeans. "On my way," he said, his tone grim. Ending the call, he turned to Kathy, who was watching him with worried eyes.

"What happened?" she asked, sitting up against the headboard.

"Body downtown," Roger replied, pulling his boots on. "Centennial Plaza. Sounds like it's serious."

Kathy's concern deepened, but she nodded, understanding. "Be careful."

Roger paused long enough to press a kiss to her forehead before grabbing his jacket and heading out the door.

The flashing lights of patrol cars illuminated the edges of Centennial Plaza as Roger arrived. He parked near the fountain, stepping out into the biting wind that whipped through the empty streets. Liz was already there.

"What do we know?" Roger asked as he approached her.

Liz shook her head, her breath fogging in the cold air. "A jogger found him about an hour ago. Called it in thinking it was some kind of display, but…" She trailed off, motioning toward the stage. "It's bad, Roger. Real bad."

Roger followed her gaze, and his stomach dropped.

Suspended high above the stage, District Attorney Bennett's body hung in a grotesque tableau. His arms and legs were splayed wide, hooked to winch-like mechanisms that stretched each limb taut, forming the horrific image of a human star. His neck was looped in another cable, pulling his head back at an unnatural angle. His suit was torn and bloodied, and the cables creaked softly in the wind, the only sound in the otherwise silent plaza. Blood had dripped from his wounds, staining the stage below.

"Jesus Christ," he muttered.

"What kind of sick bastard does this?"

Roger didn't respond, his mind racing as he took in the macabre display. His instincts told him this wasn't just about the DA. This was a message, a deliberate and horrifying statement—a declaration meant to instill fear.

The sound of a car door slamming drew their attention, and Roger turned to see the Mayor hurrying toward them, his coat flapping in the wind. His face was pale, his expression a mix of anger and disbelief.

"What the hell is going on here, Hartley?" the Mayor demanded, his voice sharp but unsteady. "I got a call saying it was Bennett. Please tell me that's not true."

Roger didn't answer immediately, his jaw tightening as he motioned toward the stage. "See for yourself."

The Mayor's gaze followed Roger's gesture, and when his eyes landed on the scene above the stage, his breath hitched. "Dear God..." he whispered, taking a step back. "What... what is this?"

"This is what happens when you ignore the warning signs," Roger said, his tone cold. "This is a message."

Liz's voice cut through the tense silence. "Sir, you might want to step back. This is an active crime scene."

The Mayor didn't respond, his eyes fixed on the DA's body. "I... I didn't think..." he stammered, his voice trailing off.

Roger exchanged a look with Liz, then turned back to the Mayor. "We need to focus," he said firmly. "You should go back to City Hall. We'll keep you updated."

The Mayor hesitated, then nodded mutely, retreating to his car without another word.

When the ladder was in place, Roger climbed up cautiously, each step creaking under his weight. The bitter wind stung his face as he neared the suspended body. The cables had dug deep into the DA's flesh. His face was swollen and bruised, barely recognizable. Roger noted the way the cuts crisscrossed over Bennett's skin, the calculated cruelty in each slice.

As Roger examined the horrific display, something caught his eye—a folded piece of paper tucked into the DA's bloodied shirt pocket. He reached out carefully, the bitter cold making his fingers stiff. Pulling the paper free, he unfolded it with a sense of dread.

The message was written in typewriter-like font, pasted together from letters cut from magazines:

"THE MAYOR SHOULD HAVE LISTENED TO HIS HEROES. I HAVE A JOB TO FINISH."

Roger's stomach turned as he read the note, his hands shaking with anger. "Son of a bitch," he muttered under his breath. This wasn't just a murder—it was a declaration.

As he leaned in closer to examine the DA's face, Roger saw it—a faint twitch of movement. His chest rose and fell in shallow, ragged breaths.

"Jesus," Roger muttered, his heart hammering in his chest. "He's alive!"

The officers below froze, the weight of Roger's words sinking in. Liz's voice cut through the stunned silence. "Get EMS here now!"

The plaza erupted into motion, officers shouting into radios as paramedics were called to the scene. Roger climbed back down, his hands shaking. "I don't know how he's still alive," he said, his voice low. "But we need to move fast."

The sterile corridors of Midland Memorial Hospital were quiet except for the occasional beep of medical equipment and the soft murmur of voices behind closed doors. Roger and Liz stood outside the ICU, their faces pale and etched with exhaustion. The weight of the DA's horrific injuries hung heavily between them, the gruesome scene from Centennial Plaza replaying in their minds.

Through the glass window of the ICU, they could see DA Bennett lying motionless in his hospital bed. His arms and legs were swathed in thick bandages, suspended slightly to relieve pressure on the mangled limbs. Monitors beeped rhythmically, tracking his vital signs, and a breathing tube snaked down his throat. His face was swollen beyond recognition, the bruising so severe it seemed almost painted on.

"He looks like he's been through a war," Liz murmured.

Roger nodded, his jaw tightening. "It's a miracle he's alive at all."

Deputy Garcia approached them from the far end of the hallway, his expression grim. "Sheriff, Deputy," he said, stopping just short of them. "We've got an update on Bennett's wife."

Liz asked, "What about her?"

"She was found tied up in the master bedroom closet at their house," Garcia explained. "She's alive but beaten pretty bad. Paramedics brought her here about an hour ago."

Roger's brow furrowed. "She's here? Where?"

"Room 212, down the hall," Garcia said. "She's asking to talk to you both."

Liz exchanged a look with Roger, her lips pressing into a thin line. "Let's go."

Room 212 was dimly lit, the heavy curtains drawn against the early morning light. Margaret Bennett sat propped up in bed, her face battered and bruised. Cuts lined her swollen lips, and dark purple rings encircled both eyes.

Her right arm was in a sling, and her trembling fingers clutched a cup of water.

"Mrs. Bennett," Roger began softly, taking a seat beside her bed. Liz stood at the foot of the bed, her arms crossed but her expression empathetic. "I'm Sheriff Hartley, and this is Deputy Trujillo. We're here to talk to you about what happened."

Margaret nodded weakly, her voice hoarse as she spoke. "You found Richard?"

Roger hesitated before answering. "We did. He's alive, but he's in critical condition. The doctors have him in an induced coma to manage the pain."

"I was so scared they'd killed him," she whispered. "I didn't know if he was dead or alive."

Liz stepped closer, her voice soft but insistent. "Can you tell us what happened, Margaret? Anything you remember might help us find who did this."

"It was the middle of the night," she began, her voice shaking. "I woke up because I heard something downstairs—like glass breaking. I thought it was Richard, but when I called for him, he didn't answer."

Her fingers trembled as she raised the cup to her lips, taking a small sip before continuing. "I got out of bed to check, but before I even got to the stairs, someone grabbed me from behind. I didn't hear him coming."

Her voice cracked, and she paused, her eyes dropping to her lap. "He was tall, strong. He slammed me into the wall so hard I thought my shoulder was broken. Then he dragged me into the bedroom and started hitting me… over and over."

"Did he say anything while he was attacking you?"

Margaret nodded faintly. "He kept saying that Richard had to 'pay for the Mayor's ignorance.' That he was sending a message."

Roger exchanged a look with Liz, their expressions hardening.

Margaret's voice dropped to a whisper. "I tried to fight back, but he was so much stronger. He beat me, tied my hands and feet, and threw me into the closet. I could hear him dragging Richard out of bed, and then… then he started beating him. I could hear it all."

Tears spilled down her bruised cheeks, and she covered her face with her free hand. "He was screaming," she said, her voice trembling. "Begging him to stop. And I just… I couldn't do anything."

Roger leaned forward, his voice steady but filled with urgency. "Margaret, do you remember anything about him? His voice, a tattoo, anything at all?"

Margaret shook her head, frustration etched into her features. "He didn't say much after that," she admitted. "And it was dark. He was wearing gloves, a mask… I couldn't see his face."

Liz softened her tone, her voice gentle. "Did he take anything from the house? Anything that might give us a clue?"

Margaret frowned, her brow furrowing in thought. "I don't think so," she said. "He didn't seem interested in anything except Richard. It was like… like this was all planned. Like he knew exactly what he wanted to do.”

Roger sat back, his jaw tight. “Thank you, Margaret,” he said quietly. “You’ve been through hell, but you’ve given us a place to start.”

Margaret looked up at him, her eyes filled with desperation. “Please… find him,” she whispered. “Don’t let him do this to anyone else.”

Roger nodded firmly. “We won’t stop until we do.”

Roger and Liz stepped out of Margaret Bennett’s room. The sterile hospital corridor seemed colder now, the faint hum of fluorescent lights adding to the oppressive silence.

“‘Pay for the Mayor’s ignorance,’” Liz repeated under her breath, her voice sharp with frustration. “He’s targeting people connected to the explosion and anyone standing in his way. The Mayor might be next.”

Roger rubbed the back of his neck, his expression grim. “The Mayor’s been playing politics this whole time. Ignoring the warnings, dismissing the evidence… if the killer’s fixated on him, he’s painted himself as the ultimate target.”

Liz’s eyes narrowed. “And what about the Mayor’s connection to the explosion? Do you think he knows more than he’s letting on?”

Roger’s jaw tightened, his mind racing. “He’s certainly acting like a man with something to hide,” he admitted. “But whether he’s hiding guilt or just fear is the real question.”

Back at the sheriff’s office, the tension was palpable. The team had gathered in the briefing room, each member looking worn and tense. Roger and Liz stood at the front, the weight of leadership pressing heavily on their shoulders.

"DA Bennett is barely clinging to life, and his wife's testimony confirms what we suspected," Roger began, his voice steady but grim. "The killer isn't done. This isn't random—he's picking targets connected to the Marathon explosion and the fallout that followed."

Liz stepped forward, holding up a photograph of the note found on Bennett. "The message is clear: this isn't just about revenge. He wants us to feel powerless, to question every move we make."

Deputy Garcia raised his hand. "Sheriff, do we have any leads on the tire tracks found near the Bennett residence?"

Roger nodded. "Forensics is analyzing them now. They found partial treads matching a heavy-duty vehicle, possibly a van or SUV. We're cross-referencing that with surveillance footage from the surrounding streets."

Liz added, "We're also reviewing the files from the break-in at the records office. If the killer's trying to cover up or expose something specific, those files might hold the key."

Roger scanned the faces of his team, seeing determination mixed with fatigue. "This bastard wants us to falter," he said firmly. "But we're not going to give him that satisfaction. Stay sharp, stay focused, and watch your backs."

Later that afternoon, Roger and Liz drove to City Hall to meet with the Mayor. The ride was silent, the tension thick between them. The streets of Midland, usually bustling with activity, felt subdued, as if the city itself was holding its breath.

When they arrived, the Mayor's secretary ushered them into his office. The Mayor sat behind his large oak desk, his face pale but defiant. He gestured for them to sit, though his demeanor was far from welcoming.

"What's this about now?" the Mayor asked, his tone sharp. "Haven't we had enough excitement for one day?"

Roger didn't sit. "You're on the killer's radar," he said bluntly. "The note we found on Bennett made that clear. You're in danger."

The Mayor scoffed, though there was a flicker of fear in his eyes. "You're overreacting, Hartley. This guy's a lunatic. He's targeting people involved in that old Marathon mess. I wasn't part of that."

Liz stepped forward, her voice firm. "You've been ignoring the warnings and pushing to close this case prematurely. That makes you a target in his eyes."

The Mayor bristled, his fingers drumming on the desk. "I've been trying to keep this city from falling apart. The last thing we need is more panic."

"Panic won't matter if you're dead," Roger said coldly. "We need to take this threat seriously."

The Mayor stood, leaning across the desk. "I'm not going to let this killer dictate how I run this city," he snapped. "If you're so convinced I'm a target, then do your job and protect me."

Roger's jaw tightened, his frustration bubbling beneath the surface. "We're doing everything we can," he said evenly. "But you need to work with us, not against us."

The Mayor waved them off, his face hard. "Fine. Do what you need to do. But don't expect me to cower in fear."

As Roger and Liz left the office, Liz muttered under her breath, "He's going to get himself killed."

Roger didn't respond, his thoughts already racing ahead. The killer was always one step ahead, and they couldn't afford to fall any further behind.

That evening, Roger sat in his truck outside Kathy's house, the events of the day replaying in his mind. He pulled out his phone and called Liz.

"Anything from forensics on the tire tracks?" he asked when she answered.

"Not yet," Liz replied, her voice tired. "But they're working on it."

"Keep me posted," Roger said. "And get some rest if you can."

"You too," Liz replied. "And Roger… be careful."

He ended the call and leaned back in his seat, his gaze drifting to Kathy's front door. The warmth of her presence was a small comfort in the midst of the chaos, but even that felt fragile now.

CHAPTER THIRTY FIVE

The winter sun struggled to pierce through the heavy clouds that blanketed Midland. The town, still reeling from the string of brutal murders, seemed to carry an unnatural quiet. The streets, though busy, were devoid of their usual chatter, as if everyone was waiting for something—something dark that could not be named.

Roger took a moment to check in with the hospital before starting his day. District Attorney Bennett was still in the ICU, his condition stable but critical. The doctors were cautiously optimistic, but the damage was severe. His wife, Margaret, was also in the hospital, recovering from her own injuries after being found tied up and beaten in their home. She was in Room 212, and though she was badly bruised, she was determined to help. Margaret had spoken to Roger and Liz, recounting what little she could remember of the night they were attacked. The strain was evident in her eyes, but there was a flicker of determination that matched Roger's own. Seeing her struggle while Bennett lay unconscious added another layer to the already heavy burden Roger carried.

The hospital hallway smelled of antiseptic and carried the low hum of medical equipment. Roger stood outside Margaret's door for a moment before leaving, taking in a deep breath. The sterile environment made him uneasy—he'd spent too many hours in hospitals during his time in the military, waiting for news that was rarely good. The past few weeks had dragged him back to those old feelings, each new body and each desperate face a reminder of how fragile everything truly was.

Later that morning, Roger stood in front of the sheriff's office. He watched as Deputy Garcia pulled up in his patrol car, the engine humming as it idled for a moment before shutting off.

Liz arrived not long after. She walked up to Roger, her arm still in a sling. "Morning, Roger," she said, her voice a little hoarse. "You look like you haven't slept."

"I could say the same for you." He gestured towards the door. "Let's get inside. We might have something new to work with."

They walked through the station doors. The officers on duty gave them nods of acknowledgment, and Roger could feel the tension in the room, the unspoken questions that hung in the air. Everyone knew that the case was far from over, and that the worst could still be ahead of them.

Deputy Garcia approached. "Sheriff, we just got something from the lab. Partial tire prints from one of the crime scenes—looks like we have a match."

"A match? Where?"

Garcia handed Roger a file. "The tire treads match a vehicle seen near the Withers crime scene. It's not a full print, but it's enough to narrow it down to a specific type of vehicle—an older model dark-colored SUV, maybe early 2000s. We also managed to pull some traffic camera footage from around the area."

Liz leaned in, her eyes brightening. "Do we have anything useful from the footage?"

Garcia nodded, gesturing for them to follow. "Come on, I'll show you what we've got."

Roger and Liz followed Garcia to the small tech room, where a computer monitor displayed grainy footage from a traffic camera. Garcia clicked on the play button, and the footage began to roll. The timestamp showed it was from the night of the Withers murder, just minutes before the estimated time of death.

"There," Garcia said, pointing at the screen. A dark-colored SUV drove through the intersection, its headlights cut through the foggy night. The footage was grainy, but the shape and model of the vehicle matched the description they had.

Roger leaned closer, studying the screen. "Can we get a better look at the plates?"

Garcia shook his head. "It's too blurry, but we might be able to enhance it a bit. I've already sent it to the tech guys to see if they can clean it up."

Liz crossed her arms, her mind racing. "If we can get a partial plate, we might be able to narrow it down further. How many of these SUVs are registered in the county?"

Garcia handed Liz another sheet of paper. "We ran a preliminary search. There are about thirty older model SUVs registered in Midland County that match the color and general description. It's not much, but it's a start."

Roger nodded, a spark of determination in his eyes. "Alright. Let's start by cross-referencing those registrations with any known associates of Withers, Simmons, or Lawson.

We need to see if anyone in their circles owns a vehicle like this."

Liz looked at the footage again. "Whoever did this was careful, but they slipped up. If we can trace this SUV, we might finally have a lead that takes us to whoever's orchestrating all of this."

Roger looked pleased with this new lead. "Good work, Garcia. Let's get the tech team on that footage and start digging into those registrations. We've been running in circles, but this might be the break we need."

Garcia nodded, his face lighting up with a hint of hope. "I'll get right on it, Sheriff."

As Garcia left the room, Roger turned to Liz. "We're finally getting somewhere," he said, his voice filled with resolve. "Let's keep pushing. Whoever's behind this is starting to make mistakes, and we're going to catch them."

Liz gave a determined nod. She said, "We should also check in with any local repair shops. If that SUV's been in an accident or had any work done recently, someone might remember it."

Roger smiled. "Good thinking. Let's divide and conquer. You take the repair shops, and I'll follow up on the registrations. It's time we bring whoever's behind this out into the open."

They spent the next few hours combing through the list of SUVs, cross-referencing names with known associates of the victims, including Eli Chambers. Liz made calls to local repair shops along Andrews Highway and Rankin Highway, trying to see if anyone had recently worked on an SUV matching their description. The responses were varied—most were dead ends, but a few promised to check their records and get back to her.

Roger, meanwhile, focused on the list of registered vehicles. He made his way through the files, cross-referencing names with any known connections to the Deep Surge project. There were a few that seemed promising—individuals who had worked for Marathon Oil in some capacity, or who had ties to the local business community that had benefited from the project.

It was nearly noon when Liz walked back into Roger's office, her eyes alight with excitement. "I think I've got something," she said, dropping a notepad onto his desk. "One of the mechanics on Rankin Highway said they worked on a dark SUV about two weeks ago. The guy was acting nervous, paid in cash, and didn't want to leave any personal information. The mechanic remembered because the guy insisted on getting the work done fast—something about replacing a damaged bumper."

"Did he get a look at the plates?"

Liz shook her head. "No, but he remembered the guy mentioned he was heading out towards an old warehouse on the outskirts of town—somewhere near the old industrial area off FM 1788."

Roger leaned back, a sense of urgency building. "The warehouse... that could be something. It might be where they're hiding, or at least where they're keeping whatever they don't want found."

Liz nodded. "I think it's worth checking out. If nothing else, it might give us a lead on who's behind all this."

Roger stood, grabbing his coat from the back of his chair. "Alright, let's move. We'll take a couple of units with us but keep it quiet. Last thing we need is to tip them off."

As they made their way out of the station, Roger felt a surge of determination. They were finally making progress, and he wasn't about to let this lead slip through their fingers. The streets of Midland passed by in a blur as they headed towards the outskirts of town, the cold wind whipping through the gaps in the truck's windows.

The warehouse off FM 1788 loomed ahead, a relic of a bygone era when the oil industry had been booming. Now it stood silent, its windows dark and its walls weathered by years of neglect. Roger pulled the truck to a stop a safe distance away, the crunch of gravel under the tires the only sound breaking the stillness.

Liz glanced at Roger, her eyes filled with determination. "Ready?"

Roger nodded, his hand resting on the handle of his door. "Let's see what we find." They stepped out of the truck, the cold air biting at their skin as they approached the old warehouse. The sense of anticipation was thick, and Roger knew they were close—closer than they had ever been.

CHAPTER THIRTY SIX

Roger and Liz moved cautiously towards the warehouse. Its rusted walls and broken windows told the story of years of abandonment. The wind carried the scent of old oil and dust, hinting at what this place had once been.

"Let's keep it quiet," Roger murmured, motioning for Liz to follow closely. They made their way around the side of the building, looking for a point of entry that wouldn't immediately expose them. The front door was padlocked and chained, but Liz spotted a side entrance that had long since been pried open, a gap just wide enough for them to slip through.

Roger went in first, ducking under a low-hanging beam before helping Liz inside. Once they were both in, they paused, letting their eyes adjust to the dim light. Dust motes floated in the air, illuminated by the occasional shaft of sunlight breaking through holes in the roof. The place was eerily quiet, the only sound coming from the creaking of old metal as the wind blew through.

"Looks like nobody's home," Liz whispered. She moved forward, and flicked her flashlight across the floor. It was cluttered with debris—old oil drums, broken crates, and pieces of rusted machinery scattered everywhere.

Roger nodded, though he kept his guard up. "Yeah, but let's not take any chances. If someone was using this place, they left in a hurry." He pointed to a series of tire tracks etched into the dusty ground, leading deeper into the warehouse. "Those tracks are recent," he said. "Maybe there's more in the back."

They followed the tracks and the further they went, the darker it got. Roger couldn't shake the feeling that they were being watched. It was a prickling sensation at the back of his neck, an instinct honed by years in the field. He kept his hand close to his sidearm, ready to draw at any moment.

"Did you hear that?" Liz whispered. There—a faint rustling, like someone shifting their weight on an unstable surface. He exchanged a look with Liz, and they both knew they had to be ready for anything. Roger gave her a brief nod, signaling to keep moving, but cautiously.

They rounded a corner, coming into what seemed to be a makeshift office space—wooden boards had been hastily set up to form a small enclosure, and inside, a desk with papers strewn across it. The space had an unsettling feel—Roger couldn't shake the sense of desperation that seemed to linger here. A broken chair lay on its side, and a few empty bottles of water were scattered across the floor. The air was heavy, almost suffocating, as if the walls themselves bore witness to the horrors that had unfolded within them.

Liz moved towards the desk. "Looks like someone's been keeping records," she said, her voice low but excited. She held up a stack of yellowed papers, her eyes scanning them quickly. "These are invoices... and look here, shipping manifests. They're addressed to 'E. Chambers'."

Roger's eyebrows shot up at the mention of the name. "E. Chambers. They really want us to keep thinking he's involved." He looked around the small space, his eyes catching sight of a map pinned to one of the wooden boards. He moved closer, examining it. "This map… it's a layout of Midland, and there are marked locations," he said, tracing his finger over several points. One of the locations was the Green Tree Country Club.

Liz joined him. "We knew they had plans beyond just Chambers. Look here," she pointed to another mark on the outskirts. "That's the old caliche pit near Highway 349. Maybe they were using Chambers to distract us while they moved through these places."

Roger took a deep breath, the pieces slowly clicking into place. "This isn't just a rogue operation. They're well-organized, and they're using Chambers as a scapegoat." He pulled out his phone and snapped pictures of the map and the documents. "We need to get this back to the station, analyze it properly. There's no telling what else we might find here."

Liz continued to search the makeshift office, opening a metal filing cabinet that stood against the wall. Her flashlight revealed more papers—documents tied to Marathon Oil, references to the explosion that had happened years ago, and even schematics of drilling operations. She turned to Roger, her face tense. "These people are connected to everything. Marathon Oil, the explosion... We knew it was all linked, but this just confirms how close they've been watching us."

Roger's gaze shifted to a stack of photographs half-hidden beneath a file. He picked them up, his stomach churning as he recognized the faces. "Liz," he said, his voice barely a whisper. He spread the photos on the desk—pictures of himself, Liz, Kathy, and Jason. Each one had been taken recently, some clearly without their knowledge. The realization sent a chill down his spine. "They've been watching us. They know everything."

Liz frowned, her expression hardening as she looked over the photographs. "We knew they were close, but seeing this—it's different. They're definitely planning something big."

Roger turned his flashlight to the floor, where dark stains caught his attention. He knelt down, his heart sinking as he touched the dried, rusty patches—blood. "Looks like they used this place for more than just planning," he said grimly, pointing to a nearby set of heavy chains bolted to the wall. The chains were stained as well, and the sight of them left little doubt about their purpose. "This was a torture site."

Liz swallowed hard, her eyes darting around the room. "Whoever was here, they were interrogating and hurting people too. We need to find out who else they had here and what they were after." She glanced at a stack of notebooks on the ground, quickly flipping through the pages. They were filled with cryptic notes, times, locations, and what appeared to be coded messages.

"We're taking all of this. Every document, every photo. Let's not leave anything behind." He quickly started gathering the papers, stuffing them into his bag. Liz did the same, her eyes scanning the room one last time, making sure they weren't missing anything important.

Suddenly, Roger's flashlight caught something glinting in the corner of the makeshift office—an old metal toolbox, partially hidden under a pile of broken wooden boards. He moved towards it, pulling it out and opening the lid. Inside were various tools, but what caught his attention was a blood-stained knife, along with zip ties and rolls of duct tape. Roger's expression darkened as he held up the knife for Liz to see.

"It's possible they even killed people here," he said grimly. He set the knife back in the box, his mind racing with the implications. "We have to get this to the lab. Maybe there are fingerprints, something we can use."

Liz nodded, her face pale but resolute. "We need to get out of here before that guy comes back. Whoever he is, he's part of this operation, and we're not equipped to take him on alone."

Suddenly, the sound of footsteps echoed through the warehouse, faint but unmistakable. Roger turned, his hand immediately on his weapon. He motioned for Liz to stay quiet. They backed up, positioning themselves behind an old stack of metal crates.

The footsteps grew louder, closer, and Roger could see a shadow moving across the far wall. Someone was here. He exchanged a glance with Liz, her eyes wide but steady. The tension between them was electric, an unspoken understanding passing between them—they had to stay calm and ready.

Then came the sound—a soft scraping, almost like metal against metal. Roger's pulse quickened. Whoever it was, they were trying to stay quiet, but they weren't quite careful enough.

Suddenly, the figure turned towards them, and without warning, gunfire erupted. The sharp crack of bullets filled the warehouse, ricocheting off the metal walls and sending shards of debris flying around them. Roger's heart pounded as he ducked lower, pulling Liz down with him. The shots were wild, but they were close—too close. Roger and Liz exchanged a quick look, both coming to the same unsettling realization: the shots were too random, as if the gunman meant to miss them. He was trying to scare them, not kill them. Bullets whizzed past, clanging off the crates, and the air filled with the acrid smell of gunpowder.

"Run!" Roger shouted. He and Liz moved quickly, staying low as they made their way back towards the exit. The figure kept firing, but the shots seemed to be growing more erratic. Then, as suddenly as it had started, the gunfire stopped.

Roger risked a glance back, but the figure had disappeared into the shadows. The silence that followed was almost deafening, the only sound the echo of their own frantic breaths. They both knew what was at stake.

"We need to move," Roger whispered. "If we can get out without being seen, we'll have the element of surprise."

Liz nodded, and they began to creep back the way they came. They slipped out of the warehouse and moved quickly to the cover of their truck, parked a short distance away. Roger made sure they hadn't been followed. He turned to Liz, a grim smile on his face. "Looks like we've got more than we bargained for. We need to get this evidence back to the station, and we need to move fast. Whoever that was, they won't be happy we were here."

"We've got something real now, Roger. Let's use it."

Roger started the truck, the engine roaring to life as they pulled away from the warehouse, the tires kicking up dust as they sped down FM 1788. The weight of what they had just found settled in—marked locations, ties to Chambers, evidence of torture, and now a mysterious figure who was clearly keeping watch.

"We'll take this to Garcia, get the team working on these locations," Roger said, glancing at Liz.

Suddenly, Roger's phone rang, the shrill sound cutting through the silence of the truck. He glanced at the caller ID, his brow furrowing. It was a blocked number.

Roger exchanged a wary look with Liz before reaching for the phone.

CHAPTER THIRTY SEVEN

Roger hesitated for a moment, his thumb hovered over the answer button. He had been through this before. The killer's taunts echoed in his ears long after the calls ended. Liz gave him a firm nod. With a deep breath, Roger pressed the button and put the phone on speaker so Liz could hear.

"Hartley," he spoke.

A familiar, chilling laugh crackled through the line, followed by a voice that oozed malice. "Roger, Roger... you really do know how to poke your nose where it doesn't belong, don't you?"

"Whoever you are, you're not going to get away with this," he said, keeping his voice calm, but the anger simmered beneath the surface.

The voice on the other end grew sharper, more agitated. "Oh, but I already have, Sheriff. You're always one step behind, stumbling through the dark while I set the stage. Finding that warehouse? That was a mistake. You weren't supposed to get that far. If you would have stayed out of this, it would already be done and it wouldn't have affected you at all. The extra deaths are on your hands."

Roger glanced at Liz, whose eyes narrowed as she listened intently to the conversation. She clenched her jaw, her hand resting near her sidearm, ready for action. "You seem pretty rattled for someone who's supposedly in control," Roger retorted, his voice edged with defiance.

There was a moment of silence on the line, followed by a low growl of frustration. "You think you understand what's happening here, Roger? You think you have it all figured out? You and your little deputy, poking around where you shouldn't?" The killer's voice rose, anger crackling through the receiver. "You were never meant to see the warehouse. I let you leave, Hartley. I could have ended you both right there, but that would have been too easy."

Roger's pulse quickened. He already suspected the truth, but hearing it confirmed made his blood run cold. He felt a chill, not from the winter air outside, but from the malevolence on the line. "You missed on purpose," he said, his voice barely above a whisper.

The killer's voice oozed malice as he responded. "Of course I missed on purpose. Killing you would be too merciful. I want you to see how this ends. I want you to watch as everything you've fought to protect crumbles. Your town, your friends, your family—all of it. You won't be able to stop what's coming."

The killer paused, then laughed again, the sound devoid of any real mirth. His tone shifted, becoming darker. "If you had just stayed out of this, Roger, things would have been simple. It would have been over—clean, quick, no loose ends. But now you've made it personal. Maybe I'll make an example out of DA Bennett—just one final push to take him off life support. Or maybe I'll pay Margaret a visit and finish what I started. And then there's Kathy... Imagine her fear when she realizes what you've dragged her into. Sweet Emily—maybe I'll make her watch as her mother begs for mercy. Or perhaps Jason—Liz's fiancé. I know all about him. I could make him watch as I take Liz apart piece by piece, or maybe I'll start with him while she listens, helpless. Imagine his screams, Liz. Imagine him calling out for you, knowing you can't save him. Do you really think you can protect them all, Roger? No one is out of my reach."

Roger's heart felt like a vice was squeezing it, but he steadied his voice. "You come after them, and I promise you, I will find you," Roger said, his voice low, filled with barely restrained fury. "You want me? Come at me. Leave them out of this."

The killer laughed again, the sound almost gleeful. "Oh, Roger, you still don't get it, do you? This isn't about what you want. This is about what I want. And I want you to feel helpless. I want you to see just how little control you have." The voice paused, the silence on the line heavy. "Tick tock, Sheriff. Time is running out. I hope you're ready to watch it all burn."

Then the line went dead.

Roger quickly dialed Kathy's number, his heart pounding as he listened to the ringing. After what felt like an eternity, she answered, her voice groggy. "Roger? It's early, what's going on?"

"Kathy, listen to me," Roger said, his voice tight. "I need you to stay inside and keep the doors locked. Don't go anywhere until you hear from me. Is Emily still in Dallas?"

"Yes, she's in Dallas," Kathy replied, her tone now filled with worry. "Roger, what's happening?"

"Just do as I say, Kathy. I'll explain everything later. I promise," Roger said, his voice softening. He could hear the fear in her voice, and it tore at him. "I love you. Please, stay safe."

As soon as Roger hung up, Liz pulled out her own phone and quickly called Jason to confirm his safety.

After Liz ended her call with Jason, Roger immediately called the hospital. "This is Sheriff Hartley," he said, his voice urgent. "I need to double the protection on DA Bennett and his wife, Margaret. No one goes near them without my explicit permission. Understood?"

The nurse on the other end hesitated for a moment before answering, "Yes, Sheriff. We will increase the security detail right away."

"Thank you," Roger replied, his voice softening slightly. He took a deep breath, trying to push away the knot of fear that had formed in his chest. "Just make sure they're safe."

Liz watched Roger, her face a mix of empathy and determination. She could see the weight of this situation pressing down on him, the burden of keeping everyone safe. "We'll make sure they're protected, Roger. He's trying to scare us, to make us react without thinking. We won't let him win."

Roger saw the resolve there, the trust she had in him, and it gave him strength. "No, we won't. We're going to make sure everyone we care about is safe. We're doubling security on all of them—Kathy, Emily, Jason, and the Bennetts. And then we're going to end this—whatever it takes."

"First thing, we get back to the station," Roger said, his voice filled with resolve. "We need to get this evidence secured and get more eyes on this. We're not letting this bastard slip away again."

Roger pressed down on the accelerator, the truck speeding up as they drove towards the station.

They reached the precinct which was already bustling. Roger pushed open the station doors with Liz close on his heels. The room quieted as they entered, all eyes turning towards them.

"Listen up, everyone. We had another direct contact from the killer early this morning. He knows we found the warehouse, and he's furious. He's also made it very clear that he's targeting our loved ones—Kathy, Emily, Jason, even the Bennetts. We've already increased security, but we need to be on high alert."

Deputy Garcia approached them, his expression serious. "Sheriff, we had a new lead come in about an hour ago. There was a report of a suspicious vehicle seen leaving the old caliche pit off Highway 349 early this morning. Witnesses said it looked like a dark SUV, and it was moving fast."

Roger exchanged a glance with Liz. "The caliche pit... that's one of the marked locations from the warehouse documents," Roger said, his mind racing. He pictured the pit—a vast, desolate place where the earth had been gouged out, leaving sharp ridges and loose rock. A place easy to hide evidence, or worse. "Alright, Garcia, I want a team down there now. Secure the area and see if we can find anything— tire tracks, evidence, anything that links back to our suspect."

Garcia nodded, already moving to assemble a team. Roger turned back to the gathered officers. "We're not letting this guy slip away again. Stay sharp, stay vigilant, and report anything out of the ordinary immediately. We're getting close, and we can't afford any mistakes."

The officers had a direction, they had a lead, and this time, they weren't going to let the killer stay ahead. Roger knew the stakes had risen—the killer had made it personal. But he also knew they had something the killer couldn't take from them—the resolve to fight, to protect the people they loved, and to bring this monster to justice.

Roger and Liz moved to the command center, where a map of the city was pinned up, with various locations marked. Roger traced his finger to the caliche pit, then looked at Liz. "Let's get down there ourselves once Garcia secures the site. I want to see it with my own eyes."

"I'll grab our gear. We need to be ready for anything."

As Liz left, Roger took a moment to collect himself. He looked at the pictures pinned to the board—photos of the victims, of Kathy, of Emily. He felt the familiar ache of fear and anger, but he let it steel his resolve. This was his town, these were his people, and he was not going to let some twisted psychopath tear it apart.

Liz returned, her eyes meeting his. "Ready?"

Roger nodded, his jaw set. "Ready. Let's finish this."

CHAPTER THIRTY EIGHT

At the station, Roger stood near his desk, reviewing the new evidence while Liz leaned against the wall, her arms crossed, her eyes focused on every movement in the precinct. They had a lead, and they weren't going to let it slip through their fingers.

"Deputy Garcia's taking a team down to the caliche pit now," Liz said, her voice cutting through the din of the room. "I hope they find something solid. We need a win, Roger."

Roger gave her a tight nod. "We need to keep pressure on all fronts. He's slipping up, and we have to be ready to capitalize on every mistake he makes." He paused for a moment. The threats against Kathy, Emily, Jason, and the Bennetts echoed in his mind. He clenched his jaw, looking at Liz with determination. "We also need to make sure our people are safe, Liz. The killer wants us to be afraid—wants us to be distracted. We can't let that happen."

Liz nodded, her eyes hardening. "We won't. But we need to stay sharp, too. He's escalating, and that means he's feeling cornered. We've got to use that to our advantage."

Just then, an officer rushed over, holding a printout. "Sheriff, I think you need to see this." The young officer handed Roger a sheet of paper. "We got another tip. It's about a property out near the state line—a cabin. It matches some of the descriptions from the warehouse documents. It looks like it might be one of the places they were using."

Roger read through the document. The location matched some of the clues they'd pieced together, but it was the remoteness that struck him. He handed it to Liz, who took it with a furrowed brow. "A cabin near the New Mexico state line," she muttered. "If they're hiding out there, it could explain the movement we've been seeing. It's remote, hard to find, and easy to defend."

Roger looked up, his gaze meeting hers. "We need to follow up on this right away. I don't want to lose any time."

Liz nodded, already moving towards the map pinned to the far wall. She traced her finger along the state border, spotting the general area described in the report. "It's isolated. Perfect place to lay low if you don't want anyone to find you."

Roger grabbed his radio, his voice steady as he spoke. "Garcia, this is Hartley. We've got a new lead—a cabin near the New Mexico state line. I want you to split the team. Half stays at the caliche pit, the other half follows up on this cabin. I want both locations secured and scouted."

Garcia's voice crackled through the radio, acknowledging the orders. "Got it, Sheriff. We're on it."

Roger turned back to Liz, who was already marking the location on the map. "We'll go ourselves," he said, his tone leaving no room for argument. "If the killer's been using that cabin, there might be something there that ties this all together. We need to see it firsthand."

They gathered what they needed—flashlights, radios, extra ammunition, and the marked-up maps of Midland and the surrounding areas. Roger could feel the eyes of the department on them as they moved towards the door, the weight of the situation evident on every face. The entire team was counting on them, and they couldn't afford to fail.

They pulled out of the station, the sense of urgency pushing them forward. The town was waking up, people going about their mornings, unaware of the danger that lurked in the shadows. Every second counted, and they both knew it. The killer had made it personal, and now it was their turn to make sure he understood just how big a mistake that had been.

The drive out towards the state line felt like an eternity. The roads became narrower, the surroundings more desolate as they approached the area indicated in the report. The cabin, if it was out here, was hidden among the rolling dunes and rocky outcroppings, blending into the arid landscape that could easily swallow anyone who wasn't careful.

The wind whipped across the open land, carrying with it the dry scent of dust and desert. Roger could feel the tension building, each mile bringing them closer to something that could either break this case wide open or end in another dead end. Liz checked her weapon, the familiar weight providing a sense of reassurance. "We'll approach quietly," she said, her voice low. "No telling what kind of setup they have out here."

Roger slowed the truck as they neared the turn-off that led towards the cabin. The path was barely visible, overgrown with weeds and lined with thick underbrush. He pulled the vehicle to a stop a safe distance away. "We go on foot from here," he said, opening his door slowly to avoid making any noise.

The air was crisp, each breath visible as they moved through the brush. Liz led the way, her steps deliberate, her eyes scanning the surroundings for any signs of movement. Roger followed close behind, his revolver clutched tight.

Finally, they caught sight of the cabin—a small, weathered structure partially hidden by the barren desert landscape. The wood was cracked and bleached from the sun, the windows dark, boarded-up in places. A rusted metal chimney rose from the roof, and a pile of discarded beer cans lay strewn around the entrance. There was no sign of activity, but that didn't mean it was empty. Roger motioned for Liz to stop, pointing towards the ground. There were fresh tire tracks leading up to the cabin, and alongside them, footprints. Someone had been here recently.

Liz met Roger's gaze, her expression grim. "This is it."

Roger took a step forward, his eyes locked on the cabin door.

They moved closer, each step bringing them nearer to whatever answers waited inside. The air was thick with anticipation, the sense that they were finally closing in on the person who had turned their lives upside down. He looked back at Liz, his hand hovering over the knob. She gave him a nod, and Roger then pushed the door open.

The interior was dim, the air stale. Dust hung in the beams of sunlight that filtered through the gaps in the boarded-up windows. The cabin was sparse—a table, a few chairs, papers scattered across the surface. Roger stepped inside, his eyes quickly scanning the room. Liz followed, her weapon raised, ready for anything.

Roger moved to the table. Strewn among the scattered documents were receipts for fuel and hardware supplies, a crude sketch of the town with key locations circled, and a series of disturbing, handwritten notes. The notes described Kathy's daily routines, Emily's schedule at school in Dallas, and even details about Jason's recent proposal to Liz. It was as if the killer had been standing in the shadows of their lives, documenting every intimate moment. Maps of the town, photographs—some of Kathy, some of Emily, and others of Liz and Jason. There were also candid shots of Roger, taken from angles that suggested he had been followed, his face captured in moments of frustration, exhaustion, and anger. One photo of Liz and Jason was particularly unsettling—it showed them at a quiet dinner, completely unaware of the eyes watching them. His stomach turned at the sight, the realization of how closely they had been watched hitting him hard.

Liz stepped closer, her eyes widening as she spotted the photographs. "They've been planning this for a long time," she whispered, her voice laced with anger. "They know everything about us."

Roger's gaze hardened as he rifled through the papers, finding a handwritten note with today's date. The note read: "Roger, this gives you an idea as to how close I have really been to you. You are wasting your time chasing me. Justice will be done. P.S. Thanks for the extra time with no officer presence." Next to it was a checklist, partially crossed off, with ominous items like "cover tracks at the pit" and "prepare the cabin for final phase." It was clear they were still in the middle of whatever twisted plan they were executing.

Suddenly, Roger's eyes fell on something that made his breath catch—an old war medal, placed deliberately on the table. It was his, a relic of a past he hadn't thought about in years. The medal had been missing for a long time, and now, here it was, sitting amid the killer's plans. The killer knew about his past, had gone through his things. This wasn't just about scaring them—it was personal.

"He's close, Liz. He knew we'd come here." He looked up, his eyes meeting hers. "We need to move. He's not far, and we can't let him slip away."

Liz nodded, her jaw set. "Let's finish this."

The sense of urgency pushed them back out of the cabin, their steps quick as they retraced their path to the truck. Roger's mind raced, the pieces of the puzzle clicking into place faster now. The killer was close, and they had to act before he had another chance to disappear.

As they reached the truck, Roger's radio crackled to life. Garcia's voice came through, tense. "Sheriff, we found something else—an abandoned vehicle, looks like it matches the description from the warehouse footage. It's hidden near the tree line at the caliche pit."

Roger exchanged a glance with Liz, tension evident in his eyes. "Be careful, Garcia. Every move we make is playing right into the killer's hands. He's anticipating us. We need to be careful—they could have traps or be ready for anyone following."

"Understood, Sheriff," Garcia replied. "We'll keep you updated."

Something in Roger's gut twisted, a feeling of dread creeping in. The way everything was laid out, the meticulously placed clues—it felt orchestrated. "Something's not right, Roger," Liz said, her voice barely above a whisper.

Roger nodded, his expression grim. "No, it doesn't." He grabbed the radio. "Garcia, hold your position. We're on our way."

Liz settled into the seat beside him, her hand gripping the dashboard as Roger floored the accelerator. The engine roared, the tires kicking up dust as they sped back towards the caliche pit. The adrenaline coursed through Roger's veins, his focus narrowing on one thing—bringing this nightmare to an end.

As they sped down the desolate road, Roger's mind flashed back to the medal—the way it had been deliberately placed, almost like a taunt. The killer knew him, knew his past, his vulnerabilities. This wasn't just a game; it was a calculated effort to dismantle everything Roger held dear. The realization only hardened his resolve.

CHAPTER THIRTY NINE

Deputy Garcia adjusted his grip on the steering wheel as he led his team deeper into the caliche pit. The terrain was rough, rocky, and unforgiving. Dust kicked up behind their convoy, blurring the already hard-to-see path. His eyes scanned the area, taking in every detail, every out-of-place rock or shadow. They had already found tire tracks, and now they were following them further in. He had a bad feeling about this.

"Alright, everyone, keep your eyes open," Garcia said into his radio. The sun was beating down hard, but the caliche pit felt eerily cold, shadows stretching long across the barren, dusty landscape. He could feel it in his bones—something was about to happen.

His partner, Deputy Morales, sat beside him, the tension evident in her eyes as she kept her gaze fixed on the surroundings. "Feels too quiet," she muttered, her fingers brushing against her radio. Morales had always trusted her instincts, and right now, they were screaming that something wasn't right. She thought of her family—her parents, her younger brother who had just gotten into college—and pushed the worry aside. She needed to stay focused.

Garcia nodded in agreement, his instincts screaming that something was wrong. He grabbed the radio and gave it a quick call. "Sheriff, we found something—tire tracks leading into an overgrown area, like they tried to hide where they were going. We're following it now."

Static crackled, and Roger's voice came through, his tone filled with urgency. "Be careful, Garcia. Every move we make is playing right into the killer's hands. He's anticipating us. We need to be careful—they could have traps or be ready for anyone following."

Garcia swallowed, glancing over at Morales. "Understood, Sheriff," he replied. He could feel his pulse quicken, Roger's warning only adding to the weight of his gut feeling.

Suddenly, there was a deafening boom. The ground shook violently, dust and debris erupting into the air, obscuring their vision. Garcia's truck swerved, the tires skidding as he fought to keep control. An explosion—a trap had been triggered. "Ambush!" he shouted into the radio. "Everyone, get back!"

Another explosion rocked the pit, and this time, the truck lurched to the side, slamming into a pile of rocks. Morales was thrown forward, her seatbelt locking her in place with a hard snap. Her thoughts flashed briefly to her mother's worried face that morning, as if she somehow knew today would be dangerous. "Garcia!" she screamed, her hand fumbling for her weapon.

Garcia's head spun, the world a blur of dust and chaos. He tried to reach for the radio, but another explosion threw him against the door, pain shooting through his side. He could hear shouting, the panicked voices of the other deputies as they tried to regroup, but the sound was drowned out by the ringing in his ears. He looked over at Morales, her face pale, her eyes wide with fear, blood trickling down from a cut on her forehead.

He grabbed the radio, his voice hoarse as he yelled, "Sheriff! It's an ambush! They knew we were coming!"

The line crackled, but before Roger could respond, another explosion sounded, closer this time. The force knocked the radio from Garcia's hand, and it fell somewhere in the chaos of the overturned truck. Morales was trying to move, her face twisted in pain as she clutched at her side. Garcia could feel the heat of the explosions, the acrid smell of smoke filling his nostrils, making it hard to breathe.

"Stay down!" Garcia managed to shout, his vision blurring as he struggled to stay conscious. He could hear gunfire now—sharp, rapid pops echoing through the caliche pit. His team was trying to fight back, but it was clear they were caught off guard. They were in a death trap, and there was no easy way out.

And then, silence. The sudden absence of noise was almost as jarring as the explosions. Dust settled slowly, the once clear air now thick and suffocating. Garcia's world darkened around the edges, pain radiating from his side and chest. He blinked, trying to keep his eyes open, the muffled shouts and sounds of movement around him fading.

Roger gripped the steering wheel so tightly his knuckles turned white. The radio had gone silent after Garcia's last desperate message, and Roger's heart pounded with each second that ticked by. The caliche pit came into view, dust clouds still hanging in the air, and a deep sense of dread settled in his stomach.

"Something's not right," Liz whispered, her eyes wide as she took in the scene. Smoke curled up from several locations, and the twisted remains of a truck lay on its side near a pile of rocks. "Roger..."

Roger didn't wait. He slammed the truck into park and both of them jumped out, their weapon drawn as they moved towards the wreckage.

The scene was chaos. Two of the patrol vehicles were damaged, their doors open, the windows shattered. The ground was scorched black in places, still smoldering from the blasts. Shards of metal and glass littered the area, and the acrid smell of burnt rubber hung heavy in the air. Roger's eyes darted around, searching for any sign of Garcia or the others.

"Over here!" Liz called, her voice urgent. Roger turned, following her to where Deputy Garcia lay on the ground, propped up against a rock. His uniform was torn, his face streaked with dirt and blood. His breathing was shallow, a painful wheeze escaping his lips.

"Garcia," Roger knelt beside him, his hand going to the deputy's shoulder. "Hang in there, kid. We're here now."

Garcia's eyes opened slowly, his gaze unfocused. "Sheriff... it was... they knew," he managed, each word a struggle. "They were waiting... traps everywhere."

Roger nodded, his jaw clenched as he looked around. He could see the devastation—the ambush had been precise, calculated. The killer had planned this, knowing exactly how they would approach. Roger could feel the anger building inside him, the realization that they had walked right into a trap gnawing at him.

"We're going to get you out of here. Just hold on," Roger said, his voice gentler now, trying to reassure the young deputy.

Liz was already on her radio, calling for backup and medical assistance. "We need EMTs at the old caliche pit off of 349 now. We have multiple officers down, repeat, multiple officers down."

Roger looked over to where Morales lay a few feet away, another deputy kneeling beside her, applying pressure to a wound on her leg. The deputy met Roger's eyes, shaking his head grimly. "It's bad, Sheriff. They hit us hard."

Roger turned back to Garcia, the young deputy's face pale, his eyes half-closed. "Stay with me, Garcia. We need you."

Garcia gave a weak nod, his hand clutching at Roger's arm. "Don't let... don't let him win, Sheriff," he whispered, his voice barely audible.

Roger swallowed, his throat tight. "We won't. I promise you that." He squeezed Garcia's shoulder gently, then looked up at Liz, who was scanning the horizon, her face a mask of determination and fear.

"We need to secure this area," Liz said, her voice hard. "This was planned, Roger. He's watching us, playing us."

Roger nodded, his eyes narrowing. The killer had anticipated their every move, laid a trap, and waited for them to walk right into it. But this wasn't over. Not by a long shot. The twisted metal, the injured officers, the smoldering remains of the ambush—it all painted a clear picture of the killer's ruthlessness. But it also fueled Roger's determination. He wouldn't let fear dictate their next steps.

Roger turned back to Garcia, nodding to one of the other deputies who had come to assist. "Get him stabilized. We're not losing anyone today." He looked out over the barren landscape, the sun now high in the sky, casting harsh shadows across the pit. The killer might have planned this ambush, but Roger knew one thing for certain: they were getting closer. And he wouldn't stop—not until the man who had done this was brought to justice.

Roger and Liz made their way back to the sheriff's office. The ride back was silent, both of them lost in thought, replaying the chaos at the caliche pit, the injured deputies, and the ambush that nearly cost them their lives. As they walked into the office, the atmosphere was somber, the officers present exchanging uneasy glances.

Roger made his way to his office, Liz close behind. He sank into his chair, his eyes scanning the scattered papers on his desk, the map of Midland still pinned to the wall, covered in hastily drawn circles and lines. Liz leaned against the doorframe, her arms crossed, her expression unreadable.

Suddenly, the door to the office burst open, and Mayor Thompson stormed in, his face flushed with anger. "Hartley! What the hell is going on?" he shouted, his voice echoing through the small room. "Another ambush? More injured officers? You said you were close to catching this guy, and now look at what's happened!"

Roger's eyes narrowed as he stood, his exhaustion giving way to anger. "We are close, Mayor. But this killer isn't playing by any rules, and he's anticipating every move we make. We're doing the best we can with what we have."

The mayor shook his head, his voice dripping with frustration. "The best you can? People are scared, Roger. They want results. They want this guy caught! And all I see is chaos and injured deputies. If you can't handle this—"

Roger's patience snapped. He slammed his hands down on the desk, his voice rising as he cut the mayor off. "If you would have let us continue the investigation the way we wanted to, maybe this would already be over!" he shouted. "You think I don't want results? You think I don't want this bastard behind bars? My men are out there putting their lives on the line every day, and all you care about is your political image!"

The mayor's eyes widened, stunned into silence by Roger's outburst. Liz watched, her eyes flicking between the two men, her expression tense.

Roger stepped around the desk, his voice lower now but filled with a cold, steely edge. "If you cared about catching this guy as much as you care about how this looks for you, we might be further along. But instead, we're dealing with red tape and bureaucracy while this psychopath is out there targeting our people."

The room fell silent, the tension thick in the air. The mayor opened his mouth to respond but found no words. He stared at Roger, his face a mix of shock and anger.

Roger took a deep breath, his gaze unwavering. "You want results, Mayor? Let us do our jobs. Let us do whatever it takes to bring this guy down. Or get out of our way."

The mayor looked between Roger and Liz, his face still flushed, but he said nothing more. With a final glare, he turned on his heel and left the office, slamming the door behind him.

Liz let out a breath she hadn't realized she'd been holding. "You really let him have it, Roger," she said, her voice almost amused despite the tension still hanging in the room.

Roger shook his head, his anger slowly subsiding. "I'm done tiptoeing around, Liz. This ends now. We regroup, we plan, and we take this guy down—no matter what it takes."

Liz nodded, a determined glint in her eyes. "No more playing by his rules. It's time we take control."

Roger looked at her, a flicker of hope rekindling in his chest. "Damn right."

CHAPTER FORTY

Roger sat behind his desk, recalling the remnants of his confrontation with the mayor. The ambush at the caliche pit had left them shaken but not broken. He could still hear Garcia's weakened voice echoing in his ears, telling him not to let the killer win. He wouldn't. He couldn't. Roger knew it was time for them to take the offensive.

Liz entered the room. She carried a stack of documents, her face set with determination. "I've gathered everything we have on this guy, all the evidence, every lead we've followed up on, and every piece that's been left behind," she said, dropping the pile onto Roger's desk with a thud. "We need to figure this out, Roger. He's playing us, and we have to turn the tables."

Roger leaned forward. Maps of the area, lists of potential hideouts, reports from officers. It was a mess, a collection of dead ends and close calls. He shook his head. "We're missing something. He's always a step ahead of us, like he knows exactly how we'll react. We need to change our approach."

Liz sat down across from him, her expression thoughtful. "Maybe it's not what we're missing, but what we're overlooking. We know he's been watching us, and he knew we were going to that caliche pit. What if there's a pattern in the way he's been predicting us? Something we're not seeing."

Roger nodded slowly, rubbing his temples. The exhaustion was starting to weigh on him, but Liz was right.

There had to be something they were overlooking, a thread they hadn't pulled. "You might be right. He's got inside knowledge, or he's tapped into something. We need to find out what. Get a team on tracking any surveillance cameras near the caliche pit, and see if anyone noticed anything unusual in the last few days. This guy's leaving crumbs—we just have to be smart enough to find them."

Liz scribbled a note on her pad before standing. "I'll get right on it. We also have the reports from the cabin near the state line. The tech team found some interesting documents—some encrypted files that might take a while to crack, but they're working on it. There was also some evidence that pointed to financial transactions—payments made to someone in the area. If we can track that money, we might have a lead."

"That's something we can work with. Follow the money, Liz. Find out who's been receiving those payments. Maybe it's someone local, someone who knows the area and has been helping him stay hidden."

Liz nodded, already heading for the door. Roger picked up one of the maps, his eyes tracing the routes the killer had taken, the places he had hidden. There had to be a connection somewhere, a clue they had missed. He just needed to find it.

A knock at the door pulled Roger out of his thoughts. He looked up to see Deputy Garcia standing in the doorway, his face pale but determined. His arm was in a sling, and he moved slowly, but he was upright and that was what mattered.

"Sheriff," Garcia said, his voice still a bit weak, "I wanted to come in. I can't just sit around while this guy's out there."

Roger stood, crossing the room to clap Garcia on the shoulder. "You should be resting, kid. But I'm glad to see you up. We could use every hand we've got."

Garcia nodded. "I want to help. I've been thinking about the ambush. There was something off about it. It was like he knew exactly where we were coming from, what route we'd take. I think he's got a scout, or someone feeding him information."

"A scout? Someone local?"

Garcia shrugged, wincing at the movement. "Maybe. Or someone with access to our communications. We should check for any compromised lines, any chatter that's been picked up. If he's been listening in, that would explain a lot."

Roger nodded, a new determination settling over him. "Alright. We'll get tech on it. We're going to tear everything apart until we find out how he's getting his information."

Garcia gave a tired smile. "We'll get him, Sheriff."

"Yeah," Roger said quietly. "We will."

Hours later, Roger and Liz sat together in the briefing room, the large map of Midland and the surrounding areas spread out before them. Red lines crisscrossed the map, marking routes, possible hideouts, and areas where the killer had been sighted. Pins marked key locations, and photographs of evidence were scattered across the table.

"We've got to think outside the box," Roger said, his eyes scanning the map. "He's anticipating us, which means we need to do something he won't expect. We need to find a way to catch him off guard."

Liz tapped her pen against the map. "What if we set a trap of our own? Leak some information, make him think we're going somewhere or planning something, and then wait for him to show his hand."

Roger considered it, his brow furrowing. "It's risky. If he catches on, we could be leading our people into another ambush. But if we're careful... if we control the flow of information... it might just work."

Liz nodded. "We'll need to be smart about it. Only a few trusted people can know what we're really doing. We need to make sure he buys it."

"We'll use the media. Feed them a story—make it sound like we're moving in on a big lead, like we've finally found his hiding spot. He'll come to us, try to stop us, and that's when we'll have him."

"It could work, Roger. It's a long shot, but it might be what we need."

"Alright. Let's get to work. We're not letting him stay one step ahead of us anymore. It's time we take control of this game."

"One way or another, this ends soon."

Roger watched her leave, the determination in her stride giving him strength. He turned back to the map, his eyes narrowing. They were done playing by the killer's rules. Now, it was their turn to set the trap.

The hours dragged on, the day fading into evening, then into night. Roger and Liz worked tirelessly, poring over the evidence, piecing together the puzzle that seemed to constantly elude them. The tiredness was beginning to wear on them both—48 hours without sleep, fueled only by coffee and sheer determination. The lines on the map blurred before Roger's eyes, and Liz's pen hovered aimlessly over the paper, her focus slipping.

Roger let out a heavy sigh, leaning back in his chair, his body aching from fatigue. "Liz," he said, his voice hoarse, "we need to get some rest. If we keep going like this, we're going to miss something important."

Liz rubbed her eyes, nodding slowly. "Yeah, you're right. We're no good to anyone if we can't even think straight." She looked at the clock on the wall—almost midnight. The realization of just how long they'd been at it finally hit her. "Alright, let's call it for now."

Roger stood, his body protesting every movement. "Go home, Liz. Get some sleep. We'll regroup in the morning, see if we can't finally get a step ahead of this guy."

Liz gave him a tired smile. "You too, Roger. Don't think you're invincible."

Roger chuckled, a hint of warmth returning to his eyes. "I learned that a long time ago. Be safe."

Roger unlocked the door to his house, stepping inside as the quiet of his home enveloped him. Kathy emerged from the kitchen, worry etched across her face, her eyes searching his for any sign of good news.

"Roger," she said softly, crossing the room to him. She took his hands, her gaze fixed on his tired face. "Are you alright? You look exhausted."

Roger nodded, squeezing her hands gently. "I'm fine, Kathy. Just tired. It's been... it's been a long day." He sighed, the stress evident in his voice. "We're trying to catch up, but he keeps slipping away. I think we might be getting closer, but I'm not going to lie—it's been rough."

Kathy pulled him into a hug, her arms wrapping around his weary frame. "You'll catch him, Roger. I know you will. Just promise me you'll take care of yourself too. I can't lose you."

Roger closed his eyes, resting his head against her shoulder. "I promise, Kathy. I'm doing everything I can. I just need a little more time."

She pulled back, looking up at him, her eyes filled with love and concern. "Then get some rest tonight. You need it. We'll get through this."

Roger managed a small smile, leaning down to kiss her forehead. "I will. Thanks for believing in me."

Meanwhile, Liz stepped into her house, the fatigue hitting her like a wave as she closed the door behind her. The soft sound of the TV greeted her, and she found Jason sprawled on the couch, half-asleep, a worried expression crossing his face as he looked up and saw her.

"Liz," he said, sitting up quickly. "You're finally home." He rubbed his eyes, trying to shake off the sleep. "I've been worried sick. You weren't answering your phone."

Liz dropped her bag by the door, walking over to sit beside him. She took his hand, her fingers brushing against his. "I'm sorry, Jason. It's just been... nonstop. We've been working around the clock, and we're still not any closer to getting this guy."

Jason cupped her face gently. "You're doing everything you can. But you need to take care of yourself too. You're not alone in this, Liz."

Liz leaned into his touch, closing her eyes for a moment. "I know. I just hate feeling like he's always one step ahead. Like no matter what we do, we're just playing catch-up."

Jason pulled her into an embrace, holding her tightly. "You're going to catch him. I know you will. You're the toughest person I know, Liz. But tonight, you need to rest. You're no good to anyone if you're running on empty."

Liz nodded, her exhaustion finally catching up with her. "You're right. I just... I can't let him win. Not after everything."

Jason kissed the top of her head. "You won't. Not you. Just sleep tonight, okay? We'll face tomorrow together."

Liz let out a deep breath, the tension slowly easing from her shoulders. "Okay," she whispered. "Tomorrow."

Jason smiled, pulling her closer. "Tomorrow."

CHAPTER FORTY ONE

Roger jolted awake at the shrill ring of his phone. He fumbled for it on the nightstand, glancing at the clock—5:27 AM. The number on the screen told him it was dispatch.

"Sheriff Hartley," he answered, his voice thick with sleep.

"Sheriff, we just received a 911 call from the Lawson residence," the dispatcher said, urgency lacing her tone. "It was cut off. We're not sure what happened, but it didn't sound good."

Roger was instantly alert, throwing off the covers as he swung his legs over the side of the bed. His mind snapped into focus, adrenaline surging as the grogginess dissipated. "I'm on my way," he said, hanging up before the dispatcher could respond. He grabbed his badge and gun, his heart racing. He knew he needed Liz.

Roger dialed her number. After a couple of rings, Liz picked up, her voice groggy. "Roger? It's barely morning."

"Liz, it's Lawson's place. Dispatch got a 911 call, and it was cut off," Roger said, already moving through his house, pulling on his boots. "We need to get over there now."

There was a brief silence before Liz's tone shifted, the sleepiness replaced by urgency. "I'm on my way. Meet you there."

Roger hung up and rushed out of the house, the cool early morning air biting at his skin as he stepped onto the porch. He jumped into his truck, the engine roaring to life, and peeled out of the driveway, his tires squealing on the gravel.

The streets of Midland were empty at this hour, the city still wrapped in the quiet of dawn. The sky was a dull gray, the first hints of sunlight just beginning to peek over the horizon, casting long shadows across the deserted roads. As Roger sped towards the Lawson residence, flashes of worst-case scenarios played out in his head. Henry Lawson had been on edge lately, paranoid even, and Roger couldn't shake the nagging feeling that this was exactly what he feared. A nagging fear lodged in Roger's chest—the thought that he might be too late. Again.

The Lawson house came into view, and Roger felt a pit form in his stomach. It was dark, the front door slightly ajar, swaying with the morning breeze. He parked hastily, gravel crunching under the tires. The stillness of the scene only deepened the unease gnawing at his gut.

Liz pulled up seconds later, her patrol car skidding to a stop. She jumped out, her eyes wide with concern, her hair pulled hastily into a ponytail. "Roger, what do you think we're walking into?"

Roger shook his head, his eyes locked on the darkened doorway. "I don't know. But I've got a bad feeling about this. Let's go."

Together, they approached the house, their guns drawn, their steps cautious. The living room was dim, the early morning light barely filtering through the ripped curtains. The air was thick with the metallic scent of blood, and Roger's stomach twisted as his eyes adjusted to the darkness.

And then he saw it.

Henry Lawson lay sprawled in the middle of the living room, his body twisted and broken, blood pooling around him, soaking into the carpet. His face was unrecognizable—a mass of bruises, cuts, and congealed blood, swollen and battered beyond recognition. One arm was bent at an impossible angle, the bones clearly broken beneath the skin, his fingers still curled as if grasping at something that wasn't there. His legs were shattered, positioned with jagged bone protruding from one shin, and his chest—Roger felt his stomach churn—looked like it had been caved in, ribs snapped inward, leaving a gruesome hollow.

The metallic stench of blood mixed with something fouler, a testament to the brutal struggle that had taken place. The room was in complete disarray—furniture overturned, the coffee table shattered into splinters, its pieces scattered across the floor. Blood spattered the walls, streaked in arcs that suggested wild, frenzied blows. A lamp lay shattered near the far wall, its shade dented and stained with dark splatters. Books were scattered, their pages torn and trampled, and the curtains had been partially ripped from their rods. It was a scene of pure, unrestrained violence—rage made manifest, a deliberate display meant to shock anyone who found it.

Liz let out a sharp gasp, her hand flying to her mouth. "Oh my God," she whispered, her eyes wide with horror.

Roger forced himself to step closer, his eyes examining every gruesome detail. Henry's eyes were open, staring blankly at the ceiling, his mouth twisted in a silent scream. Roger knelt beside the body, his gut churning, and it was then that he noticed the way Henry's body was positioned. It wasn't random. It was deliberate. The twisted, mangled form—he'd seen it before.

It hit him like a punch to the gut. The Marathon Oil explosion. The old photo flashed in his mind—the bodies of the victims, twisted and broken, staged deliberately, left as a message. This was no coincidence; this was the killer's signature, tying the murders of the old board members together in a grim pattern. Roger clenched his jaw, the realization filling him with a cold, hard rage.

"Roger, this is exactly like the Marathon case," she said, her voice steady, despite the horror in her eyes. "He's finishing what he started. There's only one left now—Gerald Simmons."

Roger nodded, his jaw clenched so tightly it hurt. "He's sending a clear message. He's telling us that he's almost done, that he's in control, and that we're too late."

Liz looked around the room, her expression hardening. She kicked aside a piece of broken furniture, her eyes blazing with determination. "We need to act fast, Roger. He's going after Simmons next. We need to get to him before it's too late."

Roger stood, his eyes never leaving Henry's lifeless form. The brutality of the scene was overwhelming, but beneath the horror, Roger felt something else—rage. Pure, unfiltered rage. The killer had taken another life, someone who had trusted Roger, someone who had been under his protection. The killer had challenged him, and Roger wasn't going to let it stand.

Roger looked around the room. The killer had left a message, but maybe, just maybe, he'd left something else. A clue. A mistake. Roger knew they were dealing with someone who was always a step ahead, but this time, he was determined to catch up.

Marla, the county coroner, arrived not long after, her team trailing behind her, carrying their equipment in heavy cases. She stepped into the living room, her eyes scanning the scene, her face hardening at the sight of Henry's mutilated body.

"Jesus, Roger," she muttered, shaking her head. "This guy doesn't leave anything to the imagination, does he?"

Roger nodded grimly. "No, he doesn't. We need anything you can give us, Marla. Even the smallest mistake could help us catch this bastard."

Marla nodded, slipping on her gloves as she gestured for her team to start setting up. They moved with practiced precision, unfazed by the horrific scene, as they began taking photographs, carefully documenting every detail—the angles of the blood spatter, the position of the body, the damaged furniture. The flash from the camera punctuated the heavy silence, each burst of light illuminating the brutality.

Marla knelt beside Henry, studying the body's broken form. She gently prodded the body, her gloved hands moving with care as she checked for any foreign objects or signs of a struggle that might reveal more about the killer.

After several minutes, Marla paused, her hand hovering over Henry's chest. "Wait a second," she said, her voice sharp. She reached into her kit, pulling out a pair of tweezers, and delicately extracted a small fragment of something from the wound on Henry's chest.

Liz leaned closer, her eyes narrowing. "What is it?"

Marla held it up, her brow furrowed. "Looks like... a piece of cloth. It's embedded pretty deep, like it got caught during the struggle." She examined it closely, then paused, her eyes narrowing further. "Wait—there's a hair tangled in it." She used the tweezers to carefully pull the hair free, holding it up to the light. "This isn't Henry's. It's too dark, and the texture's different." She glanced at Roger and Liz, her expression serious. "This could be from the killer. If we're lucky, it might still have a root. We could get DNA from this."

Roger felt a surge of hope, his heart pounding. "A mistake," he muttered, his eyes locking on the small fragment and the dark hair. "He finally made a mistake."

Marla nodded. "I'll get this back to the lab, see if we can get anything off it—DNA, fibers, anything that might give us a lead."

Roger's jaw tightened. "Do it fast, Marla. We don't have much time."

As Marla and her team continued their work, Roger's radio crackled to life, the dispatcher's voice cutting through the tense silence.

"Sheriff Hartley, we just received a 911 call from one of Gerald Simmons' neighbors. They reported a disturbance at his house."

Roger's heart skipped a beat, his eyes meeting Liz's. "It's him," he said, his voice filled with urgency. "He's going after Simmons."

Liz's face hardened, her eyes blazing with determination. "Let's move, Roger. We can't let him finish this."

Roger nodded, turning on his heel, his boots thudding heavily against the floor as he rushed out of the house. The race against time had begun again, but this time, they had something—a piece of the killer. And Roger was going to make damn sure it was enough.

CHAPTER FORTY TWO

The truck roared to life, the tires kicking up gravel as Roger and Liz sped towards the Simmons residence. The tension in the air was thick, every second that ticked by feeling like an eternity.

"We can't be too late," Roger muttered, his voice barely audible over the engine. "Not again."

Liz nodded, her hand resting on her weapon. "We'll get there, Roger. We have to."

The Simmons house came into view, and Roger's heart sank. The front door was slightly open, swinging slightly in the morning breeze. The neighborhood was eerily quiet and still. The only sound was the soft clatter of wind chimes from a nearby porch, their hollow notes contrasting with the tension in the air.

Roger and Liz exchanged a glance before jumping out of the truck, their weapons drawn as they approached the house. Roger pushed the door open wider, the hinges creaking as they stepped inside. The entryway was dark, the air thick with tension, and an unsettling stillness clung to every corner of the home. The smell of stale air and something metallic lingered, making Roger's stomach twist. The silence was broken only by the soft creak of the door as it closed behind them.

And then they heard it—a faint, muffled scream, coming from somewhere below them.

"Help! Somebody, please!"

Liz's eyes widened, and she pointed towards a door at the far end of the hallway. "The basement," she said, her voice urgent.

They quickly made their way down the hall. Roger yanked the basement door open, the smell of dampness and mildew hitting him as he flicked on the light switch. The dim bulb overhead illuminated a narrow staircase leading down into the darkness. The basement walls were made of rough concrete, and the stairs creaked beneath their weight.

The scream came again. "Please, help me!"

Roger and Liz descended the stairs, their guns leading the way. At the bottom, they found her—Lisa Simmons, tied up and hanging upside down from a rafter, her face streaked with tears, her eyes wide with terror. Her wrists were bound, her ankles tightly fastened to the rafter, the rope digging into her skin, leaving deep red welts. Her clothes were torn, and her face was smeared with dirt, her lips cracked and trembling.

"Oh my God," Liz whispered, rushing forward. She holstered her weapon and quickly began working on the knots, her fingers moving with frantic precision. Roger scanned the basement, his eyes darting from corner to corner, looking for any sign of the killer. The basement was cluttered—boxes were stacked haphazardly, old furniture was pushed against the walls, and a damp, musty smell permeated the air. Every darkened corner felt like it could be hiding something sinister, each shadow a potential threat. But it was empty—just Lisa, suspended like a fanciful trophy.

"We've got you," Liz said, her voice gentle as she finally managed to loosen the ropes. Lisa fell into her arms, her body trembling, her breaths coming in ragged gasps, her face streaked with dried tears.

Roger knelt beside them, his eyes meeting Lisa's. "Where's Gerald? What happened here?"

Lisa's eyes filled with fresh tears, her voice breaking. "They... they attacked him. In the bedroom. I heard them... I heard them..." Her voice trailed off, her body wracked with sobs, her voice barely a whisper. "The screams... I couldn't do anything."

Roger exchanged a look with Liz, dread settling in the pit of his stomach. "Stay with her," he said, his voice tight. "I'm going upstairs."

Liz nodded, holding Lisa close as Roger stood and made his way back up the stairs, his heart pounding. His mind flashed back to scenes from his past—a dimly lit room overseas, the acrid smell of gunpowder, the lifeless faces of comrades lost. He forced the memories down, focusing on the task at hand.

Marla entered the basement, her face grim. She had left the Lawson scene to her assistant, knowing the gravity of what might be happening here. Roger caught her eye, and she gave a determined nod, following him up the stairs. Every step felt like it carried the weight of the world, his mind already bracing for what he might find. They moved down the hallway together, towards the master bedroom, the door slightly ajar. The metallic smell of blood hit him before he even pushed the door open.

He pushed it open, and the scene that met his eyes was worse than anything he could have imagined. The room was an absolute nightmare. Blood covered every surface—splattered across the walls, dripping from the ceiling, pooling on the floor. The metallic stench was overwhelming, filling Roger's nostrils, making his stomach turn. The bed was a mangled mess, the sheets soaked in crimson, twisted and torn as though they had been fought against. Gerald Simmons lay sprawled on the bed, his body beyond recognition. His internal organs were torn out, strewn across the room like a whimsical display of trophies. Pieces of what once were parts of a human lay scattered around—a liver, intestines, parts of a lung. His skull had been crushed, bone fragments piercing the skin, his face barely distinguishable beneath the blood and carnage. The brutality was almost surreal, like a nightmare brought to life.

Roger's eyes took in every gruesome detail—the torn flesh, the deep gashes, the dark pools of blood soaking into the carpet. On the wall above the bed, written in Gerald's blood, were the words: "It Is Finished. Justice Is Done."

Marla's face was etched with a mix of shock and disgust—she had seen many horrific things in her career, but this was beyond anything any of them had encountered. The sheer violence, the rage—it was all too evident. She moved closer to examine the body, her hands trembling slightly, her gaze darting over the gruesome details.

"He staged it... just like before," Marla whispered, her voice barely audible. "He wants us to see his message, to know he's in control."

Roger forced himself to step closer, his eyes narrowing as he scanned the scene. Gerald's body was posed, his limbs arranged deliberately, his face turned towards the door. Roger recognized it immediately—it was identical to the last body in the Marathon Oil explosion photo. The killer had finished what he'd started, leaving no doubt that this was the final act in his twisted game. Marla's voice broke the silence again, filled with grim determination.

"We need to find anything he might have left behind—something he missed. He's gotten overconfident, and that might be his downfall."

Roger nodded, his jaw clenched. "He thinks it's over, but we're not done yet. We're going to find him."

Roger's eyes moved to Gerald's shirt, where something caught his attention—a piece of paper, sticking out of the pocket. Marla carefully reached for it, her gloves protecting the evidence from contamination. "Roger," Marla said, her voice trembling slightly, "there's something here." She pulled the note free, holding it out to him, her expression a mix of fear and determination.

Roger reached for it, his fingers trembling as he pulled it free. Marla watched, her face pale, her eyes locking onto the note with a mix of fear and determination. He unfolded it, his heart pounding as he read the words written in neat, deliberate handwriting:

"Roger, thanks for letting me finish. Justice has finally been done. I am leaving you a bonus present at the door of the Sheriff's office."

Roger's blood ran cold. He crumpled the note in his fist, his jaw clenched, a mix of rage and dread flooding through him. He could feel his pulse in his temples, the adrenaline kicking in as his entire body tensed.

He turned, rushing back down the hallway, his footsteps echoing off the walls, his voice echoing through the house. "Liz! We need to go—now!"

He found Liz at the bottom of the basement stairs, her arm still around Lisa, who was trembling and barely holding herself together. Liz looked up, her eyes meeting Roger's, and she saw the urgency in his expression.

"What did you find?" she asked, her voice strained.

"He's left us a message," Roger said, his voice tight. "A note—it says he's left us something at the door of the Sheriff's office. We need to get there now."

Liz's eyes widened, and she glanced down at Lisa, who was still sobbing quietly. "We can't leave her here, Roger. She needs help."

Roger nodded, his mind racing. "I'll call it in. We'll have EMTs here in minutes." He grabbed his radio, his voice firm as he relayed the situation to dispatch. "This is Sheriff Hartley. We need medical assistance at the Simmons residence. Victim is alive but needs immediate care. Also, we need units to secure this scene."

Dispatch responded, confirming that help was on the way. Roger turned back to Liz. "We need to move. We can't let this bastard get away."

At that moment, two officers entered the basement. One was young, his face pale, eyes wide with a mix of fear and determination—this was likely one of his first major calls. "Sheriff, we got your call," he said, moving over to Lisa, his voice wavering slightly.

Liz looked up, relief washing over her face. "Take care of her. EMTs are on the way, but she needs support now."

The officers nodded, one kneeling beside Lisa, speaking to her in a soothing voice, while the other helped to stabilize her. The younger officer's hands shook as he worked, his eyes betraying his inexperience, while his partner—older, more grizzled—guided him, his voice steady.

Liz turned her attention back to Roger, her eyes reflecting both exhaustion and determination. Roger and Liz moved quickly, leaving the basement and heading towards the front door. Whatever the killer had left at the Sheriff's office, it was part of his twisted game, and Roger knew they were running out of time to stop it.

Roger slammed the door shut, the engine roaring to life as he sped away from the Simmons residence. Liz glanced over at him, her face set in grim determination. "Roger, whatever he left... it could be a trap. We need to be ready for anything."

Roger nodded, his eyes locked on the road ahead. "I know. But we can't let fear slow us down. Not now." He gripped the steering wheel tighter, his gaze hard and unwavering. "He's been ahead of us every step of the way. But this time, we're going to catch him."

The truck raced through the empty streets, the siren blaring as they made their way towards the Sheriff's office, the weight of what awaited them pressing down like a storm cloud. Roger's mind raced, the note's words echoing over and over again.

"Justice has finally been done."

The killer thought it was over. But Roger knew better.

It wasn't over until they stopped him.

CHAPTER FORTY THREE

Roger pulled the truck up to the Sheriff's office, the sirens dying down as they came to a screeching halt in front of the building. Leaning up against the front door, barely able to hold himself upright, was Mayor Thompson. His face was a mess of bruises, his skin swollen and discolored. Blood ran down from a gash on his forehead, and his shirt was torn and stained with crimson. He looked like he'd been through hell—and somehow, he was still standing.

"Oh my God," Liz gasped, her eyes widening as she threw her door open. Roger's heart pounded as he jumped out of the truck, rushing over to the mayor. The sight of him—alive but barely—filled Roger with a mix of shock and rage. They had been too late to save Simmons, but somehow, the mayor had survived.

"Mayor Thompson," Roger called out, his voice filled with urgency as he knelt beside him. The mayor looked up, his eyes glassy, his breath labored. Roger caught a glimpse of a piece of paper pinned to the mayor's shirt. He carefully reached for it, his heart sinking as he read the words:

"You're welcome. This asshole was just a bonus. Thanks again for letting me finish."

Roger's blood boiled as he crumpled the note in his fist. The killer had used the mayor as a twisted parting gift—a taunt, a reminder that he had been in control the entire time. Roger looked up at Liz, his eyes filled with fury.

"Call EMS," he barked, his voice tight. "Get them here now."

Liz nodded, her hand already on her radio as she called for medical assistance. Roger turned back to the mayor, his eyes narrowing. "Mayor Thompson, can you hear me? Who did this to you? What happened?"

The mayor's eyes fluttered, his breaths coming in ragged gasps. He tried to speak, his voice barely a whisper. "It... it was him... he came out of nowhere. Said... said I was part of the problem." He winced, a pained groan escaping his lips. "He... he knew everything. About the board, about what we did."

Roger's heart pounded in his chest, his grip tightening on the mayor's shoulder. "What else did he say? Did you see his face?"

The mayor shook his head weakly, his eyes closing for a moment as if trying to gather his strength. "No... he wore a mask. But his voice... he said... he said it was all about justice. That we had to pay for what we did." He paused, his eyes welling up with tears, his voice trembling. "He knew about the deals. About the money. Everything we covered up. He said we were all guilty."

Roger exchanged a glance with Liz, who was now standing beside him, her face pale but determined. "The board... he's targeting all of you. Did he say anything about where he's going next?"

Mayor Thompson's eyes opened again, tears welling up as he looked at Roger. "He said... he said it was over. That he'd done what he came to do." He swallowed hard, his voice breaking. "But... but he also said... there's more to come."

Roger felt a chill run down his spine. More to come. The killer was not done, even after all the carnage he had left behind. Roger clenched his jaw, his eyes locking with Liz's. There was still a final act that hadn't yet played out.

The wail of an approaching ambulance broke through the tense silence, and Roger looked up, seeing the EMTs rushing towards them. "Over here!" he called out, waving them over. The EMTs moved quickly, lifting the battered mayor onto a stretcher.

Roger stood, his hands on his hips, his eyes narrowing as he watched the EMTs work. The mayor's face was bruised beyond recognition, his clothing torn and stained with blood. His breathing was labored, each breath a painful effort.

Roger took a deep breath, trying to steady himself. He watched as the EMTs carefully loaded Mayor Thompson into the ambulance, the stretcher wheels clattering against the pavement. The mayor groaned, his face contorting in pain, and Roger could see the fear in his eyes. The killer had reduced a powerful man to this—a broken, battered shell.

"You're welcome."

The killer had thanked them—as if they had allowed him to complete his mission, as if they had somehow helped him. It was infuriating, and it was enough to fuel Roger's determination even further. He glanced at Liz, her face set in a mask of cold fury.

"We need to regroup," Roger said, his voice hard. "We need to figure out what his next move is. We can't let him disappear again."

Liz nodded, her eyes filled with the same fire. "We will, Roger. We won't let him win. Not this time."

Roger watched as the ambulance pulled away, the mayor inside, fighting for his life. The siren wailed, the sound fading into the distance as the vehicle turned the corner and disappeared from view. The street fell silent, the weight of everything that had happened pressing down on them. Roger turned back to Liz, his jaw set, his eyes filled with resolve.

"We need to get everyone back to the station," Roger said. "All hands on deck. I want every piece of evidence we have laid out, every possible lead. He thinks he can outsmart us, but we're going to show him just how wrong he is."

Liz nodded, determination flashing in her eyes. "We need to hit him where it hurts. He's cocky—he's making mistakes. The note, the way he left the mayor alive... he's slipping."

Roger took a deep breath, letting Liz's words sink in. She was right. The killer's arrogance was showing, and they had to take advantage of that. He turned back to the door of the Sheriff's office, the sight of it filling him with a renewed sense of urgency. They couldn't waste any more time.

"Let's get inside," Roger said, his voice firm. "We need to move fast."

As they stepped into the Sheriff's office, the familiar hum of activity greeted them. Officers moved with purpose, their faces etched with the same determination Roger felt. Roger turned to Liz. "Get everyone in the briefing room. We need to go over everything—every note, every clue, every detail. We can't afford to miss anything."

Liz nodded and moved off, her voice ringing out as she called the officers to gather. Roger watched her for a moment before heading to his office, his mind still replaying the mayor's words.

More to come.

The killer wasn't done, and Roger knew that whatever was coming next would be worse. But they would be ready. They had to be. For the mayor, for Simmons, for everyone who had suffered at the hands of this madman.

Roger clenched his jaw, his eyes hardening as he stepped into his office. He grabbed the board where they had pinned every piece of evidence they had—photos, notes, maps. He stared at it, his eyes scanning every detail, every connection.

This ends now.

CHAPTER FORTY FOUR

The briefing room was buzzing with tension. The fluorescent lights cast a harsh glare over the gathered officers, their faces reflecting determination. Roger stood at the front, his hands resting on the edges of a table covered in documents, maps, and photographs.

Roger cleared his throat and began, "Alright, everyone, listen up." The room quieted immediately, all eyes turning towards him. "We all know what happened this morning. The killer left Mayor Thompson at our doorstep, alive but barely. He left us a message—a twisted thank you, to remind us that he thinks he's in control."

Roger paused, then leaned forward and continued, "But he made a mistake. He's getting cocky, and that means he's slipping. We're going to take advantage of that. He thinks he's untouchable, but we're going to prove him wrong."

The room seemed to vibrate with a silent energy. Officers shifted in their seats, their attention unwavering. Sanders, a young officer near the back, clenched his jaw, tenacity visible even through his fatigue, while Jenkins, the older officer beside him, gave a subtle nod, his eyes steely with resolve.

Liz stepped forward, her voice strong. "We need every piece of evidence laid out. Every note, every detail, every inconsistency. He thinks he's outsmarted us, but we know better. We have his patterns, his targets, and his signature. It's time we start using that to our advantage." She could see

Officer Mendoza frowning, his brow furrowed, and she gave him a brief nod, acknowledging his doubt but pressing on.

Liz paused, glancing at the gathered officers. "I want someone to go through the Marathon Oil explosion step by step," she said. "We need to break it down, reexamine every single detail. The explosion is at the core of this entire thing, and I have a feeling there's something we've missed—something that can point us to who this guy really is. If the clue is there, we're going to find it."

Roger nodded in agreement. "Sanders," he called out, pointing to the young officer near the back of the room. "I want you to take the lead on this. Go through everything we have on the Marathon Oil explosion—witness statements, the original investigation, photographs, anything and everything. If there's something in there that will tell us who this bastard is, I want it found."

Officer Sanders nodded, his face showing a mix of determination and focus. "Yes, Sheriff. I'll get right on it."

Roger turned towards the board behind him, where photos of the Marathon Oil explosion and victims were pinned in a chaotic but intentional manner. Strings connected the faces of the board members in red ink, creating a web that looked as tangled as the case felt. He pointed at the explosion photo, the faces of the board members circled. "This has been his focus from the beginning. Every one of these victims was part of the old board. He thinks he's completed his mission, but we know there's more to come. He said it himself—this isn't over."

"Sheriff, do we have any idea what 'more to come' might mean? Any indication of what he plans to do next?" The voice belonged to Officer Reynolds, who looked as if he hadn't slept in days.

Roger shook his head. "Not yet. But we know his MO. He likes to send messages, and he likes to taunt us. That means he's going to make a move that gets our attention. We need to be ready for anything. We need eyes everywhere— every public figure, every known associate of the board. He's going to strike where it hurts, and we need to be there first."

Liz stepped in. "We also need to look at any connection we might have missed—something that ties all of this together beyond the board members. There has to be a reason he's doing this. Something personal. Find out what turned him into the monster we're dealing with."

The room was silent, the gravity of the situation hanging heavy over everyone present. Roger could see the exhaustion in their eyes, but he also saw the perseverance. They were not backing down—not now, not ever. The stakes were too high, the cost of failure unimaginable.

"This is going to take everything we've got," Roger said, his voice low but firm. "We're dealing with someone who's always a step ahead, but we're not going to let that stop us. We owe it to the victims, to DA Bennett, to Mayor Thompson, to everyone in this town."

He looked at Liz, who gave him a slight nod. She turned back to the officers. "Let's get to work. Split into teams— one group will reexamine the crime scenes, look for anything we might have missed. Another will go through the victim's files again, see if there's a connection we didn't catch. The rest of you, I want patrols increased in all key areas. No one moves without us knowing about it."

The officers nodded, murmurs of agreement spreading through the room as they began to split up, each person knowing their role. The tension shifted, turning into a sense of purpose, a resolve to take action. Officer Jenkins placed a reassuring hand on Mendoza's shoulder as they moved to their stations, while Sanders rushed to grab his files.

Roger watched them for a moment before turning back to the board. His eyes locked on the photos of the crime scenes, his mind racing. There was something there—something they were missing, something the killer was using against them. He could feel it, just out of reach.

"Sanders," Roger called out as the young officer began to gather his materials. "Start with the initial investigation reports. Go through them with a fine-toothed comb. I want every detail reexamined—no matter how small. This guy's gotten too comfortable. He thinks we've forgotten something, and it's time we prove him wrong."

Sanders nodded, stubbornness written all over his face. "Yes, sir. I'll get right on it."

Liz placed a hand on Roger's shoulder. "We're going to get him, Roger. We're closer than we've ever been. He's scared—that's why he's taunting us. He knows we're closing in."

Roger nodded, his jaw tight, the weariness evident in his eyes. "I know. And when we find him, we're going to make sure he never hurts anyone again."

Liz gave him a small, reassuring smile. "We will. But for now, you need to get some rest. We've all been running on empty, and we can't afford any mistakes."

Roger hesitated, his eyes still fixed on the board. She was right—they had been going nonstop, and the case was starting to take its toll. He let out a long breath, nodding. "Alright. But only for a couple of hours. We need to stay on top of this."

Liz nodded, her eyes softening. "A couple of hours. I'll hold you to that." She squeezed his shoulder before turning and walking away, her voice calling out orders as she joined the others.

Roger took one last look at the board before stepping away. The killer thought he was in control, but Roger knew better. They were getting closer—every piece of evidence, every clue, was leading them to him. And when they found him, Roger would make sure that justice was finally served.

He opened the door to his office and stepped inside, the room dark and quiet. He sank into his chair, his eyes drifting to the stack of reports on his desk. He knew he needed rest, but his mind refused to shut down. There was still too much to do, too many questions left unanswered.

Roger leaned back, closing his eyes for a moment, the hard days finally catching up with him. He took a deep breath, letting it out slowly. He could hear the muffled sounds of the station, the voices of officers organizing, the shuffling of papers. They were getting closer. The killer had made a mistake, and Roger was going to make sure they used it to bring him down.

This wasn't over—not by a long shot.

Suddenly, a knock on the door pulled Roger from the edge of sleep. He opened his eyes, the dim light casting shadows across the room. The door opened slightly, and Sanders peeked inside, his face a mix of excitement and urgency.

"Sheriff, I think I found something," Sanders said, stepping into the room. He was holding a stack of files, his eyes wide. "It's about the Marathon Oil explosion. There was a witness statement that was disregarded in the original investigation. It might be nothing, but it sounds like it could be a lead."

Roger sat up, his tiredness suddenly forgotten. "A witness statement? What did it say?"

Sanders moved closer, laying the files on Roger's desk and flipping through them. "This statement came from a worker at the site. He mentioned seeing someone hanging around the area a few days before the explosion—someone who didn't seem to belong there. The guy said it looked suspicious, but it was never followed up on properly. The description... it matches someone we've seen before."

Roger's heart pounded as he leaned over the file, scanning the statement. "Who does it match?"

Sanders pointed to a photo in the file—a grainy image of a man with a dark hoodie, his face partially obscured. "It's not definitive, but the build, the posture... it matches the description given by some of the witnesses from the recent crime scenes. I think it could be him, Sheriff."

Roger's eyes narrowed as he studied the photo. It was far from clear, but there was something familiar about the figure. His instincts told him Sanders was onto something. "Good work, Sanders," Roger said, his voice filled with a renewed determination. "Get Liz and meet me in the briefing room. We need to go over this with everyone. This could be the break we've been waiting for."

Sanders nodded, a flicker of excitement crossing his face. "Yes, sir. I'll get her right away."

As Sanders hurried out of the office, Roger stood, his lack of energy replaced by a sense of purpose. He grabbed the files and made his way back towards the briefing room. The station was still bustling, the energy tense but focused. Officers were moving with urgency, determined to find the killer before he could strike again.

Roger entered the briefing room, the fluorescent lights flickering slightly as he placed the files on the table. A few officers looked up, their curiosity piqued by Roger's determined expression. Moments later, Liz walked in, followed by Sanders, who was practically vibrating with energy.

"What have we got, Roger?" Liz asked.

Roger gestured to the files on the table. "Sanders found a witness statement from the original Marathon Oil explosion investigation. It was overlooked back then, but it could be the key we've been missing. There was someone seen hanging around the site before the explosion—someone who matches the descriptions we've been getting from the recent crime scenes."

Liz's eyes widened, and she moved closer to look at the photo Sanders had pointed out. "This could be it," she said, her voice tinged with hope. "If we can identify this guy, we might finally have a name."

Roger nodded. "We need to move fast. I want everyone on this—see if we can enhance the image, cross-reference it with any known associates of the board, or anyone with a grudge against them. We need to know who this bastard is, and we need to know now."

The room buzzed with activity as officers moved to their stations, their focus sharpened by the possibility of a breakthrough. Roger looked at Liz, the resolve in her eyes mirroring his own.

Roger took a deep breath, his eyes scanning the room as his team worked tirelessly. This was it. They were finally closing in, and Roger knew that no matter what it took, they were going to end this nightmare once and for all.

CHAPTER FORTY FIVE

Liz sat at her desk, scrolling through the list of maintenance workers they had pulled from various job sites. Most had clean backgrounds, a few with minor records, but one stood out.

Walter Perell.

No tax records. No social security number. No birth certificate. No driver's license. Nothing.

She frowned, leaning forward. "Roger, look at this."

Roger walked over, squinting at the screen. "What are we looking at?"

Liz tapped the name. "Walter Perell. He's listed as a maintenance worker at several of the buildings tied to our victims. But he doesn't exist."

Roger rubbed his jaw, his gut telling him something was off. "How the hell does a guy get hired with no background?"

From the back of the room, Sanders suddenly straightened, flipping through his notepad. His brow furrowed as he flipped back a few more pages, then a few more.

Liz and Roger both turned toward him.

"Sanders?" Roger asked.

Sanders didn't answer at first. He muttered something under his breath, then abruptly grabbed a pen and started scribbling letters down.

He exhaled sharply. "No way…"

Roger took a step closer. "You got something?"

Sanders flipped his notepad around.

Walter Perell.

Then, directly beneath it:

Peter Weller.

Liz's stomach dropped. Roger inhaled sharply.

They had seen that name before.

It had been buried in one of the old Marathon Oil records—Peter Weller, a name that had come up but hadn't seemed relevant at the time. But now, staring at the letters rearranged in front of them, it all made sense.

"Shit," Liz whispered.

"It's an anagram," Sanders said, his voice steady. "Walter Perell is just Peter Weller, rearranged. He didn't disappear—he changed his name."

Roger's hands clenched into fists. "That's why the background check came back wrong. The son of a bitch reinvented himself."

Liz exhaled. "He's been hiding in plain sight. Working under a false identity. No records because he erased his past."

Roger sat down heavily, shaking his head. "We need to find everything we can on this guy. I want to know every damn place he's worked, every person he's talked to, and what his next move is."

Liz was already on it, fingers flying across the keyboard. "Pulling up old Marathon Oil employee records now."

Seconds later, the screen flickered, and an archived photograph loaded onto the monitor.

The Marathon Oil board members. Taken twenty years ago.

Roger straightened as Liz enlarged the image and cast it onto the wall. The old projector hummed as the grainy picture flickered to life.

And there he was.

Peter Weller.

A younger version of the man they had just uncovered. He stood near the corner of the group, his expression unreadable, his posture rigid. The photo might have been two decades old, but there was no mistaking it.

Roger exhaled sharply. "Alright, listen up, everyone. We have a name—Peter Weller. He was a site manager at Marathon Oil twenty years ago, and he lost everything in that explosion. His father, two uncles, and his brother were killed that day. And when Marathon refused to compensate his mother, she spiraled until she took her own life."

Liz shook her head, eyes still locked on the image. "He's been harboring this hatred for twenty years."

Roger's voice was grave. "And now we know he's the one behind all of this."

Sanders, still flipping through old files, suddenly stiffened. "There's more."

Roger turned. "What?"

Sanders placed a worn, yellowed statement on the table. "This witness statement. It was never followed up on back then. A worker reported seeing a man who looked like Weller hanging around the site a few days before the explosion. No one thought much of it at the time, but it matches the descriptions we've gotten recently."

Liz's heart pounded. "He's always been in the shadows."

Roger's eyes remained on the grainy photo of Peter Weller, the man they had finally unmasked.

"We need every available officer on high alert," Liz said, her voice unwavering. "We need to get ahead of this before he kills again."

Roger nodded, jaw set. "Let's find this son of a bitch before it's too late."

The tension in the room was thick, but Roger could feel the resolve in his team. They were ready to act, to end the nightmare that had gripped their town. He nodded towards Sanders. "Get this information out to every unit. I want patrols on every road leading out of town. We need to prevent any further attacks."

Sanders nodded, moving quickly to relay the orders. Liz turned to Roger, her eyes reflecting both determination and exhaustion. "We've got this, Roger. We're getting closer."

Roger gave her a small, tight smile. "Yeah, we are. But we can't let up. Not for a second." He looked back at the photograph of Weller, the image burned into his mind. The haunted eyes of a younger Weller stared back at him, a man whose grief had festered into something twisted and unrecognizable. "This ends now."

The room erupted into activity, officers rushing to their stations, phones ringing, and the hum of persistence filling the air. Roger watched as his team mobilized, a sense of urgency propelling them forward. He turned back to Liz, his eyes catching hers. "Let's go over what we know and try to predict Weller's next move."

Liz nodded, her voice taking on a tone of focus. "We have to assume he's escalating. With Simmons gone, he's targeting anyone he holds responsible—that includes us. He's going to try and make a statement."

Roger took one last look at the image on the wall, the face of a man driven by grief and vengeance. He understood that kind of pain—the way it hollowed you out, turned you into something you didn't recognize. The cold emptiness that consumed you from the inside. But Weller had chosen his path, and now Roger had to put an end to it.

As Roger walked out of the briefing room, his phone buzzed. It was dispatch. "Sheriff, we just received a report— a suspicious vehicle has been spotted near the old Marathon Oil explosion site."

Roger's heart skipped a beat, adrenaline flooding his veins. He pressed his radio. "Liz, change of plans. We're heading straight to the old explosion site. Weller might be there."

Liz's voice came back immediately. "Got it. I'm on my way."

Roger pushed through the station doors, and broke into a run towards his truck. There was no time to waste. This was it. Weller was making his move, and Roger had to be there to stop him.

He climbed into his truck, slamming the door shut and starting the engine. The tires skidded against the asphalt as he pulled out, the siren blaring as he sped through the streets. The landscape blurred by, the barren mesquite trees and wide-open fields a backdrop to the urgency pounding in his chest. Roger's focus was solely on getting to the site before it was too late.

The minutes felt like hours, each second ticking away as Roger's truck roared down the road. He could see Liz's car ahead, her lights flashing as she sped towards the location. They were close—too close for comfort. Roger's mind raced, running through every possibility, every outcome. They had to get there in time.

As the old Marathon Oil explosion site came into view, Roger's heart pounded in his chest. He could see the outline of a vehicle parked near the rusted remains of the site, the skeletal remains of machinery casting long shadows across the barren ground. Roger pulled up behind Liz's car, jumping out of his truck and drawing his weapon.

Roger and Liz exchanged a glance, the unspoken understanding passing between them. This was it. They had to move cautiously but quickly.

Roger nodded, his voice low. "We do this by the book. Watch for traps."

They moved in tandem, their weapons raised, approaching the vehicle. The air was thick with tension, each step measured. The wind howled through the rusted beams, carrying with it the scent of decay and old oil. The vehicle's door was open, and inside Roger saw a mess of papers— maps, photographs, and what looked like a handwritten note.

It was all hastily thrown about, as if Weller had left in a hurry.

Roger's eyes scanned the area, and then he saw it—wires running along the ground, leading towards an old control shed. His stomach dropped. "Liz, look—wires. He's rigged something."

"We need to fall back and call in the bomb squad. This whole place could be a trap."

Roger pressed his radio. "Dispatch, this is Sheriff Hartley. We have a potential explosive device at the old Marathon Oil site. Requesting immediate bomb squad assistance. All units stay clear of the area."

Minutes felt like hours as they waited for the bomb squad, every second a reminder of just how close they were to the edge. The chill in the air seeped into Roger's bones, but he remained steady, his eyes scanning the site, looking for any sign of movement.

Finally, the sound of sirens approached, and Roger saw the bomb squad vehicles pull up. A tall woman approached Roger. "Sheriff, I'm Lieutenant Harris with the bomb squad. Can you brief me on what you've found?"

Roger pointed towards the shed. "Wires leading into that structure. There could be explosives inside. We need to secure this area."

Harris nodded, her eyes narrowing as she assessed the situation. "Alright. We'll take care of it. I need you and your team to keep a safe distance. We'll let you know once it's neutralized."

Roger and Liz stepped back, watching as Harris and her team moved with precision and calm. The seconds dragged by, each one filled with a sense of anticipation so thick it was hard to breathe. Roger knew what was at stake—if those explosives went off, it wouldn't just be a building that was lost. It would be another scar on a town that had seen too much pain.

Finally, after what felt like an eternity, Harris's voice crackled over Roger's radio. "Sheriff, we've disarmed the explosives. The site is secure."

Roger let out a long breath, a sense of relief washing over him. He turned to Liz, who gave him a nod, a small smile breaking through the tension. They had done it. They had stopped Weller from inflicting one final wound on Midland.

Roger pressed his radio. "Good work, everyone. Let's start wrapping this up. We're done here."

As the officers began to move, Roger stood still for a moment, his eyes fixed on the old control shed. This was where it had all begun—the site of the tragedy that had driven a man to madness. And now, it was where it ended. Weller was still out there, but they had foiled his plan. For now, the town could breathe a little easier.

For the first time in what felt like forever, Roger felt a sense of hope. They had faced down the darkness, and they had won.

It was time to go home.

CHAPTER FORTY SIX

Roger and Liz pulled away from the Marathon Oil site, their vehicles navigating through the winding roads leading back towards Midland. The adrenaline was slowly wearing off, leaving tiredness in its place. Roger's eyes flickered to the rearview mirror—watching the site grow smaller.

Just then, Roger's phone buzzed, the sound cutting through the silence of the drive. He glanced down at the screen. Unknown Caller. He answered, "This is Sheriff Hartley."

The voice on the other end was chilling, smooth but dripping with malice. "You thought you could stop me, didn't you?"

Roger's heart skipped a beat. It was Weller. "Weller. What do you want?"

Weller chuckled, the sound echoing through the phone like a ghostly taunt. "You really think that little bomb was my grand finale? That was just a distraction, Roger. While you and your deputies were busy playing hero, I was finishing what I needed to do in town."

Roger's jaw clenched, a cold dread spreading through his veins. He quickly pressed the button on his radio, connecting to Liz. "Liz, patch in. Weller's on the line." He switched back to the call. "What did you do, Weller?" Roger demanded, his voice tight with anger.

Weller's voice took on an edge of mockery. "You've always been a step behind, Sheriff. While you were out there defusing my little surprise, I paid a visit to some old friends. You know, the ones who deserved to suffer just as I did."

Roger's stomach churned. He knew exactly who Weller was referring to—the people on his list, anyone who had wronged him in the past. "Where are you, Weller? If you hurt anyone else, I swear—"

Another dark laugh interrupted him. "Swear what, Sheriff? You're too late. You should have stayed out of it, Roger. If you had, none of this would have touched you. But now, everything that happens is on your hands. You couldn't save them, and you won't stop me."

Liz's voice crackled through the radio, her tone urgent. "Roger, what's he saying? What did he do?"

Roger switched to speakerphone so Liz could hear, his eyes narrowing as Weller continued. "If you hurry, maybe you'll make it in time to see the aftermath. I'd hate for you to miss the ending. You see, Sheriff, I want you to see what justice really looks like."

"This isn't justice, Weller. This is madness. You think killing more people will bring your family back?"

There was silence for a moment, then Weller's voice dropped to a cold whisper. "No, Sheriff. But it'll make them pay. And it'll make you understand what it feels like to lose everything."

Roger heard the line go dead. He slammed his fist against the steering wheel, the frustration boiling over. He pressed the radio. "Liz, we need all units mobilized—Weller's still out there, and he's targeting someone in town. We need to move now!"

Liz's response was immediate. "Copy that, Roger. I'll get everyone on it." Her voice was steady, but Roger could hear the tension beneath it. They were running out of time.

Roger sped up, the engine roaring as he pushed the truck to its limits. The roads blurred past, and all he could think about was getting back to Midland before Weller struck again. His mind raced, trying to piece together Weller's next move. Who was left? Who would he target?

As the town's lights appeared on the horizon, Roger's mind drifted to the past. He remembered Kathy, her face filled with worry, and the way she'd begged him to leave this case alone. He had promised her—promised that he would always come back to her, that he wouldn't let the darkness consume him. But that promise felt so fragile now, hanging by a thread.

Roger stormed into the conference room, Liz right behind him. The photos of the Marathon Oil board members and other targets were still pinned to the board, each face a reminder of Weller's twisted vendetta.

Liz pointed at the board. "He said he paid a visit to someone in town. We need to figure out who's left on his list—someone we haven't accounted for."

Roger stared at the board, his mind racing. He could feel the weight of the moment pressing down on him, the lives that hung in the balance. "It's not just about the board members," Roger said, his voice strained. "He wants to make a statement. He wants to hurt anyone connected to what happened."

Roger's phone buzzed again—this time it was dispatch. He answered quickly. "Sheriff, we just got a call—there's been a disturbance at the home of Margaret Bennett. Neighbors reported hearing screams."

Roger's heart sank. Margaret Bennett—the wife of DA Bennett, who was still in the hospital recovering. She was on Weller's list. He looked at Liz, his face set in grim confidence. "We need to go. Now."

Liz didn't hesitate to act quickly. As they ran, Liz's mind flashed to her childhood, growing up in Midland—her father had been a good man, but one who often let his anger get the best of him. She had learned from an early age how quickly everything could fall apart, how thin the line was between safety and chaos. It was what had driven her to this job, to protect the people who couldn't protect themselves.

They could tell signs of forced entry when they arrived at the Bennett house. They moved in tandem, pushing the door open and stepping inside. The house was eerily quiet, the kind of silence that made Roger's skin crawl.

"Margaret!" Roger called out. There was no response.

They moved through the house. The living room was a mess—furniture overturned, picture frames shattered on the floor. Roger's heart pounded as they reached the back of the house, where a faint noise caught his attention—a muffled whimper.

Roger motioned for Liz to follow as they approached the closed door of the bedroom. He took a deep breath, then kicked the door open, his weapon raised. Inside, Margaret

Bennett was tied to a chair, her face pale and streaked with tears. Her eyes widened in terror as she saw them.

"Roger," she whispered, her voice barely audible. "He's… he's still here."

Roger's gaze swept the room, but Weller was nowhere in sight. He moved quickly to Margaret's side, untying her as Liz covered them, her eyes scanning for any sign of movement. "Margaret, where did he go?" Roger asked, his voice urgent.

Margaret's voice trembled as she spoke. "He said… he said he was going to finish it. He mentioned the courthouse… something about making sure everyone knew."

Roger's blood ran cold. The courthouse—Weller was planning something bigger. He looked at Liz, his expression hardening. "We need to get to the courthouse. He's going to make his final stand there."

Liz nodded. "Let's move."

They hurried Margaret out to the waiting paramedics, then jumped back into their vehicle, the sirens blaring once more as they raced towards the courthouse. Roger's mind was focused, his determination unwavering. Weller wanted to send a message, but Roger was going to make sure it ended here.

As they approached the courthouse, Roger could see the flashing lights of patrol cars already on the scene. Officers were setting up a perimeter, their weapons drawn, patrolling the area. Roger pulled up, jumping out of the truck, his eyes fixed on the imposing building before them.

He pressed his radio. "All units, Weller is inside. He's armed and dangerous. We need to move in, but proceed with caution. He's desperate, and there's no telling what he has planned."

Roger and Liz led the way up the courthouse steps. The massive doors loomed ahead, a barrier between them and the man who had terrorized their town for far too long. Roger took a deep breath, then pushed the doors open, stepping into the dimly lit foyer.

The courthouse was eerily silent, the kind of silence that made every creak and echo feel amplified, reverberating through the empty hallways.

"Weller!" Roger called out, his voice echoing off the marble walls. "It's over. There's nowhere left to run!"

His voice faded into the silence, and for a moment, there was nothing. Then, a faint rustling echoed from somewhere deeper in the courthouse, followed by a soft, almost mocking laugh.

"You really think you can stop me, Sheriff?" Weller's voice called out, the sound bouncing off the walls, making it impossible to tell where it was coming from. "You think you can undo everything they did to me?"

Roger tightened his grip on his weapon. "This isn't about undoing anything, Weller. It's about stopping you from hurting anyone else."

He moved forward, his steps careful, his eyes scanning the darkened corridors. Liz was right beside him, her gun drawn, her eyes sharp. They moved as a unit, each step measured, each breath steady. The courthouse felt like a labyrinth, the shadows playing tricks on their eyes, every creak of the old building putting them on edge.

"Roger, over here," Liz whispered, motioning towards a hallway to their left. Roger nodded, following her lead. The hallway was long, lined with closed doors, the air heavy with the scent of old wood and dust. They moved slowly, checking each door as they went, the silence pressing in around them.

Suddenly, a door at the far end of the hallway burst open, and Weller stepped out, his face twisted in a mix of rage and despair. In his hand, he held a detonator, his finger hovering over the button. "Stay back!" he shouted, his voice cracking with emotion. "I'll blow this place sky high, and everyone will finally understand what they did to me!"

Roger raised his hands slightly, trying to keep his voice calm. "Weller, listen to me. You don't have to do this. We can end this without anyone else getting hurt."

Weller's eyes were wild, tears streaming down his face. "You don't get it, Sheriff! They took everything from me! My family, my life… and they just walked away like it meant nothing!"

Liz took a step forward, her voice steady but gentle. "Peter, we know what happened. We know how they failed you. But this isn't the way to make it right. This won't bring them back." Her voice softened, a hint of her own pain leaking through. "I've lost people too, Peter. I know what it's like to feel like the world's abandoned you. But you don't have to let that define you."

For a moment, Weller hesitated, his eyes flickering between Roger and Liz. The rage in his expression seemed to falter, replaced by something else—something that looked almost like doubt. Roger seized the moment, his voice softening. "Peter, put it down. Let us help you. We can make sure your story is heard, but this isn't the way."

Weller's hand trembled, the detonator shaking as he looked down at it. Roger could see the conflict in his eyes, the pain that had driven him to this point. For a brief second, it seemed like he might listen, like he might surrender.

But then, his face hardened once more, and he shook his head, his eyes filling with renewed decisiveness. "No. They need to pay. They all need to pay."

Before Roger or Liz could react, Weller's thumb moved to press the button. Liz lunged forward, her body colliding with Weller's just as his thumb came down. The detonator flew from his hand, skittering across the marble floor, coming to a stop several feet away.

Roger rushed forward, his heart pounding as he grabbed the detonator, his eyes locking onto Weller and Liz as they struggled on the floor. Weller fought with a desperate strength, his screams echoing through the empty hallway, but Liz held on, her determination unyielding.

"Roger!" Liz shouted, her voice strained as she tried to keep Weller pinned. "Get him in cuffs!"

Roger moved quickly, pulling the handcuffs from his belt and snapping them around Weller's wrists. Weller thrashed beneath him, his screams turning into sobs, the fight finally draining from his body. He collapsed against the floor, his breath coming in ragged gasps, tears streaming down his face.

"It's over, Peter," Roger said quietly, his voice almost lost in the vast emptiness of the courthouse. "It's over."

Weller let out a choked sob, his body trembling as the weight of everything he had done seemed to crash down on him all at once. Roger looked at Liz, her face smeared with dirt, her eyes weary but filled with relief. She nodded at him, a small, tired smile tugging at her lips.

They pulled Weller to his feet, his head hanging, his shoulders slumped in defeat. The courthouse, once filled with echoes of fear and anger, now felt empty—almost peaceful. The nightmare was finally over.

They led Weller out of the courthouse. The flashing lights of patrol cars illuminated the night, painting the scene in red and blue. Officers moved in to secure the area, their faces a mixture of exhaustion and relief. Roger looked at Liz, her expression mirroring his own—a blend of fatigue and quiet triumph.

"You okay?" Roger asked, his voice soft.

Liz nodded, brushing a strand of hair out of her face. "Yeah. I'm okay." She glanced at Weller, now being loaded into the back of a patrol car. "I just wish it hadn't come to this."

Roger sighed, his gaze following hers. "Me too. But at least it's over. No more killing."

Liz gave a small nod, her eyes glistening. "Yeah. No more killing."

Roger turned, looking out at the horizon, the first hints of dawn beginning to break, casting the sky in shades of orange and pink. The nightmare that had gripped Midland was finally over. There would be healing, there would be rebuilding, but for now, there was peace.

"Let's get back to the station," Roger said, his voice carrying a note of finality. "We've got a lot of work to do."

Liz smiled faintly. "Lead the way, Sheriff."

CHAPTER FORTY SEVEN

Everyone at the precinct believed it was finally over. The exhaustion on the officers' faces was mixed with a sense of relief as they started to dismantle the heightened security measures and return to some semblance of normalcy.

Roger drove home, his body aching with fatigue, his mind racing but also filled with a strange sense of hope. He allowed himself to imagine that this chapter was closed, that the town could heal, that he could heal. When he finally pulled into the driveway, the sight of his home filled him with an emotion he hadn't felt in a long time—comfort.

As Roger stepped out of his truck, the door creaked open, the cool morning air biting at his skin. He paused for a moment, taking in the sight of the house—the faded paint on the porch railing, the wind chimes gently swaying in the breeze, the small garden Kathy had insisted on planting last year, now dormant in the winter chill. He let out a breath he hadn't realized he'd been holding, the fog from his exhale mingling with the cold air. The scent of coffee drifted towards him, the rich aroma cutting through the crisp morning. Kathy stood in the doorway, her eyes filled with both worry and relief. She stepped down the porch steps as he approached, her arms opening before he even reached her.

"Roger," she said, her voice cracking. She wrapped her arms around him, pulling him in tight. Her embrace was warm, strong—filled with all the love that had seen them through their toughest days. Roger could feel her trembling slightly, the pent-up fear and anxiety finally escaping in this moment of connection.

Roger closed his eyes, his chin resting on her shoulder, savoring the warmth of her hug. He took a deep breath, letting the tension release from his body. "It's over, Kathy," he murmured, his voice hoarse. "Weller's in custody. It's finally over."

Kathy pulled back slightly, her eyes searching his face for the truth in his words. Her eyes were red-rimmed, evidence of sleepless nights and silent prayers. "Are you sure? I was so scared..." She shook her head, biting her lip to hold back tears. "I just want it all to be over. I want you to be safe."

Roger nodded, giving her a gentle smile. "I know. I'm okay now. We can finally breathe again." He reached up and brushed a tear from her cheek with his thumb. Her skin was cold to the touch, her vulnerability making his chest ache. "No more looking over our shoulders. No more threats."

She smiled. "I'm just glad you're home." She took his hand, her fingers intertwining with his, leading him towards the door. "Come on. I made coffee, and I think we both could use it."

Roger let her lead him inside, the warmth of their home enveloping him like a heavy blanket. The small kitchen looked exactly as he had left it, cluttered with the little messes of daily life that he found himself appreciating now—a dish towel slung over the back of a chair, a few unopened letters on the counter. The smell of freshly brewed coffee filled the space, and the faint sound of the radio, playing softly in the background, added a sense of normalcy that felt almost foreign.

He sat down at the kitchen table, the craziness of the past days catching up to him as Kathy poured two cups of coffee and brought them over. She set his mug in front of him, the warmth of the ceramic seeping into his tired hands.

They sat together, sipping their coffee as the first rays of sunlight filtered in through the curtains, casting long shadows across the kitchen. Kathy watched Roger, her eyes softening as the tension in his shoulders seemed to slowly ease. "How's Liz?" she asked gently, her voice barely above a whisper.

Roger took a sip of his coffee, setting the mug down with a sigh. He leaned back in his chair, the creak of the wood loud in the quiet room. "She's holding up. She's tough, but… it's been a lot for her. For all of us." He looked up at Kathy, his gaze filled with sincerity. "I don't think I could have done this without her. She's been a rock through all of this."

Kathy smiled, a warmth spreading across her face. "I'm glad she was there for you. It sounds like you two make a good team."

Roger nodded, a hint of a smile touching his lips. "Yeah, we do. But I'm ready to leave all this behind. I'm ready for some quiet days."

Kathy reached across the table, taking his hand in hers. Her touch was gentle, a reminder of everything he still had to live for. "Then let's focus on that. On us, on the future."

Roger smiled, a warmth spreading through his chest. For the first time in what felt like forever, he believed in the possibility of a peaceful future. They sat there for a while longer, talking, letting the reality of the moment sink in. The sun had fully risen now, its light bathing the room in a golden glow, and for a brief while, the world seemed bright again.

Meanwhile, across town, Liz pulled into her driveway. She stepped out of her car, her breath coming out in small clouds. Her body ached, her muscles sore from the adrenaline-fueled confrontation with Weller. The events of the past few days played over in her mind, each memory a blur of fear, determination, and moments where she wasn't sure she'd make it out alive. All she wanted was to collapse into bed and let the tension fade, even if just for a few hours.

The door opened before she could even reach for the handle. Jason stood there, his expression filled with relief, his eyes widening when he saw her. He wasted no time, pulling her into his arms, his hold on her tight as if he never wanted to let her go. "Liz," he murmured, his voice thick with emotion. "You're home. You're safe."

Liz rested her head on his shoulder, her arms wrapping around him. She closed her eyes, the familiarity of his embrace a balm to her weary soul. She could feel his heartbeat against her cheek, steady and strong. "It's over, Jason," she whispered, her voice barely audible. "We got him. It's finally over."

Jason leaned back, his hands resting on her shoulders as he looked her over, his eyes searching for any sign of injury. "I knew you would. I knew you'd stop him." His eyes softened, a proud smile touching his lips. "You're incredible, you know that?"

Liz smiled, a tear slipping down her cheek. She brushed it away quickly, nodding. "I couldn't have done it without Roger. But I'm so glad to be home." Her voice cracked slightly, the weight of everything finally catching up to her.

He kissed her gently, his lips lingering on hers for a moment, before he pulled away, taking her hand and leading her inside. "Come on. You need rest. Let's sit for a while."

They moved to the living room, Jason handing her a steaming mug of tea before sitting down beside her. Liz wrapped her hands around the mug, the warmth seeping into her skin. She took a sip, letting her eyes drift closed for a moment, the promise of sleep pulling at her. The living room was quiet, the soft ticking of the clock the only sound, a stark contrast to the chaos she had just left behind. "It's hard to believe it's all done," she said softly.

Jason nodded, his gaze steady on her. "You've been through so much, Liz. You deserve a break. Maybe a vacation? Somewhere far away from all of this?"

Liz chuckled, the idea of a vacation sounding like a dream. "Yeah," she murmured. "Maybe a vacation." She took another sip, her eyes wandering around the room until they landed on Jason's boots, sitting by the door. A light coating of gray dust clung to the soles, almost like concrete dust. She frowned, her curiosity piqued.

"What've you been up to?" she asked, nodding towards the boots. "Looks like you've been busy."

Jason glanced at the boots. "Oh, that? I was fixing up the planters in the backyard for spring. Figured it was about time to get them ready for the warmer weather." He shrugged, his expression casual. "Wanted to make sure everything was perfect for when you got home."

Liz smiled, her gaze softening, but something in the back of her mind nagged at her. "You're always taking care of everything, aren't you?" She reached out, touching his arm. "I don't know what I'd do without you."

Jason leaned in, kissing her forehead gently. "You're never going to have to find out. I've got you. Always."

Liz sighed, leaning back against the couch, her eyelids growing heavy. She let herself relax, her body finally succumbing to the body's want of sleep that had been building for days. The warmth of the tea, the comfort of Jason's presence—all of it lulled her towards sleep. She allowed herself to believe that the nightmare was over, that they were safe, but a small voice in the back of her mind couldn't quite let go of the image of that dust on Jason's boots. For now, though, she pushed it aside, letting herself drift into sleep, trusting that, just maybe, the worst was truly behind them.

CHAPTER FORTY EIGHT

The sun's rays stretched across the rooftops as if waking the town from a long nightmare. Roger blinked his eyes open, a rare moment of tranquility washing over him as he lay in bed. He turned his head to see Kathy still asleep beside him. The events of the last few weeks had been relentless, but for the first time in a long time, he felt like they had finally turned a corner.

He slipped out of bed carefully, trying not to disturb Kathy, and padded into the kitchen. The air felt lighter, and as he poured himself a cup of coffee, Roger allowed himself to savor the quiet. This was a morning he had earned, a morning that spoke of normalcy. He took a sip of the coffee, the warmth spreading through his chest, grounding him. His gaze drifted to the pictures hanging on the wall—snapshots of his life, of Kathy, of their past when things were simpler. He traced his finger along the frame of a photo from their younger days, back when they thought Midland was just a sleepy town and not a place filled with nightmares.

On the other side of town, Liz slowly stirred from her sleep. Jason's reassuring presence beside her was an anchor. She blinked in the early morning light, the tiredness still lingering but tinged with the sweet promise of relief. She turned her head, catching sight of Jason's sleeping form, his chest rising and falling rhythmically. His face was peaceful, the lines around his eyes softened in slumber, and for a moment, Liz allowed herself to believe that everything was as it should be. She allowed herself a moment to watch him, her heart swelling with gratitude.

She slipped out of bed, careful not to wake him, and made her way to the bathroom. As she splashed cold water on her face, she caught a glimpse of herself in the mirror— dark circles under her eyes, the toll of everything they had been through etched into her skin. Her gaze lingered on her reflection, her fingers tracing the tired lines along her cheeks. But despite the weariness, there was something else there— hope. They had made it through. At least, she hoped they had. The faint sense of unease had yet to leave her, lingering in her chest like a dull ache, but she pushed it aside. Today, they needed to move forward.

Roger sat at his kitchen table, his phone buzzing beside him. He glanced down, seeing Liz's name light up the screen. He smiled as he answered, "Morning, Liz."

"Morning, Roger," Liz replied, her voice sounding brighter than it had in days. "I just wanted to check in. How are you holding up?"

Roger leaned back in his chair, glancing out the window. "I'm okay. Tired, but I think that's a given. Kathy's still asleep. I think we're all just catching our breath."

Liz sighed, and Roger could hear the smile in her voice. "Yeah, same here. Jason's out like a light. I think he was more worried than he let on."

Roger nodded, a sense of camaraderie in their shared exhaustion. "I can believe that. Listen, I was thinking about heading into the station for a bit, just to wrap up some of the paperwork, put a bow on all this."

Liz chuckled. "You mean you couldn't stay away even if you tried?"

Roger grinned. "Something like that. Want to meet me there? We can finally close this thing up."

"Sounds like a plan," Liz replied. "I'll see you in a bit."

Roger ended the call, finishing his coffee before getting ready. It was time to put the final pieces of this nightmare behind them.

The sheriff's office was quieter than it had been in days, the tension that had hung in the air replaced by an atmosphere of cautious relief. Roger and Liz walked in together, exchanging nods with their colleagues as they made their way to the main office.

Deputy Garcia sat at his desk. He looked up as Roger and Liz approached, offering a tired smile. "Morning, Sheriff. Morning, Liz. Didn't expect to see you both here so early."

Roger smiled, shaking his head. "Well, you know us, Garcia. The job never really ends, does it?"

Garcia chuckled. "You got that right. Though, I have to say, it feels good to be wrapping things up for once."

Liz nodded, her eyes drifting over the piles of paperwork on his table. "Feels like it's been a long time since we had a morning that wasn't filled with chaos."

Garcia leaned back in his chair. "You and me both. Oh, by the way, some good news—DA Bennett woke up this morning. He's still got a long road ahead of him, but the doctors say the outcome looks positive."

Roger's face lit up with a genuine smile. "That's great news. I know his family must be relieved. It's been tough on them."

Liz smiled. "Yeah, that's the kind of news we all needed right now. It's about time something went our way."

Garcia nodded in agreement. "Exactly. A little bit of hope goes a long way." He paused, glancing at his desk before looking back at them. "Anyway, we're getting Weller processed now. He was pretty out of it when they brought him in last night, but the guys at booking mentioned something weird."

Roger frowned, exchanging a glance with Liz. "Weird? How so?"

Garcia scratched his head, flipping through the notes on his desk. "They said Weller had this concrete-like dust all over him. Thing is, there wasn't anything like that around the place where you caught him. It's like he picked it up somewhere else."

Liz froze, the color draining from her face as Garcia's words registered. Concrete-like dust. Her mind flashed back to the night before, to Jason's boots by the door, covered in that same gray dust. Her heart skipped a beat, her stomach twisting in sudden dread.

The memory of Jason's easy smile, his casual explanation of fixing the planters—it all came rushing back, but now it felt wrong, sinister even. The dust had seemed so harmless, just a sign of someone working around the house, but now the connection with Weller made it impossible to ignore.

"Liz?" Roger's voice cut through her thoughts, his brow furrowed as he watched her. "You okay?"

Liz forced a smile, nodding quickly, though her heart was pounding in her chest. "Yeah, I'm fine. Just... tired, I guess." She managed to keep her voice steady, but inside she felt like the ground had shifted beneath her feet.

Roger didn't look entirely convinced, but he let it go, turning his attention back to Garcia. "Concrete dust, huh? We'll have to look into that. Maybe he was hiding out somewhere we didn't know about."

Garcia nodded, making a note in his paperwork. "Could be. We'll dig into it, see if we can figure out where it came from. Might give us a lead on any places he was using before we caught him."

Liz barely heard the rest of the conversation. Her mind was racing, her thoughts tangled in a chaotic web of doubt and fear. She tried to focus on the task at hand, to compartmentalize the rising anxiety, but it wasn't easy. The dust on Jason's boots, his easy smile, his explanation—it had all seemed so innocent at the time. But now, with Garcia's words echoing in her ears, a chilling realization began to take hold.

What if Jason wasn't who she thought he was?

She swallowed hard, her mouth suddenly dry. Her fingers felt cold, her palms damp with sweat. The concrete dust wasn't a coincidence—it couldn't be. But what did it mean? Was Jason connected to Weller somehow? Was he hiding something from her?

Liz felt the weight of uncertainty settle over her like a heavy blanket, pressing down on her chest. She needed to get home, needed to talk to Jason, needed answers. She couldn't let her mind spiral into worst-case scenarios—not yet. Not without knowing the truth. But the fear that had started as a whisper was growing louder, a gnawing dread that refused to be silenced.

She forced herself to finish what she needed to do at the station, her interactions with colleagues a blur as she went through the motions. Every time someone congratulated her on the job well done, Liz could only manage a tight-lipped smile, her thoughts consumed by the question that had taken hold of her mind.

By the time she finally walked out of the station, the midday sun was high in the sky. Roger gave her a wave as he headed to his truck, and she returned it half-heartedly, her focus elsewhere. She climbed into her car, her hands trembling slightly as she gripped the steering wheel.

The drive home felt longer than usual. She replayed every interaction with Jason over the past few days, looking for clues, for anything that might explain the concrete dust. But nothing stood out—nothing except his smile, his reassurance that everything was fine.

When she pulled into the driveway, Liz took a deep breath, trying to steady herself. She needed to be calm, needed to approach this logically. There might be an innocent explanation—Jason could have easily been working in an area with concrete dust, and she was just letting her imagination get the better of her. But deep down, the fear gnawed at her, an instinct that something was very, very wrong.

She stepped out of the car, her eyes immediately going to the boots by the door. The gray dust was still there, faint but unmistakable. Liz's heart pounded as she walked inside, her footsteps echoing in the quiet house. Jason was in the kitchen, humming softly to himself as he prepared lunch.

"Hey, there you are," he said, turning to her with a smile. "How was the station?"

Liz forced herself to smile, her throat tight. "It was fine. Just some paperwork." She hesitated, her eyes flickering to the boots. "Jason... where exactly were you working yesterday?"

Jason's smile didn't falter, but there was a slight pause before he answered. "I told you, I was fixing up the planters in the backyard. Why do you ask?"

Liz studied his face, searching for any sign of deceit. She wanted to believe him, wanted to believe that everything was as simple as he made it seem. But the doubt wouldn't let go, and she could feel the fear creeping back in, stronger now, more insistent.

"Just... curious," she said finally. She turned away, her mind spinning. She needed time to think, to figure out her next move. Because if her instincts were right, the nightmare was far from over—and it was standing right in her kitchen, smiling at her as if nothing had changed.

Liz slipped her phone from her pocket and quickly typed out a text to Roger: "Call me immediately. Say it's dispatch and I need to go. I'll explain later. Meet me at the office."

Within moments, her phone buzzed, Roger's name flashing on the screen. She answered, trying to sound casual. "Hey, Roger."

Roger's voice came through, steady. "Liz, I just got a call from dispatch. They need you back at the office right away."

Liz took a deep breath, glancing at Jason, who was still focused on making lunch. "Got it. Thanks, Roger. I'll be there soon." She ended the call and turned to Jason, forcing a smile. "Dispatch just called. They need me back at the office."

Jason looked up, his brow furrowing slightly. "Already? I thought you were done for the day."

Liz shrugged, trying to keep her tone light. "You know how it is. Something always comes up." She moved towards the door, her eyes briefly flickering to the boots. "I'll see you later, okay?"

Jason nodded, his expression softening. "Alright. Be careful, Liz."

Liz gave him a quick kiss on the cheek before turning to leave. As she reached the door, she grabbed a small Post-it note from the desk. With her heart pounding, she discreetly pressed the sticky note onto the dust on Jason's boots, making sure it picked up a sample. She then slipped out the door, her mind racing.

She needed answers, and she needed them now.

CHAPTER FORTY NINE

Liz drove to the sheriff's office, her heart pounding in her chest. She could still feel the sticky note with the dust on it pressed against her palm. It felt like a piece of her world had been torn apart—her mind a tangled mess of doubt, suspicion, and fear. She needed Roger, and she needed to figure out what was really going on.

As she pulled into the parking lot, she spotted Roger standing by the entrance, his face lined with concern. He pushed himself off the wall as she parked, watching her approach. Liz stepped out of the car, her gaze meeting his as she tried to hide the turmoil she felt inside.

Roger walked up to her, his brow furrowed. "What's going on, Liz? You sounded urgent."

Liz swallowed hard, looking around the nearly empty parking lot before motioning for Roger to follow her inside. "Not here. Let's get to your office," she said, her voice low. Roger nodded, a flicker of worry passing over his features as they made their way through the precinct.

Once inside Roger's office, Liz closed the door behind them, the click of the latch sounding louder than it should. Roger crossed his arms, his eyes fixed on Liz as she turned to face him. "Liz, talk to me. What's going on?"

Liz took a deep breath, holding up the Post-it note she had pressed onto Jason's boots. The faint gray dust was stuck to the adhesive. "Roger, I think we might have a problem. This dust—it was all over Jason's boots this morning. He said it was from working on the planters outside. I didn't think much of it at first, but then Garcia mentioned Weller had the same concrete-like dust on him." She paused, her voice cracking slightly as she tried to maintain her composure. "Roger, what if Jason is involved in all of this?"

Roger's eyes widened. He looked from the note in her hand to her face, seeing the fear and desperation there. He stepped closer, his voice softening. "Liz, are you sure about this? It could be a coincidence. Maybe he was really just working on the planters."

Liz shook her head, her eyes welling with tears. "I want to believe that, Roger. I do. But something feels off. The way he paused when I asked him about it. The dust… it matches what they found on Weller, and there wasn't any concrete dust near the place we caught him. Jason's been acting normal, but what if he's hiding something? What if he knows more than he's letting on?"

Roger let out a slow breath, his hand resting on her shoulder. "Alright. We need to be careful here. We can't jump to conclusions without evidence, but we also can't ignore what you're feeling." He paused, looking her in the eyes. "You know Jason better than anyone. If something's wrong, we'll figure it out together. But we need to approach this carefully. We can't risk tipping him off if there's more to this."

Liz nodded, wiping her eyes. "I know. I just… I can't believe I'm even thinking this. He's been with me through everything. He proposed not long ago, Roger." Her voice broke. "How could I have been so blind?"

Roger tightened his grip on her shoulder, his voice steady. "Hey, listen to me. We don't know anything for sure yet. We need to take this one step at a time. We'll have the dust analyzed, see if we can find any connection. But until then, we keep this between us. We don't want to compromise anything."

Liz took a shaky breath, nodding. "Okay. I'll keep it together. I just... I need to know the truth."

Roger gave her a reassuring nod. "We'll get to the bottom of this, Liz. Whatever it takes. You're not alone in this."

Liz looked at Roger, the gratitude evident in her eyes. "Thank you, Roger. I don't know what I'd do without you."

Roger gave her a small smile. "You'd do just fine, Liz. You're stronger than you think." He glanced down at the sticky note in her hand. "Let's get that to the lab. If there's anything there, we'll find it."

They made their way to the lab. Liz couldn't help but glance at her phone, a picture of her and Jason smiling at her from the lock screen. Her heart ached with uncertainty, but she knew she couldn't let her emotions cloud what needed to be done. She had to find out the truth, no matter what it cost.

Liz sat at her desk. She could hear the muted conversations of the other deputies, the phones ringing, the tapping of keyboards. It was the sound of normalcy, a rhythm she used to find comfort in. But today, it felt disconnected, like she was watching from a distance.

She glanced over at Roger's office. He was on the phone, his expression serious, likely talking to someone about tightening security around the people they cared about. She was grateful for his support—it felt like he was the only one keeping her grounded right now.

Garcia approached her desk, holding a steaming mug of coffee. "Hey, figured you could use this," he said with a smile.

Liz looked up, managing a small smile. "Thanks, Garcia. You always know when I need a caffeine fix."

Garcia chuckled, leaning on the edge of her desk. "You doing okay? You seemed a bit on edge earlier."

Liz hesitated, her fingers brushing against the edge of her coffee mug. "Yeah, just... you know, wrapping up loose ends. It's been a lot."

Garcia nodded, his expression softening. "I get it. We've all been running on fumes. But hey, at least we're seeing some light now, right? DA Bennett waking up, Weller in custody... we might actually get back to normal soon."

"Yeah. Normal. That would be nice." She took a sip of the coffee, the bitterness grounding her for a moment.

"If you need anything, just holler. We're all in this together." He gave her a reassuring nod before heading back to his desk.

Liz watched him go, her mind drifting back to Jason. She pulled out her phone, her thumb hovering over his contact. She wanted to call him, to hear his voice and convince herself that everything was okay. But she couldn't. Not yet. Not until she knew for sure.

The door to Roger's office opened, and he stepped out, catching her eye. He gave her a nod, motioning for her to come over. Liz set her coffee down, her legs feeling heavy as she stood up and walked over to him.

Roger closed the door behind her once she was inside. "I talked to Marla again. She's going to expedite the analysis. We should have something by tomorrow morning."

Liz exhaled, a mix of relief and fear swirling inside her. "Good. I just need to know, Roger. This waiting… it's eating me alive."

Roger nodded. "I know. We'll get through this. Just try to keep your distance from Jason for now, as much as you can without raising suspicion. We don't want to tip our hand too early."

"I'll do what I have to. But it won't be easy. He knows me too well. He'll know something's off."

Roger placed a comforting hand on her shoulder. "You're strong, Liz. And you're smart. You'll handle this. And if you need me, I'm just a call away."

Liz nodded, her eyes meeting his. "Thanks, Roger. I don't know what I'd do without you."

Roger gave her a small smile. "You'd be just fine. But you don't have to do this alone. We're a team."

Liz felt a small spark of hope ignite inside her. Maybe, just maybe, they would get through this. Together.

As Roger watched Liz leave his office, he couldn't help but be reminded of his own past. There had been a time, years ago, when he had been in a similar position. Back when he was deployed overseas, he had been forced to question the loyalty of someone in his unit—a friend he had trusted with his life. The memory of that betrayal still haunted him, the way it had unraveled everything he thought he knew. He could see that same fear in Liz's eyes now.

He clenched his jaw, determination hardening his resolve. He wouldn't let Liz go through this alone. He knew what it felt like to have the ground ripped out from under you, to question everything you believed in. He had faced it before, and he would face it again—this time for Liz.

CHAPTER FIFTY

The next morning came with an overcast sky, the sun hidden behind a thick layer of clouds. The air was damp and cold, as if the world itself was holding its breath. Liz hadn't slept much. When her alarm went off, it felt as though she had barely closed her eyes. The faint hum of traffic outside her apartment and the distant sound of barking dogs had done nothing to soothe her anxieties. Today was the day they might finally get some answers. No matter the cost, she had to know the truth.

Liz arrived at the sheriff's office early, the parking lot nearly empty except for a few of the night-shift officers finishing their duties. She made her way inside, her footsteps echoing in the quiet hallway. She found Roger already there, sitting at his desk, a cup of coffee cradled in his hands.

"Morning," Roger said, giving her a small smile. His face was lined, the creases on his forehead deeper than usual. "You look about as rested as I feel."

Liz attempted a smile, but it didn't reach her eyes. "Barely slept. I just kept thinking about everything… about Jason." She paused, her voice faltering as she took a deep breath. "Are we ready for this?"

Roger nodded, setting his coffee down and standing up. He placed his hand on her shoulder briefly, giving her a reassuring squeeze. "Yeah. Marla said she'd have the preliminary results ready first thing this morning. Let's head down there."

They walked down the hallway to the lab. The hallway seemed colder with each step, and Liz's hands were damp with sweat as she clutched her phone. She glanced at Roger, his grim expression providing a measure of strength, but even his steady presence couldn't erase the growing sense of dread.

As they reached the door to the lab, Marla was already waiting for them, her face serious. She had dark circles under her eyes, suggesting she'd been up most of the night. She gave them a quick nod and motioned for them to follow her inside.

"Morning, you two. I've got some results for you," Marla said, leading them over to her worktable. Marla picked up a sheet of paper, her eyes scanning her notes before she spoke. "So, the dust sample you brought in, Liz, matches the concrete dust found on Weller almost exactly. Same composition, same source." She paused, her gaze lifting to meet Liz's. "This type of dust is specific—it's not just any concrete dust. It comes from an industrial site, the kind that's used for major construction, not something you'd find in a backyard garden."

Liz felt her heart drop, her breath catching in her throat. She glanced at Roger, her eyes wide with disbelief. "An industrial site?" she repeated, her voice barely a whisper.

Marla nodded, pointing at a diagram of the chemical breakdown on the table. "Yeah. It's from a specific kind of blend, probably used for large-scale construction projects or abandoned buildings. There's a chemical additive in it that makes it unique—something not used in most residential mixes. It's more durable, meant for extreme conditions."

Roger exchanged a look with Liz. "So, this dust... it could mean that Jason was somewhere near an industrial site recently. Somewhere that Weller might have been."

Liz swallowed, her throat tight. The room seemed to spin for a moment, her mind struggling to process what this meant. Jason had lied. He hadn't just been fixing planters like he'd told her. He had been somewhere connected to Weller, somewhere that had left that distinct dust on his boots.

Marla could sense the shift in the room, her gaze softening as she looked at Liz. "Do you think he's involved, Liz?" Marla asked, her voice gentle, her eyes filled with concern.

Liz took a deep breath, her hands trembling as she tried to find her voice. "I don't know. I... I thought I knew him. But now, I'm not sure of anything." She looked at Roger, her eyes pleading for guidance. "What do we do now?"

Roger stepped closer, his presence steady and strong. "We take this slow. We don't confront him directly—not until we have more to go on. If he's involved, we need evidence. And if he's not... we need to be sure before we ruin his life."

Liz nodded, her eyes welling with tears. "I just can't believe this. How could I have been so blind?"

Roger placed a comforting hand on her shoulder. "You weren't blind, Liz. You trusted someone you love. There's nothing wrong with that. But now, we need to protect ourselves and everyone else. We'll get to the bottom of this."

Marla cleared her throat gently. "I'll keep working on the analysis, see if I can find anything else that might help. If there are other traces, maybe we can figure out exactly where that dust came from."

Liz wiped her eyes, nodding. "Thanks, Marla. We need all the help we can get."

Marla gave her a reassuring smile. "We'll figure it out, Liz. One way or another."

Roger turned to Liz. "Let's go back to the office. We need to plan our next steps carefully. We'll start digging into Jason's recent activities—discreetly. We don't want to tip him off."

"Okay. Let's do it."

At the sheriff's office, Liz sat down at her desk, her hands still trembling as she tried to focus on the task at hand. Roger was across from her, typing on his computer as he began to pull up records—any information they could use to track Jason's movements without drawing attention.

The minutes ticked by. Liz stared at her computer screen, her eyes blurring over the documents in front of her. She wanted to believe there was a logical explanation, that Jason wasn't involved in any of this. But the evidence was mounting, and she couldn't ignore it any longer.

She pulled up Jason's recent phone records. Most of them were familiar—friends, work contacts, her own number. But there were a few calls to numbers she didn't recognize. She jotted them down, making a mental note to cross-reference them later. Every small piece of information mattered now.

"Liz," Roger called softly, pulling her from her thoughts. She looked up to see him motioning her over. "I found something. Take a look."

Liz moved to his desk, her heart pounding as she peered over his shoulder. On the screen was a list of recent purchases made on Jason's credit card—construction-grade gloves, heavy-duty boots, and a rental fee for a storage unit on the outskirts of town.

Liz felt her stomach twist, her heart sinking even further. "Why would he need those things?" she whispered, her voice filled with dread.

Roger shook his head, his eyes narrowing as he looked at the screen. "I don't know. But we need to find out what's in that storage unit. It could be nothing… or it could be everything."

"Then let's go check it out. I need to know, Roger. I need to see for myself."

Roger studied her for a moment, then nodded. "Alright. We'll do this together. But we have to be careful. If Jason's involved, he might be watching. We can't afford any mistakes."

Liz took a deep breath. "I understand. Let's go."

The drive to the storage facility was tense, the silence between them thick with unspoken fears. Roger drove, his eyes fixed on the road, while Liz stared out the window, her mind racing. She replayed every conversation she'd had with Jason, every moment that seemed normal at the time but now felt tainted by suspicion. The buildings and barren fields of Midland blurred past her, the gray sky pressing down on them like a shroud.

As they pulled into the storage facility, Roger parked the car a short distance away, giving them a clear view of the rows of units. The place was deserted, the only sounds the distant hum of traffic and the occasional bird. Roger turned to Liz, his expression serious.

"We need to be careful. If Jason's been coming here, he could have set something up to watch the place. We don't know what we're walking into."

Liz nodded, her heart pounding in her chest. "I understand." She took a deep breath, steadying herself. "Let's go."

They exited the car, moving quietly along the gravel path between the rows of storage units. Roger led the way, his hand resting on the grip of his gun, just in case. Liz's eyes scanned their surroundings, every shadow feeling like a potential threat. She could feel her pulse in her ears, the tension making every muscle in her body ache.

They reached the unit listed in Jason's records—a dull, gray metal door with a heavy padlock. Roger looked at Liz, his expression questioning. She nodded, and he pulled out a set of lockpicking tools from his pocket. He worked quickly, the click of the lock echoing in the stillness.

The padlock gave way, and Roger slowly lifted the door, revealing the dim interior. Liz held her breath as they stepped inside. The air was stale, filled with the scent of dust, oil, and concrete. The light from outside cast long shadows across the floor, revealing a few items scattered around—construction tools, rolls of plastic sheeting, and a set of blueprints spread across a worktable.

Liz's eyes widened as she stepped closer, her gaze falling on the blueprints. She recognized the building—it was the courthouse. Her stomach twisted, a cold chill running down her spine. She reached out, her fingers trembling as she picked up the edge of the blueprint, her eyes scanning the markings.

"Roger… this is the courthouse," she whispered, her voice trembling. "Why would Jason have this?"

Roger moved beside her, his eyes narrowing as he looked at the plans. "I don't know. But this isn't good, Liz. It looks like he's been planning something. We need to get these back to the office and figure out what the hell is going on."

Liz felt tears welling in her eyes, her heart breaking. She had hoped—prayed—that there was an innocent explanation. But now, standing in the dim storage unit, surrounded by evidence that Jason was involved in something far more sinister, she felt her world shatter.

Roger placed a hand on her back, his voice steady. "We'll get to the bottom of this. I promise you, Liz. Whatever's going on, we'll stop it."

Liz nodded, her throat tight with emotion. "I just don't understand why… why would he do this?"

Roger didn't have an answer. He could only offer her his support, his resolve to see this through. Together, they gathered the evidence, their hearts heavy with the realization that the nightmare was far from over—and that someone they trusted might be at the center of it all.

As they looked around the storage unit, it dawned on them how Jason had managed to stay ahead of their every move. He had access to their plans, their strategies. He knew their next steps before they even made them. The blueprints, the tools—it all made sense now. Jason had inside knowledge, and that was how he stayed ahead of them, no matter what they did.

CHAPTER FIFTY ONE

The sheriff's office was buzzing with activity the next morning, but Liz felt detached, as if she were observing everything through a fog. The betrayal felt like a punch to the gut, the disbelief twisting her insides. She had spent the entire night replaying their time together, searching for clues she might have missed, signs that Jason wasn't the person he had claimed to be. Every tender moment, every late-night conversation—it all felt tainted now, a painful reminder of how much she had trusted him.

She remembered the first time they met—Jason had been different from anyone she'd ever known. He was gentle, caring, and, most importantly, seemed to understand her. They had bonded over their shared love for long drives on the empty roads outside Midland, where the horizon seemed endless and the silence was comforting. He had held her hand and told her that being with her made him feel less alone. Liz could almost hear his voice now, echoing through her mind, telling her that she was his safe place. The memories stung like salt in an open wound.

Roger approached her desk, his face set in a determined expression. He handed Liz a cup of coffee, his gaze searching her face for any sign of how she was holding up.

"You alright?" he asked.

"I don't know, Roger. I just can't believe it—everything we found yesterday. It's all so much to process."

Roger nodded, his face grim. "I know. But we need to stay focused. We still don't know exactly what Jason is planning, but whatever it is, it's big, and it's coming fast." He gestured for her to follow him into his office.

Liz followed, her heart heavy as she stepped inside. Roger shut the door, then opened a file on his desk. He motioned for Liz to come closer. "I've been going over the notes we found at the industrial site—Jason's notes about the courthouse. I think I figured out what he's planning."

Liz leaned over the desk, her eyes scanning the blueprints and notes. The courthouse layout was meticulously detailed—every security checkpoint, every camera, every entry and exit point. Jason had written notes in the margins, indicating times and vulnerabilities. She could almost see Jason, hunched over these blueprints, meticulously planning his next move, and it made her heart ache. There were annotations in his familiar handwriting—little details, timings, vulnerabilities. It felt so personal, seeing the evidence of his betrayal laid bare.

Roger tapped on one specific note. "Look at this. He marked a specific date and time. His plans doesn't seem random. He's targeting the courthouse for that exact moment."

Liz's heart sank as the pieces fell into place. He had always said he was an orphan, that he had no one left. But now she knew that wasn't true. Roger flipped through another page, showing an old photograph of a family—Jason as a young boy, standing beside Peter Weller.

Liz's breath caught in her throat. "Peter Weller... that's Jason's father?" she whispered, her voice cracking.

Roger nodded solemnly. "Yeah, Liz. Jason lied about being an orphan. His real name is Jason Weller. He's been hiding this connection from you and from everyone. Everything we've found points to him wanting revenge for what happened to his family in the Marathon Oil explosion. He blames the system, and he's planning to take matters into his own hands."

Liz felt her knees go weak, and she gripped the edge of Roger's desk for support. "He lied to me about everything," she said, her voice filled with anguish. "He made me believe he had no one, that he was all alone. But all this time, he was planning this... plotting to attack the courthouse, to cause chaos when it mattered most." Tears welled in her eyes, but she blinked them away, anger slowly replacing the sadness.

Roger's expression was filled with empathy, but his voice was firm. "He's trying to disrupt the system. He must blame everyone for what happened. He's going after the judge, maybe even others involved in the courthouse."

Liz clenched her fists, anger and sadness coursing through her veins. "We can't let that happen. We need to stop him, Roger. We have to protect those people."

Roger gave her a firm nod. "We will. I've already alerted courthouse security. They're doubling up on personnel and going over the security measures again. But we need to make sure we cover every angle. Jason knows too much—he's been one step ahead of us this whole time. We have to be smarter."

Liz took a shaky breath, trying to keep her emotions in check. She had trusted Jason with her heart, and now she had to be the one to bring him down. The weight of it all threatened to crush her, but she couldn't let that happen. Too many lives depended on her now.

"What's our next move?" she asked, her voice steadier than she felt.

Roger picked up a map, pointing to the courthouse and several key locations surrounding it. "We need to station officers at every possible entry point—every place he marked on those blueprints. We also need undercover officers inside the courthouse. We can't let Jason slip through the cracks."

Liz nodded, her resolve hardening. "I'll help coordinate the teams. We need to make sure everyone knows what's at stake here. He's dangerous, Roger, and he won't hesitate if he thinks he can get what he wants."

Roger gave her a grim smile, his eyes softening as he looked at her. "I know this is hard, Liz. I wish it didn't have to be you going through this. But we're going to stop him. Together."

Liz gave a small nod, appreciating Roger's support more than words could express. She knew they had to act fast, but she also knew she couldn't let her emotions cloud her judgment. This was bigger than her, bigger than her relationship with Jason—it was about stopping a man who had chosen a dark and dangerous path.

After leaving Roger's office, Liz returned to her desk, her thoughts swirling with everything they had discussed. She barely had time to sit down before her phone buzzed. It was

Jason. Her stomach twisted at the sight of his name on her screen.

She hesitated for a moment, then answered, her voice shaky. "Jason?"

His voice came through the line, calm but with an edge that sent a shiver down her spine. "I know you know, Liz. I know what you found."

Liz's breath caught in her throat. "Jason, you need to stop this. Whatever you're planning, it's not too late. We can figure this out."

Jason let out a bitter laugh, the sound cold and filled with pain. "Figure this out? There's nothing left to figure out, Liz. You wouldn't understand. You can't understand what they took from me. They tore my family apart, and everything that happened was because of them. My uncles, my brother—gone, and nobody cared. My father, Peter Weller, you all arrested him. And before you start accusing me of lying, I didn't know he was my father for most of my life. I really thought I was an orphan, Liz, until last year when Peter found me and told me the truth. Everything I've done since then has been about making things right. This is the only way to make it right."

Liz clenched her jaw, her heart pounding. "Jason, please. We can help you. You don't have to do this. There are other ways—ways that don't involve more violence."

Jason's voice was quiet for a moment, and she could almost hear his breathing on the other end of the line. "Do you really think you can help me? After everything? The system let my family die, Liz. They covered it up, they moved on, and no one paid the price. You think there's any justice left in that courthouse?"

Liz swallowed hard, her voice cracking. "I know you're angry, Jason. I can't even begin to imagine how much pain you're in—finding out Peter was your father, seeing him arrested, losing your family—but this isn't the way. If you go through with this, you'll only be hurting more innocent people. Please, just come in and talk to us. We can find a way."

There was a long pause, and Liz could hear Jason's breathing becoming uneven. When he spoke again, his voice was softer, almost vulnerable. "I love you, Liz. I always have. You were the one thing that made everything bearable. But they took everything from me—my family, my future. They destroyed everything I had, and they never paid for it. This is the only way I can make things right."

Tears filled Liz's eyes, her throat tightening. "Jason, I love you too. I never stopped. But if you go through with this, there's no coming back. You'll lose everything—us, your chance to make a new life. Please, Jason, don't do this."

Jason's voice broke, and for a moment, Liz thought she might have gotten through to him. "I wish things could be different," he whispered, his voice filled with raw emotion. "I wish I could just walk away and be with you. But it's too late for that, Liz. I can't turn back now. Not after everything that's happened. I hope one day you understand why I had to do this."

"Jason, please," Liz pleaded, her voice breaking. "You don't have to be alone. We can figure this out together."

"No, Liz. You made your choice. You chose them. Now I have to make mine. I have to make sure they pay. All of them."

Before Liz could say anything more, the line went dead, leaving her staring at her phone, her heart racing. She knew then that there was no turning back. Jason was committed to his plan, and she had to do whatever it took to stop him. She took a deep breath, wiping the tears from her eyes, and stood up, her resolve hardening. She had to protect everyone, no matter how much it hurt.

She walked back to Roger's office. They had work to do, and time was running out.

Roger looked up as she entered, seeing the determination in her eyes. He nodded, knowing she had made up her mind.

"We've got a lot to do," he said, sliding the map back across his desk towards her. "We're going to make sure every last detail is covered. We won't let him slip through our fingers."

Liz nodded firmly. "Let's get to it. We need to stop him before anyone gets hurt." She picked up the map, her fingers tracing over the points Jason had marked. "This time, we're not letting him get ahead of us."

As the day progressed, the sheriff's office worked like a well-oiled machine, each officer briefed and ready. Roger and Liz worked side by side, ensuring every officer knew their role, every corner of the courthouse was covered. The courthouse security was on high alert, and the team was ready for anything Jason might try.

Liz caught herself glancing at the clock every few minutes, her anxiety building as the hour drew near. She couldn't shake the image of Jason—his eyes filled with pain, his voice laced with regret. She had to believe they could stop him before he made a mistake that would cost even more lives.

Roger approached her, giving her a small nod. "Everything's in place. Now we wait."

Liz nodded, her heart heavy but her resolve strong. They had done everything they could. Now it was time to face whatever came next.

CHAPTER FIFTY TWO

The courthouse was on high alert. Officers were stationed at every entry and exit point, and security cameras were monitored closely throughout the building. They thought they had it covered; every contingency seemed planned for. But there was something they hadn't anticipated—old tunnels beneath the courthouse, relics of a forgotten time, long since abandoned and unmarked on the blueprints they had studied.

Jason knew about the tunnels. He had spent months researching every possible way in, every vulnerability the courthouse had. The tunnels were dark, damp, and filled with the stale smell of earth and mildew. Rats scurried in the shadows, and debris from years of neglect littered the ground. The walls were narrow, the ceiling low, forcing Jason to crouch his way through the darkness. He moved with purpose, his flashlight illuminating the crumbling walls and broken support beams. His path was carefully planned as he knew the layout by heart. He had studied old maps, uncovered city blueprints from decades ago, and he had used the knowledge to find a way that no one else would think of.

Jason remembered walking hand in hand with Liz, her laughter echoed in his ears. Those were the days when he had hope, before everything had been taken from him. The thought sparked anger in his chest, pushing him forward. The sound of dripping water echoed around him as he moved deeper into the maze of tunnels. The atmosphere was almost suffocating, and every step he took kicked up dust that lingered in the air. Jason breathed steadily, trying to stay focused on his goal. He was running out of time, and every second counted. The weight of the explosives in his bag pulled at his shoulders, but he pressed on, his eyes fixed ahead.

He knew exactly where he needed to go. The courthouse basement was directly above, and he had already mapped out the points where he could plant the bomb to do the most damage. He wanted to send a message through the bomb, to make them all understand the pain he had carried for so long. His fingers brushed against the cool metal of the detonator in his pocket, manifesting what was to come.

Liz was pacing the halls. She felt the tension thrumming through her body, her instincts telling her that something was wrong. She couldn't shake the feeling that Jason had found another way in. He had always been clever—always one step ahead of them. She thought back to the times they had shared, the nights spent talking about their dreams, the warmth of his embrace. She shook her head, forcing herself to focus. As the minutes ticked by, her worry grew, a gnawing sense of dread settling in her chest.

Roger stood near one of the entry points. He had assigned officers to every vulnerable spot, and yet, something still didn't feel right. He glanced at his watch, then back at Liz across the hallway. She caught his eye, her expression mirroring his concern. They had been through so much together, and in that moment, they both knew—Jason was still out there, and he was dangerous.

Jason finally reached the access point that led to the basement. The tunnel ended in a rusted ladder that stretched upward. He climbed slowly, the metal creaking under his weight, his flashlight tucked between his teeth. When he reached the top, he pushed against the old grate, the heavy iron giving way with a groan. He slowly emerged into the basement, the dim light barely illuminating the space around him. The basement looked like a labyrinth of forgotten storage rooms, old records, and disused equipment. It was quiet, the kind of silence that felt thick and impenetrable.

He moved quickly, his footsteps muffled by the layers of dust that coated the floor. The bomb was heavy, but he carried it with purpose, as he looked for the spot he had picked out on the blueprints. He found it near one of the old support pillars, the concrete cracked and worn with age. Jason knelt, setting the bomb down carefully. His hands moved deftly as he armed the device. As he worked, he thought of the people who had wronged him, the ones who had taken everything from him. His face twisted in anger, the pain of loss driving him forward.

Above the basement, Liz's radio crackled to life, a panicked voice cutting through the static. "We've got movement in the basement—unidentified male. We need backup!"

Liz's heart sank. She locked eyes with Roger, and they both moved simultaneously, running towards the nearest stairwell. They couldn't afford to waste any time.

The basement was dimly lit, the air musty and cold. Liz and Roger reached the bottom of the stairs, their flashlights cutting through the darkness. The walls were lined with old pipes, some of them rusted, the concrete floor cracked and uneven. They could hear movement ahead, faint footsteps echoing off the concrete walls. Liz's heart pounded, every muscle in her body tensed. She thought about Jason, about the man he used to be, the man she had once loved. She couldn't believe it had come to this.

They moved cautiously, their weapons drawn, scanning every shadow.

Jason heard them coming. He knew his time was running out. He finished arming the bomb, his fingers lingering on the detonator for a moment before he stood, his eyes narrowing as he listened to the approaching footsteps. He moved into the shadows, his heart pounding, his mind racing. He couldn't afford to be caught—not now, not when he was so close.

Roger turned, his flashlight catching a glimpse of Jason just as he lunged out from the darkness. There was a flash of metal, the glint of a knife, and before Roger could react, Jason had the blade pressed against his throat.

"Drop it!" Jason shouted. He pulled Roger closer, using him as a shield.

Liz froze, her flashlight illuminating Jason's face. His eyes were wild, filled with a mixture of rage and desperation. Roger winced, his hands raised slightly, his gun still in his grasp but useless in his current position. Jason's face was twisted, the anger and pain evident in the deep lines on his forehead and the tension in his jaw.

"Jason, let him go!" Liz called out, her voice cracking. She slowly lowered her weapon, trying to keep her voice calm. "You don't have to do this. Please, just let Roger go. We can still fix this."

Jason shook his head. His knuckles were white, the blade pressed dangerously close to Roger's neck. "There's nothing left to fix, Liz! They have to pay for what they did. They took everything from me!" His voice broke, the pain evident in every word. His eyes were glassy, tears threatening to spill over. "You don't understand. None of you do."

Liz took a step forward, her eyes locked on Jason's. She could see the tremble in his hands, the strain in his voice. "I do understand, Jason. I know what you've lost. But this isn't the way. Hurting more people won't bring them back. It won't make the pain go away."

Jason's eyes flickered, uncertainty crossing his face for a brief moment. His grip loosened slightly, the knife wavering. But then his expression hardened again, his jaw clenched. "It's too late for that, Liz. It's too late for me."

Liz glanced at Roger, his eyes meeting hers, a silent plea for her to be careful. She could see the fear in his eyes, the understanding that Jason was beyond reasoning. She had to act—and quickly.

The seconds felt like hours as Liz steadied her breathing. She knew she only had one shot, one chance to end this without Roger getting killed. Her heart pounded in her ears, her focus narrowing on Jason's face. She could see the anguish there, the brokenness that had driven him to this point. The man she had once loved was buried beneath layers of rage and sorrow.

"Please, Jason," she whispered, her voice trembling. "You say you love me. If you ever did, let him go. Don't make me do this."

Jason's eyes met hers, and for a split second, she saw the man she had loved—the man who had once been kind and gentle. The way he used to look at her, the way he smiled when he spoke of their future. But that moment passed, and his gaze turned cold, his resolve returning. He shook his head slowly. "You made your choice, Liz. Now I've made mine."

Liz didn't hesitate. She squeezed the trigger, the gunshot echoing through the basement, the recoil jolting through her arm. Jason's eyes widened in shock when the bullet passed through his head, his grip on Roger loosening as he stumbled backward. Roger twisted away, falling to the ground as Jason crumpled, his body hitting the cold concrete with a finality that sent a shiver through Liz.

For a moment, there was silence—a heavy, suffocating stillness. The smell of gunpowder hung in the air, mingling with the musty scent of the basement. Liz rushed forward, her heart pounding as she knelt beside Roger, her hands shaking. "Roger, are you okay?"

Roger grimaced, nodding as he pushed himself up, his hand brushing against his throat where the knife had been. "Yeah... yeah, I'm okay," he managed, his voice rough. He looked over at Jason's lifeless form, his expression a mixture of relief and sorrow. "You did what you had to do, Liz."

Liz swallowed hard, her eyes stinging with tears. She looked down at Jason, her heart aching. The man she had loved was gone, lost to his own pain and hatred. She had wanted to save him, but in the end, there had been no other choice. She reached out, her fingers brushing against his, a silent goodbye.

Roger placed a hand on her shoulder, his grip gentle but reassuring. "Come on," he said softly. "Let's get out of here."

Liz nodded, her throat too tight to speak. She helped Roger to his feet, her eyes lingering on Jason one last time before she turned away. They made their way back up the stairs, the weight of what had happened pressing down on her with every step. She had saved Roger, saved countless others—but the cost had been more than she could bear.

As they emerged from the basement, the bright lights of the courthouse hallway felt blinding. Officers rushed towards them, concern etched on their faces. Liz barely registered their voices, her mind still reeling from the events of the last few minutes. She could hear the murmur of questions, the frantic radio chatter as officers were updated on the situation.

Roger gave her a small nod, his eyes filled with gratitude. "You did good, Liz. You saved my life. You saved a lot of people today."

Liz forced a smile, though it felt hollow. "I just wish it didn't have to end this way," she said, her voice barely a whisper.

Roger squeezed her shoulder. "Sometimes, we don't get a choice. You did what you had to do."

Liz nodded, though the ache in her chest remained. She had done what she had to do—but the cost of that choice would stay with her forever. She glanced back at the stairwell, the darkness beyond feeling like a weight pressing on her heart. She knew that this moment would haunt her, that Jason's face would stay with her for the rest of her life.

An officer approached, his expression serious. "Sheriff, Deputy Trujillo, EMS is on their way. Do you need medical attention?"

Roger shook his head. "I'm alright," he said. He looked at Liz. "We're both alright."

Liz nodded, though the words felt empty. She wasn't sure if she would ever truly be alright again. But as she looked at Roger, at the officers around her, she knew she had done the right thing. And maybe, just maybe, that was enough for now.

CHAPTER FIFTY THREE

The aftermath of the courthouse confrontation settled over the town like a heavy fog. News spread quickly, and the entire city of Midland was buzzing with talk of what had happened—how Jason had used the old tunnels to bypass security, how he had almost succeeded in his plan. The heroic actions of Roger and Liz were at the forefront of every conversation, but the toll it took on those involved was more profound than anyone outside could understand.

Liz sat on her couch at her house. She couldn't shake away Jason's final moments from her mind— an interaction she never she would see. She had done what she had to do, but it didn't feel like a victory. It felt like an irreplaceable loss.

She closed her eyes, leaning her head back against the cushions, trying to drown out the memories. But they wouldn't stop—the sound of the gunshot, the sight of Jason crumpling to the ground, the emptiness in his eyes as the life drained from him. He had been the man she loved, the man she thought she knew. And yet, in the end, he had become a stranger—someone consumed by hatred and pain. She remembered their laughter, the warmth of his embrace, the nights they spent lying under the vast Texas sky, dreaming of a future together. All those memories now felt tainted, twisted into something unrecognizable.

A soft knock on her door pulled her from her thoughts. She stood, her body heavy with exhaustion, and opened the door to find Roger standing there, his arm in a sling, his face drawn and tired. He offered her a small smile, his eyes filled with empathy.

"I brought some food," he said, lifting a bag of takeout. "I thought you might not feel like cooking."

Liz stepped aside, letting Roger in. He set the food on the table, glancing around her house. It was neat, organized—almost too perfect, as if she had been trying to distract herself by cleaning. The books on her shelves were perfectly aligned, her coffee table spotless, not a single thing out of place. It was as if keeping her environment in order was her only way of coping with the chaos in her mind.

"You didn't have to do this," Liz said softly.

Roger shook his head. "I wanted to. After everything that happened today, I figured we could both use some company."

Liz nodded, her throat tightening. She sank onto the couch, her hands clasped in her lap. Roger joined her, the silence between them thick with unspoken words. He opened the takeout bag, handing her a container of food. She took it, staring at it for a moment before setting it aside, her appetite nonexistent.

"You did the right thing, Liz," Roger said gently, his voice steady. "You saved my life. You saved a lot of people."

Liz swallowed hard, her eyes stinging with tears. "I know," she said, her voice cracking. "But it doesn't make it any easier. I wanted to save him, Roger. I really did."

Roger nodded, his expression somber. He had seen that look in her eyes before—the weight of taking a life, even if it was justified. "I know you did. But Jason made his choice. He put everyone in danger—including you. There was nothing else you could have done."

Liz looked down at her hands, her fingers trembling. "I just keep thinking about everything we went through together—all the moments we shared. I thought I knew him. I thought he was..." She trailed off, her voice breaking. She thought of the nights they spent together, the laughter, the plans they had made for the future. It all felt like a cruel joke now.

Roger placed his good hand on her shoulder, his grip gentle. "He fooled everyone, Liz. Not just you. But what he became... it wasn't your fault. He let his pain consume him. You did everything you could."

Liz nodded, tears slipping down her cheeks. She wiped them away quickly, taking a shaky breath. "I just don't know how to move on from this. How to keep going." Her voice cracked as she spoke.

Roger sighed, leaning back against the couch. "One day at a time. That's all we can do. We lean on each other, we remember why we do this job, and we keep going. Because that's what makes us different from people like Jason. We don't let the darkness win."

Liz looked at him, her eyes searching his. She could see the weariness there, the pain etched into the lines of his face. But she could also see the strength that had kept him going through all the hardships they had faced. It was that strength that gave her hope, that made her believe that maybe, just maybe, she could find a way to move forward.

"Thank you, Roger," she said in a whisper.

Roger gave her a small smile, nodding. "We're in this together, Liz. Always."

The two of them sat silently for a while, the weight of the day slowly lifting as they shared a quiet meal. It wasn't much, but it was enough for now—enough to remind them that they weren't alone, that they still had each other. The food was lukewarm, and Liz barely tasted it, but the simple act of eating together brought a semblance of normalcy that she desperately needed.

The next morning, Liz stood in front of the mirror, her uniform neatly pressed, her badge gleaming in the light. She took a deep breath, her reflection staring back at her. There was still pain there, still a deep ache that she knew would take time to heal. But there was also stubbornness—a resolve to keep going, to keep fighting for the people who needed her.

She walked out of her house, the crisp morning air filling her lungs as she headed to her car. The streets were quiet, the sun just beginning to rise over the horizon. It was a new day, and with it came new challenges, and new opportunities to make a difference. The sky was painted in hues of orange and pink, the first rays of sunlight casting long shadows across the empty streets. It was peaceful, a stark contrast to the chaos that had consumed her life just hours ago.

As she drove, her mind wandered to the places that held memories of Jason. The park where they had picnicked on lazy Sundays, the diner where they had shared countless meals, the hilltop where they had once watched the stars. She passed each place, feeling a pang of loss, but also a sense of closure. She needed to see these places, to confront the memories, to let go of the past piece by piece.

When she arrived at the sheriff's office, Roger was already there, his arm still in a sling but his expression resolute. He looked up as she walked in, giving her a nod of acknowledgment. There was a sense of camaraderie between them, a bond forged through the trials they had faced together.

"Ready to get back to work?" Roger smiled.

Liz took a deep breath, nodding. "Yeah. I'm ready."

"Good. We've got a lot to do."

Liz nodded, her heart a little lighter. She knew it wouldn't be easy—there would be days when the weight of what had happened would feel unbearable. But she also knew she wasn't alone. She had Roger, she had her team, and she had a purpose.

And that was enough to keep her moving forward.

As they walked into the office, the phones were already ringing, officers bustling about as the day began. Life moved on, and so would they. Together, they would face whatever came next, one day at a time.

A junior deputy approached them, holding a stack of papers. "Sheriff, Deputy Trujillo, we've got a briefing in ten minutes. There's a lot to go over regarding the courthouse incident."

Roger took the papers, glancing through them before handing a few to Liz. "Alright, we'll be there," he replied, his voice steady. He looked over at Liz, his eyes softening. "You up for this?"

Liz scanned the papers, her focus shifting to the task at hand. There were details about the investigation—evidence to catalog, statements to take. The reality of the work ahead was daunting, but it was also grounding. It gave her something to hold onto, a way to channel her pain into something productive.

"Yeah," she said, her voice strong. "Let's get to it."

The briefing room was already filling up when they arrived. Officers stood around, talking in low voices, their expressions a mix of lack of energy and tenacity. Liz and Roger took their seats at the front, the room quieting as they entered. The lead investigator stood at the front, clearing his throat as he began.

"Alright, everyone. We have a lot to cover. First, I want to commend all of you for your hard work yesterday. It wasn't easy, and we faced a lot of challenges, but we made it through."

Liz listened, her gaze focused on the notes in front of her. The investigator went on, detailing the evidence they had recovered from the basement—the bomb Jason had planted, the tunnel entrance he had used. Each piece of information was another reminder of how close they had come to disaster. But they had stopped it. They had saved lives.

After the briefing, Liz lingered for a moment, watching as the others filed out of the room. Roger stayed by her side, his presence a comforting anchor. He gave her a gentle nudge, his expression softening.

"You did good today," he said quietly.

Liz looked at him, her eyes searching his. She could see the exhaustion there, the toll the past days had taken on him. But she could also see the pride, the unwavering belief in her. It was that belief that gave her strength, that made her believe she could keep going.

"Thanks, Roger," she replied, her voice steady. "I think... I think I'm going to be okay."

Roger nodded, his lips curving into a small smile. "I know you will be."

They walked out of the briefing room together, the noise of the office surrounding them once more. There was still so much to do, so much to process, but for the first time since the incident, Liz felt a glimmer of hope. She had faced the darkness, and she had survived. And now, she was ready to move forward—one day at a time, with Roger and the rest of her team by her side.